Fated Beginnings

The McKay Series

Karen Muir

Fated Beginnings

Dedication

It is my pleasure to dedicate my book to
my amazing Godchildren:
Lindsay, Egan, and Tommy,
who have always believed in me.
And to my other wonderful nieces and nephews
Sarah, Bryan, Scott, Lindsay, Gregory,
Riley, Kate, Sam, and Victoria.
Always follow your dreams, you never know
where they may take you.

A special thanks to my family and critique partners
who made this book possible.

~Chapter One~

1886 – Boston, Massachusetts

Allison Monroe prayed no one could hear the drumming of her heart as she hid among the shadows in St. Joseph's Church. She sucked in a deep breath, craned her neck around a wide oak pillar, and scanned the room until her gaze locked on two priests conversing in whispers in front of the altar.

When the last of the parishioners rose from their pews and headed toward the exit, Allison melted further into obscurity. Had her life really come to this, hiding in darkened corners, too afraid to be seen? The past few months of self-imposed seclusion burned in her memory. Before it was too late, she needed to share her secret with someone she could trust.

A floorboard creaked. A door closed. Little by little, she eased around the pillar. Finally, the gray-haired priest was gone, and the man she yearned to speak with stood alone.

She darted from her hiding spot and hurried noiselessly down the aisle. As the priest turned toward the side door, she came up from behind.

"Father Peter, may I have a word with you?"

He spun on his heels in one swift motion. Eyes wide, his palm flew to his chest and thumped his heart. "By all that is Holy, I had no idea you were there."

"Forgive me, Father. I didn't mean to startle you. I only wanted a moment of your time to discuss...a personal matter."

He placed a soft hand on her shoulder. "Of course. It's been a while since we last spoke. I've missed your company."

"And I've missed yours, as well." She took a cleansing breath. His warm smile calmed her thundering heart.

"Shall we take a turn through the flower garden?" He extended his bent elbow. "The day is balmy for spring, is it not?"

"Indeed, it is." She hooked her fingers in the crook of his arm. He guided her through the double oak doors, down two rock steps, and into the small enclosed yard alongside the church.

Once they reached the flat stone pathway, he slowed his pace and glanced down at her. "I'm glad you stopped by today. I've been concerned for your welfare. You've kept to yourself of late."

"I sought you out to explain." She inhaled deeply. The fresh scent of Spring flowers tickled her nose.

As they strolled along the path, Allison studied the priest's familiar face. He was eight years older than her nineteen years, yet he'd risen so fast in the church. From the first day he arrived at St. Joseph's a little more than a year ago, the congregation welcomed him with open arms. It wasn't only his smile that captivated the parishioners, but also his gentle and caring nature. She was no different. Drawn to his pleasant disposition, she visited him regularly and they'd become good friends. Up until two months ago, she accompanied him weekly when he volunteered at the local hospital or tended the sick in their homes.

Would he despise her for her sins? Or, would he find it in his heart to forgive her?

She hoped for the latter.

"Miss Monroe, you're trembling. Come, sit beside me, and tell me what troubles you. God will guide us." Father Peter halted in front of an almost hidden bench in the middle of the shrubbery.

Allison stepped away from his side and perched on the edge of the stone form, ready to flee, if need be. How she wished she was home right now, curled up on her bedroom window seat, looking out over the uneven cobblestones of the roadway in front of her family's three-story brick townhouse. Lately, the padded cushion served as her sanctuary, a place to hide.

She wrung her hands, and then laid them in her lap. Bowing her head, she waited for him to sit beside her. When he did, she looked up.

"I fear you will be quite disappointed in me for I've sinned against God." Her strained voice broke sharply through the peace of the garden. The world around her hazed, as her eyes filled with unshed tears.

"Is this why you've been avoiding me? Fear not, my friend. God is very forgiving. Tell me what you've done that you consider so bad."

His tone insinuated he doubted she could do anything wrong of a serious nature. How she hated to let him down. The back of her hand quieted a sniffle.

"I'm afraid I find myself with child." Her hoarse whisper sounded strange to her ears.

Father Peter stiffened.

Heaviness surrounded them. Allison steeled herself from looking away. She held her breath, preparing for the disappointment surely written on his face. As the silence grew, a bird chirped merrily from a low hanging branch mocking the seriousness of the situation.

Father Peter tugged at the clerical collar molded around his neck. "Where is the man responsible?"

She struggled to keep the pitch of her words even, so he wouldn't see the depth of her distress. "He has abandoned me and left me to manage on my own."

"His behavior is unacceptable," Father Peter's voice rose with fury. "You are a young lady from one of the most distinguished families in Boston. We shall speak with your father. Together, I'm sure we can convince this young man to do right by you."

"Please...don't tell my father," Allison begged, locking eyes with his. "I do not wish him to know. As it is, I'm mortified I have shared my secret with you."

Father Peter placed his hand over her clenched fingers. "Tell me who this man is and why he has forsaken you."

How could she tell Father Peter that the man she'd fallen so deeply in love with was nothing more than a scoundrel? For the past few months, she'd tried to convince herself that Robert Winston Winthrop III couldn't be such a blackguard. But now, in her heart, the truth was undeniable.

"I refuse to say his name. He said he loved me. We planned to marry. Unfortunately, before we could make it so, we shared a few stolen moments of impropriety." Her cheeks burned. "When I told him I was with child, he said he wanted us to take our vows right away."

"What changed his mind?" Father Peter asked.

"He went home to inform his father of our plans." She withdrew a small silk purse from the hidden pocket in her gown and removed a crumpled parchment. "I received this the next day. A letter explaining that, although he cared for me, his father didn't feel I was a good match." Allison glanced at the priest. "Our families don't travel in the same social circles, you see."

Father Peter frowned. "Do you mean to say this so-called gentleman is from one of Boston's founding families? A Boston Brahmin." His lips puckered as if he had something sour in his mouth. "They would be the only ones to dare look down upon your family."

Allison lowered her head and nodded. "His father threatened to disinherit him if he went ahead with his plans to marry. He chose his inheritance over me and our baby." A stream of hot tears slid down her cheeks. She held up the letter. "He wishes me luck."

How could she have believed in such a man? A man whose affection was so fleeting?

"Tell me all of it," Father Peter urged.

"At the very end of his letter, he went so far as to question whether the baby was even...his." How dare he have the audacity to question her love and devotion? How dare he try to sever his responsibilities by suggesting he was not the father? She wiped the wetness from her face and struggled to regain her composure. "He enclosed some money. 'A small pittance, to help with the raising of the child', he wrote."

"The man should be horsewhipped!" Father Peter pounded a fist into his open hand. "He should be made to honor his promise."

"I want nothing to do with him ever again. I cannot stay in Boston. If I have this baby out of wedlock, my child and I will be shunned from society. My family's good name will be ruined. Such a scandal will destroy any chance my sister, Lillian, has of making a good marriage. And as for me, no man of merit will want a soiled wife and a bastard child."

Allison blinked back more tears. Her heart squeezed uncomfortably under the weight of rejection. She had spent too many hours grieving her lost love, but no more. There was nothing left inside her but an empty void.

Never again would she trust a man with her heart.

"How can I help?" he asked, his voice kind and gentle.

"I think it best if I leave Boston, as soon as possible. I've waited too long as it is. I'm starting to show. I thought I would take a train out West. I've heard people are less judgmental on the other side of the Mississippi River. I could find a job as a schoolteacher before the baby comes."

She knew her idea was unrealistic. Who would hire an unmarried, pregnant woman? "Maybe I could settle in a town where no one will care about the baby's father. I could let them believe he's dead."

Father Peter's eyebrows drew together.

Her next words came out in a rush. "I know you were born and raised in the Montana Territory. I'm hoping you can point me in the right direction. Maybe give me a contact?"

Allison returned the letter to her purse. It was the first time she'd voiced her plans out loud. She didn't want to leave the only life she knew, but she refused to let her family pay for her mistakes. They needed to be protected from wagging tongues and cold stares. People in the city were vicious and unyielding in their judgment of others. Especially, the Boston Brahmins who were the members of Boston's elite upper class. The thought of leaving those she cared for to go off and raise her child alone terrified her, but life would be worse if she stayed. Sacrifices needed to be made.

Father Peter ran his fingers through his thick brown hair and shook his head. "I'm afraid it's my duty to dissuade you. West of the Mississippi can be harsh country. In some areas, women are scarce. It's not a place for a young lady, all alone, with a baby. I'm afraid some men would consider you fair game, placing you in a vulnerable position. I must insist we think of something else."

"There is nothing else," she wailed. "Time is running out. I can't stay here much longer. I cannot—will not—bring such shame upon my family." She raised her chin and straightened her back. "I will go, with or without your help."

Father Peter heaved a deep sigh and patted her arm. "Don't worry. God will guide us." He rose to his feet and paced up and down a short path between the colorful rows of blooming tulips. "Let me think," he muttered under his breath, clasping his hands in prayer. Brown eyes stared into nothingness as he proceeded at a slow and thoughtful gait.

Suddenly, he stopped. A smug look crossed his face. "You need a husband."

"I told you, I will never take him back. I feel nothing but loathing for him. He revealed his true nature. He heartlessly tricked me into believing he cared for me. Thankfully, he's no longer in Boston, but visiting New York City. There is no hope for us, nor do I want there to be."

Father Peter put up a hand. "I'm not talking about the baby's father."

Her mouth dropped open.

"Hear me out." Father Peter gave her a silencing look. "Last week I received a letter from my brother who lives in Flat Rock, Montana. In his letter, he wrote about how the men still outnumber the woman and how his wife wishes there were more women in town to keep her company. I know a man living close to town who would make a good husband."

"Are you suggesting I marry a stranger?"

"He's an honest, hard-working man. He would protect you and the baby from any dangerous situations. I'm sure he'd have no problem raising your child as his own. I've seen him with children, and he takes to them well. His family owns a cattle ranch and he lives there with his three younger brothers. They have a big beautiful house that would accommodate a large family. After you're married, you can write home to let your parents know you are with child. They need not share with others the circumstances of your pregnancy, as you'll already be married. Jayson McKay could offer you a good life. Such a venture would allow you to start over. And, most importantly, you wouldn't have to raise your child alone."

Being in the company of any man was the last thing she wanted. "How do you know this Mr. McKay would consider such an arrangement?"

"We've been friends since childhood. He had been engaged a few years back, but the relationship ended poorly, and he's remained single since then. If I explain your situation, I have every confidence he'll be agreeable. There are few available women of marrying age in town, and he may welcome a chance to start a family of his own."

"I don't know. I never imagined myself married to a stranger. I'm not sure I can do that."

"Please reconsider. I can't in good conscience let you travel out West to live alone. It's much too dangerous. As I see things, the only other choice is to stay here in Boston, tell your father and mother what happened, and take your chances society will be lenient with their judgment."

Allison looked away and considered Father Peter's words. She could never hurt her parents when other arrangements were available. If she accepted his offer, she could shield her family from the truth until after she was married. But, was she willing to enter a loveless marriage for the sake of her child and those she held dear?

When she turned back, she gave Father Peter a weak smile. "Write the letter to your friend, but make sure he understands what I offer is a business arrangement. I'll be the best wife I can, but I can't offer anything more."

"I have a good feeling. If I'm not mistaken, I can feel the hand of God in this."

"Do you mean you think He forgives me?" she asked hopefully and then reconsidered, "Or, does He mean to punish me?"

"I'm sure He forgives you. You are one of His children. Go home. Get some rest. We should know in a few days. We can finalize our plan then."

~Chapter Two~

Allison pushed aside the dirty cloth covering the narrow stagecoach window and peeked out into the bright sunlight. She brought a soiled handkerchief to her parted lips, warding off the dust stirred up by the six-horse team. Every inch of her body ached as it bounced from one solid surface to the next. Thankfully, Father Peter, with Mr. McKay's funds, purchased three tickets for the two of them. The extra seat between them allowed her room to spread out.

She let the ragged material fall back into place and glanced across the aisle at her fellow travelers. They weren't so lucky. Unfortunately, Mr. Bates, Flat Rock's only saloon owner, was a rotund man and squeezed himself quite snuggly between his two new saloon girls. Each bump in the road more than not augmented the women's discomfort.

A movement in her stomach caused her to rub her rounded belly. Today was her five-month mark. Fortunately, unlike some women, she carried her child high, so her pregnancy was less obvious this far along. Because her wardrobe of tailored fashions did little to hide her forming bump, her sister, Lillian, whom she had told about her baby only a few days ago, insisted she purchase a few new dresses with flowing skirts to cover her growing stomach before she left Boston. As far as she knew, her parents were still unaware of her condition.

This last part of the journey was the hardest, and she wished for the trip to end. The nausea that had plagued her all morning finally hit full force at their last rest stop. If not for the kindness of Jasmine Rose, one of the new saloon girls, who saw fit to hold her flowing skirts off the ground while she heaved her breakfast, her stink would be unbearable.

Allison stole a glance to the opposite side of the stagecoach where her new acquaintance dozed. She watched the raven-haired head weave and bob to the sway of the carriage.

Jasmine was the first Cheyenne Indian she'd ever met. Actually, the young woman explained she was what some people called a half-breed but had the looks of a full-blood, which was why Mr. Bates sought her out to add to his girls. Allison wanted to tell the young lady that she had never laid eyes on a woman so beautiful but held her tongue. She didn't want to embarrass a potential new friend.

Allison had experienced a lot of firsts lately. She didn't dare close her eyes for fear of missing something new. The entire world suddenly cleared from a thick blanket of fog and she could finally see through the haze. Misconceptions she once harbored about people from different classes and races were torn down, giving her a sense of freedom. She was not in Boston anymore and no better than anyone else. Robert and his family's narrow-minded prejudice had prevented her from living the life of her dreams. During her journey west, she vowed to never let such evil interfere in her life again. Her new-found humility let her breathe easier and she embraced the fresh air.

She peered at Father Peter who pressed himself into a corner to give her extra space. How could she ever thank her friend for all he had done to make this journey possible? A few days ago, she'd received a letter from him saying Mr. McKay agreed to the marriage. The priest arrived at her parent's townhouse and begged them to let her go with him to the Montana Territory to help care for his sick sister-in-law. He made all the arrangements, including procuring Mrs. Elliot, who acted as her chaperone until she disembarked at a stop earlier in the day with plans to visit her sister.

As their eyes met, Father Peter sent her an apologetic look, as if he was at fault for her discomfort. "I assure you, we really are almost there. If I'm not mistaken, I just caught a whiff of Mrs. Pearson's chicken stew," he teased.

Allison couldn't help but flash him a sweet smile. Father Peter had been nothing but considerate, attentive, and amusing the whole trip. He alone made the past few days of travel in various coaches and trains bearable. She was safe while in his care and once when a drunken gambler tried to take liberties, it was Father Peter who threatened the man with physical harm. The gambler backed off visibly shaken. Just for an instant, she caught a glimpse of the young priest's dangerous side. Had she been anywhere but traveling across the country through rugged territory, maybe the fine line between mild-mannered priest and formidable adversary would have frightened her, but instead, she found the differences exciting, if not reassuring.

"Whoa, whoa!" A shout rang out from the driver's seat, urging the team to slow their pace.

"What did I tell you? I could find Mrs. Pearson's chicken stew in the dark." Father Peter chuckled.

"I have learned never to doubt you."

The stagecoach jerked to a stop. The passengers seated across from her roused from their slumber. She couldn't wait to leave the cramped quarters and nearly pushed her escort through the doorway before it opened. Father Peter quickly helped her down the few steps to the dirt road. When her feet touched solid ground, she resisted an urge to drop to her knees and thank God for delivering her to her destination.

The other two ladies descended from the stage with help from Mr. Bates. As they stepped into the sunshine, she marveled at the stark difference between the two women. Miss Missy's exaggerated manner and bold-colored dress with its low décolletage, demanded everyone's attention. Jasmine, on the other hand, wore a high-necked, drab-colored gown making one believe she preferred to vanish into the woodwork, rather than be noticed.

Allison made eye contact with her new acquaintance. "Miss Rose, thank you for your assistance earlier."

"Glad to help, Miss Monroe." Jasmine shifted uncomfortably as if not accustomed to kindness.

Allison gazed into Jasmine's soft, sad eyes, and her heart went out to the young woman. "Maybe I will see you around town. Take care until then."

"Thank you, Miss Monroe." Jasmine hesitated, and then added quietly, "Good luck with your baby."

Allison smiled warmly, nodded her head, and turned to the other travelers. "So nice to meet you, Miss Missy."

"Take care of yourself, doll," Miss Missy drawled as she batted her heavily made-up eyelashes. The woman then caught the attention of the dirt-crusted men on the top of the stage, and with practiced expertise, she asked in a deep, raspy voice if they would find her bags first. As expected, they scurried to do her bidding.

The corners of Allison's mouth turned up in a smile. Here was a woman who knew how to get what she wanted. She stepped over to their last traveling companion and dipped her head in a quiet good-bye to Mr. Bates. He returned the gesture by tipping his hat to her and Father Peter before he collected his bags and ushered his girls off to the Lucky Ace Saloon across the street.

Allison's heavy trunk was the last piece of luggage unloaded, and the men carried it into the stage office for safekeeping. While Father Peter gathered their carpetbags, she glanced around Flat Rock for the first time. The clapboard buildings lining the dirt street appeared well-maintained. A hitching post stood before every dwelling, with a few saddled horses tethered to the wooden poles. At the edge of the town, she spied a little church easily recognizable due to the steeple. Instantly, she remembered why she was here. A sudden chill raced through her veins, and she trembled.

"The stage was early. Jayson won't expect us for a little while. He reserved a room at the hotel, so you could freshen up after the long ride. I'll escort you to the hotel before I visit my family. When he arrives, I'll return to make the introductions."

She smoothed down the front of her dress. "That sounds wonderful. I could use a little time to wash off the dirt."

Father Peter remained standing in place. He removed his hat and raked his fingers through his brown hair. "I fear I must tell you something before you meet Jayson."

Allison held up her hand to stop his words. Her belly knotted uncomfortably. "I've been waiting for you to share what's bothering you. Over the past few days, you've avoided talking about Mr. McKay. Please don't tell me he's a woman beater. I'm not sure I could stomach such a man." Her nerves were interfering with her clear thinking.

"Oh, no. You have it all wrong. Jayson is an admirable man. He would never lay a hand on you. As your friend, I would never subject you to anything like that. I want only the best for you. Although, there is something I've held back because I wasn't sure how you would react."

"You do realize it's a little late for me to change my mind." She opened her lace umbrella to keep the hot afternoon sun from beating down on her head as she stared at her tall escort.

Father Peter fiddled with the brim of his hat, bending it in all directions. "Honestly, I'm not sure you'll be the least bit troubled by this, but I want to forewarn you before you meet my friend. You see, he survived a fire a few years ago and sustained a scar on his cheek from his injuries. Some people are surprised by the looks of it. I just wanted to prepare you. I assure you, once you get to know him, you won't even notice it."

She considered his words. "Is that what you've been hiding? You could've said something sooner. You know very well I'm not easily disturbed by such a sight."

"I'm sorry I failed to mention it earlier, but I didn't want his scar to be the reason you turned back. I can't think of two more suitably matched people and wanted to make sure you had a chance to meet," he said, visibly relaxing.

"Ease your mind. I'm way past judging others, lest I be judged myself," she reassured him with a half-smile.

Father Peter nodded in silent understanding. He offered her his bent elbow and guided her across the street to the only hotel in town. It was a quaint two-story whitewashed building. The upstairs rooms opened to a wraparound balcony overlooking Flat Rock. The first floor boasted a covered porch with rocking chairs lined up along the front. A disheveled old man with an oddly shaped hat gave her a toothless grin as he rocked back and forth in a chair next to the door. Since the hotel doubled as a restaurant, the large front windows gave diners an unobstructed view of the goings-on. The wooden and glass-paned double doors opened wide, encouraging guests to step inside.

As they made their way through the doorway, Allison was delighted by the simple yet elegant décor, something she hadn't expected out here in the wilderness. A big mahogany desk, used to welcome guests, stood in the corner of the foyer. Mail slots lined a wall cabinet behind the desk. Colorful carpets covered the wooden floors in the foyer and adjoining rooms. A charming floral-patterned wallpaper decorated the walls. Inside the dining room, a floor-to-ceiling, glass-front curio cabinet displayed hand-painted teacups and saucers.

A door swung open and a short balding man with an ear-to-ear smile stepped behind the desk and extended a hand over the rich wood counter. "Father Peter, it's good to see you again. Jayson said you'd be arriving today along with a young lady from Boston. Welcome."

The man's familiar use of her future husband's Christian name piqued her interest. Boston was much more formal.

Father Peter extended his hand and gave the man a firm handshake. "It's good to be home. You look well, Timothy."

The jolly man rubbed his belly and laughed. "I'm afraid I've been sampling too much of my wife's mouth-watering cooking since you've been gone." He turned to Allison. "This must be Miss Monroe. Jayson asked me to take good care of you."

Father Peter placed one hand on the small of her back and swept his other arm open for introductions. "Miss Monroe, may I introduce you to Mr. Pearson, the proprietor of this fine establishment."

"I'm so pleased to meet you, Mr. Pearson."

"The pleasure is mine. Ever since Jayson told us of your pending arrival, all my wife talks about is how exciting it will be to have a fancy young lady from Boston in our midst. She said something or other about the newest fashions. She had to run across to the general store, but she'll be back shortly."

"I'm happy to be here and look forward to meeting her."

Mr. Pearson's face beamed with delight.

Allison wondered if Mrs. Pearson and the townsfolk were aware of the circumstances surrounding her arrival. When they discovered the truth about her pregnancy, how would they receive her? She hoped they wouldn't shun her.

"Let me show you to your room." Mr. Pearson grabbed a key and stepped out from behind his desk. He picked up her carpetbag and made his way to the first step of the stairs. "We're putting you in our finest room. Your bedroom has double doors out onto a porch. You can walk up to the rail and look out over the whole town. A little while ago, I set out a bowl of cool water and clean linens, so you can freshen up before Jayson gets here."

Allison listened to Mr. Pearson's baritone voice as he rambled on about the room's comforts. Before she reached the staircase, Father Peter's hand closed over her upper arm, stopping her short.

"I'm off to see my family who owns the general store. If you need me, I'll be across the street. Don't worry. I know getting married to a man you don't know is difficult, but I'm sure everything will work out for the best. You'll see. Have faith."

Allison felt a tug at losing his kind and loyal company. In a few hours, she would truly be on her own, with a stranger for a husband. "If I don't get a chance to tell you later, I want you to know I appreciate all you've done. I'm sorry I entangled you in this mess." Her eyes watered as her sincere emotions bubbled to the surface. "Please accept my heartfelt thanks."

Father Peter stepped in front of her and clasped her other arm. In a faint voice, he replied, "You're a good woman, Allison. I'm touched you've blessed me with the honor of being your friend. I would do anything to keep you safe and happy. You have no idea how you touched my heart when you volunteered to help me with the sick. Few in your social circle would lower themselves to do some of the tasks you ventured to do. You made me so proud. I was beside myself with worry when you refused to leave your home and no longer accompanied me. I didn't know what ailed you and prayed you hadn't taken ill from the sick you nursed."

Allison hung her head. She hadn't felt worthy enough to be in her friend's presence after she learned she was with child.

"Your road ahead will be hard and, unfortunately, it will require a lot of courage on your part, but I have every confidence you will rise to the occasion." He loosened his grip and pulled away.

"Thank you," she said in a hoarse whisper.

Mr. Pearson stood at the top of the stairs, waiting for her to follow.

"I'll be back in a little while," Father Peter promised.

Allison nodded and watched him exit through the doorway. Turning to the stairs, she took a deep breath, raised the hem of her skirts, and began her climb.

~Chapter Three~

Allison's room was small but cozy.

"The missus will return to the hotel directly. She's sure excited to meet you." Mr. Pearson laid her carpetbag on the navy and white hand-stitched quilt covering the feather mattress. "She's gonna be mad as a hornet she didn't meet you proper-like. Our darn stage is never on time."

"Please, assure your wife that you made me feel quite at home." She unpinned her small hat and held it in her hand.

Mr. Pearson grinned like a young schoolboy. "It's my pleasure, Miss Monroe." He gave a little bow and left the room, closing the door behind him.

She took in her surroundings with a keen eye for detail. Unlike some of the other hotels in which she'd stayed recently, this one spoke strongly of a woman's touch. Fresh flowers in hand-blown vases graced the bedside table and the top of a chest of drawers. Blue-flowered wallpaper covered the walls. White lace curtains adorned a tall window next to the double doors.

Allison walked over to the open window. She pushed aside the billowing curtains to get a better look at the town. A warm breeze brushed against her face. From her vantage point, she could see all the way down the main road. At the far end, the livery was framed by lush green mountains that seemed to reach up and touch the clear blue sky. A blacksmith, standing under a roof attached to the side of the barn, banged on a piece of metal with a methodical rhythm. To the far-right stood Thomas's General Store. Displayed out front was an assortment of supplies, ready to catch the eye of an eager customer.

The Lucky Ace Saloon, where Jasmine Rose would start her job as a new saloon girl, stood across the street from the mercantile. Faint piano music drifted through the louvered saloon doors. At the sheriff's office, a man sat on a bench outside the door whittling a hunk of wood. His silver badge flashed in the sunlight. On the outskirts of town, across from the church, stood a small red schoolhouse where peals of laughter rang out as children played a game of kick the ball in the yard.

Flat Rock was nothing like Boston. Wooden buildings lined the main street. No brick or stone town houses in sight. The dirt road looked bleak compared to the cobblestones covering the streets back home. Where hundreds of people a day strolled by her three-story home on their way to the public gardens, here she couldn't see more than a dozen people walking along the wooden walkways. There were no fancy carriages pulled by high-stepping matched pairs, only a handful of saddled horses tied to hitching posts, a few two-wheeled carriages, and a buckboard waiting for a load in front of the general store.

Allison unbuttoned the tiny pearl buttons on her snug waistcoat and breathed a sigh of relief, grateful to be free of the bindings. The breeze blowing through the open window was a pleasant change from the stuffy stagecoach she had endured during the early part of the day. Closing her eyes, she inhaled deeply of the pine-scented air.

Soon she would meet the man who had agreed to be her husband. Ever since Father Peter suggested such a union, she dared not imagine what kind of man would marry a pregnant woman, sight unseen. Now she had her answer; a disfigured man who was as desperate as she. Of course, their marriage would only be a business arrangement. She had come to terms with that reality.

Never again could I trust a man with my heart.

As she stroked her belly, a fierce protectiveness flowed through her veins. Maybe Robert Winston Winthrop III found it easy to turn his back on his child, but she never would. She'd gather all the courage she could muster and do whatever she had to do to protect her little one, even if it meant marrying a stranger to give her baby a name. As long as her new husband wanted her for a wife, she would endure a loveless marriage and be the best wife possible for the sake of her unborn child.

A refreshing gust of wind blew a few loose tendrils of hair about her face, bringing her back to the moment. She moved to the glass-paned doors and opened them wide. As she stood in the doorway, a lone rider cantered past the livery, toward the hotel. There was something about the way the man carried himself on his fancy black mount that appealed to her senses. She couldn't take her eyes off him.

Back in Boston, she had seen some fine horseflesh. Many of Boston's gentlemen spent their days buying and selling beautiful animals. A game they played. Her father dabbled in such a pastime and had a keen eye for a well-bred animal. She'd always had the same skill. Even from a distance, she could tell this man's horse was exceptional. His lines were perfect, his muscular frame was one of power and poise, just like his master.

She craned her neck to get a glimpse of the man's face, but the brim of his hat hid him from view. As he passed the sheriff's office, he touched his hat in greeting. The man wore a tight black leather vest over a bright white shirt with a black bandanna wrapped around his neck. On top of his black trousers, he wore a gun holster belted around his waist with a six-shooter strapped to a thick thigh. When he neared the hotel, he slowed his horse and, in one graceful swoop, dismounted.

A sound of thunder made her glance toward the end of the street. Three riders bore down on the man dressed in black. Allison stepped onto the porch and hurried to the rail. She opened her mouth to call out a warning, but before she made a sound, the man spun around to meet them.

Their horses slid to a halt a few feet away from the man. The sheriff put down his carving and stepped off the walkway.

"I'll make ye pay fer what ye did tae our sheep!" the youngest cowboy yelled with a Scottish burr as he pulled his gun from his holster and pointed the weapon at the man's middle.

In less than a blink of an eye, the man in black grabbed the young cowboy by the front of his shirt, pulled him off his horse and threw him to the ground. He placed a knee on the young man's chest and knocked the gun out of his hand.

"Don't ever pull a gun on me again unless you intend to use it, boy," the man growled at the startled young Scotsman.

The scene unfolded so fast the other two men never had time to react, and now, with the sheriff standing over them with his gun drawn, they were unable to do anything to help their friend.

Another roar of thunder exploded into town as an older man, followed by two more riders, raced to the middle of the fray.

"McKay get off m'boy!" the gray-haired man bellowed with a thick Scottish accent.

They called him McKay.

Allison inhaled a quick breath and leaned a bit farther over the rail.

"Kincade, you better warn your son that I don't take kindly to guns pointed in my direction. Next time, he could end up dead," the man in black snarled, easing off the young man. The sheriff retrieved the young Scotsman's gun from the road.

"Bran get back on yer horse," the older man ordered.

"Pa, ye know as well as I. He did it. Him or his brothers." The young man mounted his animal.

"What are the McKays supposed to have done this time, Kincade?" A tinge of disgust edged the cowboy's voice.

"Slaughtered our livestock. Three sheep. Butchered and left tae rot."

"What makes you think the killings were the work of the McKays?" The sheriff holstered his gun, stepped forward and handed the young man's revolver to his father.

"They were found dead, scattered all over on the back corner of their property where it abuts ours. We all know how they feel about our sheep," Bran roared.

The man in black ignored Bran and looked to the older man when he spoke. "We don't hide how we feel. Your sheep strip the land bare, they smell bad, and they don't belong beside cattle. Even so, I can promise no McKay or any of my men killed your animals. You better look somewhere else for your answers and leave my family alone."

"We'll see. Boys get back tae the ranch," Mr. Kincade said.

There was a frenzy of movement as the riders reined their horses around to head out of town.

The sheriff called to Mr. Kincade, "Lachlan, I'll look into the slaughter of your sheep and see what I can find out."

"I'd be much obliged, Sheriff. I'd like tae get tae the bottom of this."

"Kincade, keep your pup on a short leash, or he's gonna get hurt," the man in black said gruffly as he picked up his horse's reins.

Allison leaned her hips heavily against the upper porch rail while she watched the men below disburse except for the one they called McKay and the sheriff. They talked in muted tones before parting company.

Her heart pounded in her chest. Could this be the man she was to marry? As if he had read her mind, the man looked up to where she stood at the rail. The scar on his cheek stood out in the sun light. His deep blue eyes bore into her soul. Caught spying on her future husband, she at once whirled about and rushed into her room.

~Chapter Four~

Out of the corner of his eye, Jayson caught a glimpse of rose-colored fabric fluttering in the wind on the upper porch of the hotel. When he looked up, he locked gazes with the comeliest young woman he had ever laid eyes on. Her clothes were too fashionable and her bearing too sophisticated for the West. His heart pounded with excitement. This must be his bride.

Her delicate features turned hard before she reeled around and disappeared into her room.

How nice. The woman I'm set to marry is repulsed by the very sight of me. The next fifty years should be interesting.

He had been foolish to let Peter talk him into an arranged marriage to a woman of social standing from Boston.

Jayson led his horse to the hitching post outside Pearson's Hotel and wrapped the reins around the pole. He untied his black jacket from behind his saddle and tugged it on over his vest. His brothers were going to be furious with him for not telling them of his plans.

Why should he? He didn't need their permission. Nor did he want them to talk him out of getting married. As the head of the family, he did everything for their sake—and the ranch's, even getting hitched. It was time they had a woman in the house. The place lacked warmth since his mother had passed. The laughter was gone. His brothers were getting too boisterous and wild. They needed a woman around, especially his youngest brother, Daniel, who was still at that gawky age of not quite a man.

When Peter first wrote about a young woman in trouble, Jayson didn't want to get involved. It wasn't his problem. But once he thought about Peter's proposal, he decided this might be the only way he could ever start a family of his own. Since the accident two years ago, ladies weren't lining up for a chance to be Mrs. Jayson McKay. Most women couldn't get past the grotesquely scarred skin running down the side of his face from below the corner of his left eye, to the base of his neck. Never mind the scars he always kept covered on his left arm and hand. It's not like he could just go to the city, court a woman, marry her, and bring her back to the ranch. None of the ladies would make it past the first meeting. He hadn't tried but was sure of the outcome.

Jayson took the front steps of the hotel two at a time. He had to finish his business in town, so he could get home and check on those slaughtered sheep. It gnawed in his belly that the Kincade's would accuse his family of something they hadn't done.

"Jayson," a friendly voice called from the street.

Peter rushed across the thoroughfare from the direction of the general store.

As Peter climbed the wooden steps, Jayson removed the glove on his right hand and extended it. "Good to see you again, my friend."

Peter clasped his hand and gave a firm shake. "It's been too long."

Jayson patted Peter's shoulder.

"I guess you haven't had a chance to see her yet?" Peter removed his hat and brushed back his hair with his fingers.

"Actually, I caught a glimpse of her standing at the upper rail. You weren't kidding. She's a looker, all right."

"Wait until you meet her. She's more than a pretty face."

"That remains to be seen," he said with an edge in his voice.

"Thanks for taking me up on my proposal."

Jayson removed his Stetson and swiped dust off the brim with his hand. "I'm not sure I had much choice with you threatening to break your vows to marry her yourself."

"Desperate times needed desperate measures." Peter chuckled.

"You've been plotting to get me hitched for years. You must be proud of yourself."

"Strutting around like a peacock ever since you agreed. What's the point of you and your brothers building up your spread if none of you marry or have children? The way you all were going about settling down, no one would inherit the ranch. I'm just getting things started. First you. Then your brothers."

"Are you sure she's up for this? I'm hoping she doesn't get married this week and then hightail it back to Boston next week."

"I don't believe she'd do that. Once she makes up her mind, she won't change it without good reason." Peter gave him a pointed look. "Don't give her a reason."

***

Allison washed away the morning's grime and then made her way to the top of the stairs. The rich sound of male voices rose from the lobby below. Although she was unable to see their faces, she knew the voices belonged to Father Peter and Mr. McKay. She couldn't quite make out all their words but discerned warmth and mutual respect in their tone.

She straightened her back, lifted her skirts, and began her descent. When the men came into view, they were standing face to face next to the entrance of the hotel dining room. She slowed her steps and took a moment to study the stranger unnoticed. He was a tall and powerfully built man who differed from the men back home. Self-confidence surrounded him, not arrogance. He reminded her of a man who made his own way in life and didn't depend on wealth or connections.

Her gaze raked her future husband. He could almost pass as a gentleman in his stark white shirt and midnight-black slacks, vest, and jacket. That was, if one failed to consider the curved shape of his hat, the gun holster sitting low on his hips, and the pointed boots with silver spurs. Each piece painted a daunting picture.

From where she stood, she saw a slight distortion of the skin flowing down Mr. McKay's left cheek into the black handkerchief knotted around his neck. She reminded herself to stay calm when he looked at her with those beautiful almond-shaped eyes she'd glimpsed earlier and hoped she wouldn't stumble over her words.

He manifested an unexpected rugged handsomeness. She'd pictured a more ordinary man. Someday she might feel comfortable in his presence, but it wasn't today.

She grabbed hold of the handrail and continued to the lobby. In unison, the men turned and looked at her as she came into view.

Father Peter took a few steps forward and held out his hand. "Miss Monroe, I hope we gave you enough time to freshen up."

"Yes, plenty. Thank you." She took the offered support.

Stepping down off the last step, she gave the men one of her brightest smiles as she pried her fingers from the safety of the railing. If Mr. McKay looked formidable from a distance when yanking a full-size man off a horse, he looked even more so up close. She bit at her trembling lower lip, disengaged her hand from Father Peter's, and offered it to her soon-to-be husband. "Mr. McKay, I presume."

"Call me, Jayson." He extended his bare hand to meet her halfway and gave her fingers a gentle squeeze.

"Please, call me Allison." She quickly pulled away from their contact, for with his touch came unexpected heat that traveled up her arm and filled her chest with surprising warmth.

"Now that you've finally been introduced, I'll leave you two to get to know each other over an early supper while I visit with my family. Send word if you need me." Father Peter gave the couple a nod.

Allison's stomach knotted. She hadn't expected to be left alone with this man quite so soon and almost reached for Father Peter's arm when he spun around to leave.

"I have a table waiting. Come join me for a bite to eat. You must be hungry after your journey." Jayson waved her through the dining room archway.

"It would be my pleasure." Allison hid her unease behind a well-trained mask of social graces. "I have heard from a reliable source that Mrs. Pearson makes the best chicken stew in the territory." She chanced a quick sideways glance for his reaction. To her delight, the corners of his lips curled up in a slight grin. He had a nice shaped mouth, but she doubted he smiled a lot. Something told her his manner was more of a serious nature.

"Mrs. Pearson would be thrilled to hear such news. I myself have traveled out of my way for just a morsel."

She found his demeanor gentlemanly but reserved. He was extremely hard to read, which frustrated her. Usually she could tell if a man found her attractive, but her future husband appeared indifferent. He guided her toward a big window overlooking the street. A clean red-checkered linen tablecloth covered the table. He pulled out her chair.

Before he joined her, a stout older woman hurried through the back door with a giant smile on her face. "Jayson, are you going to introduce me?"

He stepped aside and extended an arm for introductions. "Miss Monroe, let me introduce you to the best cook in all of Flat Rock, Mrs. Pearson."

"I'm pleased to meet you," Allison said. "I've already been enlightened to the fact that your chicken stew is quite renowned. How did Father Peter phrase it? Oh, yes, he said he 'could find Mrs. Pearson's chicken stew in the dark'."

The gray-haired woman pressed an open hand to her belly and hooted with laughter. "These boys are always teasing me. I'm pleased to finally meet you. Call me Margaret. I understand Father Peter escorted you here all the way from Boston. Will you be leaving in a few days when he does, Miss Monroe?"

"Please, call me Allison. My intentions are to remain here in Flat Rock." She glanced at Jayson in case he wanted to correct her statement.

"The rumors are true then." Mrs. Pearson beamed. "Welcome to our town. It'll be nice to have a new young lady in these parts. An educated woman is a rarity around here. I'm afraid most of the young ones head off to the cities and never return."

"The city no longer holds my interest." Allison knew she shouldn't color the truth, but she didn't want to start her new life by giving the impression she longed for what she'd left behind, even if she did.

"Would you care for a bowl of my chicken stew?"

A wafting aroma of roasted chicken, sweet sauce, and baked pastry hung on the air, tantalizing Allison's nostrils with every inhalation. "Yes, please. My mouth is watering already."

"I'll have a bowl, too," Jayson added as he took a seat.

Mrs. Pearson hurried off to the kitchen.

Sitting across from Jayson McKay, she realized how little she knew about this man dressed in black. On their way to the Montana Territory, she had avoided the subject because her future seemed too daunting to think about. The only thing she really knew about the rancher was that Father Peter held him in exceedingly high regard. Such knowledge should have been sufficient, but at that moment, it wasn't enough to quiet her unease. Since they were alone, she needed to confront Jayson with her nagging questions and set ground rules for their union. Her heart raced. Over the past few days, she'd spent many hours imagining how their first meeting would go and how her future husband would react to her stipulations.

Jayson watched her with intense blue eyes, the kind that never missed a detail. His quiet perusal unbalanced her. She couldn't guess what his thoughts were. His brows furrowed, and she wasn't sure if his expression was a good thing or a bad thing.

"First off, Mr. McKay..." she began but stopped when he raised an eyebrow at her slip.

"I mean, Jayson," she corrected.

He visibly relaxed with the use of his Christian name.

"I would be remiss if I didn't come right out and thank you for even considering my request. It must have been difficult to agree to attach yourself to a tarnished woman. I want you to know I'm not usually one to indulge in improprieties and will not embarrass you or your family with any behavior unbefitting a married woman. I know the circumstances surrounding our union are highly unusual and, if we decide to pursue our course, I'm sure it will cause some disruption in your life and the lives of your family."

"We'll be fine."

"There will be those who will frown upon me for my past sins and, through your marriage to me, you may also be frowned upon."

"I can handle that." He placed his hands on the table and laced his fingers, one hand gloved and the other bare.

"On our journey here, Father Peter disclosed only a few details about your life."

"What did he tell you?" He leaned forward.

"He told me you and your brothers have a ranch on the outskirts of Flat Rock. You raise cattle and horses. He said your parents have passed. As the eldest, you watch out for your younger brothers. He said the two of you have been friends since birth. Is there anything else I should know?"

"No, reckon that just about does it," he drawled, reclining back in his chair.

That was it? She was supposed to marry a man who was only willing to share a few scraps of information about himself. She wanted to stamp her foot and complain.

"Is there anything you want to know about me?" She waited expectedly.

"No, I'm sure if I get curious about something, I'll come right out and ask."

Frustrated by his lack of cooperation but determined to pull something out of him which painted a picture of what kind of man he truly was, she continued, "May I ask your reasons for agreeing to such an arrangement?"

He shrugged. "My friend asked for my help."

"You agreed to marry a pregnant woman, who you don't know, because your friend asked you to?"

"He's a good friend."

***

Jayson knew she was annoyed with him. He didn't trust her. She was far too pretty and sophisticated for the rough country life of Montana. Far too good for a scarred man like him, whose looks would never return to what they were before. He reminded himself not to get too attached as he stared into her doe-like brown eyes. A week from now or maybe a month or two, she would tire of this life, tire of him, and return to the city.

To go back on his word was not an option. He'd told Peter he would marry the woman and he wouldn't back out now. He would provide a name for her child and if she chose to eventually leave him, then so be it. If, for whatever reason, she chose to stay, there would be children to inherit his portion of the ranch.

His future bride fidgeted in her seat. Obviously, there was a topic she wanted to touch upon but was having trouble with the words. He sank back further in his chair, crossed his arms over his chest, and waited for what she would say next. So far, she had remarkable candor.

She inhaled deeply as if to beef up her courage. "Before I agree to this union, I need a few assurances from you. I'm concerned for the welfare of my unborn child. Will you raise the child as your own, whether it's a girl or boy?"

"Most definitely," he replied without hesitation.

Mrs. Pearson came out carrying two bowls of stew and a basket of fresh bread, which she placed in front of them. From a teapot on the side table, she poured Allison a cup and left them with an all-knowing smile plastered on her face.

***

Once they were alone again, Allison waited until Jayson looked up from his meal and gave her his full attention. "There is one other thing I must speak with you about. I would have your promise that we wait until after I deliver the baby to consummate our marriage. I only ask this of you because I'm afraid of harming my child."

Jayson's jaw muscles tightened. "So, you'll agree to marry me as long as I promise not to bed you until after the baby is born," he said with a biting edge.

She nibbled on her bottom lip. "Yes, that's what I propose. I will have a room to myself until the baby is born. For the sake of my child."

"Of course. Why else would you suggest such a thing?" he drawled.

"Will you agree to my terms?"

"I will," he said tersely and returned to eating his lunch.

Allison breathed a silent sigh of relief. Their conversation had gone better than expected. He'd agreed to abide by her stipulations, although he wasn't happy with her conditions. It was shameful to use her unborn child as an excuse to put off the inevitable. But, she couldn't bring herself to lie with a stranger and needed time to come to terms with being with a man, even one she called her husband. She lowered her head and focused on her food as she tried to regain her composure. On the outside, she presented herself as a well-spoken, confident woman, but on the inside, she quaked with innocence and insecurities.

~Chapter Five~

With a trembling hand, Allison placed her finely painted teacup on the matching saucer. Jayson, who sat across the table, removed his pocket watch, opened the engraved cover, and glanced at the hour.

It was time.

Their stilted exchange grew stale. Her company no longer held his interest. He seemed eager to leave. There was no reason to put off the wedding any longer. Jayson had agreed to her terms. Soon they would wed.

He sent a young boy to the general store to tell Father Peter they were ready to take their vows.

Allison placed her clammy hands under the table and rested them on top of her satin skirt. She stroked her rounded belly until a small thrust nudged her open hand. Her gaze dropped to her lap. A rush of pure wonderment stole her breath, as it did every time she felt movement. The baby wouldn't be long now, just a few more months. Hopefully, she was making the right decision.

"It's time we made our way to the church," Jayson said, breaking the silence.

"Of course," she replied evenly, determined to keep the fear from her voice.

"If I were a betting man, I'd say Peter is already waiting for us. I'm sure he's anxious to get this over and done with." A hint of amusement crossed his face.

Allison imagined he was right about Father Peter. Their journey west was long and now that they arrived safely at their destination, it was time to hand her over to her new husband. She shivered at the thought.

Jayson rose to his feet and pulled out her chair. He took hold of her elbow with a light touch and guided her to stand.

The brush of his fingers upon her arm caused torrents of tingles to travel to the pit of her stomach. Her reaction to his nearness surprised her. She thought herself accustomed to a gentleman's assistance. Was it his size causing such a stir? Or the way he'd stood up to those men in the street and yet walked away unscathed?

She wasn't quite sure.

He pushed in her chair. "I know the wedding seems rushed, but it's best not to drag out our engagement since we've come to an understanding. The sooner we say our vows, the sooner you can settle in at the ranch."

She nodded as she gazed into brilliant blue eyes that studied her with wariness. He didn't trust her pledge to see their wedding through to the end. What he failed to consider was she had no other options. No matter how uncomfortable their union, she had to make the best of it.

There was nowhere else for her to go.

"Margaret," Jayson's raised voice resounded in the empty dining room. "If you and Timothy close for a few minutes, you could meet us over at the church and bear witness to our marriage."

Mrs. Pearson stepped through the kitchen doorway wiping her hands on the apron tied around her waist. She laughed deep in her throat, the excitement twinkling in her green eyes. "I thought you'd never ask. I'll gather my bonnet, and we'll be there directly." Before disappearing back into the kitchen, she shook a chubby finger at them. "Don't you dare start without us."

Jayson turned to Allison. "I hope you don't mind if the Pearsons and the Thomases witness our vows. Somehow, they know all about our plans, and I suppose they'd feel put out if they weren't invited."

"Not at all. I would be honored to have your friends present." Allison cringed. She knew this day would come. Jasmine was the first to find out about her shame, but soon all the people living in Flat Rock would know of their hurried marriage. In no time, everyone would be privy to her sins. The humiliation of her past actions was hers to bear for the rest of her life. There would be no escape.

She inhaled deeply to quiet her quaking stomach. Thank goodness her parents hadn't found out about her disgrace before she married. Their disappointment would've been the hardest to endure.

Allison grasped Jayson's bent elbow and followed along as he led her to the church at the end of the street. He was tall, at least three inches taller than her previous suitor, and twice as broad. A bitter taste soured her mouth at the thought of Robert Winston Winthrop III, her unborn baby's father. Thankfully, Robert and Jayson shared no obvious similarities. She prayed her memory of her former suitor faded quickly. She longed to forget the man who, without remorse, had left her broken-hearted.

Squinting against the glare of the afternoon sun, she chided herself for forgetting her lace parasol in the hotel room. Since her small fancy hat offered no protection from the bright rays, she placed a hand against her forehead to shield her eyes and glanced up at her future husband, whose head was properly covered.

Was it her imagination or had Jayson purposely placed her on the side where the scar on his cheek was not visible? She wondered if women had reacted poorly to the sight in the past. She couldn't fathom how anyone would bother with the scar once they stared into his beautiful, almond-shaped eyes, which held the weight of responsibility in their depths and pleaded silently for salvation. It would take a lot to miss his perfect cheekbones, straight nose, and thick sun-kissed brown hair.

As they reached the wooden steps, she lifted her rustling skirts. Jayson grasped her elbow with a strong, supportive hand and helped her with the short climb to the open double doors leading into the church.

Her world darkened the minute she entered. She halted over the threshold until her eyes adjusted to the dimness. A friendly voice called her name, and she turned toward the sound.

Father Peter stood at a simple altar in the front of the church. He wore an ear-to-ear grin, obviously pleased with himself and gestured to a couple standing at his side. "May I have the honor of introducing you to Mr. and Mrs. Thomas, my brother and sister-in-law."

Mrs. Thomas stepped forward and reached her arms around Allison for a hug. "Formalities mean little to friends around here. Please call me Hannah. Everyone else does."

Such a warm welcome from a stranger took Allison by surprise. "Nice to meet you, Hannah. I'm Allison."

Hannah stepped back and waved her hand. "This is my husband, Frank."

The man tilted his head and gave her a friendly smile. The resemblance between the two brothers amazed her, with Frank being an older version of Father Peter.

Hannah patted Allison's shoulder. "We're mighty glad you decided to come to Flat Rock and be part of our community, no matter the circumstances."

A wave of heat flowed over Allison's face. It shouldn't surprise her that this woman knew the real reason for their rushed marriage. Still, a flood of mortification gushed through her veins and shook her core.

"No need to fret," Hannah reassured her. "Not a one of us can call ourselves perfect. Not even Peter. The stories I could tell you would make you wonder how they ever gave him a white collar."

Father Peter tugged at his neck as if to loosen the binds. "Unfortunately, Hannah, I don't believe we have time for storytelling."

Jayson and Frank chuckled. Each gave Father Peter a quick pat on the back, plainly aware of his transgressions.

As a clear ploy to change a sore subject, Father Peter asked, "Are we waiting on your brothers?"

"No," Jayson said.

Father Peter took a book off the altar and held it tucked against his waist. "Did you tell them you planned to marry today?"

"No," Jayson said emphatically.

"Your plan is to bring a wife back to the ranch and surprise them with the news. Are you sure that's wise?"

"They have no say in the matter. I didn't feel like listening to any of their bellyaching."

"They're going to be angry," Father Peter said evenly.

The men's conversation baffled Allison. Why was Jayson keeping her a secret from his younger brothers? She didn't know anything about his siblings, but something told her she'd missed something.

Her eyes narrowed. "How old are your brothers?"

Jayson shrugged his shoulders. "Daniel is barely eighteen. Nathan and Chase are a few years behind me."

Allison's head spun like a top. She reached for a nearby pew to steady herself. When Father Peter told her Jayson took care of his three younger brothers, she assumed they were young boys. She never expected she'd be living with not just one, but four grown men.

What would they say when they found out she'd married their brother while pregnant with another man's child? How would she adjust to a family of men who might treat her with little or no respect? Jayson had agreed to take her and her baby in, but would they?

Hannah, who seemed to be the only one aware of her dilemma, took her arm and guided her to sit on a pew.

Hannah whispered in what seemed like a faraway voice, "Nothing to worry about. Everything will work out fine. You wait and see. The McKay men are good people."

***

Am I dreaming?

The next few minutes were a blur. Mr. and Mrs. Pearson arrived. Allison didn't know how she came to be positioned in the right spot facing the front of the church, but imagined Hannah had something to do with it. She gripped a small bouquet of wildflowers Margaret had placed in her hands. Somewhere in the back of her mind she knew both couples sat in the front pews.

Jayson stood ramrod straight at her side with a serious expression on his face. His hands clasped in front of him, one gloved and the other bare. He didn't flinch.

Father Peter's lips moved, but she only made out a few of his words over the loud beating of her heart in her ears. "Better...worse...richer...poorer...sickness...health...death."

Jayson reached for her clenched hands and loosened the grip on her drooping flowers, until he got one hand free. He turned her toward him.

A few barely distinguishable words poured from his lips.

Allison focused on Jayson's eyes. Bright and intense, they stared into hers, searching for something, but she knew not what. Then came her turn.

Father Peter nudged her to respond when appropriate.

She licked her dry lips and repeated "I will" and "I do" when cued or recited the priest's words when prompted, until Jayson placed a ring on her finger.

At the end of the ceremony, Jayson wrapped a thick arm around her back. His other hand tilted her chin up a notch. Surprised, she tried to step back, not sure what he was about. He pulled her closer until she was intimately pressed against his hard body. When his head came down with his lips slightly parted, she pushed against him, but he didn't budge.

His moist lips brushed against her dry ones, and then he kissed her deeply.

This was not part of their agreement. She had until the baby was born before they shared familiarity of a husband and wife. *He'd promised.* Had he not understood? Why would he behave so boldly in front of witnesses? Shouldn't he have given her the expected quick peck and been done with it?

She shirked from his touch, but he wouldn't allow her to wiggle out of his unyielding embrace. His lips pressed firmer against hers, and a flicker of his tongue searched the depths of her mouth. His warm breath mingled with her own. He smelled of the earth, fresh and pure.

Never had Allison experienced such intoxication. There rose an underlying promise of intense passion that Robert's stolen kisses never had. A quivering sensation surged through her body and settled deep within. Suddenly, she no longer wanted to step away but yearned to be nearer.

She coiled an arm around his thick neck. With a heightened awareness of his touch alone, she explored his mouth in the same way he delved into hers. She molded her breasts against his rock-hard chest and pressed her body along the length of his.

For a blessed moment, there was no one else in the world.

Allison instantly knew when his desire waned. He stopped his probing and withdrew. As he moved away, a sharp sense of loss caused a swell of disquiet to bubble up in her belly. Comprehension of time and place returned. With her awareness came a flood of mortification for her unexpected physical response in front of onlookers.

Instead of parting from Allison completely, Jayson surprised her by lining up cheek to cheek and breathing in her ear, "I have conceded to your demands for the time being but be forewarned, this is not a marriage of convenience only...I want more children. Do not for one minute think I will not hold you to your promises."

Allison's heart pounded like a drum as she tried to steady her jagged breath. Her face flamed with embarrassment, or was it indignation? She wasn't sure, but he sent a clear warning; he would not stand for games when it came to his marriage vows. He expected to bed her.

Jayson loosened his hold and abruptly moved away.

She struggled to regain her balance on wobbly legs. Without a backward glance, her new husband turned to shake hands with Father Peter. Thankfully, Margaret grabbed one of her arms to keep her from toppling over.

Shouts of well-wishes resounded throughout the room. Timothy, Frank, and Father Peter circled Jayson and offered their congratulations. A round of tumultuous laughter rang out. Sure the men's merriment was at her expense, she glared at Jayson's broad back and chafed under barely suppressed infuriation. How dare he kiss her like that in front of others and put her in a position to be ridiculed.

"All right, enough." Hannah wagged her finger. "You menfolk need to step out of the church and let us women have a moment alone."

"You heard the lady. Jayson, you too. We'll send the new bride out directly after we have a word with her." Margaret waved a hefty arm from side to side as if sweeping the men out from under her feet. "Don't give me that look, now get."

Once the men were gone, Allison put a hand to her mouth and skimmed her fingers across her tender lips.

What just happened?

Allison let Hannah lead her to a first-row pew where she plopped down with a loud thud.

Margaret stood in front of her and brushed a loose tendril of hair off her face. "I guess you weren't expecting such a thorough going over after you recited your vows."

"If I'm not mistaken, I believe you just got branded," Hannah chuckled. "It seems Jayson wanted you to know you are his."

Allison exhaled slowly to calm her racing heart. "He's an infuriating man. As bold as can be."

"Jayson sure has the power to set a woman aflame. I daresay." Margaret fanned her face with her open hand. "You're sure a lucky woman. All he needs is a little taming and he'll trot around like the perfect saddle pony."

"I'm not so sure he can be tamed. Even if he could, I doubt I'm the woman for the job. I know almost nothing about men, especially a rancher from Montana. I wouldn't know how to go about taming someone like that." She ran the tip of her tongue over her lips.

"Oh, honey." Hannah waved her arms around in the air. "It's as easy as making a pie. All you do is to get him to fall in love with you."

"I'm afraid I have no luck with matters of the heart." She sighed heavily. "That's why I stand here today, married to a man I don't know. Right now, I cling to little hope we'll ever be more than acquaintances living under the same roof."

Hannah scooted Allison over on the pew. "You can't give up before you've even started."

"You don't know me. I have very little to offer such a man," she said.

"You're wrong on both fronts." Hannah patted the top of her hands lying in her lap. "We do know you. Quite well, in fact."

"How can that be?" she asked, perplexed.

"Well, I'm afraid it's Peter's fault. He happens to be a devoted letter writer and when he arrived at St. Joseph's Church, he began writing about some of his parishioners, you in particular. Margaret and I waited every day for the mail, so we could read his letters together."

Allison turned to Hannah. "He wrote about me? What did he say?" Should she be angry about his betrayal of her confidence?

Margaret patted Allison's arm. "Don't you worry, my dear. He thinks highly of you and was so happy when you agreed to help him tend the sick."

"And then he told us about how you stopped going with him on his rounds, stopped going to parties, and never left your parents' house. We were so worried about you," Hannah said.

"Hannah thought you had succumbed to some illness from the sick you were nursing." Margaret swept another loose strand of hair out of Allison's face and placed it behind her ear.

"We were relieved when we found out you weren't dying," Hannah said. "I guess what we're trying to say is we do know you, and we're glad you've chosen to come here to be part of our lives. We're simple folks who enjoy each other's company. We kick up our heels now and then, but you won't find too many of those fancy parties. No matter the circumstances, we know your character and welcome you to our home. We hope you'll be happy here."

Could it be true? She scarcely dared to believe her ears. Were these women offering friendship and acceptance? Her heart ached with hope that this was so.

Margaret straightened her back and placed her hands on her hips. "Jayson is a very headstrong man. He takes his position as the head of his family most seriously. He might be a little difficult to sway because a woman hurt him terribly bad in his past, but mark my words, he'll soon fall for you. When he does, he'll give you a good life."

"Thank you, so much. You've managed to put some fears to rest." They were being so nice to her. Allison couldn't find the words to explain that their union was nothing more than a business deal.

"If you need anything, anything at all, we're here for you. We'll help you in any way we can. After all, we women need to stick together," Margaret said.

The door opened with a creak, causing all three ladies to turn toward the sound. Jayson stuck his head in the tiny church and removed his hat in a sweeping motion. "Ladies, do you think I can have my bride back? It's time to go home."

~Chapter Six~

Whatever possessed him to agree to this sham of a marriage?

Jayson stood on the top of the church steps next to Allison and watched his friends return to their respective businesses. His new wife stood so stiffly, he imagined with the least bit of provocation she might bolt from his side, high-tail it to the stage depot and hitch a ride on the first stage back to Boston. More than likely, she harbored second thoughts about marrying a scarred man such as himself.

Just like, Jacquelyn, my ex-fiancée did.

He glanced down at the profile of her pretty face and feminine form. She was a looker, all right. A woman whose beauty would be wasted on the handful of people who laid eyes on her out here in the middle of nowhere. She belonged in the big city, gracing the fancy parlors of her peers.

A tight ball of knots twisted his innards. His behavior at the end of the ceremony was abhorrent. Usually, he had better control.

Why did I kiss her like that?

He knew why. He resented her stipulation preventing him from consummating their marriage. The kiss was meant to remind his new wife that even though he had agreed to her demands, he would eventually bed her, no matter how grotesque he looked. If she stuck around, he expected her to hold up her end of the bargain.

He wanted children.

Jayson removed his Stetson and raked his fingers through his short mop of hair. His intentions had backfired, though; who knew she'd respond so passionately. He drew a quick breath and sighed heavily. Instead of leaving her wanting, he found himself wishing for more.

Peter nudged him with his elbow. "Jayson, you didn't hear a word I said."

"Sorry, you were saying?"

"I asked what your plans are now."

Jayson pursed his lips. "We'll head out to the ranch as soon as Daniel gets here. I have some business I should take care of. Can you believe Lachlan Kincade and his son are accusing us of slaughtering their sheep? We've been neighbors for five long years and not once have we ever done anything to warrant such an accusation. I need to get to the truth before they start a range war."

"It's good to see you trying to stay out of trouble." Peter placed his hat on his head.

"It seems my days of getting into mischief ended around the same time you moved away to join the priesthood." Jayson jabbed his friend in the chest with two fingers. "What a coincidence."

"I'm sure I don't know what you're talking about," Peter protested with a sly smile.

Jayson arched a brow. "Now that you're no longer enticing me into boyhood shenanigans, I go out of my way to be friendly with my neighbors, no matter our differences. You never know when you might need someone to help you out of a mess. Besides, Samantha Kincade has her sights set on Chase and I don't want to jeopardize their relationship, if there is one. He wouldn't appreciate a range war if he fancies the young lady."

Jayson scanned the horizon. A cloud of dust billowed in the distance, heading their way. His family's four-wheeled, two-seated phaeton carriage pulled by Lewis and Clarke, a matched pair of high-stepping black geldings, rolled toward the church at a quick pace. His youngest brother, Daniel, had a huge grin plastered on his face, a sure sign he'd raced the animals all the way to town.

"I haven't seen your mother's carriage in years. I forgot how handsome it is," Peter said.

Jayson stole a look at Allison and then back at the four-wheeled surrey coming their way. "We had no reason to take the carriage out before now."

Daniel halted the team of breathless and sweat-soaked horses at the white picket fence in front of the church and glanced at Jayson. "Wow, you should've seen how fast they flew here. I couldn't hold them back. I think they really like pulling this old carriage. Much more than the buckboard."

"Make sure you water them after they cool off," he said.

Daniel locked the carriage brake and tied the reins to the lever. "Howdy, Father Peter. I didn't know you were coming for a visit. Welcome home."

"Young Daniel. I almost didn't recognize you. You're all grown up." Peter descended the steps and walked toward the gate.

"Tell that to my brothers. They still treat me like a kid and make me run their mindless errands." Daniel jumped down from the seat in one agile swoop. When his boots hit the ground, he removed his hat and knocked it hard against his brown chaps, dislodging a layer of dust. "Jayson, are you ready to tell me why you ordered me to clean up Ma's carriage and bring it to town?"

"I needed the buggy, so you can take my new wife home." Jayson grasped Allison's arm and urged her forward, down the last few steps to the stone walkway.

Daniel's eyes grew wide, and his mouth dropped open. His younger brother ran his fingers through his thick brown hair and shook his head in disbelief. "You're joshing me, aren't you?"

"Nope." He stopped at the fence.

Allison extended a gloved hand. "It's a pleasure to meet you, Daniel. You can call me Allison."

Daniel walked forward, took her hand, and gave it a slight shake. "Huh...a pleasure to meet you, too, ma'am," he said, stumbling over his words.

"Take the carriage over to the stage depot and pick up Allison's trunk. Then meet us back at the hotel. We have to retrieve the rest of her belongings before we head home."

Jayson knew his barked orders would help his brother recover from his startle.

"See what I mean." Daniel smiled brightly. "All they ever do is boss me around. Nice to see you, Father Peter. Jayson, I'll meet you in front of Pearson's in a few minutes." He hopped onto the driver's seat, took up the reins, and sent the matched pair into a quick trot through town.

"Don't forget to water the horses," he shouted as the buggy disappeared down the road.

Daniel waved his hat in the air a few times before slapping it back on his head.

"He worships you, you know. He'll be the easiest one to accept your marriage. I still think you should've told Chase and Nathan in advance, so they had time to wrap their heads around the notion," Peter said as they watched Daniel in the distance.

"Like I said before it makes no never-mind to me. They either accept it or not. I'm not quibbling with them over my decision."

The news that he had got married would take his brothers by surprise. He wasn't sure what the ramifications would be for not telling them his plans. All he knew was he had to do something to get out of his funk, his dark mood. Two years had passed since the fire and moving back to the ranch. Besides the loss of his mother, not much had changed in those two years. His old life in Washington

D.C. was long gone, just a fading memory of better times. He needed something to live for, like children. His brothers would've tried to talk him out of getting hitched; they would've said he was crazy. But, he'd felt the need for a change. He knew they'd be more accepting after the deed was done. After all, it was hard to go back once it was official.

Allison looked up. "Father Peter, how long will you be staying in town?"

"I suppose I'll be here a few more days. Why?"

"I'm wondering if you might come to dinner before you leave. I could put something together." Allison glanced at him for approval.

Jayson nodded his agreement. "Come for supper tomorrow night. It'll be nice to spend some time with you before you return to Boston."

"Sounds tempting. How can I refuse? What time?" Peter asked.

"Around six." He returned the Stetson to his head.

"Looking forward to it." Peter glanced over his shoulder and his face grew grim. "Oh, no. Look who's coming this way. It's your aunt."

***

A heavy-set woman, dressed head to toe in black, hurried across the street toward the church waving her cane in the air. The hairs on the back of Allison's neck stood at attention and she stepped closer to Jayson.

"What are you boys doing with your ma's carriage? Don't you try to pull one over on me. I know you're up to something. And who's with you, Peter Thomas?" the woman called out as she closed the distance between them.

Her husband's firm hand rested in the middle of Allison's back and moved her closer to the picket fence.

Jayson removed his hat. "Aunt Beatrice, I would like to introduce you to my wife."

"Wife? Did you get kicked in the head? You have no wife."

Allison straightened.

"Well, the thing is we just got married a few minutes ago. Aunt Beatrice, this is Allison McKay."

"Pleased to meet you." Allison extended her hand. The woman ignored the friendly gesture, so she dropped her arm.

Aunt Beatrice locked eyes with Jayson. "Are you crazy? Have you no sense at all? Who is this woman, and what do you know about her? She probably only married you for your money."

Allison felt the sting as sure as if she'd been slapped. She sucked in a gulp of air, stood tall, and laced her fingers in front of her.

Father Peter stepped closer to Aunt Beatrice. "Now that's not fair. Allison isn't that kind of lady, and Jayson is a grown man who can make his own decisions."

Aunt Beatrice tapped the ground hard with the tip of her cane. "When I want your opinion, Peter Thomas, I will ask for it. Otherwise, keep it to yourself."

"The deed is done," Jayson stated flatly.

Aunt Beatrice inspected Allison up and down with a fierce scowl.

It took all the mettle Allison could muster to not shrink under the older woman's perusal. One look at the woman dressed in black and Allison knew the kind of person Jayson's aunt was. Boston was full of women like Aunt Beatrice. These were the snobs and bullies of society. Some ladies thrived on making other people's lives miserable, and she could tell this was one of those women.

A chill caused her to shiver, even though the sun was warm.

Aunt Beatrice shook a finger at Jayson. "Mark my words, you are making a big mistake. This woman has an ulterior motive for marrying you. Don't be a buffoon. Get an annulment while you still can, before she takes you for everything you have."

Heat flamed in Allison's cheeks, and she glared at Aunt Beatrice. How dare this woman have the gall to say such things? She fisted her hands at her sides. It took great control not to lunge for the woman's throat. She inhaled deeply, stomped down her anger, and gathered her courage.

"Excuse me, Aunt Beatrice," she said in a pointed and even tone. "I find your behavior boorish and insulting. It's none of your concern why we have married. In the future, if you have nothing pleasant to say to us, then hold your tongue." She hooked her arm in Jayson's and gazed into his surprised blue eyes. "Husband, please take me home."

He placed his hat on his head, tipped the brim in his aunt's direction, and led her through the gate toward the hotel with Father Peter following a few steps behind. She heard Aunt Beatrice's loud huff of irritation, but to the woman's credit, she kept her thoughts to herself.

When they were a few yards away, she turned to Jayson. "I know I promised not to do anything inappropriate as your wife, but I couldn't help myself. I have a bad habit of speaking my mind. I apologize for my behavior."

"Don't fret on my account. Frankly, we don't set limits with her as often as we should. She'll get over it," he said with a hint of amusement in his tone.

"I hope you're right." She didn't like the idea of starting a new life with an adversary in the family.

***

Daniel wasted no time picking Allison up at the hotel. In a matter of minutes, they said their goodbyes, and soon she was on her way to the McKay ranch. Jayson rode his horse a few lengths ahead of the carriage, and she joined Daniel on the cushioned leather driver's seat. The tasseled top blocked out the sun's blazing rays, and a warm breeze brushed against her face, sending loose tendrils of hair dancing around her head. The carriage had a smooth ride, and she enjoyed the buggy much more than the stagecoach she'd ridden in earlier in the day.

Her head wanted to burst with the questions she yearned to ask, but she waited until they were out of town, and Jayson rode far enough ahead to not overhear her conversation with his brother. When the time was right, she turned to Daniel in hopes he'd be willing to share.

"Why is your brother not the one driving me out to the ranch?" she asked.

Daniel smiled broadly, obviously happy to join in any discussion she had to offer. "Jayson never takes up the reins. He prefers to ride his horse. Whenever we take out the carriage or buckboard, he makes one of us do the driving."

How odd. Her new husband might never take her on a carriage ride. There was something sad about such a thought. "What are your brothers like?"

"Chase, he's two years younger than Jayson, tends to be hot-headed. If it weren't for Jayson, he'd get himself into a lot of trouble. Nathan, on the other hand, is more serious. He went to school back East and studied to become a doctor but came home when Ma got sick with pneumonia last year. He feels really bad he couldn't save her and hasn't gone back to finish his schooling."

"I'm sorry to hear she passed. It must have been hard for you." She couldn't imagine a life without her mother. Although she'd moved across the country, she hoped to one day see her again.

"It would've been harder if Jayson hadn't got burned and come home to live with us before she died. He keeps the ranch running smoothly. What he says goes," Daniel stated with adoration.

"Where did he live before his accident?"

"He lived outside Washington D.C. and went to Georgetown University where he studied the law and politics. He planned to become a senator. Our grandfather was a senator. Then the fire happened, and he got hurt pretty bad, so he came home, and Ma tended his wounds." Suddenly Daniel looked at Jayson's back sheepishly. "I'm afraid if you want to know more about what happened, Jayson will have to tell you himself. I don't think he'd like me talking about it much."

"I understand. Tell me about the ranch. What's it like?" She couldn't believe Jayson had lived in the nation's capital. At one time, he'd lived in a city and had been on his way to becoming a senator. There was more to the man she'd married than he let on.

"We're almost home. You're going to like it. The house has five bedrooms and a wraparound porch. Ma made Pa paint it white. It's like the ones she saw in Virginia when she visited Pa's family on their plantation on the Potomac River. Ma put a flower garden in the front yard. We built a white picket fence around the perimeter, so the animals can't get into her flowers. Gus has a big enclosed vegetable garden out back where he grows our vegetables. He's one of our ranch hands. He's too old to go out riding the range, so Jayson put him in charge of the vegetables and barnyard animals. I help him with the animals. Cookie is the cook for the ranch hands. He pretty much runs the bunkhouse. Hank is the foreman. We have about five other hands right now." Daniel happily rambled on as he turned the team onto a side road.

The carriage went under a timbered archway with the letters MK carved in the center of a big wooden sign. Allison sucked in her breath. She was almost *home*.

After a few more miles on the dirt road, the carriage rolled over a knoll and below, in a lush green valley, was the McKay Ranch. Allison's heart pounded in her ears, for the spread was more beautiful than she'd imagined. The white-washed clapboard home with numerous chimneys poking out the shingled rooftop sat grandly on the rich green land. In the distance, a stream ran through the valley, then emptied out into a large crystal blue pond on the side of the house before it narrowed back into a stream, breaking the land up in two halves. A huge barn stood across from the house with an attached building on the side, resembling what she imagined was a bunkhouse. Corrals filled with livestock broke up the tree-lined countryside.

Just as Daniel said, there was a closed-in front yard with red and yellow flowers poking out of the ground haphazardly. The corners of her mouth turned up in a smile; she could picture herself working in the flower garden someday.

Daniel halted the team of horses at the hitching post in front of the fence and hopped to the ground. He extended his hand to help her alight, but Jayson nudged him aside and took his place. Her new husband reached up and slid his hands under her arms and against her rib cage as she laid her palms on his shoulders for support. He lifted her off the carriage and placed her feet on the ground so gently and effortlessly she wondered about the underlying strength he possessed.

"Welcome home," he said when he let her go. "I know it's not what you're used to in Boston, but it's comfortable enough."

"Your home is lovely. I'm sure it'll suit me just fine," she replied.

"We'll show you to your room. Daniel, grab one end of the trunk." Jayson threw her travel bag on top and grabbed a handle.

Allison followed them through the front door. The first thing to catch her eye was a beautiful central staircase with a carved rail. The men began their ascent to the second floor with her belongings. She lagged behind, glanced into a formal parlor, and found an ornate central fireplace, surrounded by velvet couches and chairs. Her heart pounded in her chest when she saw a Steinway baby grand piano tucked in a corner. She climbed the stairs and joined the men in the front bedroom.

"You can sleep here. This was my mother's room. Feel free to pack up her things. I'll have Daniel bring you an empty trunk, and he'll take away anything you don't want when you're done. I have business I've got to take care of, but I'll be back in an hour or so. Daniel will be around if you need anything. The privy is in the back of the house. Don't bother with dinner tonight. The boys will fix something."

"What if your brothers come home?" she asked.

Jayson was following Daniel down the stairs when he called out, "I should be back before they get here."

She slowly shut the door and latched it closed. Her body slumped heavily against the solid wood. Pain drummed in her temple. She placed her fingers against the side of her head, but the discomfort continued.

As she looked around the unfamiliar surroundings, tears welled in her eyes. The reality of her choices hit hard. Her painted-on smile vanished along with the courage she had clung to all day. At that moment, the weight of her decision was fully realized. There she stood, alone in a strange place, with an unknown man for a husband. For better or worse, her life had changed forever.

Allison made her way to the big feather bed, climbed on top, and melted into its softness. She wrapped her arms around a fluffy pillow and hugged it to her chest as she curled into a ball. The tears she'd held back over the past couple of days let loose in one big flood and she breathed out a few quiet sobs. When she closed her eyes, the faces of her parents and sister appeared in her mind and her longing for them grew.

She missed home and the life she'd left behind.

~Chapter Seven~

"Are you crazy?" An unfamiliar, thundering male voice reverberated through the bedroom.

Allison jerked her head off the pillow and scanned the room for a threat but found none.

"It's done." Jayson's baritone voice drifted in from outside.

She sat upright, swung her legs off the side of the bed, and hurried to the open window. The men were nowhere in sight.

"Chase, I think we should ask our big brother a different question. Like, why an educated young lady from Boston decided to come to the Montana Territory? What are you hiding, Jayson?"

The questioning voice rose from below her window. She looked down, but the porch roof obstructed her view. That must be Nathan, the only brother unaccounted for. Daniel said he was smart.

"There's a good reason why she packed up and left, Nathan."

Allison held her breath. Jayson intended to share her transgressions with his family. The mortification of her past actions churned in her stomach. A wave of nausea bubbled to the surface.

"Tell us," Nathan insisted.

"She's carrying another man's child."

Jayson's deliberately worded statement slammed into her chest like a blow. She closed her eyes, sucked in a gush of air, then let it out slowly.

"Are you out of your blasted mind? Of course, you are! You married a pregnant woman, sight unseen, who's carrying another man's bastard." A different male voice, the one that woke her from her sleep. Chase, maybe?

The truth of his words stung like a thorn. When her eyes opened, unshed tears clouded her vision.

"Just because Jacquelyn jilted you, didn't mean you couldn't find another woman. You never tried," Nathan chided.

"It wasn't going to happen. Allison's my wife now whether you like it or not and, in a few months, there's going to be a baby around here."

"I kind of like her. She's pretty," Daniel piped in.

"Well, I hope you and Daniel don't get too used to her. I give her a month before she finds she's not cut out for ranch life and high-tails it back to Boston, wearing your name like a trophy," Chase said.

"Guess we'll have to wait and see." Jayson's voice sounded calm.

"Sorry, Jayson, I'm with Chase on this one. A woman from Boston won't have enough guts to live out here for long."

"She mustered enough courage to come halfway across the country to marry a man she'd never met to give her baby a name. That counts for something," Jayson said.

"I hope you're right," Nathan replied.

"Wait until you meet her before you say anything bad about her. She might surprise you," Daniel retorted.

The men's heavy footsteps moved into the house. Allison left the window and slumped on a nearby chair. She laid her head in the palms of her hands. Whatever possessed her to believe she could run away from her sins? No matter how far she fled from Boston, no matter how small the community she lived in, she would always be a tarnished woman with a bastard child. She could never really start over. Those around her who knew the truth would always consider her unworthy. Of a lesser quality.

Stop it!

Allison straightened her back. She wasn't of a lesser quality; she just made a mistake. As long as she remained married to Jayson, her child was not a bastard. No one's negative opinion of her would dampen her resolve. She was a good person and would make the best of her situation.

A lump of indignation stuck in her throat. Jayson's brothers had never met her, yet they assumed she didn't belong. In their minds, she wasn't good enough to be married to their brother. They judged her weak because of her Boston upbringing. She would prove them wrong.

She descended the stairs and walked into the front room of the house. The men were standing around the big wooden table. She glanced at the newcomers, then Jayson, whose eyes gleamed in the light shining through the dining room's glass-paned windows, producing an attractive glow.

"Allison, these are my brothers, Chase and Nathan. I've shared with them the circumstances of our marriage." Jayson cocked his head toward the two men standing a few feet away, shoulder-to-shoulder, with their arms similarly crossed over their chests.

All eyes stared at her. Suddenly, there wasn't enough air in the room. Her breath grew shallow. She didn't expect Jayson's brothers to be so handsome, with the same almond-shaped blue eyes. Or, to have such strong presences, like their older brother. They were muscular and tall. Each one had a few days of growth on their striking faces. Their working clothes were soiled from a day's hard labor, vastly different than the gentlemen she knew in Boston. These men were much more formidable.

The only chance she had for them to welcome her into their family was through honesty, sincerity, and courage. Attributes that merited respect.

She held their gazes and guessed who was who by Daniel's earlier descriptions. Chase had the fiery look while Nathan was more somber. Both men appeared wary as they watched her every move with glares of disapproval.

Lacing her fingers, she laid them over her rounded belly as if protecting her unborn child. "I hope our news hasn't upset you unduly. I can imagine what a shock this must be, but let me assure you my intentions for being here are genuine. Your brother offered me a way out of a predicament and I've agreed. Unfortunately, due to my pregnancy, some tongues will wag, and through association to me your family may not be cast in the most favorable light. I apologize for any grief my connection to your family causes as I realize you have had no say in what has come about. Although, I do hope one day you will find a way to accept me and my unborn child into your family as your brother has done."

Silence hung thick in the air as Chase and Nathan raked her up and down, their faces blank masks. Allison stood her ground, steeling herself against what might come next. She hoped she had said enough. It was disheartening to think of starting a new life with a family that didn't accept her.

Chase spoke first after a prolonged period of quiet.

"Ahh heck! Let the tongues wag. I don't care what other people think. They won't cause me grief." Her new brother-in-law walked past her on his way upstairs, tilted his head, and gave her an impish smirk.

Nathan stepped forward and shrugged. "I happen to like children," he said matter-of-factly. "Welcome to the family." He extended his hand. After a quick shake, he followed his brother up the stairs.

Allison expelled her held breath and let her body relax. She could barely believe it. They weren't going to punish and torment her for her past indiscretions. They were willing to give her a chance. Her first meeting with her new brothers-in-law had gone better than expected. She must've said something they liked.

"Looks like you're in." Jayson's devilish grin practically melted her heart. "Come, I'll show you around."

She followed him out to the bunkhouse where he introduced her as his wife to the men in his employ. Although surprised at first, the ranch hands were friendly and genuinely pleased to have her there. They congratulated Jayson on his choice, which made her blush, wished her well, and promised to be at her disposal whenever needed. Her head fairly swam with being in the company of so many big, burly men. Many years ago, she'd realized she lived in a man's world, but such a sentiment was never as apparent as out here in this rough country.

After the introductions, Jayson walked her slowly around the yard, directing her attention to various buildings and points of interest. The affection he held for his ranch came out in his voice and in his commentary. As she listened to him describe his family's ranch so proudly, she found herself increasingly drawn to him, for here was a quietly reserved man who she suspected harbored deep, rarely released passion.

Jayson's word was good, and his brothers cooked the evening meal. When the family sat down for dinner, a polite awkwardness charged the air. They talked mostly amongst themselves. Nobody quite knew what to say to her.

After a few false starts, Nathan broke the silence. "How was your trip to Montana?"

She looked up from her meal and licked her bottom lip. The fish was the best she'd ever tasted, lightly salted and flavorful. Chase and Nathan were good cooks which surprised her. "I had never been out of Boston, so the trip was very intriguing, although a bit bumpy."

Chase took a big swallow of water. "Jayson said Peter brought you to Montana. Have you known him long?"

"Father Peter and Mrs. Elliot escorted me across country via an assortment of coaches and trains. Mrs. Elliot disembarked the stage this morning when we passed through Ridgemont. She wanted to visit relatives. I met Father Peter about a year ago through the church. We usually met up once or twice a week to go out into the city to care for the sick."

"You have some medical experience?" Nathan raised a brow.

"Only a little. Just the basics. I helped where I could." She'd really enjoyed her excursions to the hospital and out into the community with Father Peter. Those had been times she could let her guard down and be herself. No one judged her actions or behavior. She didn't have to say the right thing or behave the right way. Her only concern had centered around how to keep her patients comfortable.

She would miss those times.

Allison took another bite and glanced at Jayson, sitting at the head of the table. He stared at her through lowered lids, his face a blank facade. She couldn't read his expression. Was it indifference? He didn't join in the conversation or ask any questions. Maybe he wasn't interested in their discussion.

His reserved behavior only added to his mystique. She hoped one day to get to know him better, even if it meant cracking his hard exterior.

Today she was too tired from her long journey to sustain an on-going dialog. Her new brothers-in-law struggled with making small-talk and after a few blundering attempts, they silently agreed to cease all exchange.

The rest of the meal was consumed in quiet deference and when finished, everyone at the table scattered to all corners of the house.

She helped Daniel wash the dishes before wandering back to her new bedroom. As she poked around the large and elegantly furnished room, it was clear no one had disturbed Mrs. McKay's things since her passing. Her sons doubtlessly put off the task, none of them wanting to do the job. She opened the empty storage trunk Daniel had left in the center of the room.

Over the next few hours, she methodically went through the woman's personal items, which included men's breeches, wide-brimmed hats, old dusty knee-high boots, sharp-as-could-be hunting knives, fancy gowns, and even a revolver. As she separated and packed the unwanted items away in the trunk, she wondered about Jayson's mother, a frontier woman capable of raising a family of men in an unforgiving land. She imagined a strong-willed woman with a brave heart.

On the bedside nightstand, she found a framed picture of a handsome man with soft, almond-shaped eyes who stood behind a beautiful young woman sitting on an upholstered chair. Her hair was pinned up stylishly and her fancy dress accentuated her feminine form. The photograph captured the essence of a loving couple. The man's arm, casually draped around the woman's back, settled on her upper arm, where she covered his hand with hers. Immediately, Allison knew she looked at a picture of Mr. and Mrs. McKay.

Sitting on the edge of the bed, she stared at the photograph. How much easier the transition from a city girl to a country girl would be if the older woman were still alive to help her find her way. She could use a little guidance as she trudged through her new life, living among strangers. A wistful sigh escaped her lips and she placed the picture by the door, intending to take it downstairs to display on the mantle so her new family could enjoy the memory of their parents.

One day, would there be a similar picture of her and Jayson sitting on top of the mantle next to his parents?

Only time would tell.

~Chapter Eight~

Unfamiliar noises in the distance woke Allison from a fretful sleep.
This is not home.

There was no clomping of horse-drawn carriages rolling over the brick thoroughfare under her bedroom window. Instead, she met the day with the sounds of chickens clucking and cows mooing in the distance.

Through half-closed lids, she perused her sun-lit room. She had stayed abed much longer than intended. More than likely, her new husband and his brothers were long gone. At dinner last night, the men talked about riding out in the early hours of the morning.

While she curled up under the patchwork quilt, the events of the previous day flooded her mind. Of all the memories presenting themselves, she kept settling on the kiss at the altar. When she shut her eyes, she relived the moment when Jayson's moist lips pressed against her dry ones. How his thick arms had wrapped her in an unyielding embrace as he'd pulled her against his hard chest. Her body had betrayed her by responding to his kiss in a way that had never happened before with Robert. The familiarity had left her breathless, along with an unfulfilled hunger to kiss him again.

She brushed aside her tormenting thoughts. Such things shouldn't plague her mind. All she wanted was a business deal. Nothing more. She could never go through another heartbreak. Another betrayal.

Allison fluffed the pillows behind her head and studied the wedding ring on her finger. The ring showed wear, perhaps a family heirloom. His mother's, no doubt. Did it bother Jayson to give something so valuable to a woman he'd never love? She absentmindedly rolled the ring around her finger and hoped his mother wasn't rolling over in her grave because her eldest son's marriage was a sham. How would her own mother take the news when she found out her daughter had married a stranger to cover up an out-of-wedlock pregnancy?

Allison's head throbbed. She left the bed, bathed over the basin, combed her hair, and donned a fancy silk day gown.

The men had been gone for hours. Plenty of time to talk amongst themselves. Had Jayson explained to his brothers why the newly married couple didn't share a bedroom? Would his brothers speculate about such an oddity? She hoped he'd kept the reason to himself. If he shared that she didn't want to consummate their marriage so as to not harm her unborn child, she worried Nathan, who had studied medicine, might point out her deception. She didn't want her new family to find out what a coward she really was.

She wasn't ready for Jayson to take his place in her bed as her husband. Wasn't ready for such intimacy with a man she didn't know.

Especially one so virile.

Her stomach clenched. When her new husband discovered how little experience she actually had with men, he'd be astonished. After all, she heard from more experienced friends, that most women got pregnant through repeated acts, but not so with her. How would she explain her innocence?

A loud sigh escaped her lips. She'd negotiated to forestall her inevitable consummation but would eventually have to face the dilemma of her inexperience.

Allison smoothed her full skirts and made her way downstairs with a purpose in mind. She intended to prepare her first meal in her new home. Tonight, had to be perfect. Father Peter agreed to come for dinner. She would show her new family that their reservations were misplaced, and she belonged on the McKay ranch.

There was only one problem, she'd never actually cooked before. Plenty of times, as a child, she'd sat on a kitchen stool and watched Martha, their cook, work her magic as she prepared splendid meals for the family, but she'd never asked how she did it. Martha made cooking look easy. Allison figured once she started mixing a few ingredients, she'd remember the particulars. But first, she needed to find out what food was on hand, so she could plan a menu.

She stepped out on the front porch and gazed out over the ranch. Daniel stood in the corral, brushing one of the carriage horses. She strolled across the yard to the fence, reached her hand between the rails, and patted the gelding's head.

"Good morning, Daniel."

Daniel glanced up from his task. "Good morning, ma'am."

"Call me Allison. That's what my sister calls me."

"You have a sister?" He quirked his brow.

"I do, back in Boston. Lillian's a year younger than me. We're very close."

"Maybe she can come for a visit. I'm sure Jayson won't mind."

She stroked the tip of the young horse's nose and the animal nibbled her fingers with his lips. "I'd like to see her again. Maybe once I'm settled."

"Jayson said I should stay close to the house today in case you needed anything. Is there something I can help you with?"

"Actually, there is. Father Peter is coming to dinner. I'm wondering what ingredients are available, so I can figure out what to serve."

"I can help you with that." He flashed a toothy white grin and put his grooming brush on a wooden box. "I'll show you the pantry and root cellar. As for meat, chicken is always available. If you'd rather have something else, I can have Gus cut you a portion of pork or a side of beef from the smokehouse. Or, if your heart is set on fish, I'll take my fishing pole down to the pond and see what I can catch."

Her head spun with all the possibilities. "We'll have chicken. As long as you give them to me dressed and cleaned, I'll manage fine."

"Chicken it is." Daniel hopped over the railed fence and waved his hand for her to follow. "Come on. I'll show you where we store the dry goods and vegetables."

"Do you know if your mother had a cookbook?" She suddenly had qualms about whether she'd remember exactly how Martha cooked and thought maybe she should follow a recipe.

"I don't remember Ma having one, but I'm sure you can get one at the mercantile the next time we go to town. Just tell them to put it on our account." He led her back into the house.

***

Allison was busy mixing cookie dough on the wood tabletop when she heard the clicking of footsteps in the front hall. She wiped her flour-covered hands on her apron and brushed a few loose strands of hair out of her eyes. She rounded the table when two women appeared in the archway leading into the dining area. A shiver crawled up her spine. Aunt Beatrice was one of them.

"Mama, you have no business walking into Mrs. McKay's house uninvited." The younger woman whispered emphatically to Aunt Beatrice while shaking her head in disapproval.

"Nonsense, this is my nephew's house. I can come and go as I please, until he says differently."

"Mama, please," the young woman begged, pulling on the older woman's arm.

52

"Good afternoon," Allison called out.

The young woman, who appeared only a few years older than Allison, jerked her head up, her face a rosy red. She quickly composed herself, let go of her mother's arm and stepped forward, extending a hand in greeting. "Forgive us for taking liberties and walking in unannounced. I'm Jayson's cousin, Melony. When I heard he got married, I had to come right out to welcome you to the family."

Allison instantly liked Jayson's cousin. Her cheeks displayed two deep dimples when she smiled, lighting up her whole face. "Pleased to meet you, Melony. I'm Allison."

It was clear that while Aunt Beatrice was nasty and cold, her daughter was kindhearted and warm. Melony had long straw-colored, softly curled hair, fashioned with a few loose strands in front, then the rest pulled away from her angelic face. She appeared prim and proper, wearing a stark-white, high-collared button-down shirt with puffy sleeves and tight ruffled wrists, on top of a dark green flowing skirt.

"And of course, you've already met my mother," Melony said apologetically.

"Yes, I have. How are you today, Aunt Beatrice?" Allison asked. The woman was still dressed head to toe in black and carried her cane. A big scowl crossed her wrinkled face.

"I'm no happier about this turn of events than I was yesterday. I'm going to keep a good eye on you. Don't think you can pull anything over on us just because we're country folk. I used to be a city girl, born and bred, so don't think I don't know about bored young ladies and their shenanigans." She huffed.

"Well, you needn't worry. I come from a well-respected family in Boston. I'm fully dedicated to starting a family and making this my home." Allison vowed not to let Aunt Beatrice's nasty or disparaging remarks fluster her composure and presented her guest with an outward calm, drawing strength from her upbringing in Boston. She gestured toward the kitchen where a kettle rumbled on the stove. "Ladies, would you join me for a cup of tea? I have water boiling. We could visit in the parlor. Just give me a minute to gather the teacups and teapot. I'm sure you know your way. I'll join you directly."

Her guests nodded and retreated across the hall as she took the hot water off the stove. She found a hand-painted teapot and teacups in the cupboard and arranged the items on a fancy serving tray. Since the cookie dough was ready for baking, she scooped out a few rounded spoonful's and placed the gooey mixture on a cooking pan. After stoking up the fire in the wood-burning cookstove, she placed the pan in the oven.

She reached behind her back to untie the ribbon holding her apron together but then thought better of it. Something told her she should hide her expanding belly. Aunt Beatrice wouldn't be pleased to hear of a baby. It might be better to share the news when Jayson was around. Surely, she could show a little less formality with family members and keep her apron on.

When she strode into the parlor with the serving tray, she found her new relatives sitting side by side on the formal tufted, velvet sofa. She placed the tray on the low center table and poured for Aunt Beatrice first.

"I'm so sorry for the recent loss of your husband," she said to Aunt Beatrice and then looked to Melony. "And, your father. My condolences on his passing."

"Oh, no," Melony replied. "No need to express your sorrow. Pa's been dead a good five years now. A fall from his horse is what killed him. Mama's time of grieving should be long over."

"It'll never be over. I'm still mourning your pa. If you were a more respectful daughter, you would wear black, also." Aunt Beatrice snorted.

"I choose to honor my father with bright colors and happy memories." Melony abruptly turned from her mother to Allison, excitement twinkling in her eyes. "So, Hanna says you're from Boston. How wonderful. I was born in Alexandria, Virginia. We lived there for the first few years of my life, but then we moved out here. Pa wanted adventure. Since then, I've never been out of the Montana Territory. Mama couldn't do without me after Pa died. I would've loved to have traveled. What was Boston like?"

"Boston's a big, bustling city. There's always something new and exciting going on. During the day, I visited various shops looking for the latest fashions. A few days a week, my friends and I went to Boston Public Garden to walk around. Or, sometimes my father would take my sister and me down to the waterfront where we watched the ships come in. At night, we went to plays, operas, or attended social gatherings." Her heart warmed while sharing her memories of home.

"Oh, it sounds fabulous. Exactly how I envisioned city life." Melony sighed.

"It was, but I'm sure living out here will be just as wonderful, maybe a little quieter, but still wonderful," she said enthusiastically.

Melony giggled. "Well, I can't say my life's very quiet. In fact, it gets mighty noisy. You see, I'm Flat Rock's only schoolteacher."

"You are? How intriguing. I saw the schoolhouse when I arrived. It's charming." She sipped her tea.

"I love my job. I owe it all to Jayson. When I couldn't leave town to further my education, Jayson hired a private tutor to instruct me."

"He did?" Allison said with a hint of amazement.

"Jayson insisted." Melony brought her teacup to her lips.

"Humph," Aunt Beatrice snorted. "I can't believe he put such notions in your head. If you wanted to be a good daughter, you wouldn't be spending all your time with those children; instead, you'd be staying home taking care of your ma."

"Aww, Mama, you're perfectly capable of taking care of yourself, and it's not like you don't have friends to visit."

Aunt Beatrice shook her finger at her daughter. "That's not the point. A good daughter wouldn't be so selfish and leave her ma alone."

"We've talked about this before. The children need me," Melony said.

Allison didn't like the turn of the conversation. From her own experiences of seeing older women who used guilt to rule their young daughters, she knew Melony would never come out on top where Aunt Beatrice was concerned.

She deliberately redirected their discussion. "While I boiled water for the tea, I put some sugar cookies in the oven. They should be ready by now. Shall I get them?"

"Sounds delicious," Melody said.

Aunt Beatrice stared disapprovingly at her daughter but remained silent.

"I'll be but a moment." She rose from her chair and crossed the foyer into the dining room. Immediately, her stomach churned when she saw smoke enveloping the other side of the house.

"My cookies!" she shrieked and hurried into the kitchen. Running straight for the cookstove, she grabbed a towel, opened the oven door, and removed the pan of smoldering cookies. She dropped the baking sheet on the sideboard.

The two ladies, hearing her cry of alarm, rushed into the dining room.

"Quick, the windows." Melony scurried to open a window wide.

Aunt Beatrice followed her daughter and fanned smoke out with her skirts.

"Oh, my. I've ruined them." She blew out the flames. Untying her apron, she billowed the cloth back and forth over the burnt treats, shooing a thick blanket of smoke away from her disaster.

"Please don't fret," Melony called out. "It could happen to anyone."

"I bet you've never made cookies before, have you?" Aunt Beatrice said haughtily from across the room.

Allison wafted the air with her apron. "Well, there has to be a first time for everything. Unfortunately, mine wasn't highly successful."

"Mama, you know well enough that if Mrs. Pearson didn't do our cooking, the two of us would starve to death within a week. We can't cook a lick." Melony winked at Allison. "The only time our oven gets lit is when we need it for heat."

Aunt Beatrice snorted and continued flapping her arms, chasing the ashen smoke out the window on a breeze.

Melony came to stand next to Allison and studied the blackened mess. Jayson's cousin held a hand over her mouth and giggled. "Your cookies actually caught fire."

Allison's tense muscles relaxed. "They did, didn't they," she snickered. "They're so burnt I don't even think the hogs could eat them."

At such a statement both women burst out laughing. Allison grabbed her protruding bump to support her child as she belly-laughed.

Aunt Beatrice waddled over, no doubt to break up the growing bond. Upon seeing her rounded belly cradled in her hands she exclaimed, "You're pregnant! You're pregnant with another man's child! I'm telling Jayson. You're trying to pull one over on him. How dare you!"

Allison's back stiffened. This was the moment she dreaded. She couldn't let Aunt Beatrice bully her. She sucked in a deep breath. "You're correct. I'm with child. Jayson knows. We have an agreement."

Aunt Beatrice threw her hands in the air. "This is not fitting. I'll not allow my nephew to be a cuckold."

"Madame, this is none of your concern. I've made Jayson assurances that I will be a good wife, and he will raise my child as his own."

"I cannot abide by this. I cannot allow my nephew to call another man's bastard his own. You tricked him into this. The marriage must be annulled," Aunt Beatrice squealed.

56

Allison gritted her teeth. Aunt Beatrice's behavior was too much. This was her home now, as much as it was Jayson's and she would not put up with such insufferable conduct.

"There will be no annulment." Allison walked briskly to the foyer. At the doorway, she turned and stared at the red-faced woman glaring at her from the dining room. She beckoned Aunt Beatrice toward the yard with a flick of her wrist. "I will thank you to leave. I believe there is nothing more I care to discuss with you at this time. You may speak to Jayson if you feel the need. I'll leave it to him to assure you of his knowledge and agreement. Good day."

"Humph." Aunt Beatrice stomped her way through the foyer. "This is an outrage," she hissed. "I will see an end to this marriage, if it's the last thing I do." She scowled at Allison on her way out of the house. As she neared the gate, she squawked, "Daniel. Daniel! Come help me onto the carriage right this minute."

Melony, who followed in her mother's footsteps, stopped in front of Allison. "I'm so sorry. Please don't let what Mama said bother you. She has a biting tongue. I love that you're here. It's good for Jayson to have a wife and child. He deserves to be happy. I hope you don't hold my mother's behavior against me. I would so like to be friends."

"Of course. I, too, would like to be friends."

Melony squeezed her hand. "I'll sneak away without my mother and come for a visit soon."

"That would probably be best," she agreed.

From the front porch, she watched Daniel help Aunt Beatrice and then Melony into the carriage. He handed his cousin the reins. Melony gave her a nod as the horse trotted out of the yard, but Aunt Beatrice, seated at her side, looked straight ahead, and refused to glance one way or the other.

Allison waved them off as Daniel hurried up the steps to join her.

"I'm guessing Aunt Beatrice knows about the baby," he said.

"She's not happy about the news."

"Don't pay her no never-mind. Ma used to say Aunt Beatrice is only happy when she has a bee under her bonnet. She'll make a fuss. Jayson will ignore her. Then she'll move on to something else to complain about. That's her way."

"I hope you're right." She hugged her arms around herself and cringed inwardly. Aunt Beatrice would inform everyone in town and the surrounding area of her shame.

Allison wondered how much damage the woman's nasty words would wreak on her character. Life would be much harder if most of the town shunned her. How would they treat her child once the baby was born?

She hoped coming to Montana Territory wasn't a big mistake after all.

~Chapter Nine~

Allison moved around the kitchen in a panic. Things were not going as well as she'd hoped. The grandfather clock in the corner chimed a quarter to six. Dinner would not be ready on time. She still had to set the table, change her clothes, and then deliver the meal to the table.

When horses cantered through the yard and stopped at the barn, she knew Jayson and his brothers had returned. If they expected their dinner right away, they'd be sorely disappointed.

Overwhelmed with what still had to be done and not sure what to do next, she hurried to the front porch to await Jayson's arrival.

"Dinner's not ready yet," she called out as her husband came through the gate.

A layer of dirt covered his clothes. He brushed the dust off his leather chaps with the brim of his hat before he climbed the steps. The sight of him made her forget her predicament. He was so ruggedly handsome in his work clothes, all she wanted to do was gawk.

"No worries. The boys and I are jumping in the pond to wash. No sense tracking in all this dirt. We left extra clothes on the porch this morning." He picked up a stack of folded clothes from a chair.

"The water must be freezing this time of year." They were standing so close she had to raise her chin to look at his face.

"It does have a way of waking you up." He half-grinned.

The soft curve of his lips and the sparkle in his bright blue eyes caused Allison's heart to quicken its beat. She took a deep cleansing breath and reached for the back of a nearby rocker to steady her wobbly knees.

"Do you think you can entertain Father Peter on the porch when he arrives? I have to change, finish setting the table, and ready the food."

"Sure." Jayson's eyes dropped to the bottom of her dress and his jaw fell open. "What happened?"

She followed his gaze to the blackened spots on her fancy silk gown. "I had a little accident. I must've stoked the fire in the stove a little too much, making it extra hot and when my dress brushed against its side, the material melted in spots. I need to change before dinner."

He frowned. "From now on, if you use the stove, make sure you have a bucket of water handy in case you set yourself on fire."

"I know what the problem was. I wore too many petticoats under my dress, which made my skirt too puffy. Tomorrow I'll be sure to wear fewer layers."

"I hope that works or you're going to run out of dresses."

She giggled behind her hand. "You can say that after carrying my trunk to my room yesterday? I probably have enough clothes for a good half year."

His smirk tugged at her heart. He really was fine to look at when his face was soft and relaxed.

"When dinner's ready, let us know. We'll be on the porch." He turned to go.

She touched his arm to stop him before he descended the steps. "We had visitors today." Jayson's muscles tightened under the thin fabric of his shirt. All the lightheartedness she saw moments ago vanished.

"Who came calling?"

"Aunt Beatrice and Melony." She released his arm.

Jayson faced her. "How did their visit go?"

"Your aunt knows about the baby. When I took off my apron, she noticed the bump right away." She didn't dare share that she'd removed her apron to fan smoke out of the house after burning a pan of cookies. She wanted to keep her baking failures to herself.

"She was going to find out eventually."

Boisterous laughing echoed in the valley, catching her attention. His brothers walked the path to the pond, pushing and shoving each other as they went. Seemingly, without a care in the world.

How I envy them.

Allison glanced at her husband. "As you might expect, she ranted and raved about the news. I'm sorry to say I had to ask her to leave."

"You did?" A look of astonishment stretched across his face.

"Your aunt didn't give me much of a choice." Allison felt bad about it. She'd only been Jayson's wife for a day, and already she'd had to ask a guest to leave his house. "Your aunt was none too pleased."

A low chuckle rumbled in his throat. "Aunt Beatrice got what she deserved." Then he asked, "And what about Melony?"

"As you can imagine, she was mortified by her mother's behavior and hoped we could still be friends."

"And that's all right with you?"

"Of course. Melony was nothing but friendly and kind. I'm not one to judge a person by their parent's misdeeds. No matter how bad their manners are."

"Good. Melony needs womenfolk her own age around here. It can get lonely. Especially, when your mother is Aunt Beatrice." He gave her a slight smile. "You did the right thing. Soon enough, my aunt will move on to something else. Don't worry about it."

"I'll try not to."

He went down the front steps with his arms loaded with clean clothes. "Go do what you have to do. I'll keep everyone busy. If you need help, holler."

***

Allison rushed to change and freshen up. Her stomach fluttered with excitement; this was her first dinner in her new home. She envisioned everything turning out perfectly. His brothers would see she belonged.

On her way to the kitchen, she stopped by the front porch to welcome Father Peter. Jayson and his brothers were freshly bathed and dressed in their finery. It gave her immense pleasure to see her new family present themselves in such a civilized manner. They were not in the least the barbaric creatures some woman in Boston had painted cowboys as.

Each one of them had a drink in their hands and a smile on their newly shaved faces. They appeared to be in good spirits and were settling in for a fine evening together. After assuring them that she had things well under control and supper would be on the table in no time, she retreated to the kitchen.

Allison put a bibbed apron over the front of her fancy dress and busied herself with setting the table. When finished, she checked the potatoes boiling in a pot on top of the big cast-iron cookstove. They were soft when poked and ready to mash, so she took the pot off the heat and placed it on the sideboard. She found a masher in a crock on a shelf. Martha always put milk and butter in her recipe, so she guessed at how much and mashed away.

The more she smashed, the more the potatoes turned into a watery mess. These didn't resemble Martha's potatoes. The consistency was all wrong. It looked like white soup filled the pot. A wave of panic churned her stomach and a lump formed in her throat.

"Daniel, can you come in here?" Allison called out, loud enough for the men to hear.

Footsteps sounded on the wooden floorboards as Daniel entered the kitchen.

"Can I help with something?" He seemed eager to do her bidding.

"I don't know," she practically wailed. "Tell me what I did wrong. These mashed potatoes don't look anything like they're supposed to."

"Let's see." Daniel glanced over her shoulder and into the pot.

She dropped the masher into the mess and quickly stepped aside. Her hands twisted around her apron as she stared at him.

He took her place and stirred the masher around. "Did you drain the water out of the pot before you started mashing?"

"No. I didn't know I was supposed to do that."

"They come out thicker if you take out the water before you mash them, but I think they'll be all right. I'll drain a little of the excess now." He took the pot, tipped it on its side, and emptied what liquid he could into the metal sink. "Grab me the serving bowl over there with the cover and everything will be fine."

Allison handed him the bowl. She watched in horror as he poured the mushy mess into the serving dish and put on the cover.

"What else do you have for dinner?"

"I'm cooking pickled beets on the stove and two chickens are roasting in the oven. I baked the biscuits earlier and placed them in the side oven to keep them warm while I dressed."

"All right, give me another serving dish for the beets and grab a basket for the biscuits."

She quickly followed his instructions; glad someone else was in charge.

The beets were stuck to the bottom of the pan and the only way to get them out was to scrape them free. The blackened pieces overpowered the good ones.

Daniel put a cover on the dish. "Don't worry. Just because they don't look pretty doesn't mean they won't taste good."

Allison didn't buy it. She was failing miserably. "Let's see about the biscuits."

Daniel opened the oven door. He used a cloth to take out the tray of biscuits. "These don't appear too bad." He flashed her a wide smile.

"They don't look anything like Martha's." She shook her head. "They're as flat as can be."

"Let's have a taste. I bet they're delicious." He picked one up and bit into the round biscuit. Unable to bite all the way through, he gave up without breaking off a piece.

Tears welled in her eyes. She should've sent him to town to buy a recipe book. She should never have tried to make a meal from memory. What was she thinking? She felt like kicking herself right now for being such an idiot.

"They may be a little hard, but I bet if we soak them for a while in some tea or coffee they'll fall apart easily enough."

She knew he was just being nice. He put the biscuits in a basket and told her to place the food on the table while he took out the chickens.

"Dinner." He called while carrying the covered roasting pan to the center of the table.

The rush of boots echoed off the walls as the men came into the dining room. Allison went into the kitchen and removed her apron. She imagined how hungry they must be. They hadn't eaten since Cookie, the chuckwagon cook, fed them around noontime. Each man pulled out their chair and waited until she sat next to Jayson before they took their own seat. Daniel removed the cover from the chickens.

Allison's stomach convulsed when she saw the dried-out carcasses of the once robust chickens lying in their burnt drippings. It was too much. She couldn't be present when they discovered the soupy mashed potatoes, the burnt beets or hard-as-rock biscuits. And how could she forget about the blackened cookies? She had baked another batch after the ladies left and then spent all afternoon scraping their bottoms, so no one would notice she'd burnt them, too.

I ruined everything.

There was nothing edible for her hungry family. She was a failure. If they lived with her for any length of time, they would all starve to death.

She lowered her eyes. The prospect of seeing disappointment on the faces of those around her was too much to bear.

"Please excuse me." She pushed away from the table and ran upstairs.

***

Jayson took the cover off the soupy potatoes. "This is really bad," he said in a faint voice.

"She tried so hard today." Daniel placed the metal cover on the table and stared at the blackened birds. "She's been at it since this morning."

"I don't think there's one edible thing here." Chase bit a biscuit but dropped the flattened wafer on his plate without a dent. He touched a tooth as if worried he'd broken it.

"I doubt she's ever cooked before. Her family always had a cook." Peter tasted the purple vegetable apprehensively with the tip of his tongue and then conceded, returning the uneaten portion back to his plate.

Jayson couldn't believe the spread before him. When she'd volunteered to make the dinner, she'd sounded so confident. He had no idea she was so clueless when it came to cooking a meal.

Nathan took a knife to a chicken leg but gave up and put the cover back on the shriveled carcasses. "I think she's upset."

Jayson stared at Peter. "You're going to have to go up and talk to her." His new wife was more than likely upstairs bawling her eyes out. He didn't do well with weeping women.

"I'm not going up there to talk to her. You go." Peter crossed his arms over his chest.

He knew that tick in his friend's jaw. Peter was digging in his heels.

"Why do I have to go? You're her priest. You know how to talk with emotional women."

Peter leaned forward. "She doesn't need her priest; she needs her husband. This is what you agreed to when you said, 'I do'. Or have you forgotten?"

"Well, I wouldn't have said 'I do' if you hadn't talked me into it." He glanced around the table. All eyes were on him. They weren't going to let him get out of this one.

"It's not like I twisted your arm." Peter raised his brow. "You agreed under your own free will."

He sighed heavily and rose from the table. "Thanks for the support."

At the top of the stairs, he paused and inhaled deeply. He might not have thought this marriage thing through. A city girl from Boston would always be complicated. He should've settled for a mountain girl like his mother. A woman who could shoot a gun as easily as she threaded a needle to darn a sock. Married but a day and already he recognized life would never be the same again.

He knocked lightly on the wooden door. "Allison, may I come in?" Not waiting for an answer, he lifted the latch and opened it wide.

Jayson leaned his shoulder against the door jam.

"Go away." She was side-lying across the bed with her head laying on folded arms. Her fancy dress piled up around her in a mound of petticoats and material.

The bulge in her belly was prominent against the cloth stretching over her stomach. She looked so small and alone.

"Come down and join us," he said softly.

"How can I face everyone? Dinner was a fiasco. I'm an utter failure," she moaned.

"It was one dinner. It could've happened to anyone. No one is going to hold it against you."

"I wanted tonight to be perfect. I wanted your family to see I fit in. Instead, I made a fool of myself."

"I never expected things to be easy for you. That you tried is good enough for me. I'm aware your upbringing was vastly different than the women around here." He knew she'd have difficulties. When he lived in Washington D.C., he was acquainted with plenty of young ladies. They were different from the women in Montana. If she stayed, she'd struggle with their way of life. Tonight's dinner would not be her only disaster. There would be more.

Allison lifted her head and sat upright. He expected red puffy eyes and tear-covered cheeks, but she displayed neither. Instead, he saw dejection painted on her pretty face.

"You don't mind that there's a lot I don't know about being a rancher's wife?"

"There's plenty of time to learn. Don't worry about it."

He watched Allison's eyes light up. He guessed he had said something right. "You can't stay locked up in your room forever. What do you say we go downstairs? I'm sure Peter would like to spend some time with you before he leaves for Boston."

Allison studied her feet. "I know it's bad manners to hide from a dinner guest, but I'm not sure I can face anyone right now."

"He wouldn't be offended if you decided not to come back down. But, on the other hand, he'd enjoy your company if you did."

When she scooted to the edge of the bed, he glimpsed a nice pair of well-formed ankles and muscular calves encased in form-fitting stockings. She had on a pair of fancy heeled shoes. He stepped further into the room and extended his ungloved hand, waiting for her to meet him halfway.

She only hesitated a moment before she resigned herself to her fate and took his offered hand. He pulled her forward, along with her heap of skirts, until her feet touched the rug-covered floor. Deep down, he knew she wasn't a coward.

"I still feel utterly foolish for ruining our dinner."

He couldn't help but chuckle. "Something tells me this might not be the last time."

She playfully jabbed his arm. "Watch it. Or, in the future, I'll save the worst for your plate alone."

His hand flew to his chest and he gave her a pained look. "Ouch, that hurts."

***

Allison descended the steps in front of Jayson. She turned the corner into the dining area and noticed the room was full of activity. The men were busy at work. Daniel and Father Peter were clearing uneaten food from the table. Chase and Nathan were preparing a meal.

When she stepped into the room, everyone stopped and looked her way. Heat rose from the knot in her chest and traveled to her cheeks, but she refused to focus on her shame and took a deep breath to quiet the pounding of her heart. Jayson stood at her shoulder. Somehow, his presence calmed her nerves, and she gathered strength from his nearness.

"I apologize for my poor behavior. I should never have left the table in such a manner. I knew how hungry everyone was after working all day, and when I had realized how badly I failed, I'm afraid I couldn't handle your disappointment." She took the time to look at each one as she spoke.

"No need to apologize." Nathan gave her a friendly smile.

"He's right. It could happen to anyone," Daniel piped in.

Chase brought pans around to the stove. "No worries. We're whipping up some eggs, bacon, and flapjacks to tide us over."

"We understand you didn't have to prepare meals for yourself growing up." Nathan broke a few eggs in the pan on the stove.

"Since our ma taught us how to make supper when we were this high..." Chase placed a hand at waist level for effect. "...we decided we're each going to take turns coming home early from work and teach you how to make our favorite recipes."

"That way you'll get to practice and you can ask questions." Nathan stirred the eggs.

"And I'll take you to town to get the cookbook you wanted." Daniel pumped water into the sink. "It might help if it's written down."

She didn't know what to say. They were being so kind. "Thank you, I would very much like that."

Jayson leaned in, close to her ear. "Good. It's settled then. Come sit and relax. I'll pour you a glass of wine and you can visit with Peter while dinner is made."

He guided her to her chair at the table, across from Father Peter. Then, he stepped away to pour a glass of wine from a decanter on a narrow serving table against the wall.

"What did I tell you? Good people," Father Peter whispered for her ears only.

She nodded in agreement, moisture clouding her eyes.

Jayson handed her a half-filled glass of dark red liquid. When their eyes locked, she stopped breathing. There was something in his expression. Pleasure... Pride...? Something he tried to hide when she looked deeper.

He quickly turned away and joined the frenzy in the kitchen. She watched in wonder as he flipped sizzling bacon in the skillet, seeming quite at ease with such a domestic task. No man back home would ever lower themselves to do woman's work, even if they didn't have a cook.

"I'm optimistic your new life here will work out fine. I can return to Boston with a good conscience." Father Peter patted the top of her hand as it rested on the wood table.

"Everything is so different here. I feel like I'm in a strange world. Like I'm someone else and the old me is just a memory. I was so sure of myself at home; my world had order. Now I feel like a fish out of water, flapping around on the shoreline," she murmured.

Father Peter chuckled. "It will take a little getting used to, but I know you will adjust without much difficulty."

"I hope you're right.

"I'll be leaving in a few days. I need to return to Boston. What would you like me to tell your family?"

"I have letters for you to carry back home. I wrote my parents a brief note about finding myself with child, and how I came out West to marry. I asked for their forgiveness. I told them I was safe, well-cared for, and not to worry about me. I also asked for a little time to settle in before they come for a visit. I think they will be less disapproving when they see the baby," she said flatly.

Father Peter gave her another pat on the top of her hand.

She stared at his friendly face. "You don't think God will strike me down for my sins, do you?"

"No, I think you're the least of His worries." Father Peter gave her a reassuring smile.

"I'm sorry you've gotten caught up in my web of deception. I don't know what I would've done without your guidance. I'd probably be out in the world, scared and all alone. You're a good friend. I feel bad you had to lie to my parents about your sister-in-law being sick to escort me out here. I hope you don't get in trouble for your part in my flight of shame."

"Your parents are going to be very unhappy with me when I return without you."

"What's your plan when you see them?" Allison noticed the men were getting ready to bring the food to the table. She glanced at Father Peter, waiting for an answer.

He paused to wait for her full attention. "I plan on throwing myself at their feet and begging for mercy. If that doesn't work, I'm going to flash the most charming smile I can muster until they yield."

Allison giggled behind her hand. She would miss her friend.

~Chapter Ten~

Allison clutched the brown-paper wrapped book tightly against her rounded stomach as the carriage jostled over the rutted dirt road. She hoped to find salvation in the words written on the stark white pages. Hannah had assured her that, *The American Frugal Housewife*, by Lydia Maria Francis Child, would hold many of the answers she searched for: ways to be a better cook and wife.

The carriage wheel hit a rock and bounced her against Daniel's side.

"Sorry." He pulled back on the reins.

"I'm all right." She offered him a feeble smile. Even though he handled the team of horses with skill, he was always in a hurry. She couldn't fault him for treating all his jobs with unbridled enthusiasm. Performing his tasks swiftly was one of the things she liked most about her new brother-in-law.

Today, when she suggested they take a ride into town, he immediately hitched the horses to the buggy and off they went. Now that he was more comfortable around her, she could count on him for lively conversations, usually about the ranch and his brothers, as long as the topic steered away from Jayson.

On that subject, he remained silent.

Spring was a lovely time of year in Montana. She breathed deeply of the pine scent hitching a ride on the warm breeze. As far as her eyes could see, vivid greens with splotches of various shades of blue, red, and yellow wildflowers dotted the landscape. The ride to town and back in the fresh air, under the canopy, was quite invigorating.

Over the past few days, Chase and Nathan had kept their word and returned home early each afternoon to help with dinner. The time spent one-on-one with her new brothers-in-law helped her get to know them better. Chase was quick to laugh and joke, while Nathan was thoughtful and smart. They were good men and she no longer feared they would look down on her for getting herself with child outside of the sanctity of marriage. Neither mentioned how strange it was that she and Jayson didn't share a marriage bed.

While in town earlier, she'd met Hannah and Margaret for tea. From her old life in Boston, she missed female conversation the most, and thoroughly enjoyed visiting with her new friends. The women laughed easily and were quick-witted, making their company pleasurable. At the end of their time together, the ladies shared that the town was aflutter with talk of the new Mrs. McKay. Many wanted an introduction. Hannah divulged, although regretfully, that Aunt Beatrice wagged her tongue at whoever would listen about how her poor nephew got roped into marriage and how his new bride was no good for him.

Allison expected as much from the town bully but hearing such hurtful words from a family member made the cut deeper. If she confronted Aunt Beatrice about her disparaging remarks, the woman might be even more determined to slander her name. Some tyrants thrived on discord. After much contemplation, she decided not to let Jayson's aunt get under her skin; instead, she planned to ignore Aunt Beatrice's rantings and see if the woman got bored discussing things she knew nothing about, such as the inner workings of her marriage. After all, she'd have to live with the woman for years to come and didn't need an enemy in the family.

Hannah and Margaret suggested they do something to gather the townsfolk, so they could meet her and form their own opinions. This way, her neighbors would be less swayed by Aunt Beatrice's persuasions.

Her friends came up with the idea of hosting a town-wide dance in the churchyard on Saturday night. Hannah volunteered her husband to oversee the building of a dance floor. Margaret's husband would hang the lanterns. All the ladies attending could bring a dish to share. The word would go out far and wide to come and celebrate Allison's marriage to Jayson. The people of Flat Rock would then have an opportunity to meet their new neighbor.

The thought of the whole town coming together for a dance in her honor made her uneasy. Back in Boston, she had attended plenty of parties, but this one was different. She'd be the center of attention. Curious stares would follow her around. Not everyone would be as friendly and accepting as Hannah, Margaret, Melony, or her brothers-in-law. Aunt Beatrice would make sure everyone knew her story or some form of it. All eyes would judge, some expecting her to turn into the monster they thought her to be. Some would hate her already for her sins. Others would treat her rudely or just ignore her. Either way, their behavior would hurt, reminding her of her transgressions and her fall from grace.

A chill shook her body. The gathering was only a few days away. Hannah and Margaret were so excited about the prospect of a dance; she didn't have the heart to sway them from their course. When she and Daniel left Flat Rock a short while ago, the ladies were already spreading the word around town.

Now, all she had to do was tell Jayson about the dance in their honor. Was he ready to introduce his tarnished wife to his friends and neighbors?

Does he dance?

A cloud of dust rose from the road in the distance. A lone rider galloped toward them at breakneck speed. Daniel took the reins in one hand and slowed his team to a walk. He laid his hand on the rifle strapped to the outside of the seat.

As the form grew closer, she made out the shape of a young boy on a big plow horse. His arms flapped at his sides as he struggled to stay on the beefy animal without a saddle. When the rider saw the carriage, he swung an arm over his head as if terrified he wouldn't be seen. The young boy yelled something that got carried away on the wind.

Daniel took his hand off the rifle and stopped the carriage altogether, letting the rider come to them. The boy clenched his teeth and pulled back on the horse's reins with all his might to get the massive beast to slide to a stop next to the buggy.

"Matthew, what's got you all riled up?" Daniel held his restless team of horses in check.

Allison's heart went out to the young boy, probably no older than ten. A trail of tears streamed down his cheeks, making streaks through the dirt plastered to his face.

"It's Pa. He cut his fingers off chopping wood. There's blood everywhere. Ma told me to get to town and find Doc. It doesn't look good."

"You go on and find the doctor. We'll head over to your place and see how we can help." Daniel looked at her, and she nodded her agreement.

Matthew wasted no time kicking his big old horse back into a gallop. Daniel smacked Lewis and Clarke into a bone-jarring extended trot over the uneven road.

"Let me know if you want me to slow down," he shouted over the pounding of hooves striking the dirt road. "We're off to the Simpson homestead. Their spread abuts ours in the west."

"I'll be fine. Let's keep going." She grabbed tightly to the arm of the seat to keep from bouncing out. If they weren't in such a fancy carriage with an overly soft padded seat and well-structured chassis, she'd be concerned for the baby but even the dips in the road weren't jarring enough to pose a concern. They passed the McKay turnoff and continued up the road.

Chickens scattered when the carriage flew through the Simpson's yard. Daniel reined the team back, causing their hooves to slide to a stop in front of the door to the small one-story ranch house. He jumped down and lifted his arms to help her from the buggy. Once her feet hit the ground, she ran past him up the front steps. A blood trail led her across the porch to the wide-open doorway. Daniel remained behind to tie the animals to the hitching post.

"Mrs. Simpson?" Allison's eyes needed time to adjust to the dim room after being out in sunlight. It took her a moment before she could see clearly.

"Over here," a woman's strained voice replied.

She discerned the outline of a woman hovering over a man slumped at the table, his head on the crook of his arm. To the right, three young children huddled in a corner on a bed.

"Daniel, take the children outside," Allison ordered when footsteps sounded on the porch behind her. She made her way to the pair at the table.

As she got closer, she noticed the blood trail stopped at the chair. There was a pool of thick red liquid under the man's arm which rested on the wooden table.

"I'm Allison, Jayson McKay's wife. Your son stopped us on the road. I'm here to help in any way I can."

"Oh, thank you, Mrs. McKay. I'm Gloria." The woman's voice cracked with emotion. She was a tall woman, at least half a foot taller than Allison. Her gray-streaked hair hung in a single-braid down her slender back. As she straightened behind the injured man, she restlessly twisted her hands over one another. "David has had a terrible accident. He was chopping wood for kindling. My little one let out a blood-curdling scream when she saw a snake in the grass. He looked up at the sound and the hatchet came down on his fingers. He won't let me look at his hand but there's a lot of blood."

"Mr. Simpson. I have some medical experience. May I look at your hand?" She leaned over him, ready to take a peek. Out of the corner of her eye, she noticed Daniel herding the children outside.

Mr. Simpson brought his head up from his arm and locked eyes. "I don't want any help."

"Please. Let me see how bad it is. You're losing a lot of blood. We're going to have to stem the flow."

"Go away. Like I told my wife, just let me be," he growled.

"I don't understand." She couldn't fathom what he was saying.

"David says he wants to bleed out." Gloria half-sobbed, covering her face with her long fingers. She sniffled and wiped her teary eyes on the sleeve of her dress. "He says he's not much of a man without two working hands, and we'd be better off without him. Said he'd be nothing but a burden to us."

Allison's jaw dropped. The man wanted to die. He wanted to perish all because he had a few fingers gone. How absurd.

Anger churned the pit of her stomach into a queasy mess. *He wanted to leave his family behind.*

"How dare you." She stamped her foot. "How dare you give up so easily when you have a wife and children counting on you."

Why would a man choose death over his family?

"Go away," the man croaked, his eyes glossy.

"I will not go away. I will not let you take the coward's way out. You'd only be a burden if you chose to be a burden." She looked at Gloria and saw a glimmer of hope in the woman's eyes, bolstering Allison's conviction.

"Gloria, do you want your husband to die?"

"No, ma'am. More than anything I want him to live." The woman rested her hand on her husband's back.

Allison wagged a finger. "Did you hear, Mr. Simpson? Your wife doesn't want to be left a widow with a handful of children to feed. She doesn't want the hardship of being without a man or the trouble of finding a new one to take care of your family. She wants her husband. She wants you."

"That's right, David. You'd best behave and let Mrs. McKay help you." Gloria squeezed his shoulder.

The man frowned and turned his head away.

"You're outnumbered. Gloria, stoke up the fire. I want the flames good and hot." Looking around the room to see what was available, she spied a knife on the sideboard and pointed to the sharp instrument. "When you're done with the fire, put that knife in the coals."

"I'm not going to let you do it, woman," Mr. Simpson protested.

Allison grabbed his forearm with both hands. "I'm afraid you have no choice." Using all her strength, she yanked the limb he was hiding, out in the open. She had to do what needed to be done whether he liked it or not. She was fighting for his family.

"Leave me be. I've already made peace with God." He flailed his arm to get away from her hold and struck her on the side of her face. The sting caused her eye to tear up. Spackles of warm, fresh blood hit the bare skin of her face, neck, and chest.

"Daniel, get in here!" She held onto his injured arm with all the brawn she could muster and struggled to keep the appendage vertical to lessen the blood loss.

"Let me help." Gloria came to her aid and held her husband's free arm, the one pushing Allison away. "David stop fighting and let us do what has to be done."

Daniel hurried in from outside and weighted down Mr. Simpson's shoulder.

"Where are the children?" Allison was grateful Daniel was no weakling. With her brother-in-law's help, Mr. Simpson soon gave up his struggle.

"I sent them out to the barn to collect eggs. I told them not to come near the house until I said so."

A determined look crossed Gloria's face. "Good, they shouldn't have to see this."

"What's next?" Daniel stepped into her spot and took over, so she could step back.

"I need to examine the injury. Just hold him still. Keep the arm positioned upright and the bleeding will slow." When she got a good look at the wound, she took note of the severity of the damage. The thumb and little finger remained intact. The three middle fingers were gone; chopped off down to the pad of his hand.

"How bad is it?" Gloria asked.

She pursed her lips. "Not bad. He'll be able to use it some. Did you hear, Mr. Simpson? All is not lost. Do you have any whiskey? If you do, it'll save you a bit of grief."

Mr. Simpson pointed to a cupboard with his good hand. "Top shelf in the cabinet over there."

Daniel and Gloria noticeably loosened their hold. Mr. Simpson no longer resisted the inevitable. Allison left his side to retrieve the jug. She poured the amber liquid into a mug and pushed the alcohol in front of the man. He picked up the cup with his good hand and drained the glass in one quick swallow, grimacing at the end.

"Another." He banged the cup on the table.

Allison poured him another and then another.

"Are you ready, Mr. Simpson?" She held up the jug, prepared to give one more shot if requested.

"Ready as I'll ever be." He looked at his wife through heavy-lidded eyes.

Allison liberally poured the amber liquid over the wound.

Mr. Simpson sucked in his breath and then let it out with a loud, "Oww!" He pulled his hand back. "Shit woman, are you trying to kill me?"

"I know it hurts but this needs to be done." Allison retrieved the knife from the coals and a wooden spoon from a crock on the sideboard. She handed it to her patient. "Put this between your teeth. It'll help."

"Damn. Just do it and get it over with." A layer of sweat beaded on his brow. He bit hard on the handle.

"Hold him tight." She brought the flame-reddened blade down on the wound.

Mr. Simpson growled deep in his throat, bit hard on his mouthpiece, and tensed every muscle in his body.

The smell of burnt flesh caused Allison's stomach to contract. She held her breath for a moment to ward off a wave of nausea. Inhaling deeply through her mouth, she lifted the blade and brought the metal down again over more of the open wound until all the raw skin seared closed. Thankfully, Mr. Simpson slumped forward in his chair, out cold.

"Is he all right?" Gloria held tight to her husband's injured arm.

"He'll be fine. Just passed out from the pain. It's a good sign. He'll need to rest. He lost a lot of blood. Keep holding his arm upright until I get a chance to bandage it." Allison hastily retrieved a feather pillow from the small bed in the corner to put under the man's head.

She reached down and lifted her velvet dress to her knees. It took Daniel a second to realize what she wanted to do, and he turned away. She took a section of petticoat in her hands and tore off a long strip of cloth.

"This should make a good bandage." She wrapped the clean cloth around his hand. When she finished tying the end off, they propped his arm on a pillow, on top of the table.

"Do you think we should move him to the bed?" Gloria glanced over her shoulder at a door, probably leading to the back bedroom.

"He's dead weight right now. He looks comfortable enough. Let's leave him be until we have more help. Or if he wakes, we can assist him there under his own power. In the meantime, Daniel, check on the children. Let them know their father will be fine. We'll set about cleaning up the blood. We don't want to upset them any more than they already are."

Daniel did her bidding and left for the barn.

"Oh goodness, my heart is pounding so hard I can scarcely breathe, never mind think clearly." Gloria pressed her palms against her chest.

"Your body's reacting to almost losing your husband. It'll help if we busy ourselves."

Gloria and Allison went outside into the bright sunshine and filled two pails with clean water from the pump. The fresh air was a welcome respite. They returned to the house and started their tedious task of cleaning.

Allison got down on her hands and knees to mop blood off the floor with a rag. The sound of horses skidding to a halt outside the farmhouse made her glance up. She stared at the open entryway. Loud footfalls pounded upon the wooden steps and porch planks. A broad silhouette of a man filled the doorway. Although his shadowed face was unrecognizable, she knew at once that the person was Jayson.

Every tense muscle in her body relaxed. She sat back on her heels. Her husband had arrived. He would make things right. She was no longer in charge.

As he strode into the room, he ignored Mrs. Simpson, who was busy washing down the table around her sleeping husband and stopped directly in front of Allison.

"Are you all right?" He reached down, placing his hands under her arms, and pulled her to stand.

"I'm fine." She drew in a deep breath.

Jayson guided her to sit on a chair a few feet away and examined her thoroughly. "Are you hurt? You're covered in blood."

She shook her head.

He gently stroked the sore spot on the side of her cheek. "What happened here?" he said in a clipped voice.

"I'm afraid Mr. Simpson was out of his mind with pain and blood loss. He lashed out and caught me on the side of my face before I could protect myself."

"We need to put cold water on the welt." Jayson glared at Mr. Simpson's motionless form. When he looked back, his eyes softened.

"I'll be fine. Don't worry." She found his gentle touch reassuring and liked his concern for her well-being.

Nathan came into the house and hovered over Mr. Simpson. Gloria wrung her hands at her husband's side.

"I don't understand how you came to be here?" She had no idea what prompted him to come to her aid. That he did softened her heart.

"We met Matthew on the road close to town. He told us he ran into you."

Nathan grabbed Mr. Simpson under an arm. "Jayson, help me get him to his bed. I want to take a quick look at his hand."

Jayson left her side and seized the man under the other arm. The two of them half-carried, half-dragged the limp form into the bedroom where they laid him on the bed.

Gloria fussed over her husband, pulling off his boots and covering him with a blanket.

Allison rose from the chair and stood behind Nathan while he removed the bandage from the man's injured hand.

Jayson stared at the stark white wrapping, cocked an eyebrow in her direction, and smirked. "Your petticoat?"

"I used what was available." She swiped a loose piece of hair away from her face.

His gaze swept the front of her gown. "I don't think you'll be able to save your dress. Keep this up and you won't have any clothes left." He grinned boyishly.

Allison glanced down at the blood splattered across her bodice. He was right. She doubted the stains would come out. His teasing soothed her nerves. That he joked at a time like this was comforting.

She smiled back. "Not to worry. I have plenty. The loss was for a worthy cause."

Jayson sent her an approving nod.

Nathan inspected the hand with the missing fingers. "Nice work searing the flesh. The blood loss has stopped. The wound looks good. Did you do this, Allison?"

"She sure did." Gloria looked at her appreciatively.

"I couldn't wait for the doctor. Mr. Simpson was losing too much blood. I saw it done in Boston. I put whiskey on the hand to disinfect the wound before I burned it closed."

"Well, if it weren't for you, he would've bled to death. It looks like you got here just in time. He'll be thanking you for his life, I expect." Nathan retrieved the bandage and began the process of rewrapping the hand.

Allison cringed. She hoped Mr. Simpson would eventually be happy she'd saved his life, but she couldn't be sure.

Jayson's arm encircled her back and thick fingers dug into the side of her expanding waist. "Let's get you home."

She pulled back. "I have to finish cleaning. I don't want the children to see this mess."

"Don't worry. Nathan will help clean things up." He gave Nathan a pointed look.

"Sure, I will." Nathan positioned the man's injured arm on a few feather pillows. "I'm going to stick around until Doc Thatcher comes. It'll give me something to do while I wait."

Jayson guided her out into the fresh air and warm sunshine. He stopped by the water pump and removed the black kerchief from around his neck. Placing it under the faucet, he pumped the handle until a burst of water came out, soaking the fabric.

Jayson held the wet cloth in front of her. "Blood is covering your face. May I?"

She nodded.

Jayson stepped closer and used his glove-covered finger under her chin to tilt her head. Ever so gently, he dabbed around her face with the moist bandana in his bare hand. His finger brushed against her skin, causing a flushed sensation at the point of contact that surged through her like a warm wave.

Allison didn't know where to look while he painstakingly patted her, so she focused on his well-formed lips. She glanced at the scar running from his cheek down the side of his neck. Never before had he removed the cloth around his neck while in her company. The angry marks disappeared under his shirt collar and made her wonder what else he carefully concealed from sight; like what lay beneath the glove he always wore on his left hand. When the cool cloth touched her swollen cheek, she jerked away from his touch. Not intentionally. But the spot was more tender than she'd expected.

"Sorry." He backed off her sore spot.

Allison gazed into his deep blue eyes. For a moment, the world stood still. She held his stare as heat flowed through her. The concern and tenderness he'd shown her this afternoon was unexpected and weakened the walls she'd erected to protect herself from future hurt. Up until this moment, she hadn't dared acknowledge how attractive she found him to be.

But, attractive he was.

"Mrs. McKay," a woman's voice called out, knocking her out of her stupor.

Allison turned to see Gloria coming down the steps of the ranch house. The woman had washed her face and looked fresher and more at ease.

Gloria stopped before her. "Before you leave, I wanted to thank you for all you've done. I'm so grateful you stood up to my husband. Thank you for giving him what for and not letting him give up. I didn't want to go it alone with all these children to raise. I'd rather have a husband with only two fingers than no husband at all. He wasn't thinking straight until you gave him a talking to."

"I'm glad I could help." Out of the corner of her eye, she caught Jayson staring at her. He looked as if he wanted to say something but held his tongue.

"I'm ashamed of myself. I jumped to the wrong conclusions about you after talking to Beatrice. I was ready to dislike you on her say-so alone. I want you to know she was very wrong about you. You're a good woman. You'll hear no bad-mouthing from me. I'm going to tell everyone who will listen what you did for me and mine here today. Consider me a friend."

"Thank you, Gloria. Of course, we can be friends. I hope your husband recovers well."

"He will if I have anything to say about it." Gloria turned and returned to the house.

Jayson guided Allison to the carriage and helped her get her foot onto the step. With both hands gripped around the sides of her waist, he hoisted her up, and she maneuvered around to sit on the leather seat. She grabbed her brown paper-wrapped book and held it against her belly.

Stepping back to the pump, he wetted his kerchief, then handed her the material. "Put this on the side of your face or you're going to have a shiner come morning."

She placed the cold cloth against the side of her eye.

"It sounds like something happened before we arrived." He unexpectedly stepped onto the carriage and sat on the seat beside her. She had to wiggle to the far side against the armrest because he took up a lot more space than Daniel. He gathered the reins and unlocked the wheel. Making a clucking sound, he moved the horses forward and steered them around to head out of the yard.

As they neared the barn, he called out, "Daniel. You're riding my horse home."

Daniel peeked his head out of the barn doors. "Really?"

"Really." Jayson flicked the reins to get the horses to pick up their pace, although they didn't need much encouragement once they realized they were headed home.

Jayson glanced her way as the carriage set out over the bumpy road. "Care to enlighten me about what happened?"

She clutched her book tighter and removed the cloth from her face, so she could look at him. "Mr. Simpson felt living with a deformed hand would make him less of a man, so he decided he'd let himself bleed to death. Mrs. Simpson wanted her husband to live. I was desperate to save his life, so I reminded him of the hardships his wife would go through without him and how much trouble she'd have finding a new man to take care of her and the little ones."

"Ouch, that's harsh."

"As I said, I was desperate. He's a very stubborn man. Finally, I must've gotten through to him because he grudgingly let me treat the wound. What I can't fathom is why he was so adamant about dying and leaving his family behind?"

"I'm afraid out here, where life and death hang in the balance, not being a whole man could prevent you from keeping your family alive. He probably thought his wife and children had a better chance without him."

Jayson's matter-of-fact explanation bothered her. According to her husband, Mr. Simpson tried to make a selfless decision.

Allison wondered if Jayson had ever contemplated leaving this world when he was badly wounded and in pain. Whether he ever thought of himself as not being a whole man after the fire? She didn't want to broach the subject. Not yet, anyway.

"I don't agree with his reasoning. He assumed his family would someday face danger he couldn't handle, but I believe that by leaving them without a man, even a man with only two fingers on one hand, he would've put them in even greater danger. Due to the uncertainty of this world, a woman can't survive without a man at her side. I've seen it firsthand back in Boston and don't wish such a frightening situation on any woman."

Jayson sat in silence, staring straight ahead, contemplating her words. "You do know you're a McKay now. If anything ever happened to me, my brothers would take care of you."

Her jaw dropped. Was that what she was really afraid of? Being alone in this world without a man to take care of her and her children? Did she just share her own insecurities?

All her life, society had groomed her to attract a man, acquire a marriage proposal, have a family, and run her own home in the city. It had been pounded into her head that if she wanted to survive in this world, she needed a man. She went along with her parents and society's schooling because with no brothers to care for the women in her family, if her father were to one day die, his womenfolk would be alone and vulnerable.

When she caught the eye of Robert Winston Winthrop III, one of the most eligible bachelors in Boston, she finally felt safe. He'd chosen her over all the other young ladies parading around the city in their fancy garb. Allison thought if she played her part, all would be well. She foolishly assumed he was her champion and would take care of her for the rest of her life. How wrong she was. He'd abandoned her like a coward at the first sign of complexity. Because she couldn't share her pregnancy with her parents, she found herself in the place she strived so hard to avoid.

She glanced at Jayson's profile and breathed a quiet sigh of relief. She had a husband and brothers, now. Never again would she be alone and vulnerable.

~Chapter Eleven~

Jayson paced back and forth across the bottom of the stairs. Digging into his vest pocket, he took out his father's watch. Only three minutes had passed since he last viewed the timepiece. He glanced up at the second-floor landing, shook his head, and returned the watch to his pocket.

What's taking so long?

Laughter rang out from the parlor. He walked to the archway and peered into the room. Nathan and Chase were leaning against the fireplace mantle, having a lively conversation with drinks in their hands. Seeing them in good spirits only soured his mood further.

Don't they realize the family's going to be late? To be prompt was a sign of good character.

He glared at them, but they didn't notice.

When he turned back to his pacing, he noticed movement at the top of the stairs. His breath caught in his throat. Allison's natural beauty brightened the room as she glided down the staircase. Her light-brown hair was pulled back in a fancy style with loosened ringlets framing her face. Like all her dresses of late, the richly embellished gown hugged her expanding body like a snakeskin before puffing out at her hips in a swell of shiny cloth. With every step, the draped yards of light-blue satin fabric rolled like an ocean wave shimmering in the sunlight.

As he watched her, a memory from a few years ago plagued his mind. It was of Jacquelyn in a fancy silk dress, such as the one Allison wore. The vision was as clear as if it happened yesterday. They had traveled to the ranch to share the news of their engagement with his family. Wanting to impress his mother, his fiancée had dressed for royalty. They had been so happy then.

He shook off the apparition. Jacquelyn was long gone. The instant she saw his scarred face, she knew her desire to be a senator's wife, like her mother, was no longer attainable with him as her husband. Almost immediately, she broke off the engagement and ran into another man's arms. One better suited for her life's dream.

Jayson didn't want to make the same mistake twice. He wouldn't get too attached. A man never knew if the woman he set his sights on would leave or not.

I need to stop thinking about Jacquelyn, the flash fire, and how the inferno changed my life. He was lucky to have found a wife who wasn't looking for attachments. Someone who just wanted a safe place to raise a family. He could give Allison that, if she stayed.

When Allison got closer, he stared, mouth agape, at her low décolletage struggling miserably to keep her voluptuous breasts entrapped. The small ruffled short sleeves barely offered support, leaving the exposed flesh of her ample chest, delicate neck, and narrow shoulders in plain view. He swallowed hard.

Jayson barely heard the footfalls of his brothers behind him. Allison was all he could think about when she reached out a white-gloved hand, so he could help her down the last tread.

"Wow. You look gorgeous!" Chase whistled low.

"A vision to behold," Nathan chimed in.

"There isn't another woman in town who could hold a candle to you," Daniel remarked.

"Stop teasing. You're embarrassing me." She fanned her flushed face with an open hand.

Jayson noted that her response to his brother's compliments made her even lovelier. It was refreshing to be in the company of a woman who didn't know how pretty she was. Jacquelyn, on the other hand, had been more than aware of her attributes. At every turn, she used her looks to fish out compliments from her admirers.

"I haven't seen such a fancy dress since last year in Helena, when the cattlemen got together for a ball." Chase raised his half-filled glass in her direction.

"You're going to put all the other women to shame," Daniel added.

Suddenly, her smile disappeared. Her hands shot to her face to cover a sudden look of horror.

"Oh, my. I've overdone it, haven't I? I was so worried about making a good impression, I forgot where I was. I didn't consider that most of the townsfolk would find such a garment an extravagance. I'm so embarrassed by my thoughtlessness. This was a terrible choice for a dress." She reached for the rail.

"What are you doing?" He raised his brows and stared quizzically as she lifted her skirts to take a step back up the stairs.

"I simply can't wear a dress like this to meet my new neighbors. I need to change into something less flashy."

"You look fine. We're already late."

"I'll only be a moment. I don't want anyone to think I believe I'm better than them."

Jayson stood at the bottom of the stairs and watched the light blue wave disappear out of sight. He sighed loudly.

We're going to be late. "I think I need a drink."

"Come join us, brother." Chase slung an arm around his shoulders and guided him into the parlor.

"Allison has a point," Nathan remarked. "We're going to a country dance. No matter how beautiful she looks in that dress, there would be those people, like Aunt Beatrice, who'd be resentful that she owns such a fancy gown and accuse her of flaunting herself in front of the town. If I were you, though, I'd take her to the ball in Helena this year. If only to see her in that dress again."

"I'll keep it in mind." He stood at the sidebar and poured himself a glass of whiskey from the decanter.

"Boy, she sure looked pretty though. I could've stared at her all night. That's how good she looked." Daniel gazed starry-eyed at the archway leading to the foyer.

Jayson cuffed his brother on the side of the head. "She's married."

"Doesn't mean I can't appreciate a nice-looking woman," his brother shot back, purposely keeping out of arms reach.

Chase and Nathan chuckled.

"What's the matter, big brother?" Chase drawled. "Are you going to be one of those jealous husbands?"

"No," Jayson said adamantly. He took a big swig of the amber liquid. "As long as she doesn't keep dressing like that."

His brothers hooted with laughter. The rich sound had been sorely missing since their mother's passing.

His tense muscles relaxed as the liquid warmth spread through his body. After a good ten minutes, Chase and Nathan, having had enough to drink, filled their flasks for later and left to ready their mounts. He went into the foyer to stand at his post.

When Allison finally appeared on the top landing, no memory of another woman entered his mind. Instead, he took a moment to appreciate the vision she presented. This time she wore a shiny satin dress in a soft lavender shade. The new gown was plainer but no less becoming. She glowed with upcoming motherhood. It was all he could do to keep from staring at her like a schoolboy.

He took her arm at the bottom of the stairs. "Are you ready?"

"All set to go. I just need to get my cookies."

Jayson lifted an eyebrow. "You made them yourself?"

"Don't look so skeptical." She sent him a playful narrow-eyed glare. "Daniel was kind enough to help me."

Daniel came up beside them. "I sure did. Don't worry. I tried one, and they taste great. I already packed them in a basket and put them in the carriage."

"Thank you, Daniel." Allison waited until Daniel scooted around them.

Jayson escorted her onto the front porch and through the overgrown garden. His brothers, already seated upon their horses, stood lined up on the other side of the gate, ready to head to town.

"I hope I didn't keep everyone waiting too long," she called out.

"It was our pleasure to be at your beck and call." Chase tipped his hat and bestowed Allison with a big, lopsided grin.

"From the looks of things, I'm sure it was. I can tell from the glassy eyes that more than one of you got into the hard liquor while you were waiting," she teased.

"Just a little liquid courage." Nathan removed his hat and placed it over his heart in an exaggerated sweeping motion. "After all, every unwed girl in the territory will be expecting the McKay men to be ready and willing to spin them around the dance floor tonight."

She giggled. "Sounds like you have a great deal of responsibility ahead of you."

"We take it in stride." Chase smirked.

Allison squeezed Jayson's arm and gazed up at him. "I could use a little extra courage today."

"Why do you say that?" Her disclosure bothered him. He had only known her for a brief time but considered her to be one of the bravest women he'd ever met.

"I'm nervous about meeting all your neighbors. I want to make a good impression. They may not like me," she replied flatly.

Jayson led her through the gate and to the side of the carriage. How could they not like her? Her manner was naturally engaging, and she had a charming smile. The townsfolk would be fools if they didn't warm up to her right away. "You'll be fine. They'll like you well enough."

"I'm afraid I'm not as confident as you are." Allison took his offered hand and he helped her onto the seat beside Daniel.

Jayson made his way to Griffin, his horse, tied to the hitching post. He had contemplated driving her to town in the carriage, but then decided against it. He didn't like the confines of the carriage. Better to let Daniel take her.

When they got to town, it was clear that the whole countryside had come to meet his new wife. Carriages, buckboards, and saddled horses lined the front of the church. Music played in the background. The townspeople craned their necks to get a glimpse of Allison when Daniel drove the carriage by the open-air dance to find a vacant spot at the end of the row.

Jayson hitched Griffin to the post and then helped Allison down. Her features were taut.

"There's a lot of people here," she whispered.

"Not much happens around these parts, so when people hear about a dance, they flock to it from all directions." Jayson presented her the crook of his arm and escorted her past the sleepy horses lining the walkway, waiting for their masters to return. When he glanced down, her face was pale, and her lips pressed tightly together. She held his elbow with both hands in a death grip. She wasn't kidding about being nervous.

The music stopped as they walked along the church fence. The crowd moved along with them until everyone gathered at the gate. He took note of the familiar faces, full of anticipation, ready to meet the new Mrs. McKay. He never imagined his getting hitched would cause such a ruckus.

His brothers stayed at the couple's heels, forming a protective half-circle around the two. For Allison's benefit, he suspected.

Margaret and Hannah pushed their way to the front of the crowd and met them at the entrance.

"Now, everyone, take a step back and give our honored guests some breathing room, at least until they get inside." Margaret waved a stocky arm, opening a space. "There will be plenty of time to offer your congratulations as the night goes on. Alfred," she called out, "let's start the music again so we can have ourselves a fine dance."

As soon as she had her say, the music started and those assembled scattered to find the dance floor. His brothers relaxed their stances.

Hannah stepped through the gate and hooked her arm with Allison's. "Welcome. Come on inside. There are more than a few people who'd like to make your acquaintance."

Allison cautiously let go of his arm. With a wayward glance in his direction, she allowed herself to be pulled away by both Margaret and Hannah. They were making a beeline to Melony. His wife was in good hands, even though she had her doubts. The three women were well-respected members of the community and carried more weight than Aunt Beatrice.

Daniel brushed against Jayson's shoulder as he walked by. "I'll take Allison's basket to the food table and get her a punch while I'm at it."

"I think I'll get a drink myself." Chase patted a metal flask concealed in his coat pocket and locked eyes with him. "Are you good?"

"I brought my own."

Nathan trailed behind Chase. "I'll join you for a quick one before we get dancing. After all, we have a duty to all these fancy-dressed ladies."

Chase stopped short and slapped a hand on Nathan's shoulder. "That we do, brother. That we do."

As usual, Jayson found himself standing alone on the outskirts of the party. There was a time in his life when he was the person everyone sought out for lively conversation. His peers, back in Washington, D.C., were always eager for his opinion concerning the state of affairs, or to debate one topic or another. Nowadays, unless someone had something pressing to discuss, most of the townsfolk just left him alone.

In the distance, he watched Samantha Kincade push her way through the group of women to be the first one introduced to Allison. He cringed. Even though the two women were about the same age and had a lot in common, he hoped they wouldn't become close friends. There was something about the young woman that rubbed him the wrong way. Only recently back from schooling in the East, she had become overly aggressive in her pursuit of Chase.

The sheriff came to stand shoulder to shoulder with him. "Isn't it always the way? The husband gets left behind."

"Just the way I like it. Nice to see you, Jordan." He extended his bare hand for a handshake. The sheriff was his closest friend in Flat Rock.

"Wouldn't miss a chance to tease a former bachelor about getting caught...I mean married." Jordan patted Jayson's shoulder.

"It was time. Can't start a family without a wife." He couldn't take his eyes off Allison as she giggled at something Melony said.

God, she's pretty. He could watch her all night and never tire of the sight of her.

"A woman from Boston, though." Jordan scanned the crowd.

"She came highly recommended."

"I guess she did. I saw Father Peter get on the stage this morning." The sheriff brought his drink up to his lips and took a swig.

"His visits are never long enough." Jayson watched Chase take Allison's hand and bring her out onto the wooden dance floor. Samantha Kincade stared coldly at his back when he left her standing alone.

"Appears Gloria Simpson is quite taken with your wife. There's a rumor going around that she saved David's life when he cut his fingers off."

"This time the rumors are true," he drawled.

"Seems Mrs. McKay might be a little heartier than she looks."

"In her case, looks are deceiving. As a matter of fact, just the other day she had the whole lot of us quaking in our boots."

"I find that hard to believe," Jordan retorted. "Fess up. What happened?"

A slight smile tugged on his lips at the memory. "It all began when the boys and I were looking over a new filly in the corral. Allison comes out of the house carrying a hatchet and goes to the chicken coop. It seems Daniel had explained to her how to kill and dress a chicken, so she thought she'd try it. She laid the hatchet outside the door and stepped into the pen holding fistfuls of material from her gown and petticoats bunched up in her hands. Every time she lunged at a bird, she dropped her skirts, tripped on the hems, and missed the chicken all together. Those darn birds began squawking and flapping their wings like there was a fox in the hen house. Feathers started flying everywhere."

"That must've been quite a sight." Jordan chortled.

"Never saw anything so funny in all my life. Unfortunately, we made the mistake of letting her see us laugh. She didn't take too kindly to being the butt of a joke. In her anger, she caught hold of a chicken, marched out of the pen, grabbed the hatchet–leaving the coop door open which is a whole other story– and comes to stand in front of me."

His grin grew wider. "Of course, self-preservation made me go stone-faced because she looked furious, but my brothers didn't do such a good job of holding their grins back, which only fueled her irritation."

Jordan cocked his brow. "What did she do next?"

"She shoved that flapping chicken and the flat of the hatchet against my chest. In a deadly calm voice, she says, 'From now on if you want meat for dinner, you give it to me cleaned and dressed or you'll get only eggs and biscuits.' Then she whirled around, lifted her skirts, and stomped back to the house. My brothers stopped laughing, and we all stood dumbfounded, watching her go."

Jordan hooted with laughter. "She didn't."

"She most certainly did." He chuckled. "I was really lucky she handed the hatchet to me flat side first. The look in her eyes told me she struggled with that decision."

Jordan wiped his watery eyes with the back of his hand. "Sounds like she has a little fire in her."

"She sure does. You can bet we no longer laugh at her failed attempts to figure out ranch life. We also provide her with fresh meat before every meal. No sense in getting her riled up." Jayson's arms, crossed over his chest, shook from his mirth.

The men watched Daniel take Allison for a spin around the dance floor. Jayson didn't know his brother could dance. The kid was all grown up. When did that happen? Gone were the boyish features, gangly limbs, and too large feet. Daniel moved with grace and ease as he guided Allison around. The look on his face radiated with the pleasure of being with the prettiest girl at the dance.

"Your brothers seem to like her," Jordan said.

"They get on well with her."

At the end of the dance, Allison gave Gloria Simpson a warm hug. What his wife did for the Simpson family made him proud.

Jordan chugged down the last of his drink. "Let's get over to the food table before Mrs. Mullin's fried chicken is all gone."

Jayson could smell the feast from where they stood, and his stomach rumbled with anticipation. He followed his friend to the table, grabbed a plate and filled it to the brim.

"I looked into the butchering of the Kincades' sheep. Still a mystery. No tracks. Looks like the area was swept clean." Jordan bit into a chicken thigh.

"I went up there myself. Found one of my beef cows slaughtered in the same way, not half a mile away. It must've been stabbed with a knife not less than fifty times," he said.

"Pretty gruesome, if you ask me. It seems like someone's holding a lot of anger toward the McKays and Kincades. Can you think of anyone who feels that way about you or them?"

"No one comes to mind." He pulled apart a fried chicken breast and stuffed a piece into his mouth.

"Best watch your back," Jordan warned.

"None of my family members or men are going out alone. We're riding in pairs for safety. Animals are one thing, but I'm worried whoever is doing the butchering may turn his sick behavior on people. Whether he's doing it for pleasure or revenge, let's hope we catch this guy soon." Jayson put his plate on the table and picked up his drink.

Allison strolled toward him. She looked gorgeous. Her eyes were glassy, cheeks rosy, and her plump, red lips were set in a smile. She held a half-finished punch in her hand and appeared much more relaxed than when they'd first arrived.

"Come dance with me," she begged, holding out a gloved hand. A strand of hair had come loose from her chignon and was plastered to the side of her damp neck. He wanted to reach out and touch the silky threads but held himself back. He needed to keep some distance for his own sanity.

"Not right now," he said.

Years had passed since he'd danced. He didn't want to draw that much attention to himself. After his accident, he didn't feel comfortable at social events. He'd only come tonight for Allison's sake. "I want you to meet a friend of mine, Sheriff Jordan Hollister."

"Pleased to meet you, Mr. Hollister." She held out her hand, which Jordan grasped.

"The pleasure is all mine, Mrs. McKay. Call me Jordan or Sheriff, either one will do." Jordan gave her hand a little shake before letting go.

"Are you enjoying yourself?" Jayson pointed his mug toward the center of the dance.

"Very much so. I love the music. I didn't know Cookie played the harmonica. He's so good. I'm going to have to get him to teach me sometime."

Jayson liked that she was embracing her new life. Chase joined them and handed her a full cup of punch. She chugged down the last of the one in her hand and gave him her empty cup.

90

"Sorry to steal her away, but David Simpson said he wanted a word with her. Come along." Chase held out his elbow in an exaggerated fashion.

Allison stifled a giggle. "See you, later," she called over her shoulder and went off with Chase.

"She's a very lovely, lady." Jordan tapped Jayson's shoulder.

"Indeed, she is."

"There's something I've been meaning to ask you." Jordan locked eyes with Jayson's.

"Sounds ominous. What's on your mind."

"Well, you being the head of your family and all...I was wondering if you would mind if I asked your cousin, Melony, to go on a...carriage ride with me ...sometime?" Jordan stumbled over his words.

"What are you asking? Are you asking if I'd give you permission to court Melony?" he teased.

"Well, if you put it like that, I guess I am." Jordan's face turned bright red. "I wasn't sure what you would think, considering I don't have much to offer a pretty girl, being a sheriff and all. And besides, Bran Kincade has been sniffing around her like a dog, and I know he would be better equipped to provide for her."

"Are you serious?" he said incredulously. "Do you actually think that young pup has more to offer than you? Now, I do think you might be out of your mind."

Jordan shifted his weight from one leg to the other. "I'm serious, Jayson. She's a fine woman and I was hoping to get to know her better."

Jayson couldn't wipe the smile off his face. "If Melony is agreeable, then I would gladly give you my blessing." He watched Jordan's face light up like Fourth of July sparklers.

"Thanks, Jayson, you won't regret it."

"If you're really serious about getting to know her, I suggest you get yourself out on the dance floor as soon as possible. If I'm not mistaken I think Bran is making his way toward her as we speak."

"Excuse me." Jordan took off through the crowd, making a beeline to Melony.

Jayson couldn't help but smile.

~Chapter Twelve~

Lit lanterns lined the outside dance floor, keeping the darkness of the encroaching night at bay. The twinkling of stars sparkled in the cloudless sky. Jayson savored his last bite of pecan pie before setting the empty plate on the table. He doubted he'd taste anything so delicious for a long, long time. Allison hadn't developed an aptitude for cooking, no matter how hard his brothers worked with her. He didn't hold out hope her skills would improve anytime soon.

When his aunt waddled toward him with a determined look on her face, he cringed. "Good evening, Aunt Beatrice. Are you having a good time?"

She pointed a pudgy finger in front of his face. "I want a word with you, young man. As the matriarch of this family, I feel it's my duty to inform you that you've made a terrible mistake."

"I have no idea what you're talking about," he drawled.

His aunt's face turned crimson and she thumped the tip of her cane on the ground. "You, marrying that city girl."

"Her name is Allison. She told me you came for a visit with Melony. How nice."

His aunt's lips puckered as if sucking a sour candy. "She's pregnant. You married a tarnished woman. She played you for a fool. I think you should end this sham. Get rid of her. We can fix this before it's too late. I have friends in the church."

Jayson's muscles tensed. This had to stop. He leaned forward and towered over his aunt.

She took a small step back.

"Auntie, I know about Allison's past. I knew about her pregnancy before we wed, and I still agreed to the marriage."

She shook her head. "I don't understand why you would marry such a woman. Couldn't you find a nice girl around here?"

"I did what I had to do to start a family."

She leaned heavily on her cane. "I don't trust outsiders. In my experience, they're trouble."

"You know nothing about Allison. We're having a baby in a few months. You don't have to like the situation, but I wish you'd try to get along with my wife and accept the baby for the family's sake."

"I only want what's best for you."

"I appreciate that, but I know what's best for myself. I won't be getting an annulment and I'll raise the child as a McKay, along with any other children we might have."

"Humph," erupted from deep within his aunt's throat.

"I do hope you cease with these innuendos. She's already part of the family, whether you like it or not. Every time you blacken her name with your sharp tongue, you blacken the McKay name. Which I might remind you is the same last name both you and Melony carry."

She huffed. "Well, I never."

"It's important to me that our family gets along." He reached out and placed a hand on each one of his aunt's shoulders, quirked an eyebrow, and bestowed on her the biggest, most heartfelt smile he could muster. "Please, Aunt Beatrice. Will you promise to be nice to Allison? I would appreciate it very much."

It worked. She rolled her eyes and gave him a smile that crinkled her nose. "I suppose if you want me to," she conceded reluctantly.

"Thank you, Auntie." He pulled the older woman in for a big hug and held her there. "You've made me happy."

"Enough of that." She pushed him away and waved him off, a bit flustered yet delighted by his odd behavior.

He gave her a slight nod. "Now, if you'll excuse me, I'm off to find my wife." He stepped away from his dumbfounded aunt, glad to have eased her mind.

A long time had passed since he'd shown his aunt any real affection. As the head of the family, he had made sure Aunt Beatrice and Melony lived comfortably. They resided rent-free in a house he owned in town and he gave them a monthly allowance. But, he rarely showed Aunt Beatrice genuine warmth. Since the fire, no one had been on the receiving end of that emotion. Hopefully, he had said enough to mend any family discord.

As he wandered around the fringes of the dance floor, he caught sight of Allison and Melony strolling arm in arm along the lighted walkway to the outhouses behind the church. They chatted excitedly, their heads bent together.

His talk earlier with Jordan rattled him. Someone had it in for the McKays. He found a good spot in the shadows and stationed himself on the same side as the privy, far enough away to give the ladies privacy but close enough to be available, if needed.

When the two women appeared, there was a lot of giggling. He met them on the path before they returned to the dance. "Are you ladies having a wonderful time."

"Oh, my," Melony chortled. "I can't help laughing. Allison's being so silly. If I'm not mistaken, I think she's tipsy from drink."

Allison responded to Melony's remark with a loud guffaw. Her belly shook with mirth, and she cradled her rounded stomach with both hands.

"Allison, have you been drinking?" He wondered where she could've gotten spirits because the ladies punch was free of alcohol.

His wife pursed her lips and attempted to wipe the smirk off her face but failed miserably. He stood, hands on his hips, awaiting a response.

"Only a little." Allison giggled and put a hand over her mouth to hide her amusement.

"Where did you get alcohol?"

"Shhhh. It's a secret." She placed a finger across her lips and her eyes darted from side to side. Her legs wobbled beneath her body and she grabbed Melony's arm for support.

Melony chuckled.

Jayson sent his cousin a piercing look and then glanced back at his wife. "Tell me."

"You're no fun," she complained loudly.

"So, they say," he retorted.

"Daniel put some brandy in my punch." Her voice dropped to a cheerful whisper. "He said it would ease my nerves."

Jayson scanned over the heads of those in attendance until he found Daniel. He locked eyes with his brother and with a nod of his head, he silently bid him over. Chase and Nathan noticed because they stopped socializing and joined the group in the shadows.

"What's up?" Daniel asked.

"Did you put brandy in Allison's drink?"

"Only a little," Daniel said apprehensively. "She was anxious about meeting everyone. I thought it'd help her relax. She agreed."

"I think you gave her more than a little. She's drunk."

"I'm...not. I'm just having...fun! Don't be such a...bore," she stammered, her words thick on her tongue. Letting go of Melony, she crossed her arms over her chest but swayed dangerously. He pulled her into his side where she leaned heavily against him.

"I hate to admit it, but I might've had something to do with Allison's inebriation," Nathan volunteered. "I knew she was nervous about being judged, so when I fetched her punch, I put some whiskey in her cup. I didn't know Daniel had already given her something."

Chase's chin dropped to his chest and he studied his pointed boots.

"Chase, is there something you'd like to add?" Jayson asked disgustedly.

"I'm afraid I did the same thing," Chase said regretfully. "Sorry, Allison, I wanted you to loosen up, so you'd have some fun."

Allison giggled. "Don't look so glum. I'm having a whole bunch of fun."

Jayson's irritation with his brothers grew. He stared at them narrowly. "How could you be so irresponsible? All she wanted to do was make a good impression on our neighbors. She's going to be mortified when she realizes what happened here tonight."

"Don't be silly," Allison tittered. "I feel wonderful!" She snuggled her head beneath the crook of his arm, the side of her face pressed against his chest.

Melony chimed in. "I don't think anyone noticed she's tipsy. To everyone else she looks like she's just having a good time. The only thing is, we should keep her away from my mother. You know how Ma is. She'll be very disapproving if she finds out. Jayson, I think you should take Allison home before it's obvious she's had one too many. The rest of us will stay here at the dance. If anyone asks we'll say she wasn't feeling well because of the baby. It'll all work out fine."

Jayson nodded in agreement. "Sounds like a good idea. Thanks, Melony."

"Glad to help. I'll go keep my mother busy while you head out. See you soon, Allison." Melony gave his wife a quick hug and headed off toward her mother.

His brothers fanned out in a hurry. They wanted to get as far away from him as possible. *Idiots*. That's what they were. They'd have to make things right with Allison when she was well enough to hear them. At least Daniel had the decency to ask permission. She must've been pretty desperate to turn to hard liquor. He was sure she wasn't used to anything stronger than a glass of wine.

He held Allison steady against his hip. "I'm taking you home."

"I want to dance some more," she whined prettily and tried to pull away.

"Take my word for it. That's not a good idea."

"You're no fun," she complained.

A low chuckle rumbled in the back of his throat as he led her through the darkness. "That's what my brothers tell me all the time."

When they arrived at the far corner of the white picket fence encircling the church, he swept her into his arms in one fluid motion.

"Ooh," she shrieked, grabbing his neck with both arms. She nuzzled her head under his chin. He inhaled deeply, catching a whiff of roses in her pinned-up hair. His body reacted to her touch, and his breath hitched in his throat.

"I've got you. I'm just going to place you on the other side of the fence. People are less likely to notice us here in the shadows than if we head out the front gate. We don't want to draw attention to ourselves. Not tonight." He lifted her over the barrier and gently placed her on her feet on the other side of the fence. Then, he pried her hands from his neck.

Damn, she feels good.

"Allison, hold on to the fence while I jump over." He placed her hands on the top of the pickets to keep her steady in the dark. Stepping away, he took a few long strides and vaulted over the three-foot fence.

"Oh, my!" She let go of the wooden pickets and clapped her hands in applause. "That was amazing."

"You didn't know you married such a talented man." A belly laugh quaked his innards and he smiled wide.

"Can you do it again?"

"Maybe some other time." Taking her arm, he guided her to Lewis and Clarke only to find their carriage boxed in.

"Damn." He stroked Clarke's nose with one hand.

"Oh, no. You cussed." She pointed out with concern.

"Sorry. We're in a bit of a sticky situation, but nothing I can't fix. It's going to take me a few minutes to get our carriage out of this mess." He took her arm, led her to the back of a buckboard situated a few teams away, and set her bottom on the wooden planks. "Stay here until I get our ride out."

When she remained sitting where he put her, he returned to his horses and began backing Lewis and Clarke and the carriage out of the tight spot. His rig was barely free when he noticed Allison had left the safety of the wagon and was walking out into the middle of the road.

"Is that you, Jasmine Rose?"

"Good evening, Allison," responded a shadowed figure, leaning against the side of the saloon. The woman, clothed in a tight-fitting, low-cut dress with a knee-length ruffled skirt, walked toward his wife.

Allison took a few more steps to meet her halfway.

"What a lovely night," Allison said in a sing-song voice, looking at the sky.

"That it is." The woman stopped in front of Allison.

"What are you doing out here all alone?" Allison's voice pitched with alarm.

"Just waiting for the dance to end. There'll be a bunch of rowdy men coming our way afterward."

Allison giggled. "Did you hear? I got married."

"I heard. Congratulations."

Allison swayed on her feet, and the woman reached out to steady her.

"I had too much to drink tonight," Allison confided.

"I see," the woman said evenly, without judgment.

He led the team of horses toward the women.

"Why don't you visit me sometime? It's the McKay ranch." Allison pointed west. "You take that road out of town and you can't miss it."

"I would, but I'm afraid the liveryman won't rent me a horse. He says it's too risky, renting to saloon girls. He never knows if they'll bring his horse back or not."

"You don't strike me as that kind of person," Allison said emphatically.

"Thank you. I'm not."

Jayson joined them.

Allison swung her arm wide in an exaggerated fashion. "This is Miss Jasmine Rose. We rode the stage into town together." She put a hand over her mouth to hold her merriment. "She held my skirts off the ground when I vomited. This is my husband, Mr. Jayson McKay," she said proudly.

"Jayson is good enough for me." He extended his hand. In the moonlight, he could tell she was of Indian descent. She had a single braid flowing over one shoulder, ending at her thin waist.

The young woman shook his hand warily. "Jasmine, if you will."

Jayson glanced at his wife. With the almost full moon shining on her hopeful face, he couldn't resist doing something to please her. "Allison, do you want Jasmine to come out to the ranch for a visit?"

His wife nodded vigorously, grabbed his forearm with both hands, and bounced on the tips of her toes. "Oh, yes. Please, Jayson, I would like that very much."

He smiled down at her, then glanced back at Jasmine. "In that case, I'll have a horse sent over to the livery for your use, for whenever you want to visit." He considered himself a good judge of character. This woman was no threat to his family.

Jasmine's eyes widened, and her mouth dropped open. "Really?"

"Come see me as soon as you can. We'll have tea." His wife's voice had a lively sing-song quality to it.

"Thank you. That's exceedingly kind."

Allison swayed. Jayson hooked an arm about her shoulders.

"We need to go home. My brothers snuck Allison alcohol without her knowledge, thinking it would relax her. She's not going to feel well tomorrow. Best come by the ranch the day after."

"I will. Thank you. I hope you feel better, Allison," Jasmine said.

Allison tittered. "I feel great!"

"Jasmine." He tipped his hat and guided his wife to the side of the carriage.

"Up you go." He helped her onto the seat and then forcibly slid her bottom to the other side, so he could sit beside her. Gathering the reins, he clucked the horses to get along home.

"Bye, Jasmine," Allison called out, half hanging out of the carriage. "Come visit soon."

He pulled her back before she landed on her head.

The cloudless night made their journey home easier. The moon was bright enough to light their way over the rutted road. Lewis and Clarke made good time knowing food waited in their stalls.

Allison spent the carriage ride snuggling against his side and talking nonstop about the people she'd met in town. She was giddy one minute and close to tears the next, depending on the story. By the time they reached the ranch she was clinging to his arm, and her head rested against his shoulder. Never in the past had he enjoyed the ride home from town so much. Having her sitting next to him, so full of life and touching him intimately, was exhilarating. When the buggy rolled into the yard, he was sorry their trip was ending.

"Whoa." Jayson stopped the team at the gate leading to the house. The oil lamps in the bunkhouse were still lit.

"Gus!" He tied the reins to the brake.

The older man was the only one who had opted to stay at the ranch. All his other ranch hands were itching for some fun and had high-tailed it to town earlier in the evening to join the festivities. As the night progressed, his men looked to be enjoying the evening and a few even danced with Allison, including Cookie. After the dance ended, some of them would wander over to the saloon. It was a good thing his men had the day off tomorrow because, come morning, more than one wouldn't be able to safely sit in a saddle.

He walked around the carriage and raised his arms. Allison launched herself from the seat and landed against his chest so hard he had to take a step back to keep his balance when her full weight hit him square center.

"You're strong," she chirped merrily in his ear. Her arms hooked about his neck and her feet dangled.

"It's a good thing I am, or we'd be rolling in the dirt right now."

A rich, feminine laugh sounded in his ear, jumbling his insides. Their bodies pressed tightly together. Her face was so close; he could smell the alcohol on her breath. He took his time, letting her body slide along his until her feet hit solid ground. Even then his arms lingered on her sides, not willing to give up their closeness.

"Did you want something, Boss?" Gus's gruff voice called out, cutting into the quiet of the night.

He turned to see the old-timer standing at the rear of the carriage waiting for instructions.

"I was hoping you were still awake. Could you settle Lewis and Clarke in their stalls for the night? We can take care of the carriage tomorrow."

"Sure thing, Boss." Gus smiled a toothless grin. "When it got dark, I lit some oil lamps in the house to light your way. Did you have an enjoyable time, Mrs. McKay?"

"It was lovely," Allison said gaily. "Cookie played his harmonica. Hank danced mostly with the widow, Mrs. Benson. Giles is sweet on Hillary, the banker's daughter. Although, I think she may not be right for him. She's a little bossy."

Gus grunted his amusement. "Glad you had a good time, missus."

"My husband didn't dance with me. Not once." She pouted.

"Come along, Allison." With a hand on her back, Jayson urged her forward through the gate and into the house.

"That wasn't nice of you not to dance with me." She frowned, and tears pooled in her eyes.

"I'm saving my dancing for the ball in Helena. Some of the Montana cattlemen put one on in the fall."

Allison clapped her hands and squealed. "We're going to a ball?"

"We are," he promised. The vision of her earlier, in her blue dress, still weighed heavily on his mind.

The foyer was lit by a few oil lamps on the side table and a few more on the second floor. He steered her to the rail. "Let's get you upstairs."

"I can do this myself. Let me show you." She swatted away his arm and gripped the wooden support but after a few steps she lost her balance. Not willing to chance her falling, he scooped her into his arms.

"Oh, my." Her arms flailed, and she grabbed onto him.

"You smell good." She cuddled her face into the crook of his neck. Her warm breath brushed against his throat.

A hardness grew in his loins. He never thought a woman, especially one as lovely as Allison, would ever let him get so near with the lights on. He could've put her feet on the landing, but he wanted to savor the feel of her body molded against his without the prying eyes of his family.

Using a few free fingers, he reached for a lit oil lamp on the side table. The dim light illuminated their way, while he carried her to her room. Thankfully, she hadn't closed her door completely, and he used his foot to push it wide.

With a bit of finagling, he placed the oil lamp safely on the bedside table and adjusted the wick, lighting the room in a soft glow. Ever-so-slowly, he lowered her legs until her fancy boots touched the rug covering the wooden floor. Still, he didn't let her go. He knew he should. Instead, he stroked her back, letting his hand glide over the soft satin of her light purple gown. Her full breasts pressed against his upper body, as she rested the side of her head over his heart. His racing

100

heartbeat pounded in his chest and echoed in his ears. Her outstretched arms enveloped his waist. He removed the glove on his left hand, letting it fall to the floor.

Jayson breathed in the scent of fresh roses arising from her hair. His deft fingers removed pin after pin holding her chignon on top of her head until a wave of curls cascaded down her back. Leisurely, he ran his hands through the silky tresses, something he had ached to do for a long time.

Lately, she wore her hair like Melony, with some of the front tied back but the rest left long and hanging. Some evenings he caught himself staring at her from afar when she wasn't looking. Golden streaks peppered her light brown hair when the sunlight hit it exactly right. It killed him to sit back and not touch her in those moments.

He cupped her chin with gloveless fingers and tilted her head, so he could gaze upon her lovely face. Her coffee brown eyes were glassy, lips red and ripe. He couldn't help himself. Desire burned within him. His other hand moved to her bare shoulder. The touch of her skin inflamed his yearning and his manhood hardened. Slowly, his fingers trailed to the back of her neck where they pressed lightly, urging her head forward to meet him halfway.

When their lips joined, a wave of intense pleasure flowed through his body. Never in his life had he felt this way. He deepened the kiss, and she met him passion for passion, as she had in the church. A moan escaped her lips. She cupped his face with both hands and pulled him closer. He let his tongue explore the deep recesses of her mouth. Her tangy taste was pure intoxication.

She arched her hips toward his, but her belly got in the way and she whimpered, the sound reverberating in his ears.

They had to stop. He'd made a promise. They would not share a bed until after the baby was born.

Jayson willed himself to pull away. He laid his hands on the sides of her expanding waist and gave her a gentle nudge backward. Then, he turned his head from her tempting, lush lips.

"What's the matter?" Allison asked, dazed and confused.

"Let's not get too carried away. There'll be plenty of time for this after the baby is born," he said in a husky voice.

"But it feels so good," she purred innocently.

Jayson groaned. He needed to maintain some control. She had no idea what she did to him.

Suddenly, horror materialized on her face. "Oh, no. I don't feel so well," she shrieked, covering her mouth with her hand.

Jayson rushed her to the washbasin in the corner. Gathering her hair away from her face, he held the mass of soft curls with one hand and stroked her back with the other. She hunched over the blue-flowered bowl and spewed her dinner.

His brothers were jackasses. He had hoped she would be spared this part of over-indulging, but apparently not. When she switched to dry-heaving, he reached for a clean cloth and stuck it into the freshwater pitcher on her dresser. Wringing it out with one hand, he held it on her forehead.

"Are you okay?"

"Everything's spinning. I have to lie down," she whispered.

His heart went out to her. He didn't like seeing her unwell and feeling poorly. Tears streaked her cheeks and she was as pale as a white-washed fence. Using the moist cloth, he wiped her face and mouth.

"I'm so embarrassed. Sorry you had to see that."

Jayson guided her to sit on the edge of the bed. "I feel like it's my fault. I should've kept better sights on my brothers."

"I hope the baby's all right." She grasped his forearm for support.

"I'm sure your little one will manage fine. You don't drink like this on a regular basis." He rubbed her back to soothe her anxiety. "Let me help you take your dress off. You'll be more comfortable."

"I don't know if that's...necessary." Her voice faltered. She closed her eyes and placed her hand on her forehead.

He didn't wait for a go-ahead. Standing her, he unbuttoned the crystal buttons on the front of her gown and lifted the whole satin dress over her head, leaving her in her fancy corset fastened only half-way down the front because of her expanding belly. He unhooked the stays, ignoring her breasts fighting for freedom and removed the confining garment from her middle. Soon enough, she stood before him in only her delicately embroidered chemise and lacy silk petticoats.

She crossed her arms over her breasts, to maintain some modesty in her alcohol-induced fog, but only succeeded in making her cleavage more prominent. He loved the shape of her rounded breasts, the way they were always fighting for freedom against the too-small bodices of her fancy gowns.

The tightness in his loins returned. He threw back the covers. "In with you."

Allison wasted no time and dove into the bed. He unbuttoned her leather boots and pulled them off. She let him work his hands up her legs, under her silky drawers, to remove her garters and hose. He couldn't say the task wasn't a pleasant one. His fingers lingered on the bare skin of her muscular legs, as he slowly removed her underthings. She was too worn out and had no fight left in her to warn him away.

He poured her a cup of water from the pitcher. Sitting her upright, he put the rim to her lips, so she could take a sip. "How's your head?"

"The room's spinning." She quickly lay down.

"If you keep your eyes open and focus on something, it'll help." He pulled the covers over her and started to stand.

"Please don't leave. I don't want to be alone." She reached for his scarred hand and placed it against her cheek.

He dragged a chair next to the bed. "I'll stay with you until you fall asleep."

"Thank...you," she sputtered, her eyes growing heavy as she spoke. He re-wet the cloth and placed it on her forehead.

Soon her breathing was steady, and she drifted asleep. He pulled his hand out from under her head and swept loose tendrils of hair away from her face. She looked so sweet and peaceful. A tightness squeezed his chest, and he let out a shallow breath.

His feelings for Allison had changed. There was warmth in his heart when he looked at her. Visions of her plagued his mind when she was out of sight. He could no longer stay detached. Their marriage was supposed to be a business deal. That's what Peter had proposed. Two people making a life together without attachments. It's what they agreed upon. That's what he wanted.

He'd built walls around himself, but she weakened them. The problem with Allison was that she was too easy to care for. She had a way about her that drew people in. He studied his sleeping wife and shook his head.

Besides her tenacity, what he admired most was her courage and straight talk. He found her company enjoyable. It was refreshing how she treated him normal and didn't make a big deal about his scars. He liked the sound of her laughter when his brothers teased her and even liked seeing her riled up and stamping her dainty foot.

Allison rolled half onto her back. The covers fell to her side, exposing her rounded belly under her expensive silk chemise. He laid a hand on the firm surface and ran his fingers gently back and forth over the mound while she slept, something he didn't dare do when she was awake. There was a flutter of movement and he stilled so he could better feel the rolling bump.

Someone's not happy with their mother tonight.

As he stared at his wife, a sour taste bubbled up from his stomach and caught in the back of his throat. He doubted she'd ever have feelings for him. More than likely, she was still in love with the baby's father. When they'd first met, she'd made it clear she was just looking for a name for her child and security. She had been straight-forward and honest.

In the past, he had loved a woman who didn't feel the same way about him. He couldn't live through such hurt and pain again. He couldn't continue, year after year, hoping that his wife would someday return his affection.

That would kill me.

A decision had to be made before it was too late. He was already in great jeopardy of falling hard and couldn't take such a plunge. Couldn't go through the pain again. Somehow, he had to convince Allison to leave. If she left soon, her departure would hurt less. She should go back to Boston. She didn't belong here, anyway. She was too good for this part of the country.

Too good for me.

She was better suited to living amongst her peers, where she'd be admired and cherished by all.

Of course, the two of them would remain married and she could take his name for the baby. He would make sure Allison and the baby had enough money to live comfortably. Peter could check in on them and see to their welfare. Occasionally, Jayson could make the trip into the city, see them from a distance, just to make sure they were all right. His brothers wouldn't be happy, but they would get over it.

Jayson pulled the covers to Allison's chin. He leaned in and pressed his lips against her forehead. The rose scent tickled his nose and he let his breath out slowly.

"I'm sorry, Allie. I can't take a chance you won't break my heart."

~Chapter Thirteen~

Allison tugged a weed out of the earth and tossed it on top of others piled high in a wooden bucket. How she loved being outside in the early morning sunshine, her hands digging through the dirt. She sat back on her heels and admired the colorful blooms of pink bitterroot and yellow wallflowers lined up along both sides of the stone pathway.

This was her very first flower garden. In Boston, her family hired groundskeepers to take care of the greenery surrounding their townhouse. Over the past few weeks, she'd made it her mission to come out daily to pull weeds and water the roots of the budding stems. The results were beautiful.

While she worked, memories of the town dance filled her head. Three weeks had passed and thankfully she hadn't heard any gossip about her overindulgence in spirits from those who had attended the gathering. She allowed herself to hope that no one outside of her family and Jasmine knew of the circumstances surrounding her early departure that evening.

Chase and Nathan apologized profusely for their part in getting her intoxicated...as soon as she had been well enough to hear their regrets.

How could she be mad at them? They just wanted her to relax and enjoy herself. She barely remembered more than the first hour of festivities. The rest of the night blurred in and out. Nathan told her Jayson had brought her home. She wished she could recall their time together.

Since the dance, her life had slowly settled into a comfortable daily routine. The men left before she woke. She liked sleeping late, a habit she'd developed back in Boston after too many late-night parties. The mornings were quiet and peaceful. She kept busy tidying the house, feeding the chickens, and working in her flower garden. On occasion, she visited the ladies in town. A brother-in-law or a ranch hand was always nearby to assist her with anything she wanted and they never left her alone. She suspected Jayson had something to do with that.

Every other day, Chase, Nathan, or Daniel, helped her make dinner. In between, they let her figure out how to prepare the evening meal on her own. She wasn't particularly good at cooking. No matter how hard she tried, something always went wrong. Sometimes, she'd omit an ingredient or measure wrong. Other times, she cut her vegetables too thick or thin and they wouldn't cook properly. Her lack of skill didn't seem to faze the men and they even praised her failures.

The cast-iron stove remained a mystery. She couldn't regulate the heat; the flames were either too hot or not hot enough. She lost a few of her favorite dresses to burn holes and singeing. The darn contraption had it in for her, and when it was her turn to prepare a meal, she approached the stove warily.

After dinner, Jayson retreated to his office or read in a corner by oil lamp. Her brothers-in-law provided her with nightly entertainment. When in cheerful moods, they'd cajole her to play the piano, and made her laugh as they sang along. They taught her to play Poker using dried beans for bets. She was surprisingly good at the card game and had a jar full of winnings to prove it. Some evenings she read letters from home. Of course, when reading aloud, she skipped over the embarrassing entries Lillian included.

Allison rose from her knees, stretched her back and admired her latest work. Only one small section in her garden had yet to be returned to its former glory.

The sound of a horse galloping toward the house made her glance down the dirt road. She smiled broadly when Jasmine cantered into the yard and slowed the mare in front of the gate. Her friend had visited a few times since the dance.

"Jasmine." She adjusted the wide-brimmed hat she'd inherited from Jayson's mom. "So good to see you, again."

"What a beautiful morning. The minute I woke, I knew I had to take advantage of the weather and come for a visit."

"I'm glad you did. It gets lonely being the only woman out here." She so missed female companionship. In Boston, her mother, sister, and female servants were around at all hours of the day or night, but now wherever she looked, there was a man. "Tie your horse to the post and we'll sit on the porch, out of the sun. I made some cold tea." She pulled off her soft leather gloves.

"Your garden is coming along nicely." Jasmine dismounted. She loosened the string under her chin and let her hat fall upon her back. This afternoon, her friend could pass for a respectable young lady. She wore a pristine white shirt, navy blue riding skirt, and a matching vest. Brown boots protected her calves and reached to almost her knees. Her midnight black hair was bound together in a long, thick braid that hung down her back. Bangs, swept to one side, covered part of her forehead.

"Thank you. Jayson's mother did all the hard work. I'm just nursing it along. I never had a garden before. I'm trying to get as much as I can done before I have to stop. It's getting harder and harder to bend over. My stomach gets in the way."

"I can imagine. Only a few more months." Jasmine stepped into the enclosed yard.

Allison removed her well-worn hat and gently rubbed her rounded belly. "I'm a little nervous about childbirth. Nathan's all excited because he's been reading about it in his medical books. I guess the women around here use Mrs. Benson to deliver their babies and not Doc Thatcher. Nathan said not to worry, he'd be available if anything went wrong."

"Everything will be fine. Over the years I've helped deliver a few babies and those births went smoothly." They climbed the stairs and stepped onto the porch.

She turned to Jasmine. "Do you think you could come, too? When the baby's ready. I mean if it's not too much of an imposition."

"I'd be honored to be at your side when you have the baby. As long as it's all right with your husband," Jasmine said.

"I'll ask him. I don't think he'll mind. It gives me peace knowing you'll be with me."

Jasmine reached down, grabbed Allison's hand, and gave a little squeeze. "It's normal for a woman to fret about giving birth."

"I'm sure I'll manage fine. Just jitters." She sent her friend a tight-lipped smile, then poured two glasses of cold tea.

They each sat in a wooden rocking chair.

Jasmine bobbed back and forth in an easy rhythm as she studied the hills in the distance. The runners creaked as they glided over the porch floor. "This is such a beautiful country, isn't it?"

"It sure is. There's nothing like this back in Boston." She sighed. Her eyes scanned the hills in the distance. A peacefulness came over her.

"How are you settling into ranch life?"

She chuckled. "Well, it's a little more challenging than I imagined. For one thing, I'm not used to living with four men and a handful of ranch hands. Sometimes they make my life more difficult because they overlook sharing pertinent information with me."

"What did they forget to tell you?"

She stopped rocking and smiled broadly. "For example, a few days after the dance, I noticed everyone had stacked dirty clothes outside their bedroom doors. I picked up all the clothes and toted them out back to the washing tubs. I had never washed clothes before, but I saw it done a time or two back home and thought they wanted me to give it a try. I filled the cast iron cauldron with water, lit the fire, which turned out to be an arduous task, and waited for the water to boil."

"Then what happened?" Jasmine leaned forward expectantly.

Allison stifled a soft laugh. "Mr. Chang arrived with his family in tow. He ranted at me, in what I assume was Chinese, and shooed me away. Jayson and his brothers forgot to tell me he regularly cleans everyone's clothes on the ranch. Daniel came to my rescue and explained my error. Mr. Chang takes pride in his work. When he saw me trying to do his job, he became upset that I had dared to steal his livelihood."

Jasmine covered her mouth with her hand to smother a giggle. "Oh, no."

Allison chuckled. "I thought I was helping out, only to be embarrassed because they failed to tell me what goes on around here."

"Men. Sometimes they're hard to read." Jasmine pursed her lips and shook her head.

"Sometimes? How about all the time. I come from a family consisting of my mother, a younger sister, and an overly indulgent father. Except for the one man who treated me poorly, I have absolutely no experience with men."

Jasmine laughed. "I have too much."

She smiled wide. "I must tell you, Jayson is the hardest one of all to read, and at times he can be a little intimidating. I don't remember what happened at the dance, or after, but since then his behavior has changed. If anything, he's more formal, detached, and withdrawn. He keeps saying things under his breath about me returning to Boston where I'd be happier. I don't think he appreciates all the work I'm doing and how hard I'm trying. If he does, he doesn't comment on it," she said dejectedly.

"I think your husband is a very complicated man."

"I'm not sure he likes me much." Her gaze dropped to her lap and she smoothed her skirts. "I know our marriage was supposed to be a business deal. I'd provide him with a family and he'd provide my baby with a name and me with security, but I'd feel better knowing he at least liked me a little."

"I only saw you together one time. The night of the dance. But, from what I saw, he likes you a lot." Jasmine laid a light hand on Allison's shoulder.

She raised an eyebrow at her friend. "Why do you say that?"

"Because of how protective he was of you and how he tolerated your tipsy behavior. Also, the way he wanted to please you by offering me a horse to ride so I could visit you, even though I'm not the most respectable person for a wife to associate with."

"That's not..." she began but Jasmine put her hand in the air to halt her words.

"Of course, it's true. I know I'm not. If he didn't care for you, I don't think he would've offered me a horse."

"I want to believe you're right. But, he's been so...distant...lately." Her chin dropped. When Jasmine touched her arm again, Allison raised her head and looked into her friend's warm, dark-rimmed eyes.

"Are you sure he's not staying away because he thinks you're trying to poison him with your cooking?" Jasmine chortled.

Allison laughed. "Oh, you're such a tease."

Jasmine stood and pulled her up to stand. "Come with me. Before I leave here today, I'm going to show you how to make my mother's mouth-watering chicken and dumpling stew. I guarantee your husband will notice you after he takes a bite."

"I'm holding you to your bragging," she said gaily as she followed her friend into the house.

***

For three nights in a row, creaking treads on the staircase outside Allison's bedroom door woke her from a sound sleep. In the pitch black of the night, she listened closely for any hint of who might be prowling the house at such a late hour.

Tonight, I'm staying awake to find out who it is.

The ominous sounds of the night, drifting in through her open windows on the warm breeze, resonated off her walls, as she lay wide-eyed on her bed, waiting for the footsteps to return upstairs. Eerie shapes formed in the shadows as the moonlight failed to illuminate the corners of her room, leaving them bathed in darkness. Various images formed in her mind of what lurked out of sight, but she dared not shut her eyes. If she did, she knew sleep would follow.

Finally, she could stand it no more. To ward off her overactive imagination, she struck a match and lit her oil lamp. Once the wick was raised and the room well-lit, she breathed a loud sigh of relief. Thankfully, no danger lurked in the corners.

Sitting on the edge of the bed, she reached for the timepiece on her bedside table. The hands on the clock read two-thirty. It seemed futile to lie there all night, wondering who skulked around on the first floor. If she wanted to know, all she had to do was go find out.

Allison slid her feet into sateen slippers and pulled a silk robe around her body, tying the corded belt above her non-existent waist. Seizing the oil lamp, she softened the flame, opened her door, and noiselessly made her way to the top of the stairs. A warm glow appeared around the doorway of the dining area below. She descended the steps to the foyer without a sound, taking care to avoid the creaking stair treads.

Her feet stalled at the bottom of the stairs. She hoped she wasn't too presumptuous with her curiosity. It wasn't right to invade someone's privacy.

An unbridled desire for answers compelled her forward and she stepped into the room. Jayson sat at the wooden table, shirtless. In his hand he held a clear glass filled with amber liquid. An uncorked bottle of whiskey rested at his elbow.

When he tipped his head back to gulp the contents, he noticed her standing under the archway.

"Did I wake you?" He clonked the empty cup on the table with too much force.

She stepped farther into the room. "Just the past few nights. I thought I'd come down and discover the identity of our night owl."

"You caught me." His blue eyes were glassy with drink.

"Having trouble sleeping?" she asked softly.

"Some." He poured more whiskey into his empty glass. "My skin tightens up at night when I'm not moving. Occasionally, I come down for a drink to curb the pain. It helps me get back to sleep," he said flatly.

Her heart went out to him. How he suffered, then and now. No one should go through such torment. "Have you tried laudanum?"

"I have. The medicine makes me stupid and lazy. I weaned myself off. Alcohol works better. I just need enough to get me tired. Then I'm good."

Allison turned up the light of her oil lamp and stepped closer to the table before setting it down next to his lamp. Jayson sat on a chair in nothing but his trousers. No shirt, no socks. For the first time, she saw the extent of his scars. They started on his left cheek, ran down his neck to the front of his shoulder, over his upper arm and ended above his elbow. They began again below the elbow and traveled to his wrist, then along the outside of his hand, encompassing his pinky and ring fingers. The skin looked like it had melted off. The scar tissue was pink, coarse, and raised. She imagined what a painful experience he had gone through.

"Not a pretty sight, are they?" he drawled.

"I've seen worse."

"You might as well return to bed. There's nothing you can do for me here," he stated dejectedly.

She stared hard at the angry skin. "You said you wake because your skin stiffens, causing pain. I have some salve my sister gave me. It helps to soften the skin. Let me get it." She picked up her oil lamp, turned abruptly, and hurried upstairs to get the jar from her room.

When she returned, she noticed Jayson had taken another big swig of drink.

"Don't bother, I'm fine."

"Nonsense, what will it hurt? Let me try." She stood behind him.

"I don't need any help. I'm going to bed." He grabbed the arms of his chair and made a move to stand.

"Don't be a baby. Sit." She placed a hand on his shoulder and pushed him back down. "This won't hurt a bit."

Allison unscrewed the cover and lathered her fingers with the greasy cream. She applied a thin layer to his cheek. The scar was narrow and far enough away from his eye, nose, and mouth that it didn't distort any of his facial features. She thought he had an attractive face, with his desirable lips, high cheekbones, and almond-shaped eyes.

He watched her warily as she rubbed the ointment into his neck and onto his shoulder. When she had helped Father Peter with the sick and injured in Boston, she had seen a few shirtless men, but she couldn't remember seeing a man in such good physical shape. Every muscle was well-defined. He worked hard, and his body reaped the benefits.

As she kneaded his arm, her gaze dropped to the hills and valleys that made up his chest. The smooth almost hairless skin piqued her curiosity. She wondered what his sculptured chest muscles felt like under her hands...against her lips.

Oh, my!

Her body trembled, her breathing slowed. A warmth settled between her legs. What was the matter with her? She hadn't thought her actions through. All she wanted to do was lessen his pain. She never imagined how much she'd be affected by the intimacy of rubbing salve onto her half-naked husband.

Her heart raced, and cheeks flushed.

Jayson stared at her intensely as she came around to the front and massaged his lower arm. She lifted his hand and kneaded the cream between his fingers. When she looked up, his crystal-blue eyes smoldered with something she couldn't discern. Her breath caught in her throat.

Jayson pulled his hand away as if again burned by fire. "I think you got it all." He handed her a cloth napkin from the table.

She wiped the excess lotion off her hands. "Does it feel better?"

"It sure does. You best get yourself back to bed now. Think of the baby. I'll be up directly after I put the bottle away," he said dismissively.

Allison pulled her robe tight. She picked up her oil lamp and retreated to the archway. When she got to the opening, she glanced over her shoulder and gazed at him in all his male glory as he ambled to the sideboard and placed the bottle on top. He had a gorgeous, masculine build, and she wouldn't mind staring at him all night long. If he'd let her.

She heaved a soft sigh.

He did it again. Whenever she got close, he pushed her away.

He doesn't like me very much.

She stepped into the foyer and hurried up to bed.

***

Jayson stared at his reflection in the wall mirror hanging above the sideboard where they stored the liquor decanters and crystal glasses.

She'd touched him.

No one had touched his deformed body since his mother had tended him after the fire.

She didn't flinch.

He had expected a different reaction.

Jayson peered at his image and examined the scars covering his bare skin. A long time had elapsed since he'd looked at them last. He stayed away from mirrors or anything reminding him of the accident. His brothers were the only ones who ever saw him without his shirt, and only when they swam.

An uncomfortable bulge pressed against his trousers. Allison's closeness stirred deep-rooted feelings he had hoped to avoid, especially if she was returning to Boston.

He could scarcely breathe when she leaned over him in nothing but her sheer bedclothes, for fear he'd lose control and pull her into his lap. The urge to devour her ripe lips and explore her perfect female curves was hard to resist. The alluring aroma of wild roses hovered around her, intoxicating his senses. He had to fight off his desire to snuggle his face in the nape of her neck and then kiss his way down to her full breasts.

The discomfort in his groin grew to distraction.

Two years had passed since he had held a woman in his arms. Jacquelyn was the last. He could've visited the saloon in town or even gone all the way to Helena, if he felt the need, but the thought of a woman lying with him when she didn't want to, soured his stomach.

When he'd first met Jacquelyn, she had feigned innocence around men, but he soon discovered that she was quite experienced and craved male companionship. She'd always been a willing partner, that is, until the fire. Afterward, she wanted nothing to do with him. She turned her back and walked away the moment she knew he was never going to have a career in politics.

It must've been the drink, but his thoughts abruptly turned back to Allison.

Sweet Allison.

Over the past few weeks, he had studied her from afar.

A small smile turned the corners of his mouth. The woman had such a peaceful and calming nature. He enjoyed her company immensely. He liked the way she moved with grace and ease, even while burdened with child. He admired how non-judgmental and kind-hearted she was to those she met.

A bit of mystery surrounded his wife, though. He didn't believe for a moment she was experienced with men. If she wasn't with child, he would say she hadn't lain with a man at all.

He shrugged his shoulders and wiped out his crystal glass. It was none of his business. If he had his way, she'd soon be on her way back to Boston where she belonged and things around the ranch would return to normal. His heart would be safe.

I'll miss her when she's gone. But, it's for the best.

~Chapter Fourteen~

Allison arranged the Black-Eyed Susans from her garden in a glass jar and methodically fixed them in an eye-catching bouquet. It was her turn to make supper and she decided to prepare Jasmine's recipe. When they made the meal together last week, the stew turned out delicious. She hoped it would again.

This afternoon she took extra care to make sure the flames in the cast iron stove were the right temperature before she started, and then followed the recipe exactly as taught. In her heart, she knew tonight's meal was going to be perfect. Jayson would have no cause to look at her as if she didn't belong. No cause to say she should return to Boston.

The men had gone down to the pond for their nightly swim before supper. While waiting for them to finish, she placed the jar bursting with bright yellow color in the center of the table. She stepped back and admired Mrs. McKay's fine china place settings. A heavy sigh escaped her lips. The table looked as fancy as any back East. Just because they were in the middle of nowhere didn't mean they couldn't be civilized. Heavy footfalls sounded on the porch. The men were on their way. She went behind the kitchen counter to gather the food.

"What's for dinner?" Chase entered the room first.

"Since you liked Jasmine's chicken and dumpling dinner so much, I thought I'd cook it tonight."

"Smells great," Nathan said.

She giggled nervously. "Never mind the smell, I'm hoping it tastes good."

Jayson walked through the doorway and stood by his chair. She sucked in a deep breath and let the air out slowly. His virile appearance caused a flutter in her lower belly, which had nothing to do with her baby. Curls from his damp hair, framed his face. His white shirt clung to the moisture still on his skin, pulling the cloth taut across his broad chest.

"Can I help?" Daniel stepped into the kitchen area.

She shook herself out of her stupor and pointed to the kettle on the stove. "Sure, you can take our meal to the table."

Daniel grabbed a cloth, lifted the heavy cast iron pot by the handle, and carried it to the table. He placed the pot next to the flowers. She glanced around the room full of handsome men standing by their seats waiting for her to sit and her heart skipped a beat. Out here in Montana, she had a purpose besides snaring a husband and entertaining her neighbors. There was a great deal of pride to be had in feeding a hungry family. A small smile curled the corners of her lips. She removed her bibbed apron, grabbed the heaping dish of mashed potatoes with one hand, and a basket of rolls in the other.

As Allison walked to the table with her arms encumbered, she realized she'd made a poor choice when dressing for dinner. Like most of her gowns, her yellow satin dress was too small for her enlarged breasts and expanding waistline. She didn't notice the ill-fitting bodice earlier when the bibbed lace of her apron hid her cleavage but now without a covering, the growing mounds were fighting for freedom.

She prayed the men hadn't noticed but when she glanced up, all eyes were on her chest. A blazing flush rose from her neck, into her cheeks.

"You're going to have to excuse me while I find a dress a little more...uh...appropriate," she stammered. "I'm afraid I'm running out of gowns that fit," she said in a humorous tone as she placed the basket of rolls on the table.

Jayson locked eyes with her, his expression flat. "I'm sure there are plenty of those fancy dresses back in Boston."

The hairs on the back of her neck stood straight up. Anger knotted her stomach.

He didn't just say that!

Every muscle in her body tensed. A sudden surge of scorching heat streamed through her insides, making it difficult to breathe.

One too many times lately, he had mentioned under his breath that she should return to Boston. Always pushing her to leave. Reminding her she didn't fit in. That she was unworthy. Making her feel as if she wasn't good enough. Like Robert made her feel when he abandoned her.

Her nostrils flared as she glared at her husband's smug face. Without breaking eye contact, she stepped toward him, raised the heavy dish of mashed potatoes with both arms and slammed the metal bowl down on the wooden surface so hard chunks of white pulp splattered the front of everyone standing around the table. The men's chairs scraped across the floor as they stepped back in a rush to get away from flying debris.

"That's it, Jayson McKay," she shrieked, laying shaky hands on what used to be her hips. "No more. Do you hear? I'll not put up with your sour mood and indifference anymore. I made a promise to myself when I agreed to marry you. I vowed to do my best and stick it out as long as I was wanted. Your veiled mumblings over the past few weeks have made it perfectly clear that I'm not wanted here. That I'd be better off in Boston. Well, guess what? You have your wish. I'm leaving."

Allison turned to Daniel, standing at her side. His face was as pale as a bleached sheet. "Finish your dinner and then hitch up the team, you're taking me to town." She glanced across the table. "Nathan and Chase, give me a half-hour to pack my things, then come for my trunk. I'm staying at Pearson's Hotel tonight. Tomorrow, I'll be taking the first stage back to Boston." She stomped out of the room and ran up the stairs.

***

The sound of a door slamming broke the heavy silence.

Jayson swallowed hard. This is what he'd been working toward. What he thought he wanted. "Well, it's probably for the best."

His brothers stood speechless around the table, mouths agape.

Out of the corner of his eye, he noticed Daniel move toward him.

A sharp, explosion of pain reverberated through his jaw. Knocked unbalanced by the fisted blow, he landed against Chase's shoulder.

"What the hell did you do that for?" He growled at Daniel as Chase pushed him away like he couldn't stand his touch.

"How could you?" Daniel said in a shrill, quivering voice, his fists clenched at his side. "She was the best thing that ever happened to you and you pissed it all away."

"You're a sick son-of-a-bitch." Chase shook his head.

Rubbing his jaw with an open hand, Jayson stared hard at Chase. "What are you talking about? She was never going to stay. You said it yourself the first day you heard about her. You said she would be high-tailing it back to Boston as soon as she got a chance."

Chase glared back. "I said that before I met her. She was proving me wrong."

"You never gave her a fair shake," Nathan chimed in. "What happened? Did she get too close?" A look of disgust marred his middle brother's face.

Jayson scowled at him. Nathan knew him best.

"I can't look at you right now." Chase turned on his heels to leave. "I need a drink. I'll be at the saloon. You can carry your wife's trunk down yourself. I'm outta here." He grabbed his hat and six-shooter from the peg on the wall and left the house.

"I lost my appetite. I'll be in the barn, hitching up the team." Daniel stormed out after Chase.

Jayson stared at Nathan, the only one willing to remain. "They'll get over her leaving."

"They might, but I'm not sure you will," Nathan said pointedly.

He shook his head. "I can't go through it again. It's better if she leaves sooner, rather than later. She'll never return any feelings I might have for her."

"Not if you remain boorish and unfriendly. Allison is nothing like Jacquelyn. You can't spend your life hiding out here in the middle of nowhere, pushing everyone away so you don't get hurt again."

"You're a fine one to talk. You were so close to completing your studies to become a physician, but after Ma died, you just quit."

"I don't know about you, but I'm tired of giving up when life gets hard. Having Allison around got me thinking about finishing what I started. She didn't walk away when things got tough. She found a way out of her predicament, made a commitment, and was keeping her end of the bargain, which is more than I can say for you," Nathan poured himself a glass of whiskey from the sideboard and took a sip. When he looked up, his eyes narrowed. "What about you, Jayson? Are you willing to give up on Allison, someone who could make you happy? Seems like you still have a choice here."

"She could leave me one day." He joined Nathan and poured himself his own drink.

"Nothing's for sure. We don't know our future. Sometimes, we just have to play it out." Nathan slung back the rest of the amber liquid in his glass.

Jayson's stomach knotted in a tight ball. A few weeks ago, he'd been so sure Allison should return to Boston. That he'd be better off without her, but now he wasn't so certain. "I'm pretty confident I just blew any chance I had with her."

"If I were you, I'd own up to being a jackass, beg for forgiveness, and do whatever it takes to change her mind about leaving. She's worth humbling yourself for."

***

Jayson stopped outside of Allison's closed door and took a deep breath. He'd really messed things up good. Knocking once, he didn't wait for an answer before he lifted the latch and pushed the wooden door wide. Allison stood with her back to him, rummaging through her chest of drawers. Her trunk sat open at the foot of her bed.

"Please, don't go," Jayson said hoarsely as he stood in the doorway. "I want you to stay."

She abruptly halted what she was doing and lowered her head. "I find that hard to believe after weeks of keeping your distance and muttering under your breath about how I don't belong here. Always pushing for me to return to Boston. Well, you win. I'm going." Her voice shook with emotion.

"Forgive me." He took a few steps into the room.

"I don't know if I can."

Nathan's words popped into his head. "I've been a complete jackass."

Allison removed a set of folded clothes from a drawer and placed them on the top of the bureau. Her back remained straight but her head dropped in defeat. "Why do you want me to stay? I'm obviously not what you were looking for in a wife."

"You're exactly what I was looking for," he said huskily.

Allison leaned her elbows on the high dresser. "Then why do you want me to leave?"

He took a few steps into the room. "It's complicated."

"More complicated than my reasons for coming to Montana and entering into this arrangement?"

"I was engaged to a woman who left without a backward glance." He hitched his thumbs in his front pockets. "She took one look at the scars on my face and high-tailed it out of my life. When she discarded me like that, it crushed me. I'm afraid I thought eventually you'd end up leaving, too. I wanted to protect myself from the same hurt, so I devised a plan to get you to go before I became too attached."

Jayson covered the distance between them and wrapped his arms around her, pulling her back against his chest. He rested his unscarred cheek against the side of her face. "The problem with my plan is that I'm already attached." He let his words sink in and then whispered in her ear, "Don't go, Allie. Stay...stay with me."

"Why should I?" she exhaled softly, her body trembling beneath his touch.

"So, I can make it up to you. So, we can be husband and wife."

"What happens if you change your mind again and want me gone?"

"I won't. I want to start over. Maybe our marriage could be less of a business arrangement and more like a real one." He needed their relationship to feel tangible. To be her husband in every sense of the word. He nestled his face in the crook of her neck and brushed his lips against her soft skin.

God, she smelled good.

"You hurt me. I've been trying so hard to make this my home and you've made my life more difficult. You were willing to toss me away without considering how leaving would affect my life."

"I'm sorry. I never meant to hurt you. I thought the sooner you were gone, the easier the break would be. I wasn't thinking clearly. I was being selfish."

He turned her around gently in his arms, so they faced each other.

"What happened?" She touched the side of his swollen chin with the tips of her fingers.

"Daniel blamed me for your decision to go back to Boston." He chuckled. "I never saw his fist coming. If Chase hadn't softened my fall I would've ended up on my backside. My little brother packs one mighty blow."

"You deserved it." She looked deep into his eyes.

"I know," he acknowledged. Her brown eyes were red-rimmed, and he imagined she had shed a tear or two after her decision to leave. He swept a loose tendril of hair away from her face and stuck it behind her ear, letting his fingers linger a moment on the side of her neck. "I never should have pulled back. You didn't deserve that."

Her head tilted against his hand. He leaned down and skimmed his lips against hers, kissing her tenderly. When he was convinced she believed his words were sincere, he gave her a small peck on her forehead.

"What can I do to get you to stay?" he breathed against her bare skin.

She pushed away so she could scrutinize him. "Do you promise to stop being so ill-tempered?"

"I promise." He crossed his heart with a finger.

"Will you cease making remarks about me returning to Boston and let me settle in here?"

"Most definitely." He gazed longingly at her exposed cleavage spilling over the neckline of her potato-speckled, yellow satin gown.

"Are you ready to let me get to know you?" she asked.

He sighed. "I am. I thought I'd feel relieved when you finally decided to leave. Instead, I felt like I got shot in the gut. I'll do anything to keep you here in Montana."

Allison pursed her lips and shook her head as she studied his face for the truth. Finally, she broke the long, drawn-out silence. "You're not the only one who was abandoned without a backward glance. Don't forget, I also was cast aside and left to manage on my own. The wounds run deep. You were willing to get rid of me and the baby just as easily as *he* did."

"I'm sorry. I won't ever do that again." He ran his hand up and down her back.

"You're going to have to earn back my trust. Bear in mind, there are no guarantees. I refuse to stay where I'm not wanted or appreciated."

"Understood." He leaned down to capture her lips but pulled away before he made contact. Instead, he stared into her doe-like eyes. "I'm prepared to go out of my way to show you how much I appreciate you."

"You'll have a lot of making up to do to get back in my good graces," she warned.

"Give me a chance to court you. We have a few weeks before the baby comes. Let's use that time to get to know one another. The way it should've been done in the first place."

"How do you propose to court me? I'm already your wife."

He kissed her softly, savoring the taste of her lips, and when he felt her soften against him, he broke their embrace. "I'm going to make a point to spend more time with you. We'll go for carriage rides and have picnics. I'll come home early and take my turn at teaching you how to cook. At night, I'll join you when you play poker or do whatever you want me to do. What do you say, Allie? Will you stay and give me another chance?"

Her lips tightened as she thought about his offer. She nodded. "I'll stay."

"Excellent." Jayson let out his breath, and then stepped back and held her hands in his. He couldn't repress a big grin. "If that's the case, you're going to have to learn a few new skills. Things you'll need to know to survive out here in Montana."

"What else do I need to know? I'm already figuring out how to cook."

"You need to learn to shoot a gun. Every woman out here should know how to protect herself."

"I'm afraid of guns."

"That's why we're going to practice, so you respect them, but don't fear them." He held onto one of her hands and pulled her behind him toward the stairway. Her hand was soft and small in his, the contrast pleasurable.

"Wait, I can't go anywhere. I have to change my gown," she exclaimed, digging in her heels, stopping him in his tracks.

"I kind of like the way you're dressed." He winked. "Your potato splatters match mine."

Allison tugged on the edge of her bodice, trying to cover her exposed skin.

"This is what we're going to do. I'll take the next few days off from work. I'll teach you how to shoot a gun. It's a handy thing to know out here on the ranch. Afterward, we'll have a picnic down by the stream."

He took both her hands in his and brushed his lips over her knuckles, one hand at a time. Her smile shone radiantly, his breath hitched in his throat. How did he get so lucky?

"The following day, the two of us will head to town. We'll pick out some colorful cloth at the mercantile and take it over to Mrs. Mullin's house. She'll be back from her trip by then. She's an excellent seamstress. She can fit you for some new dresses to hold you over until we can get to Helena where they have a fancy-dress shop. When you're done, we'll go over to Pearson's Hotel for lunch. What do you say?" He gave her fingers a little squeeze.

Her eyes sparkled with excitement. "I think that's a fine idea."

He turned and tugged her to the top of the stairs.

"Where are we off to right now?" she asked eagerly.

"First, we're going to inform Daniel that you're not leaving before he does something stupid to get back at me. Then we're returning to the house to have our dinner. You worked hard on our meal and it deserves to be eaten. I had a chance to taste a clump of potato stuck on my shirt and it was delicious."

"Sorry about that." Allison giggled. "You said there were a few things I should learn. What are some of the other things?"

"Swimming would be one. I love swimming and can't think of a better way to spend time with my wife."

"I never tried swimming before."

"Don't worry. I'll teach you," he promised.

They were crossing the foyer when Allison stopped him with the pull of her hand. He spun around to face her. She glowed with happiness. Her cheeks flushed, her eyes twinkled. He couldn't help but reach out and stroke the side of her face.

"If I'm going out of my way to learn all these new things, I think you should learn a thing or two, yourself," she said coyly.

"And, what do you believe I need to be learning?"

She batted her eyelashes prettily. "I think my husband needs to learn how to dance."

Jayson placed his hands on her rounded hips. "It has been a few years since I danced. I think you're going to find me an eager student. It'll give me another reason to touch you." He leaned in for a gentle kiss which was warmly reciprocated.

"I think I'm going to like this courting business," Allison said breathlessly.

~Chapter Fifteen~

"I'm in here."

Allison was halfway down the stairs when Jayson's deep voice hailed her from the library. She rounded the banister and headed to the back of the house. The heavy paneled door was ajar, and she peered through the narrow opening.

"Good morning, sleepyhead." Jayson reclined against his leather chair, behind a wide mahogany desk.

Her face heated at his teasing. "I'm sorry I slept so late. I'm still not used to Montana's early mornings."

"I find it hard to believe you can sleep through our rooster at daybreak." He chuckled deep in his chest. "That bird is loud enough to wake the dead."

"That's why I curl up with two pillows. When the ruckus begins, I put one over my ears to block out all the noise. Before I know it, I've fallen back to sleep."

Jayson's ear-to-ear smile warmed her heart. "Stay in bed as late as you want while you can. I have a feeling when the baby comes you won't have a chance to get any good shuteye."

At his mention of the baby, she rubbed her belly.

"Come sit." He gestured to the two high-back chairs facing the front of his desk.

Allison hesitated at the doorway. This was Jayson's sanctuary. She had never entered the room, except to take a quick peek. A guilty twinge pricked her innards. She hadn't seen fit to dust the bookshelves because it didn't feel right to invade his private space. She hoped he hadn't noticed.

"I heard you moving around upstairs, so I made some tea and gathered you a few of Daniel's spice muffins."

Allison strolled over to the desk and sat down on the edge of one of the chairs. She wasn't used to this eager-to-please Jayson and glanced at him warily.

He poured a cup of tea from the teapot and leaned across his desk to hand her the fine china.

"Thank you." She retrieved the cup and saucer, sat deeper in the chair, and took a sip. The hot liquid sent a warm, welcoming trail down her throat. Her gaze leisurely swept the room and paused on the hand-scrolled, decorative floor-to-ceiling bookshelves lining the wall behind him. "You appear to have a fully stocked library."

"My father was an avid reader. The winters are long if you have nothing to occupy your time."

Allison took another sip. One of the books along the wall caught her interest. She rose from the chair with her teacup in hand, walked around his desk and stood in front of the rows of leather-bound novels. Her fingers lightly stroked the embossed words on the binding of her favorite Jane Austin book. "Quite a variety of topics."

"Father wasn't fussy when it came to books. He liked everything."

"And your mother?"

"She couldn't put a good book down. Jane Austin was one of her favorite writers. I bet we have all her books." He relaxed back into his chair and made a steeple with his fingers. "My mother grew up a mountain girl. When she met my father, she couldn't read at all. Reading wasn't considered a priority when your family had to put food on the table. According to my father, they spent many winters curled up in front of the fireplace, while he taught her to read. She said one of her greatest regrets was not learning when she was young, so she made sure we all read at an early age."

She brushed a loose tendril of hair off her face. "You must take after your parents. I noticed at night you always have your nose in a book."

"I like to keep my mind busy." He rearranged the papers spread out before him.

"What are you working on?" She peered down at the piles.

"Would you like to see?" He pushed back his chair and wiggled a finger at her. "Come, I'll show you."

Allison covered the few steps between them. When she stood within arm's reach, he grabbed her waist and pulled her against his side, as he remained seated. She sucked in her breath when her leg met his muscled thigh. Even with layers of material between them, the connection was disquieting, and she had trouble focusing on anything else but where their bodies touched.

"These are drawings of buildings I'm erecting on our property." He pushed a few prints in front of her.

She took a sip of her tea and studied the pictures. "It looks like a barn."

"It is." Jayson glanced up at her from his reclined position. "But not an ordinary barn. This one is a hay barn. Chase thinks we'll save greater numbers of our herd if we feed them through the winter. Right now, we open range them. The cattle are let loose, and they fend for themselves. We round them up in the spring. Not all the animals survive a harsh season. This year we've begun fencing off fields to grow hay. Come the end of summer, we'll hire men to harvest those fields, and store the feed for the coming winter."

"Where are you building it?"

"The other side of the bunkhouse. We're going to have a barn-raising in a few weeks."

"A barn raising?"

"Neighbors from all over will come with their families. The men help build the frame, sides, and then roof. The women bring food for supper and after we complete our work, we all gather for a meal. There's usually music and dancing by the end of the day."

Allison put her teacup down on the corner of the desk and clapped her hands. "We're hosting a party."

Jayson smiled. "In a few weeks."

Her body shook with excitement. "It sounds like fun. Are you going to dance with me?" She hoped he would. At the last dance, he hadn't danced with her at all. He seemed ill-at-ease with the activity.

Did he know how to dance?

Jayson laid an open hand on the small of her back and gave her a half-grin. "Maybe."

She trembled from the intimacy of his touch. "I'll be expecting you to ask me."

"If this dance is anything like the last one, I might have to muscle my way through your crowd of admirers just to stand by your side."

"That's not true," she protested playfully. What would the townsfolk say if he begged off again?

"We'll have to wait and see." Jayson lightly stroked her back before his attention returned to the pictures. Gathering them up using one hand, he set them aside and then spread more drawings across his desk. "Would you like to see what else I have planned?"

"Show me." She was delighted he confided in her, but their close proximity unsettled her nerves. She breathed in deeply to calm her racing heartbeat.

"These are plans I drew up for a sawmill to be built downstream from the pond. I expect the population in this region to grow in the next few years, especially now that the stagecoach comes through town on a regular basis. Also, there's a good chance Montana Territory will become a state soon. If we get statehood, people will be flocking to this area. There'll be a lot of new construction and they're going to need raw lumber. We have plenty of timber on our land and I plan to start harvesting and selling it."

Allison studied the pictures with awe. They were drawn with care and in great detail. She moved the papers around for a better look.

As she considered his drawings, Jayson watched her carefully.

He pointed to one of the pages. "We'll use the stream as a power source for a water wheel that will run the saw and help with our manpower needs. This means we'll have to hire more men around here to work in the sawmill. Once it's operational we won't have to rely only on our cattle and horses for revenue."

"These are amazing. Have you seen such an operation before?" She glanced down. His slow-building smile gave her pause. He looked as if he could devour her.

Jayson wrapped an arm around her lower back and clasped her waist on the other side. "I sure have. Back East," he said in a throaty voice.

Without warning, he pushed his chair back, and with both hands on her hips, he pulled her onto his lap.

She squealed in surprise and reached an arm around his neck to steady herself. "Oh, my. What are you doing?"

"I'm courting my wife." He chuckled.

"Someone may see us," she said breathlessly, enjoying his closeness. A fragrant woodsy aroma drifted up from his shirt and she inhaled deeply.

"We're married." He laid an arm across the top of her thighs as if to keep her in place and snuggled his nose into the curve of her neck.

She giggled and lifted a shoulder to her ear. "That tickles."

"Maybe you'll like this more," he whispered huskily as he nuzzled deeper and pecked small kisses along her collarbone.

***

Jayson nearly tumbled off the edge of sanity when he heard a small, almost inaudible moan, sounding deep in his wife's throat while his lips brushed against her bare skin. She wiggled on his lap, finding a comfortable position, and his loins tightened from the onslaught. She smelled of fresh flowers, like a warm summer breeze. He knew he shouldn't, but his gaze dropped to the creamy skin spilling over her bodice. He bit back a groan. Her bright eyes sparkled, and his innards melted to mush.

With the tips of his fingers, he beckoned her chin forward. When in range, he kissed her plump, ripe lips. She responded with her usual unbridled enthusiasm. While he explored and teased her mouth, she did the same to his. There was an alluring curiosity in her kisses that arose from inexperience, which he found refreshing. Her free arm hooked around the other side of his neck and she twisted her body toward him, as far as she could go with her protruding stomach in the way. Her pure and simple passion made his pleasure grow.

When the throbbing between his legs became downright uncomfortable, he pulled back and placed languid pecks on her cheek, throat, and collarbone. He let his pounding heart return to a leisurely rhythm.

Allison rested her parted lips on his forehead, her breath jagged.

Placing the palm of his hand against the side of her face, he tenderly kissed her one last time before pulling away. Her soft brown eyes, framed by long, black velvet lashes stared at him with yearning.

"Well, wife. We better stop now or we're apt to give Daniel an eyeful."

Allison sighed softly. "We wouldn't want to do that."

Jayson would've loved to take their intimacy further; it had been so long since he'd held a woman in his arms, but he couldn't count on his self-control in this heated state, so sadly he backed off while he still could. He had made her a promise when they'd first met and aimed to keep it.

"Day's a wasting. We better get out to the shooting range. I packed us a lunch. If we have time I'll take you by the spot where the sawmill is going."

"Sounds wonderful." Allison tried to scoot off his lap but her expanding body and the yards of fabric of her gown made the task difficult.

He grabbed her under her arms and lifted until she stood. The loss of her warm bottom was sorely missed, and he regretfully let her go. As she busied herself with straightening her clothing, he remembered the agreement he'd made to himself last night. He'd vowed to win her back. The plan was to make up for all the distance he'd put between them over the past few months. Get her used to being near him. Make her want to stay.

He grinned to himself. *Today is going to be a fun day.*

***

The carriage stopped under a lone pine tree on the top of a rolling hill. Allison glanced around in all directions. The land spread out like an ocean of blue-green waves. The air in her lungs caught in her chest, the vastness of the rugged country stole her breath away.

Jayson locked the brake, tied the reins to the handle, and jumped down from the buggy. "This is where we practice shooting. It's far enough away from the livestock so we don't spook them." He held up his arms to help her down.

She leaned forward to meet him halfway, but her stomach prevented her from bending that far. Resigned to her limitations, she turned, held onto the seat, and stepped back onto the foot support.

Jayson grabbed her around her waist, to guide her down. "What's the matter? Having a little trouble?"

"How would you like to carry around all this extra weight in your belly?" She was mortified to show him her backside, and she quickened her pace.

"I like the way you move," he said in a deep voice.

Her cheeks flamed from the off-handed compliment. When her feet hit the ground, she turned in his arms to face him but found herself too close for comfort. Only inches apart, she raised her chin and gazed into his dark, fiery eyes. Tingles coursed through her body. She shivered as she held onto his biceps, well-defined under her open hand.

"Are you ready?" A boyish grin lit up his face.

"I suppose." She let go of his arms and he stepped away.

He secured the horses' lead rope to the tree and lifted a wooden box from the back of the carriage. "You wait here while I set up our targets."

Jayson crossed the open ground and stopped at the first log, less than ten yards away. He lined up a few dozen tin cans and empty bottles along the top.

"The distance doesn't seem too far," she called out.

"After you get used to hitting these targets, we'll move them farther away, to the other logs."

His long strides covered the ground quickly as he returned to the carriage. A happy smile curled his lips. Her heart skipped a beat. He was dressed handsomely in his stark white shirt, black vest, and matching trousers. His black hat sat back on his head, cocked a bit to one side. She breathed in deeply and let the air out slowly. Never in her life had she dreamed of being in the company of such a man. One so virile and sure of himself.

Memories of the first day they'd met at the hotel came to mind. He had been so intimidating. An air of dangerousness had surrounded him. At the time, she hadn't been sure whether the threat was emotional or physical, but it had been clearly present. With his broad shoulders and at a height greater than most men, he was physically powerful and, she supposed, a force to be reckoned with in a fight. Strength and confidence emanated from him. If he stood in a room full of men, they would look to him to lead.

Her face heated at the recollections of that morning's kisses. He wanted her. She had seen the look before on Robert's face. More than anything, she wanted Jayson to desire her but feared that someday she'd care for him more than he cared for her. She couldn't handle him casting her aside again. She couldn't handle him abandoning her *like Robert did*. Robert had never loved her as much as she'd loved him; if he had they'd still be together.

Last night almost broke her heart. Every day she grew more and more fond of living in Montana, on the McKay ranch, with her brothers-in-law *and him*. Unlike Boston, out West she had a greater purpose in life. She ran a home, helped put food on the table, and men asked for her opinions. The feeling was exhilarating. She didn't want to leave.

Jayson held out a small revolver.

She glanced at his weapon holstered at his hip. "I'm not going to use your gun?"

"Mine is heavier with a longer barrel. You're going to learn to shoot with my mother's gun. It's a Colt 45 revolver, but this version has a shorter barrel than most. It's lighter and will be easier for you to handle. Some men draw from their hip and shoot with one hand, but I'm going to teach you to grip the handle with both hands, cock the hammer, take aim, and squeeze the trigger. It'll take you more time, but with practice your aim will be more accurate. After we're done with the Colt, we'll switch over to the Winchester repeating rifle."

She rubbed her belly. Doubts about her abilities plagued her mind. She didn't want to disappoint him. "Are you sure it's necessary I learn all this?"

He wrapped his arms around her back and pulled her close. "Are you planning on staying here with me?"

"Yes," she whispered.

Jayson swept a tendril of hair from the side of her face and put it behind her ear. "I'll always do whatever I can to protect you, but you never know what situations will arise. The law out here is spotty. I wouldn't be doing right by you if I left you without the means to protect yourself."

She nodded. "I understand."

"You'll do fine." He gave her a peck on the nose and a broad grin. He stepped aside and showed her the parts of the revolver and how to load and handle the weapon safely.

She listened intently, absorbing all he said. His teaching method was mesmerizing. He explained everything in detail, patiently. As he talked, she wondered if his father had taught his mother to read the same way on those cold, wintery nights.

When done explaining how a gun works, he demonstrated how she should stand. "I want you to put your strong foot forward. You're going to aim with both hands." Stepping behind her, he pressed his chest against her back. His burly arms encircled either side of her body and he pulled her arms straight up to shoulder height. His hands covered hers and he held the gun with her. His cheek rested on the side of her face. "Look down the barrel with one eye. When you have the first tin can in your sights, I want you to pull back the hammer with your thumb and cock the gun. Then, put your finger on the trigger."

He completely enveloped her in his arms, his strength cradling her body. She steeled herself against reacting to his touch. She concentrated on what she was doing. Learning to shoot was important if she stayed in Montana, so she wanted to do her best. She lined up the target and followed his directions. His fingers and hands covered hers every step of the way.

"Now squeeze," he said.

She pulled her finger and an explosion sounded. Automatically, she jerked back but his body softened her jolt. She quickly recovered from the startle. "Oh, my. I didn't hit a thing."

"You did great. All you need is a little practice and that's what we're here for. The first shot was just to get you used to the feel of the gun in your hands and the power behind the weapon when fired."

"Are you sure I can do this?"

"Most certainly. Let's try again." He still had his arms wrapped around her body and she melted into his chest.

Allison took her stance. She held the gun in both hands and raised her arms to shoulder height with light guidance from her husband. Looking down the gun barrel, she cocked the hammer, eyed her target, and squeezed the trigger. This time she was ready for the noise and the power behind the blast. She stood her ground.

The tin cup flew off the edge of the log and landed a few feet away.

"I did it. I did it," she squealed, being careful not to whip the gun around.

"You did. Do you want to try again?"

"I think I'd like that." She couldn't stop smiling.

***

Jayson gazed out over the clear blue water of the pond.

I have a second chance.

The night before, he'd almost ruined everything. His brothers were right; what an idiot he'd been. Fear of rejection had almost cost him Allison. He was done with his self-imposed isolation and loneliness. He wanted to be with a woman.

He wanted to be with his wife.

Today he planned to convince her he had changed his ways. No more boorish and unfriendly manners. A long time had passed since he'd courted a woman, but damned if he wasn't going to try. Hopefully, she'd end up so smitten she wouldn't think of leaving. So far, the day was going better than expected. Some of her wariness was evaporating.

Allison stood next to him on the outer edge of the dock, looking down at the water below. A rowboat used on the pond when fishing, was tied on one side. "I never learned to swim."

"Not to worry, I'll teach you."

Allison crossed her arms over her chest. "Are you sure swimming is necessary? I could just sit here at the end of the dock and soak my feet."

"You want me to dance. I want you to swim." He knew she balked at the intimacy of swimming together, especially since he swam unclothed, but it was that familiarity he wanted, something bonding her to him, ensuring she'd stay.

"What will I wear?"

"You could go buck naked like me." He flashed her his most mischievous smile. "Or, if you're feeling a little more modest, you could go in your camisole and drawers. That's the way my mother swam during the day. I can turn my back, if you insist. I won't see a thing."

"What if someone happens by?"

"Everyone on the ranch is working and Daniel is making dinner. We're pretty well hidden from view by the bushes. I wouldn't worry about anyone seeing us."

She wrung her hands. "Are you sure?"

"Positive. You can undress behind those shrubs. I brought down some blankets to wrap up in when we're done." He placed an open hand on the small of her back and gave her a reassuring rub. "I think you're going to enjoy this. Nothing to fret about."

"I guess...I could try." Allison turned and walked down the wooden slabs until she was back on dry land. She picked up a blanket on the grass. "I'm using this to cover up with when I'm done undressing."

"Sure."

She went behind the bushes along the water's edge.

Jayson took off his clothes and dived into the pond. He crested the surface spitting a mouthful of water into the air. As always, the feel of the cool water was medicinal on his sore muscles and tight skin. He floated on his back and kicked his feet.

Last night, as he'd contemplated a plan, he concluded he didn't have to jeopardize his heart to get her to stay. If he gave her what she wanted most, *attention, appreciation, and security*, she'd remain with him in Montana. She said no guarantees. He could court her but didn't have to fall for her completely. He could hold back some of his feelings, just enough to keep himself sane if somewhere down the line she left him. They could live together happily if he met her halfway. They could have a good life together.

Allison appeared from behind the bushes, the blanket wrapped tightly around her, so she looked like a mummy. She made her way to the shoreline and cautiously tested the temperature of the water with her toes. Satisfied she could stand the cold, she waded in alongside the dock. Taking care not to get the bottom of the blanket wet, she kept hiking the material up until she could no longer keep it dry.

"Would you look away, so I can get in without you gawking at me?"

He chuckled. "Surely, you don't mind if your husband sees you in your underthings?"

She sent him a pointed look.

"All right, just this once."

Jayson dunked his head underwater. When he surfaced, he stood chest-deep in the water. He shook his head sending droplets flying and brushed back his hair with both hands. He didn't face Allison, but he could make her out from the corner of his eye. She had removed the blanket and placed it on the wood planks. Keeping her chin tucked under, she concentrated on every step. With one hand on the dock, she carefully made her way farther into the water.

She was lovely with her wavy brown hair pulled away from her face and left long down her back. Her fancy chemise stretched taut around her middle. He noticed she had stopped wearing her corset; he imagined she could no longer get the edges closed.

When she got to the end of the dock, she halted and looked up. Standing on her tiptoes, the water came up to just above the peaks of her breasts. "I don't think I can go any farther."

Jayson took a few steps toward her and held out his arms. "Come to me. You can do it."

Fear danced in her wide, brown eyes. Hesitating only a moment, she launched herself at him and he met her halfway, engulfing her in his embrace.

"See, this isn't so bad."

She clung to his neck, wrapping her arms around him in a death grip. "Don't let go of me."

"I have you. You're good and safe."

"I don't think I can touch the ground," she whispered in his ear.

He bent his knees and lowered her a few inches until her toes touched the bottom of the pond. "See, you can still touch if you need to."

"Maybe this is enough for today." She continued to hold onto his neck for dear life.

"Let's get you comfortable with floating in the water before you call it quits." Her body pressed so hard against his that he could discern every curve against his torso and hips. He tried to untangle her arms from around his shoulders, but she resisted.

"What are you doing?" Panic pinched her voice.

"Don't worry, Allie. I won't let go of you. Trust me," he breathed huskily into her ear.

She stared into his eyes and slowly slackened her hold.

He stepped forward, so they were in shallower water. Maneuvering her around, he cradled her in his arms, supporting her back and legs. She again clasped his bicep.

"Just enjoy the feel of the water all around you."

He held her horizontal with her stomach submerged, but her face sticking out of the water. Her body sagged with weightlessness, and she loosened her grasp on him.

"See how if you're relaxed you can float on the surface?" He removed some of his support and she remained buoyant.

Allison nodded slightly and shut her eyes.

He looked down at the angelic figure he cradled so delicately. Now relaxed, she positioned her arms and legs slightly apart as they floated in the water. Her long black eyelashes feathered across the top of her rosy cheeks. Long strands of hair fanned out across the water's surface, not yet wet enough to sink. As he knew they would be, her thin undergarments were translucent, exposing every inch of her body and he languidly studied her feminine form. He watched her chest rise and fall in a calm, easy rhythm. She was no longer scared but enjoying the experience.

Suddenly, her eyes opened, and she put a hand on her belly. "The baby just kicked."

He brought his knee up to support her legs, while he placed an open palm on her stomach under the water. He caressed the bump until he felt movement. "I think the baby likes being in the water."

Smiling down at his lovely little wife, he watched her expression soften as she gazed at him with bright, glossy eyes.

Tight little bundles knotted in his stomach.

At that moment, he knew his plan was never going to work. He couldn't harden his feelings toward her or deny them. To do so was like asking himself not to breathe. He was on a path where his soul was in jeopardy of being lost to her forever. His world was reeling out of control and he had to trust Allison not to tear his heart to shreds.

Jayson leaned in and placed a lingering kiss on her lips.

Heaven help me!

~Chapter Sixteen~

Allison stepped out on the front porch of Pearson's Hotel; her hands clasped around the bend of Jayson's elbow. She glanced at her husband, who patted the top of her fingers and gave her a tender smile. His gaze caused a fluttering in her belly, not from her child.

He looked so handsome wearing an expensive well-tailored black suit with a stark white shirt peeking out from beneath. When he lived in the city, the outfit must have generated many head turns. No matter how he dressed, Jayson was an impressive looking man, with or without his facial scar.

All morning long, he placed her on the opposite side of his marked cheek as he escorted her around town. What he didn't realize was that when she looked at him, she barely noticed his disfigurement. She only saw his straight nose, well-defined cheekbones, and bright-blue, almond-shaped eyes.

Heat rose on her cheeks when her thoughts turned to his well-formed lips. He had kissed her a few times since he'd declared his intent to court her. Each time their lips met he teased her to respond, which sent tingles racing through her body. Robert's sloppy kisses had never caused a stir like that. She ached to experience more and blushed deeper at her musings.

Jayson had left her an emotional wreck after he'd let her believe he harbored no feelings for her and wanted her gone from his life. The initial pain of being abandoned, yet again, was severe but short-lived. He apologized profusely for his behavior and promised to make it up to her. She wanted to believe him. Now only a nagging irritation remained.

Had he been more forthright about his past hurt from the beginning of their marriage, maybe she could've assured him of her intentions to stick it out, no matter what. Once she made up her mind, she saw things through.

His request for forgiveness had her hoping their marriage might work one day. Maybe in time, they could manage a good life together. She just had to learn to trust him again. Not an easy feat. Especially, after Robert showed her how untrustworthy a man could be, even a man she loved.

Jayson halted on the porch, before descending the steps. "Let's see. I've taught you to shoot a pistol..."

"Who knew I had such good aim?" she chimed in.

"Amazingly so. I'll have to remember not to rile you up, for fear of you shooting me." He looked at her and chuckled.

She giggled. "Oh, you know I wouldn't do that."

"You might be tempted if I turn into an idiot again." He gave her a quick wink and adjusted her new wide-brimmed hat on her head, so he could see her full face.

Allison smiled at her husband's jesting. Suddenly, her stomach rolled. She stroked the spot where her tumbling baby pushed against her abdomen. Jayson stepped close and laid a big hand on her belly in such a familiar way, she breathed in a quick gulp of air to still her beating heart.

He continued, "...and I've made you breakfast, brought you to town to pick out material at the mercantile, took you to Mrs. Mullins so she could measure you for some new dresses and we've just had lunch at Pearson's Hotel. Do you know what that means?"

"What?"

"I think it's time we return home and go for another swim."

"Again?" The thought of a soak in the cool water on such a sweltering day appealed to her, but she had her reservations. Their time together yesterday had been so...intimate. Almost risqué. But, they were married so...

She nodded in agreement and, in return, he bestowed on her a brilliant, ear-to-ear smile. She'd never seen him look so carefree and happy. Gone were the daunting walls he put up when they'd first met. He was trying so hard. His usual moodiness and distance was disappearing before her eyes.

I like this man.

He helped her down the front steps of the restaurant. They walked side-by-side toward the carriage left across the street, in front of the mercantile.

Jayson tapped the top of her hand to get her to look up at him. "How about I help you make dinner tonight?"

"I thought you left such things to your brothers," she said playfully.

"I have my specialties. If you want, I could teach them to you," he said huskily.

The double meaning made her cheeks flame. "I think I would enjoy that."

Suddenly, a crash and a man's raised voice emerged from the second floor of the Lucky Ace Saloon. A woman shrieked. A man growled in pain.

"Indian bitch," a man shouted.

Jayson quickly moved Allison away from the middle of the street to the side of their carriage and stepped in front of her, blocking her with his body.

The upstairs door, attached to the side steps, flew open.

Allison's stomach churned.

Jasmine raced down the stairs half-naked and bare-footed. A look of terror skewed her usually pretty features. A huge, burly man chased after her. When Jasmine reached the wooden sidewalk, the man lunged forward and grabbed her by her unbound hair, yanking her back. Her legs flew out from beneath her and her buttocks hit the hard planks with a loud thud.

"Jasmine," Allison screamed in horror as the man kicked her friend in her side with his boot. Fighting against Jayson's arm, she tried to run to Jasmine, but her husband held her back.

"Stay here," he ordered in a tone meant to be obeyed.

He sprinted across the roadway. Before he got into the fray, Jasmine's attacker picked her up by her hair and punched her a few times in the face. Allison's stomach quaked at the sight.

Jasmine's inert body slumped to the ground.

As the brawny man let go of Jasmine's hair, Jayson launched himself forward, coiled his arm and let loose with a punch so powerful the man's head snapped backward. Jasmine's attacker, off-balance, lost his footing and careened into the side of the saloon. He let out a heavy groan. Before the man got his wits about him, Jayson hit him again and then again until the man's big body slid down the side of the building into a heap on the floorboards. The sheriff ran across the street from Pearson's Restaurant. Mr. Pearson trotted behind, as fast as his short legs could move.

"Enough." The sheriff grabbed Jayson's raised arm from behind, and forcibly pulled him away.

"No more." Mr. Pearson grabbed her husband's other arm.

Jayson struggled against his restraints. He had a look on his face that conveyed his desire to do more damage.

She hurried across the street and knelt over Jasmine's lifeless body. Blood trailed out the side of her mouth. Through the gaps in her disheveled hair, it was clear her left eye was injured. Allison struggled to hold her friend's head on her narrow lap but soon gave up, cradling it in the bend of her arm instead.

Allison inspected the eye damage more closely after she brushed Jasmine's unbound hair away from her face. Jasmine was unconscious. Her breath shallow. The young woman had a cracked and swollen bottom lip. Her battered eye was swelled shut, and already turning various shades of bluish-purple. Allison pulled the edges of the thin robe together over her friend's beaten body, covering her undergarments.

A movement at the top of the steps caught her eye. A few of the barely dressed saloon girls huddled together, too afraid to move. She glanced at her husband.

Mr. Pearson released him. "Help your wife."

Jayson shrugged off the hands holding him and stepped away. He glared at the man sprawled at his feet covered in blood, moaning.

The sheriff bent over the man. "We'll take him to jail and let him cool off. The circuit judge will be here in a few days. He'll know what to do with him."

Allison breathed easier when Jayson knelt beside her. He placed a gentle hand on her upper back. "How is she?"

"I'm worried. She's breathing, but out cold. Her body's badly beaten." Her voice cracked with emotion. A single tear rolled over her cheek and she brushed it away.

Jayson squeezed her shoulder. "We'll take her to Doc Thatcher." He scooped Jasmine up in his arms, her knees draped over the bend in his arm. Leaning forward with his free hand, he grabbed Allison's arm and helped her to her feet.

Together they headed to the doctor's residence. Allison hastened alongside, practically jogging to keep up with Jayson's long strides. Doc Thatcher's office was in the front part of his house, a white-washed building a few doors down from the bank. She remembered seeing his sign out front earlier in the day.

Jayson didn't knock. He turned the knob and walked into the foyer. "Doc. Doc," he shouted.

A rustling sound came from the back room. "I'll be right there," a man's grizzled voice called out.

Allison followed her husband into a side room, where he laid Jasmine on a raised table. She put a pillow under Jasmine's head and pushed the tangled hair from her face.

A short gray-haired man wearing round glasses walked into the room drying his hands on a cloth. He nodded to her husband. "Jayson." He then glanced her way. "Mrs. McKay. What can I do for you?"

"A young woman was beaten up in the street. Could you look her over?" Jayson gestured to the table.

"Sure, happy to oblige." Doc Thatcher stepped up to the table and glared at Jasmine. His mouth curled in a snarl. He spun around and snorted his contempt. "I don't treat Injuns. They killed my family. I can't help you. Take her and go."

Allison gasped. Her mouth dropped. How could a doctor be so cold-hearted? Didn't he take an oath? She took hold of Jasmine's hand and held it tight. Never had she seen such blatant prejudice. The man was utterly appalling.

Jayson straightened to his full height. He stared at the little man. His jaw clenched, and his mouth pinched.

She held her breath. Her husband was a formidable adversary when provoked.

"Doc, let me make myself perfectly clear," he said with deadly calm. "You will look over this young lady's injuries, and you will treat her as warranted."

A shiver traveled up her spine. A dangerous aura permeated the air.

Doc Thatcher swallowed hard. The threat was clear. The man knew he was in a precarious situation. "If you insist."

"I insist." Jayson crossed his arms over his chest.

Allison exhaled slowly. Doc Thatcher was smarter than he looked; men didn't dare go against her husband.

The doctor returned to the table and checked Jasmine's breathing and pulse. He passively moved her arms and legs. Then, he pressed and prodded all over her body, which elicited occasional whimpering moans. Jayson stood over the man's shoulder, watching every move he made.

Allison stayed at the head of the table and gently stroked Jasmine's forehead. "You'll be all right," she whispered.

Finally, Doc Thatcher turned and went to the basin to wash his hands. "She was knocked around good. Some of what we're seeing is head trauma. That's why she's still out cold. She has two cracked ribs on the right. No other broken bones. Her face is bruised and swollen, but there won't be any permanent damage. When she wakes, you can give her some laudanum. She will need to rest for a few days. No working at the saloon."

Allison locked eyes with Jayson. For a moment, unspoken words passed between them.

"Jasmine can come home with us." He looked at her for approval.

"Of course, she can," she replied adamantly. "We'll take care of her."

The doctor walked to a cabinet, took out a little vial, and handed it to her husband. "Now get her out of here."

Jayson scowled at him. "Yeah, thanks."

She grabbed a blanket off a side table and covered Jasmine in the cloth.

Jayson removed a few coins from his inside coat pocket and slapped them down on the corner of the desk. "This should cover what I owe you."

"That'll do." Doc Thatcher snatched the coins up in a fisted hand.

Jayson hoisted Jasmine's wrapped body in his arms and headed toward the door. She let out a soft moan but otherwise remained quiet.

Allison rushed to the front door and opened it wide. They stepped out onto the wooden sidewalk.

"Don't worry. She'll be fine. She needs time to heal. We'll have Nathan check her out when we get home, just to make sure nothing was missed," Jayson said in a valiant attempt to calm her fears.

She wrung her hands. How could she let Jasmine go back to being a saloon girl after what she just saw? A fierce desire to protect her friend rose up. "I don't believe Jasmine likes being a saloon girl. I'm not sure she had a choice being part Indian, and all. During the time I've spent with her, I got the feeling she only worked there to support herself."

"What are you saying?"

"I've been thinking..." Allison hesitated before she continued, "I don't know how things are financially but...uh...would it be possible for Jasmine to work for us? We know she can cook. She offered to be around when the baby came. Do you think we could hire her to help around the ranch?"

***

Jayson remained silent as he carried Jasmine the rest of the way to the carriage. The young woman seemed small and frail in his arms. He thought about what Allison asked of him. It was one thing to take her friend home and care for her until she healed. But, another thing to ask an unmarried woman to live on a ranch full of men. Then again, it wasn't likely Jasmine's reputation would suffer considering what she did for a living. He wasn't sure how his brothers would react to the news.

He placed Jasmine gently on the back seat of the carriage, propping her up against the cushion. Turning, he extended a hand to his wife. She placed her small hand in his. With their touch came a flood of warmth.

"Is this what you want?" He gazed into her big coffee-colored eyes that could make a man forget his own name.

"I do," she responded softly.

Using his other hand to support her arm, he helped her step up into the back seat of the carriage to sit by her friend. "Are you sure this is what Jasmine wants?"

"I'm sure. I've seen her out at the ranch. She's happy when she visits. I know she'd be a tremendous help. She loves cooking, and she's good at it." Allison situated herself on the seat and positioned her friend, so she leaned against Allison's side. The young woman groaned when moved.

Jayson sighed. He had a lot of making up to do when it came to his wife. His behavior of late was deplorable. Helping her friend would be a start.

"All right. It sounds like a good idea but, ultimately, it's up to Jasmine whether she wants to stay with us after she's healed. We'll at least give her a fresh start."

"Oh, yes. Of course," she said excitedly.

"You wait here. I'll be right back. I have to talk with Mr. Bates about her quitting and get her things."

She grabbed hold of his arm, giving it a little squeeze. "Thank you, Jayson."

His stomach did a quick flip as she gazed at him warmly with her sparkling eyes. This moment was well worth all the shit he was going to get from his brothers when they found out he had brought home another female.

He pulled his arm out from beneath his wife's hand and gave her a reassuring nod. "I'll be right back."

Jayson crossed the street to the Lucky Ace Saloon and pushed open the two louvered, swinging half doors. It was mid-afternoon so there were only a few patrons sitting at various round tables and only one colorfully dressed girl waiting on customers. He made his way to the wall-to-wall bar.

"Mr. Bates." He tipped his hat.

"Mr. McKay," the rotund man replied. "I understand I owe you a debt of gratitude for stopping Big Jake Maguire from killing my girl. He's a real mean one. Seems he has a deep hatred toward Indians in general. Your brother, Chase, stopped him from getting into it with her the other night. Missy said she saw you and your wife take Jasmine over to Doc Thatcher's. How's she doing?"

"She'll recover but needs a while to mend. I'm taking Jasmine out to the ranch to heal. My wife wants her to stay with us full-time."

"That could be a problem. I have money invested in her and, of course, there are future revenues to consider. It was hard enough to find an Indian girl who speaks good English. She hasn't been here very long but some of my customers like her."

Jayson had to respect Mr. Bates for being a shrewd businessman. He took out his billfold and placed a stack of bills on the wooden bar top. Mr. Bates looked at him with greedy eyes. Making his wife happy was going to cost him, but he didn't mind. "I believe this amount should cover any debt the young woman may have." He placed a few more bills on top of the pile. "And, this should cover you for any inconvenience of lost revenues in the future."

The man licked his thick lips as he scooped up the stack of money and stuffed the wad inside his coat pocket. "I think that will do, Mr. McKay."

"Now, if you would be so kind as to point me in the direction of her room so I may gather her things, I'd be obliged."

"Missy," the beady-eyed man called out. "Take Mr. McKay up to Jasmine's room to collect her stuff. Seems she's going to live at the McKay ranch from now on."

A well-endowed woman with a heavily made-up face stepped alongside him at the bar.

She chuckled deeply. "Did I hear correctly? You're taking Jasmine away from all this?" She swung her arms wide. "Won't she be thrilled. Come with me."

He heard the sarcasm in her voice. Allison was right; it sounded like Jasmine wasn't too fond of her profession. He followed Missy up the stairs, her behind swung side to side like an unlatched barn door in a storm. She led him to the third room on the right. The door was wide open, the handle busted, and the casing in splinters.

The woman turned toward him. "I've never seen you at the Lucky Ace before, Mr. McKay. Why don't you stop by sometime? Try your luck," she practically purred.

He knew what she meant. "I'm married."

She belly-laughed. "That's no excuse. We get plenty of married men around here."

"Guess their wives aren't as pretty as mine."

The woman hooted with laughter and stepped into the bedroom. "Guess not."

He peered into the room and was instantly taken aback by how neat and orderly it looked. Having Jasmine help with the cleaning might not be a bad idea; she sure had a knack for it.

The woman noticed his surprise. "Jasmine's a stickler for keeping things tidy."

He stood by the doorway while Missy opened drawers in the dresser and stuffed the contents in two travel bags. She picked up a small, sharp knife off the top of the nightstand.

"Jasmine is usually never without this knife strapped to her thigh." She held up the blade. "Big Jake must've caught her totally unaware or she would've been able to at least hold him off for a few minutes until we had time to get the sheriff." Missy shook her head. "She never did like working as a saloon girl, you know. It just wasn't for her. The only time I ever saw her happy or even smile was on the days she rode out to your ranch to spend time with your wife."

She walked to the corner of the room, squatted down, and with the edge of the knife, she worked up a floorboard.

"The girls have secret hiding spots where they keep their money tucked away. No sense in having cash hanging around for their customers to steal," she said matter-of-factly as she retrieved a change purse from a dark hole.

Missy made her way to stand before him. She handed him the pouch, which he put in an inside pocket, and then she gave him Jasmine's bags.

"Do me a favor, Luv. Tell Jasmine I said, good luck."

"Will do." He tipped his head good-bye before he turned and walked out of the room, his mind already busy working on what he was going to say to his brothers.

~Chapter Seventeen~

Allison stretched her arm across Jasmine, keeping her friend from pitching forward when the carriage halted at the white picket fence in front of the house.

Jasmine whimpered softly.

"We're home," she uttered in a soothing voice. "Just a few more minutes, then I'll get you settled."

Chase stepped out of the barn and crossed the yard. "Who do you have there?"

Jayson locked the brakes on the carriage and tied the reins around the lever. "Jasmine, Allison's friend. She was beaten senseless on the street outside the saloon by some man who calls himself, Big Jake. She'll be staying with us for a while."

Allison supported Jasmine in a half-sitting position in the back seat. Chase walked around the buggy and glanced up.

"Here, let me take her." Chase wrapped his arms around Jasmine's listless form, then scooped her off the leather seat. "I'll put her in my room."

Allison's stomach clenched at the sight of Jasmine's limp body. How could anyone do this to a woman? Whether it was the head injury or the laudanum making Jasmine so sedate, she didn't know. She prayed there wouldn't be any long-standing damage.

Jayson jumped down from the carriage. "Where's Nathan? I'd feel better if he looked at her. I'm not trusting Doc Thatcher's assessment."

"He's fishing down at the pond with Daniel. They should be heading back soon," Chase replied over his shoulder, walking toward the house through the flower garden.

Jayson reached for Allison, sliding his hands under her arms. "She'll be all right, just needs a little rest, that's all." He lifted her gently and placed her feet on the ground. "Go on in. I'll take care of your packages. When Nathan returns, I'll send him to you."

She squeezed his forearm. "Thank you for rescuing Jasmine and letting her stay here."

How could she ever repay his kindness? Her earlier irritation regarding his willingness to abandon her softened. Rising on the tips of her toes, she placed a gentle kiss on his cheek. His dazed look confirmed she'd caught him off guard. Not waiting for a response, she whirled around and hurried through the gate.

Allison stopped long enough in her bedroom to retrieve a pitcher of water, a stack of clean cloths, a soft brush, and a nightgown. She was of a mind to wash away the blood splatters still covering Jasmine's skin, clothing, and hair, removing all reminders of her beating. As she stepped into the hallway, Chase was exiting his room.

"Sorry to put you out, Chase."

"No bother. I'll bunk with Daniel. He doesn't snore as bad as Nathan." He winked playfully.

"Thank you." She gave him a tight-lipped smile in passing.

Allison entered his room and placed the water pitcher on the side table. It was a good-sized room. Two cushioned chairs faced a cold fireplace. There was a braided rug covering the wooden floor on the side of the bed. The overstuffed mattress was big enough to fit two. She pulled a chair close to the bed and sat. Jasmine looked so small and fragile curled up on her side under Doc Thatcher's blanket.

It broke her heart that her friend endured so much hurt for being different. *For being an Indian.*

She soaked a clean cloth in the water, wrung it out, and placed the soft material on her friend's forehead.

Jasmine let out a cracked moan.

"I have to wash you up. I'll be gentle." She cleaned away bloody spots splayed across Jasmine's tawny skin.

"Allison?" Jasmine's swollen eye watered as she fought to open it.

"I'm here." She moved the cloth lightly over her friend's swollen face. "You're at the McKay ranch."

"A man carried me upstairs. I thought I was dreaming."

"It's no dream. That was Jayson's brother, Chase. This is his room."

Jasmine rolled slightly onto her back. "What am I doing here?"

"A nasty man was beating you in the street. Jayson stopped him. We brought you to the ranch."

Tears pooled in the corners of Jasmine's eyes, and she seemed to be coming out of her stupor. "I remember. I didn't do anything wrong. I wanted no trouble." A small, wet stream of tears ran down the side of her cheek. She brushed the moisture away with the back of her hand. "He busted down my door, ranted about his family being killed, and then came at me. He wanted me dead. I saw it in his eyes. It happened so fast. I didn't have my knife. I couldn't protect myself," she choked out, her swollen lip causing her words to sound distorted.

"Hush," Allison soothed. "It's all right. You're safe, now. I'm going to take care of you."

Jasmine rolled to the edge of the bed and tried to sit up. "I have to get back to town. Mr. Bates will be expecting me to work tonight."

She pushed her friend back down onto the bed. "You're not going anywhere. You cracked two ribs on the right side. The rest of your body is bruised and swollen."

"I'll lose my job."

"No, you won't. You don't work for Mr. Bates anymore."

"What are you talking about?" Jasmine squeaked out.

"Jayson paid your debts. He's of a mind to ask you to stay at the ranch to work for us as a cook. And, to help me with the house and the baby." Allison hoped Jasmine would accept the offer. It turned her stomach to imagine her friend returning to her job as a saloon girl. No woman should have to do something they despised just to survive. That wasn't living.

Jasmine struggled to come up on her elbows, but the task was too daunting. She melted back into the mattress. "Why would he do that?"

"Because I asked him to." Allison knew the reason he'd agreed was to make up for the way he'd treated her a few days ago. She should feel remorseful about using his guilt to manipulate him into helping Jasmine, but she didn't.

The cause was just.

"Why are you being so nice to me?"

She patted the top of her friend's hand. Jasmine wasn't used to kindness. The thought made her heart ache even more. "You might not see the similarities as clearly as I do, but we are alike in many ways. For one thing, we're both survivors. The man I once loved abandoned me without a backward glance. I thought he loved me, but I was wrong. He left me no other choice but to travel down an unknown path and fight for a new life. I expect you also have done the same."

148

Jasmine nodded, as she squinted with her one good eye.

"You also have a kind heart. Whether you like to admit it or not, you care for other people. I saw your true colors on the first day I met you."

Jasmine turned her head and swallowed hard.

Allison dunked the rag in the water and squeezed out the excess. She dabbed the cloth around Jasmine's neck, wiping away the blood dotting her bare skin. "When I look at you, I see a woman to be admired. One of great courage, strength, and savvy. I want what you have. I'm a city girl. Before I came here, my only goal in life was to find a man to take care of me. I was raised to run his home in the city, have his children, and throw lavish parties. So much has changed. I'm living in a wild place. I don't understand the rules or the way of things. Out here, I need to learn how to protect myself and if need be, my family. I have to learn to rely on myself...as you have."

"What do you want from me?" Jasmine asked.

"To be my friend. Teach me those things I know nothing about. For example, I have no idea how to tack a horse. I never had to do that myself. Or, how to cook over an open fire...or cook in general? What snakes should I stay away from?"

"All snakes as far as I'm concerned," Jasmine chimed in. "I don't like any of them."

"Okay, that's helpful." Allison giggled.

Jasmine chuckled, but then quickly grabbed the side of her face with one hand, and her ribs with the other. "Don't make me laugh. It hurts."

"Sorry." She stared hard at her friend. "I'm at a disadvantage. I don't know how to be a rancher's wife. If I'm going to make a go of it, I must learn everything there is to know about getting by out here. You can teach me. What I'd like to offer in return is my friendship, support, and a safe place to live."

Jasmine thought about her offer. "I think I can help you out."

Excitement bubbled in the pit of Allison's stomach. Her friend could teach her so much about life in the West. Allison looked forward to their blossoming friendship. There was a roughness but also a warmth and tenderness that surrounded Jasmine. The contrast was so endearing. She extended her hand. "Then it's a deal?"

Jasmine clasped it. "Deal."

She shook her friend's hand, then sealed the bond with a smile. "Now that we have that all settled, let's get you cleaned up and put you in a nightgown so you can rest comfortably and heal."

"Ahh, about nightgowns. I sleep in the nude," Jasmine said.

"Oh, my! I guess there is a lot for me to learn." Allison laughed.

***

"Are you crazy?" Chase held Clarke by the bridle in the middle aisle of the barn.

Jayson unbuckled the horse's harness and lifted sections of leather from the animal's back.

"Perfectly sane, the last time I checked," Jayson drawled.

Nathan and Daniel entered the barn with their fishing poles resting on their shoulders. Daniel clutched a rope at his side with three trout dangling from it.

"You won't believe what Jayson's gone and done," Chase said.

Nathan placed his wooden pole on a hook bolted onto the barn wall. He turned to Jayson. "What did you do this time to get Chase all riled up? Please tell me it wasn't something stupid that ruined things with Allison again?"

Clarke shook his massive head, impatient to be out of his bindings. Chase rubbed the center of the gelding's face to quiet him. "He's taken in a saloon girl from town."

Jayson brushed Clarke's back. "I rescued Allison's friend Jasmine from a beating in town and brought her here to recover."

"Is she hurt bad?" Nathan asked, concern resonating in his voice.

He caught his brother's eye over the horse's back. An image of Jasmine's limp and battered body appeared in his memory and soured his stomach. How any man could do that to a woman was beyond him. He hoped Big Jake rotted in jail. He would definitely attend the court hearing when the circuit judge came to town next week. "She has a few broken ribs, and her face is bruised and swollen. According to Doc Thatcher, no broken facial bones. I was hoping you could look in on her when you get a chance. Allison is with her now."

Nathan visibly relaxed.

"Tell him how you paid off her debt to Mr. Bates, and how you're going to ask her to work for us here on the ranch," Chase said.

"Is that true?" Nathan asked.

"What did you want me to do? You should've seen Allison. She was so distraught over seeing her friend almost get killed in the street. You're the ones who wanted me to do whatever it took to make her happy." And he would do anything, even if it meant begging his brothers to agree. He walked around Clarke to brush his other side.

"But a saloon girl?" Chase groaned.

Daniel tied his line of fish to a nail sticking out of the barn door. "I kinda like her. She's pretty."

Chase reached out to cuff his brother in the head, but Daniel dodged his hand.

"What do you have against Jasmine staying with us? Allison thinks we can hire her to help with the cooking, along with other chores, especially when the baby comes. Lord knows we could use a good cook if just to take the pressure off Allison. And, I'm sure Allison would gladly welcome the company of another woman around here. Winter is coming, and we all know what that's like out here."

"But a saloon girl on a ranch with a bunch of men," Chase said.

"I met her. She's not like the other women at the Lucky Ace. Allison says she doesn't like anything about working as a saloon girl. That her being employed there was just a means for her to support herself. Considering what she did for a living, I doubt she'd be too concerned about her reputation being damaged for staying out here unmarried."

Chase took the bridle off the gelding and put on a halter. "We went from having no women on this ranch to having two of them in a few months. This is gonna be hard to get used to. Women always complicate things."

Jayson finished with Clarke. He led the horse to an empty stall set up with water and grain. "For Allison's sake, please try to put up with the changes. Jasmine's staying here is not a sure thing. She may very well decide this isn't what she wants and leave. I'd hate to ruin any gains I've made with Allison by denying her friend a place to stay."

"I'm happy Jasmine's here. She's a good cook and not too bad to look at," Daniel said, keeping a good distance from his brothers.

"Ahh, to be young and put every woman you come across on a pedestal." Nathan snickered. "The good old days. Remember those, Chase?"

"I do not," Daniel protested.

"Yup, you do, Little Man." Chase made a gesture of swatting at Daniel again but wasn't anywhere near him. "That's just growing pains."

Jayson shook his head at their teasing. "Is it settled then? I'll ask her if she wants a job working for us. We'll see what she says."

"Agreed," Nathan said.

Chase kicked a stone. "Fine."

Daniel nodded.

Jayson smiled at his brothers. Their concession to let Jasmine stay was going get him back into his wife's good graces.

He definitely owed them one.

~Chapter Eighteen~

A trail of dust billowed behind a fancy carriage as it crested the small hill on the way down the dirt road to the McKay house in the valley.

Allison leaned heavily against the porch rail to get a glimpse of the first to arrive for today's barn raising. "Run and tell Jayson we have guests," she called out to her youngest brother-in-law.

Daniel, who was about to open the front gate, stopped short and glanced over his shoulder at the approaching buggy. He spun around and jogged across the yard to where Jayson stacked raw lumber with the help of Chase, Nathan, and some of the ranch hands.

She stepped away from the railing and hastily smoothed the fabric on the front of her new draped dress. Her body vibrated with excitement. This was her first time entertaining a crowd at the ranch, and she struggled to contain her building exuberance. She took a deep breath and reminded herself that the barn raising wasn't just about having a party. There was a higher purpose. Today was a way for neighbors to help a neighbor.

Just the same, she was so looking forward to the get-together.

Jayson met her at the picket fence. She gazed appreciatively at her devilishly handsome husband. He dressed in his usual pitch-black clothing. His stark white linen shirt presented a startling, yet appealing contrast. He swung the gate door wide. At the same time, he reached for her hand and guided her through the opening until she stood at his side.

A big grin covered his clean-shaven face. "Are you ready for a busy day?"

"As ready as I'll ever be. Jasmine and I have been cooking all morning." She watched the carriage stop halfway down the road. Their guests spoke to Hank, their ranch foreman, who was returning from checking on the herd.

"Don't overdo it today. If you start feeling tired, I want you to go up to your room and lie down. Jasmine can take over while you rest." Jayson quirked an eyebrow, giving her one of his *do as I say* looks.

"I'll be fine. I'm too excited to think about resting."

"Promise me."

She rolled her eyes. "I promise."

"Don't make me stop hammering boards to throw you over my shoulder and carry you up to your room in front of all our neighbors." His voice held a hint of playfulness.

"You wouldn't." She stifled a giggle.

He wagged a finger. "Only if you misbehave."

She sighed loudly. Although she let him think he was being annoying, it was nice to have him worry about her well-being. "I'll behave and take it easy today."

He placed an open hand on the small of her back. "That's all I ask."

Allison wrung her hands as the carriage moved toward the house. "Why is everyone arriving at noontime and not early morning, when it's cooler?"

"People have to care for their animals and do their chores first. Also, it takes time to prepare enough food. There'll be a lot of hungry men when we're done working. Most people will get here within the next hour, but those who can't help with the heavy lifting or who can only come for the food and dance will trickle in later. All day long we'll see neighbors coming and going."

She waved as the buggy rolled into the yard. "It's Hannah and Frank."

Together they stepped forward to greet their friends.

***

Soon others followed. Able-bodied men with their families arrived first. The women put their chairs from home under the maple tree on the side of the house, out of the hot sun, where they could watch the work progress. A few mothers oversaw the younger children as they played down by the pond. The youngsters stuck their toes in the water and splashed around. Squeals of joy and laughter echoed through the valley, along with the constant banging of hammers and shouts of men working on framing the barn.

Old Gus and the other men who were unable to take part sat on the bunkhouse porch smoking pipes and chatting amongst themselves. Cookie roasted a steer on a spit over an open flame in the back yard. The smell of smoldering beef, wafting up on the warm breeze, watered everyone's mouths.

Over the course of the afternoon, the women took turns lugging fresh pails of water to the sweat-soaked men. Allison blushed at the thought that when they finished, there would be a pond full of half-naked men, and hoped they planned far enough in advance to bring an extra set of clothes.

Beneath the lush foliage of the old shade tree, the ladies sat in a semi-circle around a table laden with food. From their vantage point, they had a clear view

154

of the goings-on. Aunt Beatrice loudly voiced her opinions about whether certain men were doing their jobs correctly, who wasn't working fast enough, or what she'd do if she was in charge.

No one was willing to stroke Aunt Beatrice's fire by agreeing or disagreeing with her comments. For the most part, the women seemed content to just smile and focus on the tasks in their laps. Many were either sewing or knitting.

Allison watched her female neighbors with awe. Never had she learned to sew or knit. Her polished skills were in the art of embroidery, and she stitched fancy designs on pieces of cloth used for handkerchiefs. A worthless talent on a ranch where it would be more prudent to know how to darn a sock, fix a hole in a pair of trousers, knit a sweater, or piece together a blanket that would keep one warm on a chilly winter night. On her next visit to town, she vowed she would see if Margaret or Hannah could give her lessons in those pursuits. She considered asking them today but decided against bringing attention to herself. She didn't want Aunt Beatrice to overhear and hold it against her.

The hours went by quickly. It was amazing how well-organized the McKay men were, and how smoothly the work went. She found Jayson's fluid movements mesmerizing as he lifted and hammered boards of raw lumber. His deep voice resounded above the others while he directed the men and made sure they did their jobs. She noted he was patient, yet commanding.

Her heart soared with pride.

When they finished framing the structure on the ground, the men used ropes and poles to stand the sides. Each man moved in unison. Sweat rolled down their bodies and drenched their shirts. Even though Aunt Beatrice was quick to complain that some helpers were slack in their efforts, Allison was hard-pressed to name any one of her neighbors who wasn't pulling his weight.

Before long, they erected the sides, and the new barn had an unfinished roof.

Jayson shimmied down a ladder. When he was a few rungs from the bottom he jumped to the ground and let out a shrill whistle. All building noise quieted. He called out loud enough for all to hear, "That's it, men. We're done for the day. Pack up your gear."

"Whoo-hoo!" A bevy of hoots and hollers reverberated in the air around the new building. A few dozen men alighted from ladders and exited the barn.

Jayson and his brothers stood on the path to the buckboards and carriages, shaking hands with those who helped as they put away their tools and ladders.

As expected, some of the men grabbed their extra clothes and headed to the pond. The women quickly collected their work on their laps, returning the items to their baskets.

Jayson made his way over to the women. "We're done for the day. If you ladies don't mind, we're going to clean up before we partake in your wonderful meal."

Hannah stood and slapped her hands on the table to get everyone's attention. "Well, ladies. You heard Jayson. It's time to feed our hungry menfolk." The women stirred into action.

Jayson gave Allison a boyish grin. "I'm going upstairs to wash. I'll return soon."

Allison knew he chose to wash up inside, so no one would see his scars. She stared at her husband's back as he climbed the steps to the porch and retreated into the house through the kitchen door.

Jasmine, who had stayed on the fringes of the gathering all day, sidled up and smirked. "Best be careful, or else people's tongues are gonna start wagging about you lusting after your husband."

Allison's slack jaw snapped shut, and she placed her fingers over her mouth. She turned abruptly to look at her friend. "I...ah..."

"It's all right." Jasmine chuckled low. "I'm the only one who noticed you drooling."

"You're far too observant." She grinned. How she loved watching him move. It was mesmerizing how he carried himself with his shoulders back, chest out, chin high, yet his gait was so relaxed. She had to be careful not to act like a love-struck teenager in front of her guests; such behavior wouldn't be proper.

It was nice to see Jasmine happy. Her facial injuries had healed since the beating, and her beauty had, for the most part, returned, but a hint of sadness remained. Allison endeavored to eradicate her friend's doldrums by staying cheerful. Hooking Jasmine's arm with hers, she dragged her forward. "Come. Let's see what we can do to help set up."

Daniel placed a few empty barrels strategically around the lawn. The women laid long, flat boards on top, making more tables. They covered them with cloths. Those who came in four-wheeled conveyances brought extra chairs, plates, cups, and utensils from home. They placed the items about the newly made tables. Women retrieved the food stored in the house and placed their dishes on the tables. Cookie and Daniel set out platters of cooked beef. Chase and some of the men carried out beer and wine kegs from the root cellar.

After the men returned from washing up and the food was laid out, they all sat down. Allison sat at the head of the table next to her husband. The crowd quieted and dropped their heads as Jayson recited a quick prayer.

When Jayson finished giving thanks to the Lord, he stood and lifted his mug in the air. "On behalf of myself, my wife, and my brothers, we toast all our friends and neighbors who came out today to help us raise our new barn. We thank you for your hard work and the mouth-watering meal before us. We wish you all good health and prosperity throughout the year."

Those around the table raised their drinks.

"Cheers," rang out from the guests before they took a sip.

Cups and glasses banged down on the wooden tables. Suddenly, the gathering broke out in a furor of activity as men and women loaded piles of food on their plates. Talking and laughing grew to deafening heights and lasted until their plates were clean.

Unlike some of the women, Allison stayed away from the wine. She didn't dare chance a repeat of the last dance where she had imbibed too much liquor. Tonight, was a night she wanted to remember forever.

Once everyone was sated, Jayson tapped a knife to a bottle until he had everyone's attention. "Time to dance."

Hoots rang out. The musicians collected their instruments. People rose from their seats.

Earlier in the day, Daniel had strung up lanterns around the hard-packed dirt in front of the house, which was now a makeshift dance floor.

Jayson reached for her. "Would you do me the honor?"

"The honor is mine." She placed her hand in his.

He helped her onto her feet and guided her to the center of the yard. With his hand on her back, he pulled her as close as her protruding belly would allow. His height made her raise her chin when she gazed upon his face.

A mischievous grin curled his lips. His eyes were bright and animated. She inhaled deeply as her heart melted.

When the music began, he took the lead and whirled her in a wide circle. Everywhere their bodies touched, a budding warmth grew. She forgot others watched. His high spirits encircled her in a bubble of glowing light, intoxicating her senses. Could this be the man she'd always dreamed of?

In the back of her mind, a nagging fear rose, hinting that their newfound friendly rapport was an illusion and couldn't be trusted. That the easy affinity blossoming over the past few weeks was too fragile to endure forever. From her past experience with Robert, who had supposedly loved her, she knew a man's attachments could be fleeting. A man could shower her with attention and affection and yet fall short of full commitment. She reminded herself that Jayson's heart belonged to another. He'd only agreed to their arrangement because she'd proposed they needn't be emotionally linked. She'd called it a business deal. He'd wanted to marry and have a family, but remain aloof, never jeopardizing his heart.

Their relationship had only changed when she'd threatened to leave. He had only courted her, so she'd stay. She couldn't let herself fall for him completely. Nor, could she care for him more than he cared for her. Once the courting was over, he might revert to the old Jayson. If she continued letting him break down the barriers she erected, she could find herself broken-hearted like before.

She shook her head to dismiss her negative thoughts.

Maybe their marriage wasn't exactly what she'd hoped because the foundation was built on a bargain and not on love, but that didn't mean she couldn't enjoy his company, even if just for a little while.

As long as I guard my heart.

Allison glanced up, wet her lips, and smiled warmly. His eyes were as blue as the summer sky. "Why Mr. McKay, you surprise me with your skillful steps. Here I thought you didn't know how to dance, and I was going to have to teach you."

"I never said I couldn't, I just don't like to." He pulled her closer with a firm arm.

She inhaled a sharp breath. "What changed your mind?"

His eyes smoldered a deeper, darker blue. He whispered in her ear. "Dancing gives me a reason to touch you."

Her whole body warmed at his words and she leaned closer.

He stared at her and she held his glowing gaze.

Heat brewing between them made her tremble, and she relied on the strength in his brawny arms to support her when her legs grew weak.

If he keeps this up, I'm in trouble. I will lose my heart.

Other couples joined them. The yard filled with colorful skirts swirling around and around. Laughter rang out from the couples. Children squealed in delight as they darted between dancers.

After a few songs, Allison begged her leave. Her feet throbbed. She found a chair next to Aunt Beatrice, where she watched the ladies being whirled about by handsome partners. Jayson played the perfect host, making the rounds and thanking people for coming to help.

A movement out of the corner of her eye caught her attention. Jasmine worked alone at the end of the long table, covering left-over food and rearranging things. All day long, her friend had stayed in the background, helping where needed, but never settling down and enjoying herself. Allison was sure Jasmine didn't know where she belonged. She wished she could do something to rectify her friend's insecurities and low self-esteem.

Jayson joined Allison again and offered to get her and Aunt Beatrice a fresh pot of tea from the house.

As she awaited his return, Bran Kincade staggered toward Jasmine with a bottle of alcohol held tightly in his fisted hand.

"Hey, honey. Come 'ere. I want ta share a drink with ye." He took a long swig from his bottle.

Jasmine kept her eyes averted and busied herself with picking up an empty plate.

"I'm talking ta ye," he stammered, his Irish burr thick.

Allison's stomach squeezed into a tight wad of knots. By the way he acted she guessed he was drinking something stronger than beer. This wasn't going to turn out well.

"Please, Bran. Leave me alone." Jasmine turned to walk away.

Bran grabbed her by the wrist and spun her about. "Come 'ere. I've got something for ye." A chuckle erupted from deep in his throat. "Something ye've seen before and not likely ta forget."

Jasmine tugged, but the young man had her arm in a death grip. He started to drag her toward the back of the house.

Allison's hands flew to cover her mouth. She glanced at the kitchen door, wishing Jayson would appear.

"Let go," Jasmine pleaded, digging in her heels.

"I wanna have a little fun, and yer the whore ta give me some."

Horrified by Bran's brazen behavior, Allison hoisted herself out of the chair and took a few steps forward, determined to rescue her friend.

Before she could call out and warn the man off, Chase came up from behind the couple. He placed a hand on Bran's shoulder. "Take your hands off the lady, and we'll forget this ever happened." His deadly calm voice reminded her of Jayson's, the first time she'd met him in town. She breathed a sigh of relief. When a McKay got rattled, they were a force to be reckoned with. Chase would see that Jasmine remained unharmed.

Bran stopped in his tracks and glanced over his shoulder. "The McKays think they're so much better than us. My money's as good as yers." He sneered.

People noticed the commotion and gawked. Jasmine pulled against Bran's hold but was unable to get away.

Chase wrestled Bran's arm until Jasmine broke free. She stepped back, lifted her skirts, and ran into the house through the side door.

"You shouldn't have done that, Chase," Bran spit out in anger.

"Jasmine's a guest here and no longer works at the saloon."

"Once a whore, always a whore."

Chase tensed. "Go sober up. You're an ugly drunk."

"Stop treating me like a child."

"Then, stop acting like one," Chase growled.

Bran's face turned a rosy red. He scanned the crowd of people who stopped dancing and stared at him. Blotchy spots covered his cheeks. He threw his bottle at an empty chair, and it shattered into a hundred pieces. Pulling back his arm, he let go with a wild punch aimed at Chase's face but missed when Chase ducked.

Chase rose to his full height and put his fists up in a defensive stance.

Instead of lunging and beating the brash young man to a pulp, which Allison knew Chase could do if he wanted to, her brother-in-law intentionally shoved Bran backward a few steps, to get him to move off.

Women gasped, and their men ushered them under the maple tree, out of harm's way. Allison stood next to Aunt Beatrice and covered her mouth with her hands.

Bran wasn't ready to call it quits. He regained his balance and flew at Chase. Cocking back his arm, he hit Chase in the stomach. Chase hauled back his fist and punched Bran in the nose, eliciting a muffled groan. Suddenly, fists flew in every direction and men circled the combatants on all sides, making it difficult for the ladies to see what was going on.

Jayson ran down the steps from the house and burst into the center of the fight. "Enough," he yelled. "Break it up." He forcibly parted the two. "What's the meaning of this?"

No one spoke. Both Chase and Bran averted their eyes. Blood covered their faces, Bran worse than Chase.

"Jordan, take Bran down to the pond and clean him up. Chase, come with me." Jayson placed a hand on his brother's shoulder and led him toward the house, talking in low tones. Nathan followed.

Allison watched as the rest of the men positioned themselves in a circle, reliving each blow as if they had been the participants.

"Well, I never." Aunt Beatrice huffed loudly. "That woman has no business being in our company."

The hairs on the back of Allison's neck stood straight up. Slowly, she turned and glared at Jayson's aunt. "Jasmine did nothing wrong. She was minding her own business. She rebuked Bran's advances, but he got heavy-handed. Chase did the right thing by protecting her honor. No woman should be treated that way."

"Protecting her honor? She has no honor. She's a whore," Aunt Beatrice stated.

Allison pushed her shoulders back. Aunt Beatrice's narrow-mindedness was so abhorrent. "She was a working girl at a saloon. Now she's a cook and a guest in your nephew's house. We're happy to have her here."

Aunt Beatrice grasped the top buttons on the neck of her black dress and held on tight. "If it were me, I would send her on her way. She has no business around decent folks."

Allison noticed the ladies gathered about were listening intently to their conversation. She addressed the crowd. "I know some of you think my friendship with Jasmine is surprising, but I assure you she's a wonderful and compassionate woman. Like many of you, hardships and pain have scarred her life. Sometimes, we, as women, must be courageous and make tough choices to survive. I don't judge her for what she had to do to feed herself but instead admire her for her courage and fortitude."

Margaret put her arm around Allison's shoulder. "What would any woman do to survive? I'm thinking some of us have secrets of our own we don't want anyone to know about. Things we're not proud of that are best left buried."

Hannah grabbed Allison's hand and squeezed. "I think everyone deserves a second chance. I applaud Allison for thinking well of others and for not passing judgment. I believe we should follow suit and do the same. After all, we women have to stick together."

The ladies heartily agreed, except for Aunt Beatrice who grunted her disdain. Chase went into the house.

Jayson joined the women under the maple tree. "Sorry about the commotion, ladies. Just a few young men getting rowdy. Too much liquor. It won't happen again. Why don't you find your partners and take another whirl around the dance floor? Before long, you'll be heading back home."

The women dispersed.

Allison guided Jayson away from Aunt Beatrice and said in a faint voice, "I hope Jasmine's all right."

"I'm sorry you had to see that. I think she'll be all right. Chase went to see if he can entice her to come back out."

"I hope she joins us. She has every right to be here."

"That she does." He looked down at her shoes peeking out from the bottom of her fancy powder blue dress. "How are your feet? Do you think they are rested enough for another twirl around?"

"I'm ready," she said with a smile.

***

When the dance was over, Jayson left Allison in the company of Melony. He made his way to the corner of the new barn where Samantha Kincade stood by herself, sipping a glass of wine as she watched the goings-on from a distance.

"Miss Kincade," he said with a nod of his head.

"Mr. McKay." She raised her half-empty glass.

"Sorry your father couldn't join us today."

"He's away. Should be back in a few days."

"Are you having a good time?"

"Wonderful." A sarcastic edge came out in her voice. "Great entertainment."

Jayson stood beside her, shoulder to shoulder and looked out over the dancers. His eyes settled on Chase spinning Jasmine in circles. The young woman looked like the dance floor was the last place in the world she wanted to be. He glanced at Samantha. "I would appreciate that in the future, you wouldn't goad your brother into bad behavior when he's had one too many drinks."

"I have no idea what you are talking about." She gulped a big swig of alcohol.

"I repeat. Do not manipulate your brother into doing things to make others look bad."

"My brother's a big boy. He can make his own decisions," she drawled.

Jayson glared at the woman. "Let me spell it out, Miss Kincade. Chase assures me he no longer has feelings for you. Trying to make Jasmine appear tarnished and unsuitable for polite company will not change the way my brother feels about you. You need to move on to someone more appreciative of your charms."

Samantha snorted. "He means nothing to me."

Jayson crossed his arms over his chest and stared at her. "Good to hear it. From now on, leave my family and friends alone."

"Fine," she said grudgingly.

The two stood there for a moment in silence, watching couples step in time to the music.

"Glad we could come to an agreement. I expect no more trouble. If you'll excuse me, I'm going to get back to my other guests. Good day."

As Jayson walked away, he felt the young woman's blazing eyes upon his back. A chill coursed through his veins and down his spine.

Nathan had seen Samantha riling Bran up prior to his assaulting Jasmine. As his sister whispered in his ear, Bran's face had turned beet red while he gulped down a half of a bottle of whiskey. It didn't take much to figure out that Samantha was behind her brother's actions.

Chase had made the right decision to break his ties to the young woman before it was too late. Jayson couldn't fault his brother for his attraction to the vixen, though. Besides being beautiful, there was something wild and untamed under her surface. Unfortunately, there was also something disturbing and dangerous.

Samantha's coldness reminded him of another woman.

Jacquelyn.

When they were engaged, he never saw Jacquelyn's true colors. He was so smitten with her beauty and worldliness, he was willing to do anything she asked. He honestly thought she felt the same way about him, but now he saw how distant she really was. Because he was young and naive, he followed her blindly, waiting for shreds of affection. She wanted to be a senator's wife like her mother, so he started a career in politics. Her dream, not his. She was a master manipulator and to his disgust, he let her exploit him.

He strolled over to Chase and Jasmine, on the outskirts of the yard. Jasmine led a rough life and didn't deserve any more grief. Allison really enjoyed her friendship. He had to admit he liked having the woman around as well. She was a hard worker, and easy to get along with. Her honesty and candor was refreshing. Now that she was a part of the ranch, he felt responsible for her safety and well-being.

Jayson stood next to his brother. "Do you mind if I talk to Jasmine alone?"

Chase gave him a disgruntled look but conceded. "Jasmine, I'll get you some apple cider." His brother left them standing side by side.

"Head up. Don't let them see you squirm," Jayson said.

Jasmine tilted up her chin to look at him, and he stared into her midnight brown eyes. Shame shone in their depths, but he also saw courage fighting to the surface.

She clasped her hands together at her waist and straightened her back. "I'm sorry, Jayson. I never wanted to cause a scene or embarrass your family. You've all been so good to me."

"You did nothing wrong. You were set up by Samantha Kincade. She encouraged her brother, who had a few too many drinks, to go after you for the sole purpose of embarrassing you."

"Why would she do that?"

"It has to do with Chase. She's angered he doesn't return her feelings." Jayson perused the dancers. Everyone appeared to be enjoying themselves. The fight earlier hadn't dampened anyone's fun. Jordan and Melony twirled around in front of them. Jordan had a huge grin on his face. He was happy for his friend.

Hell, the way I've been feeling lately, I want everyone to be happy.

"I can assure you, she needn't worry. I'm not the type of woman a man commits to."

"Chase is a big boy. He can decide for himself who he wants to be around."

"I'm not good enough for him. He should look elsewhere."

"Did I ever tell you my mother was a mountain girl, born and bred? My father was a gentleman farmer and senator's son from outside Washington, D.C. Vastly

164

diverse backgrounds, and a very unusual pairing. And yet, incredibly happy together." He tipped his head and grinned. "I wanted you to know you weren't at fault. You have every right to be here. I talked to Miss Kincade. She should leave you alone from here on out. Now, if you'll excuse me, I think I'll go dance with my wife. If I'm not mistaken Nathan is headed this way to take his turn at spinning you around." He leaned in. "Remember, keep your head up. But, most of all, smile and have some fun."

Jayson stepped away when Nathan arrived. He scanned the yard. His gaze settled on Allison as she talked to Hannah. His heart skipped a beat. She looked so lovely, standing there in her shiny new dress and perfectly coifed hair. All grace and warmth. A deep smile lit her face, as she laughed at something Hannah said.

Was he losing himself to her? He had an opportunity to let her go before he got too attached, but he couldn't do it. He liked having her around. It was he who'd suggested courting her, so she'd stay, but every time he touched her, he was drawn in deeper and deeper. He enjoyed his role as her husband and looked forward to being a father.

Could he trust her with his heart?

Why would a beautiful and educated woman want to stay out West with a damaged man like himself? Someone who's hard to look at. What were her real motives? Was she manipulating him in some way, like Jacquelyn? Was she playing some sort of game to get something from him? She said she was looking for a name and security for the baby. Could he believe that her intentions were true? Would he find out someday that she too was cold and calculating?

As he covered the ground between them, his head pounded with roiling self-doubt and insecurity. *She can't be like Jacquelyn? She just can't be.*

~Chapter Nineteen~

Allison strolled out onto the back porch carrying a serving tray.

"Come sit for a while. I have apple cider and cookies," she called to Gus and Jasmine who were stooped over a row of tomato plants.

They straightened and waved simultaneously. All morning, the pair had worked steadily in the garden behind the house, harvesting the ripened crop. Throughout the summer, Gus had spent many hours painstakingly nurturing his vegetables. His dedication showed, and the McKay ranch had enjoyed an abundance of fresh-grown produce this year.

Allison set the tray on the low table between two of the rocking chairs under the covered porch, out of the warm rays. She frowned at the burnt-edged sugar cookies filling the plate.

I'll never get it right.

No matter how many times she followed a recipe, her food never came out the way it was supposed to. Sometimes her attempts were even inedible. Each culinary failure made her question her worth as a rancher's wife. *Maybe I'm just fooling myself.*

Inhaling deeply, she stepped to the rail and rubbed her expanding belly.

Unfortunately, helping in the kitchen was about all she could do these days. She offered to work in the garden this morning, but Jasmine asked her to make cookies instead.

She watched Jasmine lift an overflowing basket of freshly picked tomatoes off the ground and head toward the porch.

Allison sighed. She envied her friend's graceful bearing. Of late, her own movements were cumbersome, and she likened herself to a beached whale. Nathan said the baby was going to be a big one. The thought was frightening. What if the baby was too big to come out? What if it was turned wrong? A neighbor back in Boston lost her baby in childbirth. Allison trembled.

The other day, she'd voiced her concerns about the dangers of delivering a baby. Jasmine told her not to fret and assured Allison she would be at her side for the birthing and all would go well.

I have to believe her.

If it wasn't for her friend's help these past few weeks, the whole McKay ranch would've fallen apart. Jasmine was a good worker, not to mention a great cook, and she had settled in nicely, helping where needed. She was true to her word and was teaching Allison everything there was to know about ranch life.

Jasmine climbed the porch steps. She was well-dressed in her navy vest, riding skirt and a wide-brimmed hat. Tall leather boots reached her knees and the split skirt covered the rest of her long legs. One shiny, black braid hung over the front of her shoulder and dangled below her waist where a red ribbon tied the ends together. Her shirt, as always, was pristine white, even after chores. Jasmine didn't ruin clothes the way Allison did.

Allison cringed when she recalled all her damaged and unwearable dresses stuffed in the bottom of her armoire. Maybe she should consider a lady's riding habit, like Jasmine. Such an outfit seemed more practical for ranch work, instead of her fancy parlor dresses.

The thunder of galloping horses sounded down the road.

"That can't be Jayson and Daniel. Daniel took the buckboard to town." She walked to the side of the house, hoping to catch a glimpse of the newcomers arriving in the front yard.

A gunshot rang out and then another.

She startled.

Jasmine grabbed Allison's shoulders from behind, stopping her from stepping forward.

"Careful," Jasmine said in a low tone.

Together, they slowly leaned forward and peered around the corner. Her body quaked. Two strangers on horseback and...Big Jake.

Taking a step back, out of sight, she faced Jasmine. The word *danger* screamed in her head. Her heart thumped in her chest. She clutched her trembling hands. "It's Big Jake," she whispered hoarsely, "and his men."

Jasmine's eyes grew as large as silver dollars. Horror shone on her face, mirroring Allison's own fears.

Collectively, they peeked around the edge of the house again. Another gunshot rang out. Hank was shooting at the riders from the corner of the new barn. The men dismounted and scattered under cover.

She couldn't believe her eyes. Fright turned her body to stone as she watched the scene play out as if in slow motion.

A quick volley of shots flew back and forth. Then all was quiet. Allison's stomach lurched. Bile rose in her throat. Jasmine tugged at her arm until she stepped back out of sight, behind the house. They stared at each other, both trying to process what they just saw. Her heart pounded so hard in her chest she was sure the noise sounded across the yard. Hank was no longer returning fire, which only meant one thing. He was either injured or dead. How she wished Jayson was here. Of all people, he'd know what to do.

"Come out, come out, you little Indian bitch," a gruff voice yelled at the top of his lungs.

A burst of laughter echoed in the valley. "She ain't gonna show herself unless you ask her real nice like."

"I ain't asking nice. Jasmine, you whore, get out here. Now." the man with the gruff voice shouted. "Don't make me come get you."

"We don't have time for this. Someone could've heard our shots," another man chimed in. "You two go through the front, and I'll go around back."

Jasmine pulled her toward Gus, who stood statue-still at the top of the back steps.

Allison followed Jasmine instinctively, someone she trusted above all others. Her arms wrapped around her belly, the only protection she could offer her child against the impending threat. "What are we going to do?"

Gus wrung his hands. "What's going on? Who are they, missus?"

"Very bad men, Gus. We're in danger," she said breathlessly, the dire situation realized. These men were on a vendetta to maim or kill Jasmine. Payback for Big Jake being locked up at the jail for a month.

"There's no place to hide outside." Jasmine grabbed Gus by his arm and guided him toward the back door. "The guns are in the kitchen, but we're not going to make it to them in time. The men are already off their horses. They'll be in the house in minutes. Besides, there are three of them."

Allison held the door wide for Jasmine and Gus to hurry through. "Let's hide in the root cellar. Maybe they'll tire of looking for us and leave. Daniel told me there's a tunnel to a hidden exit in the back yard. If we're at risk of discovery, we can make our way to the other opening."

They rounded the corner and stepped into the pantry. It was a small, dark room with only a tiny window filtering in a narrow stream of light. The walls on three sides were lined with shelves filled with preserves, vegetables, spices, and baskets of provisions. Stacked on the floor were sacks of flour and various sized barrels.

Jasmine fiddled with a latch on a shelf. A hidden door, disguised as floor-to-ceiling shelves, swung open. Only those familiar with the root cellar's existence would know of the entry behind the wall. Daniel said it was purposely built as a place to hide or escape through if the house was set upon by renegade Indians. How times had changed. It wasn't Indians threatening their lives, but white men.

The cellar doubled as cold storage where they kept perishable food chilled. Blocks of ice, cut from last winter's frozen pond, melted slowly in big metal tubs all around the underground room. Steep steps led down to the darkened abyss.

Allison took a deep breath to slow her racing heart. "Jasmine, go first. Then help Gus. I'll be right behind him."

Gus dug in his feet. "Let me get the guns out of the kitchen and protect you."

"There's no time." She placed a hand on his shoulder. Her desire to safeguard the elderly man, a dear family member, was strong. "Our best chance is in the cellar. Please, go."

Jasmine stopped halfway down the stairs in the black void and reached for Gus. He grabbed her hand, and she helped the older man navigate the darkened treads.

Heavy footsteps sounded on the back porch, only a few feet away. They were getting closer by the second. Allison peered into the shadows of the cellar. She wasn't going to make it down the steps, and then close the door, without them all being discovered. Her hand quaked on the disguised door. If found, they would kill both Gus and Jasmine for sure. A pregnant woman they might spare.

I hope.

In the dim light, she stared at Jasmine and Gus who gazed up at her inquiringly.

"Don't you dare," Jasmine choked out, her voice barely audible.

"Sorry. No time. They'll kill you. They may show me mercy. Stay quiet." She shut the door and pulled a heavy sack of flour and a keg of ale in front of the shelves.

A man bellowed, "Jasmine, you Indian bitch. Get out here or I'll tear this place apart." A loud crash, followed by glass shattering, echoed throughout the house.

She squatted behind a sack of rice and a barrel of molasses. Her belly got in the way when she tried to curl into a ball. Maybe she hadn't thought her actions through. In her desire to keep others safe, she'd put herself and her unborn child in great peril. Wrapping her arms around her belly, she hugged herself tightly and summoned her courage. If they found her, she had to remain calm and not physically resist.

The door to the pantry swung open with a loud bang.

Her body shook with fright. She squeezed her eyes shut.

Please, God, don't let him see me.

Boots scraped against the wooden floorboards as someone stepped into the room.

Allison's breath caught in her throat. She kept perfectly still. Her eyes remained closed, too afraid of what she would see.

"What do we have here?" A deep grating voice questioned.

Thick fingers bit into her upper arm and yanked her onto her feet. Her eyes flew open, and she stared at a craggy-faced man with a deep scar running down one cheek. He reeked of an unwashed body. A putrid smell assaulted her nostrils. Nausea churned her stomach.

"Let go of me," she ordered.

"You're in no position to tell me to do anything, Missy."

Another man stood in the doorway. She recognized Big Jake, the same man who beat Jasmine to unconsciousness, and who would've killed her friend, if not for Jayson.

"Where's the whore?" he ground out through clenched teeth. When he stepped farther into the room, the small space turned stifling.

Allison heard footsteps going through the bedrooms upstairs. She prayed Jasmine and Gus remained quiet. "I don't know what you're talking about?"

A slap landed across her cheek, jerking her head to the side. The sting brought tears to her eyes.

"Don't get sassy with me. I heard the whore was working as a cook out on your ranch," Big Jake growled.

Allison wanted to rub the pain from her fiery cheek, but Scarface held her arms behind her back. She inhaled slowly, gathering her nerve. Staring at Big Jake through blurred vision, she chose her words carefully. She hoped Big Jake wouldn't guess how close she and Jasmine really were. "The Indian woman high-tailed it out of here yesterday afternoon. Made my husband pay her what he owed her, and she took off. Said she was done cooking and cleaning up after white folks."

Heavy boots stomped down the stairs. "No one hiding on the second floor," a voice called from the front hall.

Big Jake considered her for a moment to ascertain the truth of her words.

She didn't flinch.

"Where'd she go?" he growled.

"I didn't see her leave. She didn't say good-bye. I'm not sure where she was going, but I heard she was on horseback, heading east." Allison held her breath. She prayed she was convincing enough.

Big Jake punched the door frame. "Shit. I wanted to kill the bitch."

"If she ain't here, what are we gonna do, Jake?"

"We're not leaving empty-handed. Take this one." He pointed at her. "It was her husband who got me locked in jail. If I can't get back at that Indian whore, then he's gonna pay for what he did. We'll stick to the plan. Take anything of value in the house and string up all the horses to sell."

A chill washed over her, she shivered.

"Looks like she could have a kid anytime."

"What does it matter? Bring her anyway. We'll sell her to the Mexicans, along with the horses. They'll take her, especially if the price is right. Once she has the kid, she'll make a good whore."

Allison's jaw slackened, and she gulped down a deep breath. Images of being passed from man to man, made her legs weak.

Scarface pushed her through the doorway of the pantry. She tripped on the hem of her gown and almost fell to her knees, but the man pulled her up with a quick jerk. Her arms ached from the uncomfortable position.

In the foyer, they met up with another man, who had a patch over his left eye. He gripped a bottle of Jayson's good brandy in one hand and carried a sack bursting at the seams, under his other arm. "Is that her?"

"The whore's gone. This is McKay's wife."

"What are we going to do with her?"

"I owe that bastard McKay for interfering in my business and getting me locked up. We're bringing his woman along with us. He's gonna go crazy wondering what we did with her." Big Jake stared at the sack. "What'd you find?"

"Jewels, coins, and a bunch of things we can get money for. I also swiped a few bottles of liquor."

"Good job," Big Jake said.

Scarface shoved her past the men, and out the front door. "If we're gonna git out of here in one piece, we oughtta stop yakking and git go'in. I've a mind to trade my bay horse in for the black one in the paddock. It's a real looker."

Big Jake called out. "Don't be stupid. It's got the McKay brand on it. I've done this before. We gotta get rid of the horses quick. All the horses. You can't keep any unless you want to be strung up. The Mexicans will take them all. We just gotta git the bunch to the meeting point before they leave for down South."

Allison tried to slow their progress by digging in her heels, but Scarface kept shoving her forward. With her hands held behind her back, she had no power to resist for fear of falling forward and hurting the baby.

At the barn, she stopped short. Motionless legs stuck out of the doorway. A lump rose in her throat, and she swallowed it down. The dead man's torso was hidden but she knew it was Slim. He had been fixing the corral fence earlier in the morning.

Poor Slim. Her eyes teared up and threatened to overflow. He must've been the first to go down when Big Jake and his men arrived in the yard. He was part of their ranch family. Someone who would be missed. She shivered uncontrollably. These men were ruthless.

What have I gotten myself into?

Big Jake went to catch the horses in the corral, and One-Eye saddled Bella, the horse Jasmine always rode.

Scarface pulled her arms out from behind her back and held her wrists in front. She stayed still. It was best not to provoke them.

Her first instinct was to weep but she willed herself to stay strong for her child. "Please, you don't have to do this. Leave me here."

"Shut up. I do what I'm told." He tied her hands together.

"Just take the horses. That should be enough."

"Jake's the boss. If he says you're coming with us, then you're coming with us." He tugged on the rope to make sure the knot held.

"Please, for the baby's sake." Tears stung her eyes.

"You don't get it, Missy. I don't care. If you don't stop yapping, I'll take my bandana off and stuff it down your throat."

Allison's temple throbbed. She wouldn't find a friend in this bunch of ruffians.

One-Eye led Bella to a turned-over wooden box. She spared a glance back at the house and hoped she'd placed enough barrels of ale and sacks of flour in front of the hidden door to blockade Jasmine and Gus in the cellar long enough for the group to leave on horseback.

As scared as she was to be snatched away to only God knew where, she didn't want anyone else to get hurt. She prayed Jasmine wouldn't leave the safety of the root cellar too soon. If Jasmine did muscle her way out, she'd get the guns and start shooting. Big Jake believed Jasmine was long gone. If this group of outlaws had any inkling Jasmine and Gus were alive, they would kill them on sight, just like Slim and Hank.

Allison couldn't bear the thought of anyone else she cared for being killed.

At least she had a chance for survival, she had worth.

As a whore in a Mexican cantina or brothel!

She shuddered. Big Jake wanted Jayson to suffer by not knowing what happened to her and the baby.

Would Jayson care if they were gone? When they married, he'd promised to keep her safe. Would he track her across the vast countryside? When he couldn't find her, would he give up and return to the ranch to continue his life without her? What would happen to the baby? It wasn't his child. To what lengths would he go to fulfill his promises?

A battery of unanswered questions fired in her mind and, like her drumming heart, refused to slow down. Her doubts and fears rattled away one after the other.

Scarface grabbed her from behind, lifted her off the ground, and set her feet firmly on top of the upside-down wooden box, next to Bella.

"We can do this one of two ways. You can get yourself onto the saddle under your own power, or I can throw you on it like a sack of potatoes. It's up to you."

Allison grabbed her skirts, hiking the material up one thigh as high as possible. She put the unencumbered leg over the saddle, reached for the horn, and pulled her bottom onto the seat.

Scarface took both the reins and led Bella to his horse. He hoisted himself up in the saddle.

Big Jake mounted his horse and rode up beside her. "Just so we're clear, if you give me any trouble, I'll kill you."

One-Eye got on his animal and led a string of McKay horses behind him.

Allison gripped the horn with her bound hands as the group galloped off through the field toward the mountains in the distance. She glanced over her shoulder at the ranch house fading fast. Her dry throat closed with stuffed emotion, and she struggled for a breath.

Please God, keep my baby safe.

~Chapter Twenty~

Jayson sat straight in the saddle and gave his mount its head.

As they always did, Jayson's horse, Griffin, and the carriage horses, Lewis and Clarke, walked briskly toward home. The trip to Flat Rock with Daniel to pick up supplies for the soon-to-be-built sawmill was exhilarating. He hadn't felt this alive in years. Lately, there was a spring in his steps and a fire in his belly to get things done.

There was only one explanation for his change of heart.

Allison.

She stirred in him a long-buried desire to live. Not just live, but to dream big again. Something he thought was gone forever. Her company soothed his soul, and he sought her out every chance he got. Without knowing, she'd compelled him to be a better man.

She makes me happy.

But a nagging voice in the recesses of his mind warned him to be careful, to move slowly. Their marriage had a rocky beginning, and they had only known each other for a short time. No promises had been made about her staying in Montana, or with him, just wait-and-sees. She didn't trust him not to change his mind and push her away again.

He shook his head. *Stop it.*

His insecurities and fears were getting in the way of a better life. He had to stop worrying about her leaving. Instead, he needed to show her how much he wanted her around, so she'd stay.

On the horizon, a person emerged on the rise in the road. The hat was clearly outlined, but the manner of dress was different. He squinted to get a better look.

A woman? A woman in a riding habit?

The female sprinted toward them.

Jasmine!

His stomach lurched.

He kicked his mount into a ground-breaking gallop, eating up the distance between them. As he got closer, Jasmine clutched her side and fell to her knees, gasping for air.

Jayson yanked hard on the reins. Griffin slid across the gravel, halting in mid-stride. Before his horse stopped, he jumped off and took a few big steps to the woman crumpled at his feet. His heart raced in his chest, nearly exploding from the frenzied beat.

"Jasmine." He knelt on one knee and clasped her shoulders, giving her a small shake. "What happened?"

Be strong, clamored over and over in his head, as if thinking it would make it so.

Jasmine grabbed his elbows and looked up. Her eyes were as wide as saucers. A trail of tears cleared a path down her dust-streaked cheeks. A chill coursed through his body. Jasmine wasn't the emotional type. She was fierce like his mother. A lump formed in his stomach. As she gasped for air, he waited for answers he wasn't sure he wanted to hear.

Daniel and his team of horses charged up behind. "Whoa! Whoa!" The horses' hooves dug into the dirt road sending stones flying. The buckboard bumped to a stop, shifting the supplies forward until they hit the back of the seat with a thud. "What's going on?"

Jayson glanced over his shoulder at his brother. He wanted more than anything for Jasmine to tell him at once that Allison was all right. That he had nothing to fear. But, he knew he had to be patient and give her time to recover.

"Not sure. Jasmine needs a minute. Throw me your water," he said to Daniel.

Daniel grabbed his canteen, hopped down from the buckboard, and handed it over.

Jayson put the opening to Jasmine's lips. She took a swig and coughed. With a trembling hand, she wiped her mouth. Her breaths came quick and shallow. They were a good three miles from home. From the look of things, she'd run the whole way. Why wasn't she on horseback?

"Can you talk?"

She nodded, inhaled deeper and exhaled slower.

His innards burned as if he swallowed crushed glass. "Is Allison all right?"

"I don't know. Big Jake and his men came to the ranch and took her. They killed Slim and wounded Hank," Jasmine's voice shook with emotion and her fingers bit into his arms. She laid her forehead against his shoulder. A small sob escaped her throat. "I don't know."

This can't be happening. Fear quaked his core. Big Jake was ruthless. Allison was in grave danger. His throat closed, and his breath got stuck in his chest. He gulped to open the passageway. "Tell me everything. From the beginning." His muscles tensed uncomfortably, forming hard bulges. He wanted to spring into action but drew on all the self-control he possessed and willed himself to remain calm. He needed to get all the facts.

Jasmine cleared the tears off her face. Her eyes pleaded for him to make things right. "Gus and I were in the garden. Allison came out on the back porch. We heard gunfire. Big Jake and two of his men were in the yard shooting at Slim and Hank."

She dropped her head. "They were looking for me. He said he wanted me dead."

"You're just one of many reasons for him to cause trouble," he assured her. Jayson had testified against Big Jake in front of the circuit judge. The brute was sentenced to a month in jail for beating Jasmine. Jayson remembered how Big Jake had glared at him in an I'll-tear-you-limb-from-limb kind of way when the sheriff hauled him off to jail. A knot tightened in his stomach.

The thought of Allison hurt and scared when he was not there to protect her was almost unbearable. He stomped down his desire to jump on his horse's back and blindly race across the countryside to save her from whatever might be. Guilt plagued him for not being around when she needed him most. And what of the babe? Would the child even survive? He had grown accustomed to the notion of being a father and was looking forward to the baby's arrival.

He used every bit of courage he could muster and let his more rational head prevail. He couldn't go off half-cocked. He had to focus on listening, so he could form a plan.

"We were too exposed outside." Jasmine swallowed hard. "We went inside but weren't going to make it to the kitchen to get the guns. We decided to go to the root cellar. Allison had me go first so I could help Gus down the stairs. Then she...she..."

"What did she do?"

"She shut the door on us," Her voice turned shrill. "She said there was no time. They would kill me if they found me. She said she'd have a better chance than we would."

Of course, she'd protect those she cared for. Trade her life for someone else's. Allison couldn't help it; it was in her nature to be selfless, a trait he really admired in her. He just wished she hadn't chosen to act on it today.

"They found her right away. I overheard them say they wanted to sell her as a whore to some Mexicans, the ones who are buying the horses. Then, they dragged her outside. Big Jake wanted to hurt you by taking her."

A whore. God, no. "How long ago did this happen?" His mind raced as fast as his pounding heart.

"I don't know exactly. Allison put barrels in front of the door and barricaded us down in the cellar. Gus and I had to find a match in the dark. Once we lit the lantern we made our way through the tunnel to the exit behind the house. By the time we got out, they were riding off in the distance. They took all the horses. We found Slim dead, but Hank was still alive. We dragged him to the bunkhouse and laid him on the porch, out of the sun. We stopped his bleeding. Gus is with him. I took off running to town to fetch you."

"You did the right thing." He helped her stand.

She grabbed his arm in a vise grip. "Please, Jayson. You gotta find her. I'm worried about her...and the baby."

"Which way did they go?"

"They headed toward the mountains to the west."

Jayson looked in that direction. He knew which mountains. A plan formed. He had to get to her before any permanent damage was done. She had to be so scared. He needed to be there for her. "Daniel, get the horses unharnessed."

Daniel immediately unbuckled the leather straps. "What are we going to do?"

"I'm going after them." He glanced back at the twin peaks in the distance.

"You can't go alone. There are three of them," Jasmine said.

Jayson grabbed some of the unfettered strapping from Daniel and threw the leather on the buckboard. He had to keep busy to give himself time enough to deliver Jasmine and Daniel their orders. Everything had to come together just so.

"Hopefully, I won't be alone for long. Once the horses are untethered, I want you to take one of them..." He stared at Jasmine. "You can ride bareback can't you?"

She nodded.

"Ride to town. Get Doc and the sheriff. Then, return to the ranch, help with Hank, pack some supplies, and wait for my brothers."

"What am I going to do?" Daniel asked.

Jayson hoisted himself up on Griffin, unable to wait much longer. Every fiber in his body was electrified and ready to explode. Only a ground-eating gallop in Allison's direction was going to lessen the jolts.

"Find Chase, Nathan, and the rest of our men on Rattlesnake Bluff. Tell them what happened. Have them stop by the ranch for extra ammunition and supplies before they head out. Let them know I plan to cut Big Jake off at the bend in the river. Where the only good passage through the mountains begins. If I make a straight line from here, I might be able to get ahead of them. They'll have to water the horses there if they plan to go through the mountain pass."

Griffin, sensing Jayson's energy, pranced beneath him. He reined his horse in.

"Have Chase follow their tracks in case they double back or change course. That way, we won't lose them. If I don't run into Big Jake in a decent amount of time, I'll know they went another way. I'll find Chase and Nathan's trail and meet up with them. Tell them," he choked out, "we don't stop until we find her."

"What about the sawmill supplies?" Daniel gave Jasmine a leg up onto an unharnessed Clarke.

"Leave them."

Jayson spun Griffin around and took off galloping across the land.

Please, God, let me get to her in time.

~Chapter Twenty-One~

The pace was brutal. A tear rolled down Allison's cheek, but her hands were tied, and she didn't dare let go of the saddle horn to wipe away the moisture. The baby was coming. She could do nothing about it. As she bounced around on the back of the horse, she silently prayed for the life of her child. Helplessness washed over her like a wet rag and weighed her down.

Powerless to change her fate, she struggled to accept her predicament. Despair twisted her mind. Anguish caused her insecurities to rise and jab at her heart.

Did Jayson know she was gone, or even care? Why would he want a wife who carried another man's child? What man would want a wife who couldn't cook?

He could do so much better.

She shook her head to extinguish her errant musings and reminded herself to focus on ways to keep her and the baby alive. The group slowed at a river bend and waded across the water. She lifted her legs to keep her feet dry. When they reached the bank on the other side, they stopped to let the horses drink and graze in a small, flat meadow.

The men dismounted.

She couldn't tolerate another minute in the saddle. "Please, I have to use the bushes."

Scarface scowled. "Get down."

Holding the pommel with her bound hands, she maneuvered her leg around while using all the upper body strength she could muster, and gently lowered her feet to the ground. Her legs barely held her upright after being in the saddle for the past hour or so. It had been months since she last rode a horse. She hung onto the leather strappings until she was strong enough to stand alone.

"Hurry up. I don't have all day." Scarface grabbed her upper arm and yanked her toward the biggest oak tree on the outskirts of the clearing, thirty yards away.

"You have five minutes, then we leave," Big Jake called after them.

Sticky fluid lined her inner thighs. Delivery pains had plagued her since she first sat on Bella, back at the ranch. They were evolving faster and faster. In Boston, while helping Father Peter, she had witnessed a few births. During those times, she did nothing more than hold fresh linen behind a line of women who did the real work. She had some inkling of what was to come but had no idea how she'd deliver her baby on her own.

So far, she kept her on-going distress secret from her captors by using measured breaths to quell her discomfort. Histrionics hovered just below the surface, but she strived to keep her emotions hidden. She wasn't sure what the outlaws would do when they found out the baby was arriving soon. She feared for the life of her child. A wave of helplessness engulfed her, and she cupped her belly with her trembling hands.

God, give me strength.

As she ambled toward the wide, old tree, a sob caught in her throat. She swallowed it down. While on horseback, so many scenarios of how to get away had rolled around in her head, but none seemed plausible. Now that she was in full-blown labor, and her feet were firmly on the ground, she had to try to escape.

She glanced at her bound hands. They had to be untied for her to be successful. Somehow, she needed to convince Scarface to remove her bindings and give her some privacy in the thicket. The woods surrounding the meadow looked dense. If she fled and hid, the men might give up and move on. She nibbled on her bottom lip, not sure if the plan forming was just emerging from desperation.

Another bout of pain caught her off guard. She slowed her steps, concentrated on breathing, and prayed Scarface didn't notice.

When she reached the side of the tree, she stopped, while the last of the pain dissipated. "Mister, please, can you untie me for a few minutes, so I can hike my skirts properly?" She used a soft, feminine voice in hopes of swaying the man her way.

"I don't know. I don't think Jake would like it."

"He's busy with the horses, and the other one's gulping whiskey. I'll only be a moment if you give me the use of my hands, otherwise, it will take me much longer."

"I don't know." He glanced over his shoulder at the other men.

"Please…" She batted her eyes, "it's not like I can go far with this big belly."

"Well, I guess I can unbind you. Just for a minute, ya hear?"

"That's all the time it'll take." Her face remained soft, but inside she was a ball of nerves. The plan was to take flight once she rounded the massive tree. She'd only have one chance to get away and had to make it count.

Scarface unknotted the rope and pulled it away.

Allison rubbed her wrists. Hiking up the hem of her skirts to her calves, she stepped past the side of the tree. Scarface followed on her heels.

"I'll be going with you to make sure you come back," he said.

She spun around to face him, ready to plead for privacy. Without warning, the sharp tip of a knife, at the end of a white-clothed arm, reached out from the shadows behind the tree and lodged deep within Scarface's neck. The outlaw stared at her with wide eyes as a gurgle vibrated in his open mouth. The blade was pulled out. Red blood gushed from the wound. Scarface raised a hand to cover the opening. Before stemming the flow, he crumpled to the ground.

A scream stuck in her throat. While she struggled to project the sound, a man's hand clamped over her mouth to stifle the noise. Her arms flailed through the air to protect herself and her unborn child from a new, unknown threat.

"Allie, it's me," Jayson said tenderly in her ear as he pulled her behind the tree, her back pressed against his chest. He waited for her to turn her head to look at him before he removed his hand.

"It's...you?" She whirled around as he loosened his hold. They were so close, his familiar woodsy scent reassuring. Relief turned her muscles to jelly.

He came for me. Every fiber in her wanted to jump for joy. She placed her hands upon his chest, needing to touch him to make sure he was real.

"How?"

"Jasmine found me. Told me what happened." He held her face between his hands. "Are you hurt?"

Dazed, she shook her head. Her throat squeezed with held back emotion. She reeled at the sight of him and clasped his waist to steady herself, unwilling to ease up for fear of him vanishing before her eyes.

"Come. Griffin's not far. I have to get you out of here."

A sharp pain shot through her innards. "The baby's coming." Her focus changed. She gulped hard and breathed through the discomfort.

Jayson stared at her. "Now?"

Her head bobbed up and down, a ball of air catching in her lungs.

"Okay." His eyebrows drew together. He glanced around the tree to make sure they were still safe. Squatting down, he reached for the lifeless body at their feet and took Scarface's gun out of his holster.

He straightened and handed her the gun. "Remember when I taught you to shoot? You use two hands, eye your target, cock the hammer, and squeeze the trigger."

An uncomfortable knot of fear rose from her stomach and squeezed her chest. She nodded, clasping the cold, heavy weapon between her hands.

"I'm going out there while I have the element of surprise."

Her eyes widened. He was leaving her. Abandoning her to go it alone. Her heartbeat pounded in her ears. "Please, stay with me. Don't go," she whispered hoarsely.

"We're not safe with them alive." He ran his hands along her upper arms. "If one of those men shows his head around this tree, shoot him. If something happens, Chase and Nathan are coming. They will find you. Understand?"

"I'm scared." Her hands trembled.

"Everything's going to be fine." He pecked a kiss on her forehead. "I'll be right back. Promise." He left her side and disappeared into the thick bushes.

"Hey, what the hell's taking ya so long?" Big Jake hollered from the bank of the river. "Get that bitch moving. We don't have all day. We have to stay ahead of anyone following us."

Allison stood frozen, her back against the rough bark of the oak tree. She clung to the gun with both hands and listened intently for any sounds. Her mind raced with wild imaginings. What happens if Jayson gets hurt? Or, he doesn't return? Will she be able to kill a man?

Please, Jayson. Come back to me.

Suddenly, gunfire echoed off the mountains. She didn't have much time to think about what was going on in the meadow because another round of intense pain brewed in her abdomen. Shutting her eyes, her breathing became her focus. She wrapped an arm underneath her belly and rounded her back.

The volley of gunshots ended abruptly. She held the revolver in both hands and pointed the barrel toward the side of the tree, where she expected someone to emerge if they came for her. Her discomfort waned, and her stomach relaxed. Bushes rustled. She could do this. Jayson taught her how. She pulled back the hammer and peered through one eye, lining up her shot. Her arms tensed, and she inhaled deeply.

"It's me," Jayson called out.

Relief bombarded her body, turning her muscles to rubber. She exhaled loudly and dropped her arms to her sides.

He stepped into view and covered the few feet between them.

"Are you hurt?" she asked as he took the gun out of her hand.

The corners of his lips curled up in a soft smile. "I'm fine. They didn't expect to see me so soon. We're safe. They won't bother us anymore." He grabbed her by her arms and pulled her to him until her breasts crushed against his chest.

Reacting to his touch, her body shuddered, and her legs grew weaker. "You came for me."

"Of course, I came for you. You're my wife," he said matter-of-factly, wrapping a brawny arm around her back to hold her upright.

Waves of tremors took over until she shook uncontrollably. "I don't know what's wrong with me."

He pulled her tighter and stroked her back. "It'll pass. Your body's just reacting to your fright."

A sob rose from her throat and broke free. Tears filled her eyes. She laid the side of her face against his chest.

"Let it out, Allie. You'll feel better," he whispered in her hair as he swayed side-to-side with her wrapped in his embrace.

And she did. Her body responded with a bout of guttural sounds and quaking. Her tears soaked the front of his vest. As the waterworks tapered off, she sniffled and gathered her emotions.

Suddenly, another round of pains began, and she again focused her energy on her breathing. He stayed close, stroking her back as she rode the wave of pain.

When the episode passed, she melted into the warmth of his arms and asked, "How did you find me?"

"I knew they'd stop to let the horses drink before going through the pass. I just chose the biggest tree."

"I planned to escape and hoped to run away and hide in the woods, but I wasn't sure I'd get too far." She clenched her teeth when she stopped talking to keep them from clacking.

"I'm glad I got here before you had to." He held her a little tighter.

Allison let his safe embrace soothe her nerves, her shivers calmed. "Jasmine promised she'd help me with the delivery. The baby's not going to wait."

"I'm here. I'll deliver the baby."

"You wouldn't know what to do…" Another pain robbed her of her breath.

"I know what to do."

She tilted her head up to study his face.

He brushed a light kiss on her forehead and then gazed into her eyes. "I have a confession. After you gave me that salve, I continued to wake up in the middle of the night. Maybe, I'm just used to only sleeping a few hours. Anyway, I didn't want to awaken you by going downstairs, so I brought books to my room to read. One of the books I skimmed through was Nathan's doctor book."

She concentrated on disregarding a new round of pain. Jayson cupped the side of her face, and she leaned her cheek against the palm of his over-sized hand. His touch felt so right.

"Nothing to fear. I can deliver the baby."

"Are you sure?"

"Positive. Trust me." He sent her a smile oozing confidence, something she didn't possess.

Allison gathered what nerve she could muster. She had no other options.

***

Together, in between Allison's contractions, they retrieved Griffin, secured the horses, and gathered everything they needed for the birthing.

Although moving around felt good after too long on horseback, she knew it was almost time to push. Pressure was building in her pelvis. The pains were arriving quicker and quicker, only minutes apart. She barely had time to recover from one, before another started in again.

Jayson found her a sandy spot on the riverbank, not far from the horses. On the small incline, he spread out a layer of horse blankets and placed his overcoat on top. To save her day dress for the ride home, he had her undress down to her camisole and one lone petticoat. He teased her about the number of petticoats she still wore after she'd promised him she would wear fewer in the kitchen, but then agreed it was lucky she had on so many because they would come in handy for swaddling the baby.

With his help, she squatted down, her big belly getting in the way, and reclined in an upright position against the bank, keeping her knees bent. She had no time to be embarrassed when Jayson checked the baby's progress because another wave of discomfort racked her body. Her fingers clutched tightly to the edges of the horse blankets she was propped up on. This was not the way she envisioned the birth. She never thought she'd be out in the middle of nowhere with Jayson delivering the baby.

Please, God. Help me get through this.

Jayson remained on one knee in front of her. "You're not quite ready to push yet. A little while longer."

"I'm scared," she said softly.

"I know you are." He leaned in and brushed a piece of hair out of her face.

Irrational thoughts tormented her mind, and she couldn't prevent herself from voicing them. "Maybe, I can hold out until Jasmine gets here?"

"I'm not sure we have that long. We're going to let nature take its course. My only real job here is to catch the baby when he or she arrives. The rest is just a natural process," Jayson said with assurance.

In between breaths, tears rolled down her cheeks. "The baby wasn't supposed to come for another month. What if the child doesn't survive?"

"Hush, now. You're getting yourself all worked up about nothing. The baby will be big enough. You'll see."

"I shouldn't have let them take me. Maybe there was enough time to hide in the root cellar or to get the guns. I don't know. If I hadn't gone with them, things would be different. I'd be home."

"Don't upset yourself with things you can't change. You made the best decision you could at the time. Leave it at that."

Jayson took a half-sitting position alongside her and put his arm under her neck, pulling her head into the crook of his shoulder. He snuggled against her side, intertwined his fingers with hers, and placed their clasped hands on her rounded stomach. "Tell me about your parents."

"My parents?" she asked, dumbfounded.

"Tell me about your parents, Lillian, and your life in Boston."

She was taken by surprise. He never asked her about her former life. It was a topic they never discussed.

"What are they like? Tell me," he urged.

Immediately, she pictured her parents and sister. Their smiling faces appeared clearly in her mind. In between breaths, soft moans, groans and panting, she shared how much she loved them and what her days were like in the city. He cuddled beside her, their clasped hands stroking her belly during episodes of pain as she recoiled against his chest during the worst of it.

186

He listened to her fond memories of growing up in a happy family, having picnics on the banks of the Charles River, and fancy balls full of laughter and dancing. She told him about the day she met Father Peter and how she loved going with him on his weekly visits to the hospital and through the city to help those in need. The stories spilled out in nervous chatter until it was time to push.

And, then he left her side, positioning himself in front of her.

In the random moments when her brain was clear enough to think during the last stage of childbirth, she marveled at his take-charge manner. He was patient, encouraging, and calm. He embodied confidence. She knew she could trust him.

Finally, he said, "This is it. One last big push, Allie. You can do it."

His words broke through her fog. She grabbed hold of the edges of the blankets beneath her and with a loud primitive groan, she gave him what he needed.

"You did it," he exclaimed.

Fatigue overtook her, and she melted into her makeshift bed.

A newborn baby's wail usurped nature's sounds.

"We have a son," he announced and held the small naked bundle up in his big hands for her to see.

"Is he healthy?" she whispered.

"Looks to be perfect. Just like his mother. Let me wipe him down and swaddle him, then I'll give him to you to hold."

We have a son. Not, *you have a son.*

Those words trumpeted in Allison's head. Right then and there, she knew for sure, she couldn't live without Jayson's love. A marriage in name only wasn't enough. She needed him to love her as much as she loved him.

~Chapter Twenty-Two~

Following the delivery and a brief period of needed rest, Allison begged Jayson to take her and the baby home. The kidnapping was too fresh. The many things that could've gone wrong kept repeating themselves in her head, stealing away her peace. Being out in the open like they were added a certain vulnerability to her already frazzled state. She craved four walls and the safety of the McKay ranch.

Jayson made her prove she could stand on her own before he agreed to turn his back and give her a moment of much-needed privacy. While she washed in the shallows of the river, he talked in hushed tones to the baby cuddled in his arms.

Her heart soared at the sight.

His actions today exceeded her every expectation. He didn't abandon her or falter under pressure. When danger surrounded them, and the situation grew complicated, he took on the challenges without a second thought, taking control and remaining calm.

After she finished freshening up, Jayson helped her into her dress. While he collected their things and got the horses ready, she tried to breastfeed the baby. Her first attempt was awkward, but she was able to get him to feed a little. When she finally joined Jayson, she struggled not to look as fatigued as she felt, worried he'd change his mind and make them stay longer.

She needed to go home.

They set out riding double on Griffin, leaving the stolen horses and three dead bodies behind. Allison sat sideways on a pile of blankets in front of her husband. He swore the cushioned seat would add to her comfort. She cradled her newborn son, wrapped in clean petticoats. Jayson's arms encircled her body, ensuring that she wouldn't tumble off in her weakened state. She snuggled against his chest. His familiar woodsy aroma settled her frayed nerves. Her arms remained taut while holding the baby, too afraid to drop him as their mount walked briskly along.

A few miles into their journey, a group of riders appeared in the distance, coming upon them fast.

She tensed.

Jayson squeezed her waist gently. "It's Chase and Nathan." He steered Griffin out of the sun and into the shade of an old oak tree. Taking out his canteen, he unscrewed the cap and handed her the container.

Allison gulped a few swallows of water and gave it back as they waited for the riders to join them.

Chase, riding with Jasmine seated behind him, was the first to canter up and slide to a stop under the tree's leafy cover. Jasmine jumped off the back of his horse, went around Griffin, and stepped up on a fallen log.

Jasmine touched Allison's arm. "You're alive."

"Jayson found me."

Jasmine scowled. "You locked me in the root cellar."

"I'm sorry. I was so scared they would kill you if they found you. I couldn't let that happen."

"No one ever did anything like that for me before." Jasmine's voice croaked with emotion.

Allison smiled. "That's what friends do for each other."

Jasmine rubbed her arm. "I'm so happy you're safe."

The other riders arrived and fanned out around the two horses.

"Is everyone all right?" Nathan asked.

"We're fine, and we have a healthy son," Jayson said proudly.

Hoots of congratulations rang out from the crowd of men. Allison craned her neck to get a good look at the smiling faces of her brothers-in-law, ranch hands, and Sheriff Hollister.

Jasmine stroked the baby's little fingers. "He's beautiful."

"How's Hank?" Jayson asked.

"He'll be hurting for a while, but he'll live," Nathan said.

Jayson nodded. "I left a string of horses and three dead outlaws about five miles back. Any volunteers?"

"Don't you worry, Boss. We'll go get them," Giles said. The ranch hands reined their horses down the trail.

"Congratulations, Mrs. McKay." Sheriff Hollister tipped his head, and then looked to Jayson. "I'll take the bodies back to town to be buried. Glad everything worked out. I can't say I wasn't worried."

"Thanks, Jordan." Jayson touched the brim of his hat.

The sheriff kicked his horse into a canter to catch up with the others, leaving Chase, Nathan, and Daniel behind.

Allison tilted the baby so Jasmine, who remained standing on the fallen tree trunk, could get a good look.

Her friend pushed the wrappings away from the baby's face. "I guess you didn't need me after all."

Allison lifted her chin and gazed at her husband who returned her look. "Jayson took care of things."

A big smirk crossed his striking face. "I managed fine. After all, I had the easiest part. All I had to do was catch."

Her cheeks heated with the memories of sharing the intimacy of birthing with him.

Jasmine chuckled. "You did good, Jayson."

Nathan guided his horse alongside and gave his brother an ear-to-ear grin. "I don't suppose you would've done so well had you not swiped my medical books to read at night. Good thing I had them. Huh?"

"Just like Pa always said, 'a little reading never hurt anyone'," Jayson replied. Nathan chuckled.

"Let's get you home." Jasmine took off her navy vest and unbuttoned her white shirt. She pulled out the blouse's hem from inside her riding skirt.

"What the heck are you doing?" Chase asked.

"I'm making a sling to help hold the baby. They get as heavy as a bag of boulders, even at this age." Jasmine removed her shirt and tied the sleeves together. She slipped the knotted ends over Allison's head, then helped Allison position her elbow in the material to act as an arm support.

"There. This will help hold the baby. You'll be much more comfortable this way. It's a long ride home."

"Thank you." The sling supported her son securely, without causing her arms undue strain.

"Where in the world did you learn that?" Chase asked, his mouth hanging agape.

Jasmine grinned. "You would be amazed at all the things I know." She stepped down from the log and out in the open exposing her lowcut camisole, blousing out over her form-fitting corset, showing her cleavage to its best advantage. She glanced at the McKay men staring at her. "Really. You mean to tell me you men have never seen a woman in her underthings?"

Nathan and Daniel quickly reined their horse's heads away and gave her their backs.

Allison smiled wide when Jasmine let out a loud belly laugh. The tension of the day finally faded away.

Jasmine donned her vest and strolled over to Chase. "Sorry about getting you all flustered," she teased. He gave her a hand up, and she situated herself behind him.

"What happened to Clarke?" Jayson asked.

Chase moved his horse up next to Griffin. "He came up lame."

Jasmine leaned toward Allison. "What do you say we head back to the ranch?"

"I'd like that very much," she replied.

***

"You should put me down. I'm too heavy for you," Allison protested as her husband carried her into the foyer. Jasmine walked a few steps behind with the baby.

Jayson chuckled low, deep in his throat. "This is not the first time I've toted you up the stairs."

Her cheeks burned. She melted deeper against his shoulder. "I'm afraid I don't remember."

"That was my brothers' fault."

Allison tightened her hold around his neck when he took the first step. She breathed in the earthy scent permeating his clothes and then relaxed. "I wish I could remember what happened after the dance."

"Not much to remember." As if unburdened, he mounted the stairs and carried her into her room with little effort.

The sight of her bed made her heart swell. *I'm home.*

He set her on the quilt-covered mattress, positioning her back against the feather pillows. "I have something for the baby. I'll be right back."

Allison watched him leave. She smiled softly at Jasmine, who stood inside the door, and extended her arms for her sleeping son. "It's good to be home."

"I, for one, am glad you're back." Jasmine handed her the baby as if it was the most precious package in the world.

Jayson returned, carrying a piece of furniture. He placed the wooden cradle on the floor, next to the bed. "I found this in the attic and refinished it. I thought you could use it."

She leaned down and ran her fingers over the smooth wood. The craftsmanship was exceptional. All the edges were rounded. A scroll pattern decorated the head- and footboards. Intricately shaped dowels made up the slats on the sides. Two rockers were attached to the bottom. She pushed it gently and watched it sway back and forth.

"It's beautiful. Was it yours?" She gazed at her husband. Tears stung her eyes.

He sent her a heart-warming smile. "A long time ago."

"Thank you," she said hoarsely, a lump lodging in the back of her throat.

"I made a small mattress out of a pillowcase I stuffed with lamb's wool and fitted it on the bottom of the bed. I figured that would be soft enough."

Allison glanced down at the baby in her arms. "I think he'll like it very much."

"Daniel should be up shortly with clean water, so you can freshen up. Be sure to lay down and rest. I'll check on you later." He spun on his heels and exited the room.

When he left, there was a void in his place. She stared at the doorway, hoping he'd return.

Jasmine lovingly stroked the baby's new bed. "It's gorgeous. Leave it to your husband to think ahead."

She looked down at the piece of furniture. "He does that a lot, I've noticed."

Daniel knocked on the door frame and stepped inside. "I have your water. It's only lukewarm. I didn't have time to heat it on the stove. I thought you might be in a hurry."

"It'll be fine, thank you."

He lugged two heavy pails into the room and placed them next to the washbasin. "Maybe tonight after you rest, you can have a proper bath. I'll make sure you get hot water then."

"Sounds wonderful," she said.

On his way by the bed, he touched the baby's cheek. "Jayson told me not to bother you yet about holding the baby. You need your rest. I'll wait 'til later."

She smiled softly at Daniel. "We have a few things we have to do with him first, but I'm thinking you'll have plenty of time tonight."

A lopsided grin crossed his face. "Looking forward to it."

He ambled to the door, then turned slowly, as if searching for the right words. "I'm really happy to have you back, Allison. I was so worried about you and the baby. I felt powerless when I heard you were taken, but I knew Jayson would bring you back safe. I'm glad he did."

"Thanks, Daniel."

Jasmine closed the door behind him. "That kid has a lot of heart. He's going to grow up to be one heck of a man."

"I think you're right."

Jasmine spread a small blanket on the bed and stretched out her arms. "Let me take the baby, wash him up, and put a cloth diaper on him."

"You know how to do that?" She passed the baby to her.

"I do. And you're going to learn very fast yourself." Jasmine chuckled.

She watched with awe as Jasmine wet a cloth in the pail, and gently rubbed all traces of childbirth away. The baby released a muted wail when the water hit his bare skin, his lungs not yet strong enough to project his dismay too far. She rechecked his little body to make sure everything was as it should be. A soft sigh rolled over her slightly parted lips.

He's perfect.

"The sooner you clean up and change into a fresh nightgown, the sooner you can lay down and rest. Now git." Jasmine dried off the baby.

Allison pushed herself to rise off the bed. She was so fatigued her legs were as weak as a newborn foal's. Her thoughts jumbled from all that happened, and her temple pounded in a pulsing rhythm. She walked to the basin, poured water into the bowl, and unbuttoned her day dress. Wiggling out of the arms, she let the mounds of cloth pool at her feet.

"I'm so happy you're alive and well. I feel giddy with relief," Jasmine said.

She stopped mid-task and stared down at the soap and linen cloth in her hand. "To tell you the truth, I wasn't sure I was going to make it. I have never been so scared in all my life. At one point, I had lost all hope. The pains were coming fast and furious, and I was on horseback with a bunch of outlaws who wanted to sell me to men worse than them. I feared for the life of my child, and my own life. I didn't know what to do. I've never felt so helpless."

Jasmine fastened a diaper around the baby's bottom with two big pins. "I'm so sorry. I feel responsible for what happened."

"Please don't say that. You were in no way responsible. Big Jake was evil. They all were. I'm glad they're dead. I know to think such is uncharitable, but their deaths give me peace."

"How did you get away?"

"I planned to make a run for it when they watered the horses."

"Is that how you escaped?" The baby made small grunting noises and squirmed on the bed. Jasmine swaddled him in a blanket, held him against her shoulder, and rocked him back and forth.

"I didn't have a chance to flee. One minute I was alone and scared and the next Jayson was with me. He saved my life and the baby's life. He was there when I needed him most."

"He's a very capable man."

"You found him and told him what happened. Thank you."

Jasmine patted the baby's back and smiled. "That's what friends do for each other."

Allison nodded. She finished scrubbing, dried off, and put on her nightgown. Something was weighing on her mind. But, because she was afraid of the answer, she had put off the question until she couldn't hold back any longer.

"Jasmine, the baby came early. He's so small. Nathan did a quick exam and says he's going to be fine. Jayson says the same thing, but I'm not sure if they're just telling me what I want to hear. I need to know the truth."

"Come sit."

She sat in the rocking chair. Jasmine handed over the baby. He nuzzled at her breast.

"Let me show you how to feed your son." Jasmine helped position the baby and gave her instructions.

When the baby was settled and suckling, she glanced at Jasmine sitting in the cushioned chair beside her. "You never answered."

Jasmine sighed. "First off, I'll always tell you the truth, whether you want to hear it or not. As for your question, there are never any guarantees. Your son came early, but thankfully he's big to begin with. Smaller than some babies, but bigger than others. He appears healthy. Both of you are in good hands out here on the ranch, away from the cities. There is no disease in these parts right now." Jasmine stared at the infant attached to Allison's breast. "He's taken to feeding, so that's always a good sign. But, for him to survive, you have to take good care

194

of yourself, eat right, and rest so you produce enough milk to nourish him. Every day he'll get stronger and stronger. You wait and see."

Jasmine patted her arm. "When the baby's done feeding, I'm going to get you in bed, so you can sleep for a few hours. When you wake, dinner will be ready, and the men will be waiting to see your son up close. You better start thinking of a name."

"Thank you, for telling me the truth."

"Always," Jasmine replied.

~Chapter Twenty-Three~

Faint noises woke Allison out of a sound sleep. A few seconds passed before she realized she was hearing her new son's mewling. The baby's cries were soft and muffled. Rolling to the side of the bed, she peered into the cradle where her newborn squirmed. She hung her arm over the edge and rocked the cradle back and forth.

Today her life had changed forever. Her child was no longer a notion. He was flesh and bone. The fierce protectiveness that embodied her while pregnant, driving her to abandon all things familiar and compelling her to move out West, grew deeper. From now on, her life would revolve around her son.

"I wonder if Robert will ever regret his decision to abandon us? Or will we only be a fleeting memory from his past?" She stared down into the cradle and sighed heavily.

She touched the baby's cheek with the tip of her finger. He instinctively turned his head, looking for a meal. "Jayson is your father now. He proved today he'll do everything he can to keep us safe. I trust him to do right by us. We'll have a good life here with him."

Allison sat on the edge of the mattress, leaned down, and gathered up her child. He was so light in her arms. She laid him on the bed and changed his cloth diaper the way Jasmine taught her. For the first time that day, she was alone with her infant son and the immensity of the moment took her breath away. There was a nagging fear she might do something wrong, but Jasmine assured her that taking care of a child came naturally. When he was swaddled again, she sat on the rocking chair and let him nurse.

As she rocked in a relaxing rhythm, she stared at her son's chubby cheeks. Her emotions bubbled to the surface and she swore she could feel her heart growing in her chest. She softly hummed a lullaby she had learned as a child.

Ranch noises drifted in on a warm breeze through the open windows. Men's indistinct voices sounded faint in the background. Horses neighed. Cows mooed. Chickens clucked. Metal against metal chimed in the distance. The curtains billowed and flapped in the light wind. A peacefulness enveloped her.

"You have uncles who have promised to dote on you and spoil you rotten." She caressed the side of her baby's face. "Back in Boston, you also have a grandma, grandpa, and an Aunt Lillian. I'm sure they will fall in love the minute they lay eyes on you. I haven't asked them to visit yet, because I wanted you to arrive first. I'm sure I disappointed them with my unladylike behavior with your father and then hurt them deeply when I ran away. I didn't know what else to do. If I stayed in Boston, all our lives would've been miserable. I never wanted them to suffer."

As the baby nursed, he made faint grunting noises and wiggled his tiny fingers. He didn't understand her words but sharing lessened the guilt she harbored for the past choices she'd made. She gently brushed her lips across the silky fuzz on top of his head and ended the trail with a feathered kiss. His fresh baby aroma accosted her senses with an overpowering heavenly smell, and tears materialized in her eyes, blurring her vision.

The love in her heart for her newborn was all-consuming. She could barely contain the magnitude of affection bombarding her every time she laid eyes on him.

Would it always be like this?

***

A knock sounded on the study door. Jayson glanced up from his ledgers, glad to have something to distract him from the papers in front of him. He couldn't seem to focus on them with any amount of clarity.

Jasmine stepped into the room.

The concern etched on her face made his stomach quake.

"Is everything all right with Allison and the baby?" He placed his hands on the edge of the desk and readied himself to stand.

She waved him down. "They're fine. I just need a moment of your time."

Sitting back on his leather chair, he sank into the upholstery. "What can I do for you?"

He had already thanked Jasmine earlier for the part she'd played in the day's events. Had she not made it out of the root cellar and run miles to find him, things might have ended on a different note. He doubted Allison or the baby would be alive if it hadn't been for Jasmine's devotion and courage.

I will always be in her debt.

"Would you mind if I close the door? What I want to discuss is private. I don't what your brothers to overhear."

He nodded. "By all means."

Jasmine shut the thick door with a soft thud.

He motioned to the chairs in front of his desk and waited for her to select a seat. Jasmine didn't usually go through such ceremony.

"Is someone bothering you? Is it Chase?"

"Oh, no. Nothing like that." She sat with her back straight on the very edge of the cushioned chair. Her pursed lips projected a serious aura.

His interest was piqued. "What can I help you with?"

"I want to know where you're sleeping tonight."

He cleared his throat. "Umm...in my bed?" he stammered. Not sure where their conversation was headed.

She interlocked her fingers and laid them on her lap. "I know this is none of my business, but it's time for me to speak my mind."

His brows drew together. "What's this about?"

"I'm just going to say it." She paused to take a quick breath. "Okay, I know you and Allison don't have a typical marriage. I've got eyes. I'm guessing this so-called *business deal* included some stipulation that you don't sleep together until after the baby is born. Correct me if I'm wrong."

"Uhh...maybe." He played with the collar on his shirt, opening the material wider. Suddenly, the air was stifling in the room.

"Well, guess what? The baby's here."

He stared at her. "I'm well aware of his presence. If you recall, I was there when he came into the world."

"It's time, Jayson. Time for you to get your things out of the spare bedroom and move in with Allison where you belong."

A knot formed in his stomach. This was the moment he had both dreaded and looked forward to for months. This was the point of no return. After he moved into Allison's bedroom, there was no going back.

Jasmine rose from her chair and walked to a small end table next to a leather sofa, where a decanter of brandy and two glasses sat. She pointed to the amber liquid. "Do you mind?"

"Help yourself." He watched her pour a glass and take a swig as he considered her words.

She looked up with glassy eyes.

He ran his fingers through his hair. "The baby's not even been here a full day. It's too soon."

"Can I fix you one?" She tilted her head toward the liquor.

At his nod, she filled his glass half full, strolled over to the desk, and handed it to him. He took a big gulp.

Placing her hands on the desktop, she leaned forward. "It's not too soon. You need to lie beside your wife at night and take your place as her husband."

"Shit, Jasmine. I can't barge into her bedroom with all my stuff and expect her to welcome me."

"That's exactly what you should do. Don't delay your life together any more than you have already. Stop courting her." She spread her arms wide and looked up to the heavens. "Damn it, Jayson. You're already married. The outcome's a sure thing. Get in there and commit to your marriage. You now have a little one to think of."

He rested his elbows on his desk and stared at her. "I won't be asking her to consummate the marriage so soon. God, Jasmine, she just had the baby."

"Of course, you won't. But you can lie next to her and help her in the middle of the night. Get used to being with each other in the most intimate ways."

"She drives me near crazy when I'm around her. What happens if I'm pushed too far?" He could talk to Jasmine about such things. She wasn't a typical young lady, she was well-versed about how things worked in this life.

"You have more self-control than anyone I've ever met. I have faith you'll remain a gentleman and wait for her to heal before you force your attentions on her."

"How will I know when she's ready?"

"Believe me. She'll let you know. Remember, as much as she's driving you crazy, you're driving her senseless, too. I expect you won't have too long of a wait."

"Are you sure she's going to be agreeable to this?"

"Don't ask. Just do it. Don't think about it. I heard her moving around upstairs. She's awake and feeding the baby. Gather your things and join your wife." Jasmine walked toward the door.

He closed his ledger, pushed his chair back from his desk, and stood. "I guess you're right."

She opened the door and glanced over her shoulder before she stepped out. "I know I am."

***

Less than five minutes later, Jayson stood outside Allison's closed door holding some of his extra clothes. He almost lost her today. Queasiness roiled in his belly. Over the past few months, she had become an important part of his world. Life without her would be far more brutal, than the loss of Jacquelyn a few years ago. He hoped never to experience such a thing again.

He knocked on the wooden door, lifted the latch, and pushed it open. Allison sat on the rocking chair with the baby in her arms. Her eyes widened, and her sensuous mouth dropped open at the sight of him. Guess she hadn't expected him to stroll right in.

"You startled me." She quickly covered her exposed skin with a small cloth.

He stepped into the room, laid his armful of clothing on the bed, and turned.

She quirked her eyebrow. "What are you doing?"

"I'm moving my things in."

"Why?"

He gave her a quizzical look. "If I'm going to be sleeping here, I should have my stuff."

"You're sleeping here?"

"Wasn't that our agreement?" God, she looked lovely with her hair all tussled after her nap. Her cheeks were rosy, with a light blush forming. She tried to cover her thin, white nightgown with the baby in her arms, but not much was left to his imagination.

"I just had the baby," she proclaimed.

"I've kept my end of the bargain these past months. Now it's time for you to keep yours. I won't be pushing you to consummate the marriage, but I will be sleeping here with you from now on."

She nibbled at her bottom lip. Her chest rose and fell heavily as she inhaled and released a full breath. With a shaky hand, she pushed an errant tendril of hair behind her ear.

He busied himself with putting his things away in a few empty lower drawers in the high-boy. It figured she took all the good ones. He might have to discuss with her the concept of sharing space.

Out of the corner of his eye, he saw the shock on her face as she buttoned the front of her nightgown with one hand. He'd obviously rendered her speechless and she struggled to absorb his declaration. This was not what she had expected.

200

Oh, well, Jasmine was right. He had to take charge and not let any more excuses keep them apart.

The baby fussed, and she averted her attention to the bundle snuggled against her chest.

He closed the last drawer, then sat on the chair next to her rocker.

"Can I hold him?" He held out his hands.

She passed him their squirming son. The baby's little hands and fingers moved stiffly and frantically, while he made little grunting noises.

Allison wrung her hands. "I don't know what's the matter. He just finished eating. He looks uncomfortable."

Jayson gazed down at his new son's rosy cheeks and button nose. His heart melted.

"Do you have a little burp?" he asked softly in a silly voice. He placed the baby upright on his shoulder and tapped the infant's back.

"How do you know how to do that?" Allison asked in awe.

"When I was in Washington, I spent every Sunday afternoon with my cousin, Lucille, and her family. She had a whole brood of children, of all ages. You had to learn quickly to keep up with them." He chuckled.

"You're very good at it," she remarked.

"I had a bit of practice. She made me work for my supper." He grinned as the baby let out a loud burp.

"By the look of things, you ate pretty well at Lucille's." Her smile lit up her honey-brown eyes and made them sparkle, making her tease more endearing.

"How are you feeling?" His voice turned quickly from mirth to concern.

Allison nervously covered her chest with her forearms. Perhaps, she was feeling a little awkward. They were sitting in her room, *their room*, together and she wore only a thin sleeping gown. Maybe she was thinking about sharing her bed with him tonight.

She would have to get used to it.

"I feel like I rolled down a hill, head-over-heels. I'm not sure there is a part of me not aching after the groundbreaking ride and everything else that happened." A light blush appeared on her cheeks. "The nap helped immensely. I'll be fine."

"Good to hear." He repositioned the baby in the crook of his arm and played with his tiny fingers. "I want you to know, no one will ever take you from the ranch again. I'm afraid I developed a false sense of security because my mother was always safe here. From now on, you and our family will be well-protected. Chase went to town to hire a few good men. I don't want you believing something could happen to you at any moment. I want you to feel comfortable living on the ranch, and in Montana."

Allison met his stare. "I've always felt free from harm here. I know being taken today was only a chance occurrence. Not something likely to happen again."

He let out a breath he didn't know he was holding. "I'm glad you feel that way."

"Thank you for all you did for me today."

"That's what husbands do for their wives." He smiled. "I think I smell dinner cooking. If you're up to it, we could bring the baby downstairs and properly introduce him to the family. I know Daniel is itching to hold him, and if I'm not mistaken, Chase and Nathan are also."

"I'd like that. Can you bring him down while I get changed?"

"Sure. Have you settled on a name?" They had never talked about a name. He was worried she'd choose one which reminded her of the baby's real father. That every day when she said her son's name, she would think about the man she'd left behind.

"If you have no objections, I'd like to call him Brandyn. It's my father's middle name."

He exhaled slowly and gave her an ear-to-ear grin. "I think Brandyn McKay is a good, strong name. I like it."

***

A cooing sound coming from the direction of the window woke Allison from a sound sleep. Her eyes opened slowly. A silhouette of a shirtless male was outlined clearly against the light of the full moon.

Jayson.

She remained still and watched him through heavy-lidded eyes, appreciating the sinewy male form. He held her swaddled baby in his arms and swayed back and forth.

"Your mother, she had a hard day. We'll give her a few more minutes of rest before we wake her." He whispered but she easily heard the words over the distant noises of the night.

The baby sucked loudly. In the dim light, she saw Jayson was using the tip of his pinky to pacify her son.

202

"See this," he held Brandyn up facing the yard. "This is the McKay ranch. This is your home. You'll grow up here with all your brothers, sisters, and cousins. You are a McKay now and part of our family."

Her heart grew too big for her chest and her breath caught in her throat.

Jayson's finger came out of her son's mouth and the infant fussed.

Allison sat on the edge of the bed and donned her silk wrapper. She had purposefully dressed in one of her more expensive sleeping gowns, with a line of little pearl buttons running down the front, in case her husband caught sight of her in her nightclothes. Her breasts were exceptionally full and hard. She hoped Jayson didn't notice the change in her body. If he did, she hoped he liked her new shape and found her attractive. She slipped her bare feet into silk slippers, lit the oil lamp on the nightstand, and made her way to the window.

Jayson glanced down at her standing at his side. "Brandyn woke so I was showing him the ranch."

She chuckled softly. "And I'm sure he's interested in hearing all about it at this hour."

"I didn't want to wake you. You looked so peaceful."

He watched me while I slept. Her face heated, and she was glad he couldn't see the color change in the darkened room. Would she ever get used to their sharing such close quarters? It was unsettling having a man around all the time, even if Jasmine put a screen up in the corner to give her a little privacy.

"I'm afraid I didn't hear him cry. I hope I'm not one of those mothers who's not attentive to her child's needs."

"Don't worry. I was already awake when he stirred. I changed him."

"You know how to do that, too?"

"I told you. I had practice, besides I'm a quick learner," he said in a playful voice.

She raised her arms for the baby. "Here, let me feed him and settle him back to sleep."

Jayson tilted his head toward the rocking chair. "Go get comfortable, and I'll hand him to you."

She sat in the chair and got herself into a good position. As Jayson sauntered over in his bare feet, she had a chance to admire his unclothed chest and low-slung trousers. His chiseled muscles danced in interesting patterns as both the moonlight and lamplight hit the peaks and valleys at different angles. When she reached for Brandyn, the bare skin of Jayson's arms brushed against hers. Every fiber in her body stirred. She longed to linger but knew she couldn't.

How was she ever going to reside in the same room as this man, whose every move, look, or action set her aflame with want of intimacy?

As she cuddled the baby, small whimpers broke the quiet, and her son nuzzled against her breast. She reached for a blanket to lay over her shoulder, to hide from sight.

Jayson sat on the cushioned chair next to her. "Please, don't cover up," he implored in a husky voice.

Tingles coursed through her body. She gazed into her husband's pleading eyes. All modesty dissolved. She opened her robe, unbuttoned her gown, and exposed a well-rounded breast. Positioning the baby's lips close to her nipple, she teased him to latch on. Soon enough he suckled.

Jayson stared at them in the dim light, his eyes glossy. For the next half hour, they sat in companionable silence, listening to the baby feeding and the noises of the night.

~Chapter Twenty-Four~

B ang. Bang. Bang.

The sound of hammers striking metal echoed through the valley.

Jayson pounded the last of his nails into a wooden shingle and wiped the beads of sweat from his brow with the back of his hand. Looking up, he surveyed the rolling green fields spread out before him. Being up on the roof of the newly built sawmill gave him an unobstructed view in all directions of the McKay ranch. The main house sat grandly in the distance, next to the blue waters of the pond. Across the way, a few stray cattle dotted the landscape. He'd have to remember to have Giles send men up on the ridge to round up the strays and return the animals to the herd.

The ranch's new building was situated directly over a fast-moving stream to take advantage of converting the flowing water into a source of energy. His soon-to-be-constructed waterwheel would run his saws, saving on manpower. A few more weeks and the sawmill would be completed.

He stared longingly at the pond. The heat of the day soaked his shirt and he yearned for a cool dip in the water.

"I'm done with my sack of nails. What do you say we pack up and take a quick swim before supper?"

Chase, who worked a few feet away, glanced up. "Ten more nails and I'll be right behind you."

Jayson nodded. Chase had volunteered to help him with the roof. By the end of the next day, they'd be finished with the shingles. He welcomed his brother's help. The man was an ox when it came to physical labor and did the work of two men.

Tucking his hammer in his belt, Jayson shimmied down the ladder to the ground below.

Two weeks had passed since Allison's abduction and Brandyn's arrival. He couldn't bring himself to venture far from the house. The need to protect his family was strong. A pang of nagging guilt plagued him. He should've been more vigilant. Allison should never have been put through such a fright, nor should she have been forced to deliver her baby in the woods. He'd underestimated the safety of the ranch.

Before the kidnapping, the sheriff assured him the man responsible for slaughtering his steers and Kincade's sheep was long gone. Since the weasel was identified and fled the territory, no more brutal animal killings had occurred. Jayson let his guard drop, thinking the danger had passed.

I should've known better. There's always danger.

He frowned. So many things could've gone wrong that day. He couldn't stop playing the scenarios over and over in his head, but he knew it did no good ruminating about the past. To quell his apprehensions, Chase hired six gunmen. Their job was to keep an eye on the property and guard the women.

The new hires eased his mind some, but he still watched over things himself. If his brothers thought he was being too protective, no one voiced their opinions. They harbored their own regrets for leaving the women so defenseless. He noticed they, too, stuck around the house more often than usual.

Jayson took a long swig of water from his canteen. He tidied the area around the sawmill and waited for Chase to join him on the ground.

Together, the two men walked side by side down the path toward the pond.

"I left a pile of clean clothes on the dock this morning." He swept back his sweat-soaked hair with one hand.

"I didn't think of it. Do you suppose your wife will mind if, after our swim, I run up to the house buck-naked? I'm sure she'd love to set her eyes on a perfectly-muscled male body, instead of your scrawny one."

He shoved Chase sideways off the path. "I'd mind. Don't even think about it."

Chase laughed and pushed him back.

A grin played on his lips. Lately, he noticed a change in his rapport with his brothers. The way they were all getting along reminded him of old times. Before his accident.

Over the past few years since the fire, he'd endeavored to make everyone as miserable as he was, especially those closest to him. Life had dealt him a bad hand, and he wanted everyone to suffer along with him. How selfish and self-centered he'd been. His mother buffered some of his anger and frustration when she was alive, but after she passed, all bets were off, and his brothers were the first in his line of fire. He'd bark out orders, hoping they wouldn't get it right. Just so he could get riled up at them.

So he could feel something.

206

Allison had changed that. He no longer felt trapped, unfulfilled, or angry with his situation. There was hope for a good life.

He glanced sideways at Chase. "The Cattlemen's Ball is coming up. A few months ago, I booked rooms in Helena for a few nights' stay. It's in a couple of weeks. I wasn't sure we could attend, with the baby and all, but I talked to Nathan, and he said Brandyn is strong and healthy. If Allison wants to go, I plan on renting a coach. It'll make traveling easier for her and the baby. It might be good to get away from the ranch for a few days. Take her shopping. Did you want to join us?"

"Maybe. Could Jasmine come along?" Chase asked.

"Sure. Allison would like her company. Of course, that means you'll have to share a room." He raised an eyebrow at his brother. "Either with her, or Nathan and Daniel."

"Whatever you do, don't tell her I suggested it. Let Jasmine think it's coming from you." Chase brushed his damp hair back with one hand.

"Why?"

Chase stopped in his tracks and yanked on Jayson's arm, so he'd stop too. "She probably won't go if she thinks I'm behind it. She doesn't want anyone to know we're spending so much time together."

"It's obvious, considering the way you drool after her every time you look her way."

"She has some particular notions about us being together. She says I should be looking elsewhere. She also says she respects you and Allison too much and locks me out of her room at night."

"It's tough being around a beautiful woman and not being able to bed her. Believe me, I know."

"In that regard, I think I'm doing better than you. At least, she's agreed to sneak away with me from time to time. Although, it can be dangerous. I swear, the other day I came home with a thistle in my ass. Hurt like hell."

The image of Chase struggling to pluck a thorn out of his butt made Jayson chuckle loudly.

Chase thumped his back with an open hand. "I don't know what you're laughing about, from the looks of things, you still haven't gotten to that point."

He shook his head and started walking. "I don't know what I was thinking when I agreed to Allison's stipulation of not consummating our marriage the night I married her."

"You probably got all flustered when you realized what a lucky son-of-a-bitch you were." Chase snickered.

A low groan rumbled in his throat. "I kick myself all the time for my mistake. The woman drives me absolutely crazy. Now that we share the same bedroom, one look at her in her underclothes or the smell of her nestled next to me in the middle of the night gets me unhinged. I'm sleeping less than ever. I can't even touch her like I did before the baby came. I'm worried I could lose control at any moment. Brandyn is the only thing keeping me sane. Him, and knowing Allison needs time to heal."

"Wow, you've got it bad. No wonder you've been working non-stop on the sawmill."

"A hammer in my hand is a great way to get out my frustrations. That, and a good cold swim in the pond."

The water was up ahead. Jayson untucked his damp shirt from inside his pants, undid the buttons, and opened his shirt wide. He heaved Chase off the pathway. "Race you."

"No fair," Chase yelled, struggling to regain his balance.

Jayson sprinted ahead, unbuckling his belt at a dead run. A few seconds later, Chase's footsteps pounded behind him.

A big smile crossed Jayson's face. *Just like old times!*

~Chapter Twenty-Five~

"Would you care to dance?" Allison held out her gloved hand. The musicians readied themselves to start playing after a short break and colorfully dressed couples moved onto the dance floor in preparation.

"Again?" Jayson grinned.

A soft titter sprung from the back of her throat. "Yes, again. You know very well my time at the Cattlemen's Ball is quickly coming to an end. Soon enough I'll be back in our hotel room feeding our hungry son and Daniel will be attending the dance in my place. I might not get too many more chances to dance with my husband."

Jayson bowed slightly, took her hand, and pulled her close. "My pleasure," he whispered huskily in her ear.

At their contact, she caught her breath. If possible, her husband was more handsome than usual. His black frock coat and trousers were cut from the finest imported cloth. The suit was so impeccably tailored, the material fit his muscular frame flawlessly. Under his jacket, he wore a gold silk-embossed vest over a white shirt whose stiff collar was secured by a narrow black bow tie.

Jayson stood taller than most of the men in the room. She tilted her head and stared into his sparkling blue eyes. There was a new softening of his features. The changes were very appealing.

As she savored his intimate touch, she reminded herself they were not alone and grudgingly widened the space between them. All evening long, curious stares followed the couple around the room. Jayson hadn't attended such an event in years, and his presence was causing quite a stir.

When the music began, he enclosed her in his strong arms and twirled her around with ease. For a man who didn't care to dance, he moved like he'd learned the steps before he'd learned to walk. His graceful moves put her past partners to shame. Each time he pulled her close, she inhaled his heady aroma and her legs weakened from the assault. The heat their bodies generated was so intense, small beads of sweat moistened her chest.

As they kept time with the music, she glanced around the room at the other brightly dressed attendees. The Montana Stockgrowers Association's annual Cattlemen's Ball was more elegant than she imagined and as fancy as any ball back in Boston. The room itself rose two stories tall and was illuminated by three massive chandeliers hanging from the ceiling. The walls were off-white with gold decorative trim, forming eye-catching patterns around the oversized windows and double doors. Ranchers and their wives from all over Montana were present, decked out in their finery. The ball was abuzz with excitement and energy. Many of the ranchers hadn't seen each other in a long time. They were anxious to talk about their ranches, the Montana Territory, and plans for the future.

The McKay's had arrived in Helena two nights earlier. Thankfully, Jayson had planned ahead and booked them a few coveted rooms at the Paradise Hotel, paying in advance. For their journey, he had rented a stagecoach, insisting she, Brandyn, and Jasmine would be more comfortable traveling in a fancier conveyance than their own open carriage. Jayson shared a padded seat with her and the baby, while his brothers rode their horses alongside. The trip was long, but her husband offered her his shoulder to sleep on when exhaustion rolled over her.

The day before, the whole family strolled through the bustling city streets of Helena while they shopped for a fancy dress for Jasmine. Of course, her friend balked at attending the dance, but the family wore Jasmine down until she had no other choice but to accept their invitation. The fashionable ball gown Jasmine chose was so breathtaking, Chase's face lit up like a Roman candle when he gazed upon her in the hotel lobby, making the purchase priceless.

Allison wore her blue gown—the one too extravagant for Flat Rock. For the first time in many weeks, since before the birth of her son, she felt pretty. At least her husband and brothers-in-law voiced their admiration, causing her insides to warm from their unsolicited praise.

When the dance ended, Jayson introduced her to an older couple, Mr. and Mrs. Silverstone, who owned a ranch outside Helena. She made a mental note of who they were for future reference. So far tonight she had a long list of people she'd met. She doubted she would recall everyone, but this pleasant couple deserved to be remembered.

Allison held Jayson's arm loosely as he discussed his sawmill and how the McKay ranch was harvesting hay to supplement their herd's feed supply that winter. Like the other ranchers he talked to, the older gentleman's jaw dropped in wonder. Jayson was a visionary and generated respect amongst his peers. She was proud to be on his arm.

While quietly observing her husband, she realized he was not the same man she'd met a few months ago. The man she first laid eyes on was serious, self-conscious, and standoffish. Today, speaking about things dear to him, passion resonated in his voice. He presented himself as engaging and self-assured. His scars were fading before her eyes. The difference was heartwarming, and she hoped she and the baby had something to do with his startling changes.

When Mr. and Mrs. Silverstone took their leave, Chase, Jasmine, and Nathan joined them.

"Why aren't you dancing?" she asked Nathan.

Nathan chuckled. "Because, unfortunately for me, my brothers have already claimed the most beautiful women here, and I'm having a devil of a time finding one for myself."

"I'll drink to that." Chase lifted his cup to his brothers and tipped his head to the ladies.

Allison's face heated at the compliment. When she glanced at Jasmine, she noticed her friend blushed also.

Jayson leaned close to be heard over the music. "Would you like some punch?"

She nodded.

He raised an eyebrow toward Jasmine. "Can I get you something? I'm not my brothers. You can trust me to bring you a cup that's not spiked if that's your preference."

Jasmine smiled softly. "I'm all set, thanks."

Chase and Nathan's guilt-ridden faces caused Allison's hand to fly to her mouth to cover a giggle. Her husband knew how to annoy his brothers. They gave him a dirty look for bringing up a sore subject.

"I'll be right back." He smirked as he spun on his heels and headed toward the refreshment table.

Nathan stepped in front of her and gave her a practiced bow. "Would you do me the honor?"

"My pleasure." She curtsied and gave Nathan her gloved hand. He guided her out into the crowd of revelers.

As Nathan swirled her around, she noticed how much alike the brothers were. Nathan was as agile as Jayson, and from what she'd observed, so was Chase. She enjoyed being part of the McKay family. Father Peter was right; they were good men. She was lucky to have ended up in their midst.

When the dance finished, Nathan escorted her back to Chase and Jasmine. Jayson was surprisingly absent. She scanned the outskirts of the room.

"Where's Jayson?"

"Umm...he's getting you some punch." Chase shifted his weight from one leg to the other.

"That was a little while ago." She glanced at the table set up with drinks next to the open patio doors, but Jayson was nowhere to be seen.

Chase stared at the tips of his boots. "He got waylaid by an old friend."

She placed her hands on her hips and stamped her foot. "Chase McKay, what aren't you telling me?"

He grimaced, shaking his head. "When he was getting your drink, I saw Jacquelyn follow him. They exchanged a few words and stepped outside onto the patio."

Allison's stomach quaked from the news. "Jacquelyn?" she squeaked. "His former fiancée, Jacquelyn?"

"The one and the same," Chase said flatly.

"Did you know she was here?"

"I only noticed her when you were dancing with Nathan."

She exhaled slowly. "Well, I'm sure everything's all right." The words spoken were as much for her benefit as those around her.

Nathan squeezed her upper arm. "Yes, I'm sure they're just talking about old times."

"He'll be back any minute," Chase added nervously.

She stared at the opening to the back yard. The shuddering in her belly turned to gnawing. "What do you think she's doing here?"

"Probably political reasons," Nathan responded. "Montana Territory wants to become a state. A lot of politicians are flocking to the area to help with the process. She has a fondness for those in politics."

Suddenly, a wave of uncertainty pounded in her head. She wiped her sweaty palms on the sides of her dress.

Jacquelyn was here. Her husband's first love. The one who broke his heart.

Jasmine gave her a pointed look. "You have nothing to worry about."

"Oh, I'm not worried, surprised is all." She hoped God wouldn't strike her down for the blatant lie. She crossed her arms over her chest and was startled to find her left breast was much bigger than her right. Brandyn needed to be fed soon. A growing urgency caught her off guard.

All her building apprehension regarding her husband's impromptu meeting got pushed to the back of her mind. She straightened her shoulders and lifted her head. "It's time I get back to Brandyn. If you'll excuse me, I have to let Jayson know I'm returning to the hotel. I'll send Daniel over once I relieve him. Have a good night."

Allison turned and headed toward the patio. The hairs on the back of her neck stood when she felt their eyes on her, but she kept walking, head held high. She hated to interrupt Jayson's rendezvous, but she had no other options; the baby won out over any insecurities.

When she stepped onto the stone patio, she stopped to allow her vision to adjust to the dim light. The moon, along with strategically placed lanterns, illuminated the area in a soft glow. Jayson stood a few feet from the doorway, his back toward her as he faced one of the most beautiful women she'd ever seen.

Allison swallowed hard.

Even in the shadowed light, the woman's delicately shaped face was framed flawlessly by elegantly coiffed curls which highlighted her high cheekbones and perfectly shaped lips. The lady was tall and wore an expensive gown, cut in the latest fashion, with a low bodice showing off ample cleavage. Her stance was one of grace and poise, exposing her long neck to its fullest advantage.

Allison sucked in her breath and remembered her mission. She needed to return to the hotel to feed her son before she leaked all over her bodice and humiliated herself in front of all these strangers.

Stepping up behind Jayson, she touched his arm and prayed her voice would come out strong and sure when she spoke. "Excuse me. I just wanted to let you know I'm returning to the hotel."

Jayson whirled around, sloshing the drink in his hand over the rim of his cup. He wiped the droplets off his coat sleeve and put the glass down on a nearby table.

"I'm sorry to keep you waiting for your drink. I ran into an old friend." He laid a hand on the side of Allison's waist and guided her a few steps forward.

"Let me introduce you. Miss Jacquelyn Brown, this is my wife, Mrs. Allison McKay."

Allison extended her gloved hand. "Pleased to meet you, Miss Brown."

"Likewise, Mrs. McKay." Jacquelyn grabbed a few of Allison's fingers and gave a little shake. The woman smiled, but the warmth never reached her eyes.

"I didn't see you earlier amongst the dancers. Have you only just arrived?"

"My escort and I had carriage trouble," Jacquelyn said.

"I hope you have a pleasant time at the ball." She looked up at Jayson. "I, on the other hand, must call it a night. I have to get back to our son."

"Of course, we should be on our way." Jayson's face was etched with concern.

"Oh, no, you don't have to leave on my account. Please, stay and enjoy yourself. I'll make my way back to the hotel on my own. It's only across the street. I'll be fine."

"You shouldn't be on the streets alone. I'm ready to leave."

"If you don't mind," she replied.

Jayson tipped his head in Jacquelyn's direction. "Good to see you."

Allison tilted her head. "Good-bye, Miss Brown."

"Good-bye," Jacquelyn replied.

As Allison turned, the woman's face scrunched up in a puckered frown, making her beautiful features jagged and unbecoming. Walking through the archway, she felt invisible daggers pierce her back. The woman was obviously annoyed by her interruption.

Jayson guided her through the ballroom to the front doors. They retrieved her wrap and his hat.

Nathan met them in the foyer.

Jayson laid a comforting hand on her arm when he spoke to his brother. "We're leaving. Be on the lookout for Daniel; we're sending him over."

"I'll watch for him," Nathan said.

"Ready?" Jayson asked.

She nodded.

Jayson escorted her outside, across the street, and into the Paradise Hotel. The town was busier than expected at this late hour, and she was glad she hadn't followed through with her original plan to return alone, for the crowds were loud and rowdy.

When they reached their room, she heard squawking noises on the other side of the wooden portal.

Jayson unlocked the door and they walked in. Daniel stood at the window, holding Brandyn against his chest as he patted the baby's back.

Daniel turned as they entered the room. "He started fussing a few minutes ago. I changed him and that helped, but I think he's hungry."

She made her way to her brother-in-law and removed her long gloves. "Thank you so much for taking care of him."

"You know how much I like watching my nephew. Did you have a good time?"

She reached for her son. "The best. Now it's time for you to go on over. There's still plenty of food and drink to be had, and more than one pretty young lady looking for a dance partner."

Daniel, who was already handsomely dressed in a tailored suit, grinned broadly. He leaned down and kissed Brandyn's forehead. "I'm on my way."

"Come back with Nathan and Chase," Jayson called out before shutting the door on his brother's disappearing form.

She put the squirming baby on the bed and unbuttoned the pearl buttons down the front of her gown. "I've a mind not to ruin this dress. I don't have many good ones left. Most have had the misfortune of encountering my cookstove and haven't survived."

Jayson smiled ear to ear. "I love this gown. The color suits you perfectly. Let me help."

He lifted the material over her head until she stood in just her camisole, corset, and petticoats. Sharing such close quarters with Jayson over the past month had made her comfortable being in her underthings while in the privacy of their bedroom. She tried not to think about the way she looked with only thin layers of material covering her womanly parts.

Her body had changed since the birth of her son. Because she felt rounder, she was extremely excited about wearing a corset again. She'd missed her hourglass figure. The contraptions always made her feel feminine and graceful and she hoped Jayson saw her that way.

After gathering the baby, she sat in the rocking chair Jayson and Nathan had carried up from the lobby on the first day of their stay. Jayson said she would be more comfortable nursing in the chair and talked the owner of the hotel into letting them move furniture around. He also insisted they bring the cradle along, strapping it to the back of the coach, so Brandyn felt secure in his own bed.

This was the last feeding of the night before her son settled in for a long interval of sleep. During the early morning hours when the baby woke, Jayson always got up with him. She didn't know what was wrong with her, but exhaustion ruled her lately. Her husband would wait until the last minute and then he would prod her awake. They would sit together at dawn while Brandyn fed, listening to the baby's suckling, and the noises of the waking ranch. Their early morning time together was always so peaceful.

Allison pulled down the lace edge of the camisole exposing her engorged breast and let the baby nurse. Thankfully, she hadn't leaked through to her ball gown.

I got back just in time.

Jayson removed his frock coat and silk vest, laying them over the back of a chair. He undid his tie and unbuttoned his white shirt to the waist. She viewed his muscular body peeking out through the opening and her heart skipped a beat. He plopped himself onto the bed, squeaking the mattress springs, and leaned his back against the headboard. "Did you hear Mr. Silverstone say he wanted to put up a few more buildings on his ranch? He needs some lumber and has agreed to purchase mine."

"When will the sawmill be operational?" She stroked the peach fuzz on the top of her son's head. Jayson had been working hard to finish the sawmill. It had surprised her when he decided to take time off so they could come to Helena.

"We should be up and running in a couple of weeks. I need to buy a few draft horses and a bigger wagon for delivering the lumber. I'm also going to have to hire some more men. We're going to have to add onto the bunkhouse. We might need to hire another cook to help Cookie, although I don't know how he's going to take the news. He won't like sharing the space, but I can't let him cook for all those men."

"Maybe you could call the other cook his assistant," she suggested.

He locked his fingers and placed them behind his head. "Maybe I could."

His shirt opened wider. Her breath caught in her throat. He was so gorgeous. He didn't even know it. His voice was full of excitement, and his eyes twinkled with passion as he spoke about his plans.

Allison didn't want to think about his meeting with Jacquelyn. On their walk back to the hotel he hadn't said a word about her. She wondered how the encounter had affected him. The two hadn't seen each other since right after the fire—that's what Nathan said.

He seemed unfazed, but she couldn't be certain. The woman was so beautiful. Next to Jacquelyn, Allison imagined she looked drab.

She sighed heavily and gazed at the baby in her arms.

Back in Boston, before Robert had singled her out, she'd had a few admirers of her own. She couldn't be all that unattractive, could she? It seemed like so long ago.

Allison shook off the uneasiness plaguing her, glanced up, and tried to focus on Jayson's conversation. She smiled when he looked at her for a response, but she didn't have a clue of what he was talking about.

Her thoughts drifted off again. The past month had gone by so fast. After a few awkward moments of sharing a room and sleeping in the same bed, she and Jayson fell into an easy existence. Once her head hit the pillow, she was sound asleep. Jayson wasn't so lucky. At first, she worried he watched her during the night but then stopped bothering herself about it.

The courting had stopped. Jayson no longer touched her in the flirting manner he did prior to the baby's arrival. He kept his hands and lips to himself except to peck a kiss on her forehead at night or to touch arms when they exchanged Brandyn between them. Maybe, delivering the baby and her newly rounded shape extinguished any attraction he'd had for her.

Once in a while in bed, on the rare occasions she was half-awake, and he was slumbering, he might touch her with an arm or leg. She'd lay next to him in the dark imagining what it would be like if he stroked her body on purpose. When he woke, he always pulled away, as if embarrassed by the connection. Such a reaction always made her feel undesirable.

A knock sounded on the door, drawing her out of her thoughts.

Jayson left the bed. "Who could that be?"

He grabbed her wrap and draped the covering over her shoulders to hide the sight of her nursing Brandyn from the doorway. He opened the door a foot.

From her chair, she saw an older child hand a folded note to Jayson. He gave the young boy a coin from his trouser pocket and closed the door.

"What is it?" she asked.

Jayson opened the folded paper and read the words to himself. His expression turned flat and unreadable. "A request to meet with someone I talked to at the dance. Probably some unfinished business. I have to go out for a few minutes. Will you be all right alone?"

She nodded and gave him a weak smile. A lump formed in her throat.

Jayson rebuttoned his shirt and donned his suit coat. He didn't bother to put on his gold vest or tie. At the doorway, he turned. "I'll be right back. For safety's sake, I'm locking the door from the outside. The extra key is on the bureau. Do you need anything while I'm out?"

She shook her head. "I'm all set, thank you."

Then he was gone.

~Chapter Twenty-Six~

The wooden door shut with a thud.

Dread churned Allison's stomach, making her queasy. The shawl over her shoulders grew unbearably heavy. She shrugged off the material, letting it fall to the floor. Carrying her nursing son in her arms, she walked to the window and stared at the street below. Her chest tightened with guilt for peering out from behind the curtain, but she had to know.

Scanning the lamp-lit walkways across the street, she found who she was looking for. There was no missing the tall woman, dressed in a dark cloak, walking at a fast clip toward the livery stable.

A frosty chill traveled to Allison's core as the woman removed the hood covering her perfectly coifed hair and ducked into the barn through a side door.

Allison had hoped she was wrong.

Jayson was halfway across the main thoroughfare when he turned and glanced at their window in the hotel. She backed into the darkened shadows, out of sight, and held her breath. After a moment, she gathered her nerve and peeked out again, only to see her husband disappear through the same door as *Jacquelyn*.

A quickened heartbeat pounded in her chest. The room reeled. She sat on the edge of the rocking chair, clinging to Brandyn, still attached to her breast. Her shoulders rounded as she focused on her breathing.

I'm losing him.

She was losing her husband to another woman.

Their broken marriage was all her fault. After Robert had rejected her, she came to Montana seeking only security and a name for her baby. She had been the one who forced Jayson to wait to consummate their marriage. Made him agree to her ridiculous terms. She thought she could live with a man as his wife, sharing only mutual respect, without any deep emotional connection.

How naive!

What a fool she was for never expecting her feelings for Jayson to change, and even more so for not bedding him when they did.

Brandyn's eyelids grew heavy and his suckling slowed. Holding him against her shoulder, she patted his back and returned to the window to stare at the livery's side door.

She should've agreed to consummate the marriage on their wedding night, but she had been so scared.

Having had only one experience with a man, she was afraid of embarrassing herself with inept and innocent fumbling.

At least, that's what she'd told herself.

She nibbled her lower lip. To be honest, she was more fearful of reliving the inadequacy, pain, and repulsion she felt the first time she copulated with a man.

Her only encounter had taken place with Robert at the Tucker's Ball. The night started out festive and fun. She had indulged in too much wine, so Robert escorted her out into the winter-bare gardens for some fresh air. Lanterns placed around the perimeter of the yard lit up the dark like fireflies on a warm summer's night. The sight had taken her breath away.

Robert whispered words of endearment in her ear as he guided her across the way and through the double glass doors of Mr. Tucker's study. Being outside caused the wintery cold to run through her veins and he held her close, rubbing his hands up and down her arms until she warmed. She found it odd a bottle of brandy and two glasses awaited them in the dim, fire-lit room. He checked the main door to make sure it was locked before he poured her a drink.

They sat side by side on an upholstered couch. At Robert's urging, she swallowed a few big gulps of the smooth drink. When her glass was empty, he professed his love and vowed they would one day marry and share a life together.

At that moment, even without a formal engagement, she was the happiest she had ever been. The most eligible bachelor in Boston wanted her above all others. Robert was the only son of one of the most respected founding families of Boston. Rich beyond compare. Her position as his wife would have advanced her up the social hierarchy to one of the foremost ladies in society. A challenging position, but she imagined she'd bear the responsibility well enough and make him proud.

Robert's kisses were gentle and sweet at first, but then they grew demanding and sloppy. He pressed her back into the couch, stroked her breast with one hand, and with the other, he rummaged underneath yards of satin fabric in a quest to find her most intimate parts.

She went along with his actions because she believed with all her heart they were meant to be together and would share the rest of their lives as man and wife.

How wrong she was.

Once her underthings were out of the way, he wasted no time getting on top of her. Everything happened so fast, her head swirled with uncertainty. Whether the fog clouding her good judgment was a product of the alcohol or suppressed desires, she couldn't be sure.

He exposed her breast to the air and licked her taut nipple. She remembered how her body jerked with new awareness. Never had she imagined such a sensation and she thought she might explode from want of something unknown. Without given a chance to explore her new yearnings, the sentiment was soon gone. Abruptly, he bit down hard on her tender bud...obliterating her evolving pleasure...while he mounted and plowed into her at the same time.

Even now she cringed, recalling the force of his thrusts and the stabbing pain that followed. He'd seized what he wanted without a care for her well-being. Afterward, when he'd collapsed on top of her, preventing her from filling her lungs with air, he told her how wonderful her body felt under his, and how much he'd enjoy such an act again in the future.

No words of love.

She shuddered at the memories. Robert had been the man of her dreams. Even though she loved him, she couldn't shake the feelings of disappointment and shame. The act had repulsed her. But, instead of blaming him, she convinced herself it was the alcohol and her own inexperience that had robbed her of enjoyment. On subsequent visits, she adamantly refused his further advances, insisting on waiting until after the wedding to relive their union. Always hoping the next time they joined together, the experience would be better.

But, the next time never came. Although Robert officially proposed after finding out about the baby, his father refused to give his blessing. As the daughter of a wealthy shipping merchant, she wasn't good enough for the Winthrops of Boston, one of society's elite Boston Brahmin families. Robert chose his inheritance over her and the baby. With his sudden change of heart, her life had drastically altered. Decisions were made for the sake of her child.

When she arrived in Montana, the very thought of lying with a stranger terrified her. If copulating was horrible with a man she loved, what would it be like with a man she didn't even know? That's why she was so reluctant to consummate her marriage in the beginning.

Now that she harbored tender feelings toward Jayson, she was even more terrified. What if she turned out to be a cold woman in bed? What if she hated the act? What if he didn't like her new soft curves after childbirth? Would she displease him? All these questions ran rampant in her mind and made her pull back from the intimacy she knew he craved.

Was he now fulfilling his needs with another woman?

She trembled.

Where was the courage that enabled her to leave behind everything she held dear and travel to the unknown Montana Territory to marry a stranger?

Brandyn burped against her shoulder. She inhaled deeply of his pleasing baby scent, nuzzling her nose in his fuzzy hair. His eyes were closed. He would sleep for a few hours. She swaddled him in his blanket and placed him in the cradle.

Jacquelyn might want Jayson for whatever reason, but he was already Allison's husband and she didn't intend to give him up.

A quick look outside confirmed she still had time before he returned. A plan formed to get her husband back. She opened the trunk at the foot of the bed and retrieved the softest, sheerest sleeping gown she owned. Quickly, she doffed her corset, camisole, petticoats, drawers, and shoes. She debated whether to remove her silk stockings, then rolled them off, too.

At the water basin, she poured a few drops of rose scent in the lukewarm water and sponge bathed. When finished, she donned her nightgown, letting the silky fabric slide over her body. The drape of the cloth accentuated her curves and showed off her cleavage in a most risqué way. A dress shop owner in Boston had assured her this nightdress would set any man aflame.

Of course, she had bought the garment with Robert in mind.

She winced at the thought.

Now...the sight of her near undress was for Jayson's eyes only.

Allison moved around the room and extinguished all but two oil lamps, turning the flames down low. She sat on a cushion-topped stool in front of the mirrored vanity and unpinned her hair, letting the soft curls fall around her shoulders and down to her waist. Picking up her brush, she slowly passed the bristles through the strands. Her hand dropped to her lap when footsteps creaked on the rough pine boards in the hallway.

A light knock sounded on the wood portal and the key turned in the lock.

"It's me."

Her stomach flipped at her husband's voice. She clenched the brush handle with both hands.

The door opened. Jayson stepped in and relocked the door. He slowly turned and noticed her sitting in front of the mirror. Her heart lodged in her throat when his eyes raked her up and down. He stood unnaturally still, his face taut with a masked expression guarding against any outward emotion.

Allison winced at his reserve and assumed Jacquelyn was to blame. She set the brush on the top of the vanity and entwined her fingers to keep from fidgeting. "That didn't take long."

As if her words drew him from his stupor, he stepped forward and went to the cradle. "How's the baby?"

"I fed him, and he fell back asleep." She cringed at his quick change of subject.

He leaned over Brandyn and rubbed his head. "Sleep well, little one," he whispered.

Allison's heart skipped a beat at the warm sight, but she continued to watch him warily, unsure of how he'd treat her after being with his old fiancée.

Jayson stared down at the baby for a minute longer, and then glanced over his shoulder. "There's something I wanted to give you."

A lump formed in her throat. She swallowed hard.

He took a few steps forward until he stood in front of her. Rummaging through his coat pocket, he removed a small cloth pouch. "My father always gave my mother a keepsake after each of his sons were born. I'd like to continue his tradition by giving you this."

Her eyes widened as he pulled out an oval-shaped locket. He held out the necklace, dangling from a silver chain, for her to examine. She ran her fingertips over the intricately embossed design on the front.

"It's beautiful."

"I had it made especially for you. While you were shopping yesterday, I took Brandyn to the photographer and had a picture of him taken to fit inside. We had to take a few to get the right size."

She opened the locket and saw Brandyn's little face. Her eyes misted. A rush of emotion filled her chest.

"I love it."

"Of course, we might have to take his photograph often the way he's changing every day." He grinned. "On the other side, you can put a picture of another child."

Or, one of my husband.

Jayson unlocked the clasp and stepped closer. "Let's see how it looks."

He brought the chain around both sides of her neck and under her hair. His fingertips brushed her skin as he worked the catch, sending tingles in all directions.

Once clipped, she turned to inspect the pendant in the mirror. It hung low and rested in the valley of her breasts. The piece was exquisite.

Jayson shrugged off his jacket. "It looks good."

"It's lovely."

Sitting on the edge of the flat-topped trunk at the foot of the bed, he removed his boots and socks. "I had the back engraved," he said nonchalantly, but she could tell in the reflection of the mirror that he was watching her closely.

Taking up the piece in her trembling hands, she turned it over. *To my beautiful wife. Your husband, Jayson.*

The hairs on the back of her neck prickled. The words reminded her of the intimacy she longed for. Her eyes burned. She blinked back the moisture.

Leaving the seat by the vanity, she crossed the room. Standing before him, with her knees between his legs, she placed her hands on either side of his face.

His brows arched in surprise.

"Thank you," she whispered in a throaty voice and leaned in to kiss his lips.

The touch was electrifying. Every fiber in her being sparked.

A deep groan escaped his mouth. He gripped her waist with his hands and kissed her as if devouring a sweet morsel.

Starved for such affection, she rewarded him with her own all-consuming kiss. He held her at bay when she tried to step closer.

Freeing his mouth from hers, he breathed hoarsely, "No more, or I won't be able to stop."

She tensed. Didn't he want her? After a secret rendezvous with Jacquelyn, maybe she was too late. Maybe all he wanted was the original business deal. She gazed into his darkened blue eyes, inches from her own. Her heart pounded as if part of a drum corps. When she recognized the smoldering desire burning in their depths, her fears receded.

"I don't want you to stop." Her warm, jagged breath mingled with his as she whispered her words.

A rumble reverberated from his throat. He pressed his lips to hers, exploring her mouth with renewed vigor. His hands went under the hem of her nightgown and cupped each calf as she stood before him.

I have to tell him.

She halted her kisses and withdrew to look upon his face. "There is something you should know."

He tilted his head and examined her curiously.

"I'm...I'm not as experienced as you might think," she blurted out. "I was only with Robert once. I didn't really know what was happening..."

"Shh..." Jayson placed his forehead against hers. "Tonight, we have no past. There's only you and me. No one else."

She nodded and met his mouth halfway. The weighted necklace pulled at her neck and the cold metal splayed against her bare flesh, reminding her of the rightness of their union.

As he covered her mouth with passion, his hands leisurely journeyed behind her knees, sliding up the backside of her thighs and over the curve of her buttocks, where he gently caressed and pulled her hips toward him.

Quivers coursed through her body as she anticipated where his wandering fingers might explore next. Her need to touch him grew, and she unbuttoned the first button on his shirt, at his neck. Her knuckles skimmed over his firm chest as she moved to the next fastener in line, repeating the action again and again, until all were undone. She tugged open his shirt and helped him remove the material, her hands lingering on his exposed skin. Never had she encountered anything so glorious as his bare chest with all the rolling hills and dips to discover. Memories surfaced of a time not long ago when he sat at the table, shirtless and so desirable. She broke their kiss long enough to look down at his sculptured form and knew she was looking at perfection.

Searching out his lips again, she laid her hands on the top of his shoulders. He stiffened when she first encountered the scars running down his arm. She let her soft touch show him that his scars didn't matter. He surrendered to her ministrations and she continued, endeavoring to caress his hurt away.

All of her senses came alive. The draping night dress brushed softly against her naked skin while the hem followed his hands to her ribs. He cupped the sides of her rounded breasts, providing slight pressure, and stretched his thumbs out to stroke the tips of her nipples. A shot of lightning launched through her insides, taking her by surprise. She gasped at the sensation. An unfamiliar liquid heat pooled between her legs.

At her sharp intake of breath, Jayson stopped and glanced up. His eyes took on an almost midnight blue in the dim lamplight. Her heart soared, seeing his desire. At this moment, she could tell he had no thoughts of another woman. He only wanted her.

Jayson tugged the sleeping gown over her head, letting the material fall to the floor. He brushed soft kisses on her taut nipples. At first, she tensed, expecting pain to follow but easily relaxed at the gentleness of his touch.

This is Jayson, not Robert.

Gliding her open hands over the contours of his back, she memorized every hill and valley. The light licks of his tongue caused a small moan to erupt in the back of her throat. She arched her back. Jolts of pleasure streamed through her body.

His hand traveled to her hip and he guided her bare bottom down to straddle one of his thighs. Her mind fogged as his lips trekked a path to her collarbone and then feathered kisses along the side of her neck.

She tilted her head to give him full access, her long hair tickling her naked body. He pulled her forward until her breasts brushed against his bare chest. Her skin tingled as it contacted his sculptured muscles. One hand held the back of her head, his fingers entangling in her hair. His mouth found hers, yet again. His tongue explored deeply, teasing her to respond, so she mimicked his actions as her fingers glided over every inch of bare skin she could reach.

An all-consuming need welled up inside her.

He kneaded her breast until her breathing shallowed. She waited expectantly for him to touch her most sensitive parts and squirmed on his knee. His hand slid down her ribcage, over the curve of her hip, and to the bend of her upper thigh. He smoothly stroked her inner thigh, subtly parting her legs wider as he caressed. When she thought she couldn't stand his teasing anymore, she lifted her buttocks and he slid two fingers into the wet alcove between her legs, while at the same time rolling her nipple between his fingertips.

Allison let out a whimper and shuddered at the slick feel of his long fingers delving in and out of her inner-most parts in a rhythmic dance. She pulled away from his mouth as a moan bubbled up from the back of her throat. He recaptured

226

her lips and deepened his kisses. Her muscles contracted and relaxed around his fingers and she writhed with unfamiliar want.

When his fingers left the warmth between her legs, a profound loss flared inside her, and an ache remained in their place. He stood, forcing her to stand with him. His lips and body remained plastered against hers and she felt the hardened bulge against the front of his trousers.

While kissing her senseless, he used his hands on her hips to guide her backward. At the bed, he scooped her up in his strong arms. She grabbed onto his neck as he gently placed her on the squeaky mattress that noisily protested their weight. When her head rested on the feather pillow, he stopped his tantalizing kisses and pulled away.

She clung to his shoulders. "Please don't go," she begged in a husky voice. Had she done something wrong? Had he changed his mind?

Scanning her naked body, his eyes darkened with hunger. He pecked a light kiss on her forehead. "Alli, sweetie, I'm not going anywhere. Let me get out of my trousers, then I'll join you."

A flush warmed her already hot skin. He stepped away and shed the rest of his clothing. Decorum would have her look away, but she couldn't bring herself to do so. He was magnificent undressed. Years of physical labor had chiseled his body into one of strength and power. Curiosity got the better of her and she glanced lower to the dark hair circling his erect manhood, which stood at attention as if seeking her out. She wanted to reach out to touch the part of him that was all-male but wasn't sure if it was allowed, so she kept her hands to herself.

He lowered himself alongside her. His large hand roamed every part of her exposed body as he kissed a trail along her neck.

"You're the most gorgeous thing I've ever laid eyes on," he mumbled in her ear.

At his declaration, she sucked in her breath. Goosebumps rushed down her arms.

His fingers probed between her legs, in and out, until she squirmed under his heavenly onslaught. The likes of such sensations she'd never experienced before.

When her building slickness signaled her readiness, he repositioned himself and hovered over her. His knees parted her legs. The heat of his body fueled her fire and she clung to his shoulders, pulling him closer. As the tip of his manhood penetrated her outer sanctum, her whole body stiffened. All she could think about was the pain and disappointment that was yet to come.

Jayson noticed. "If there's pain, tell me. I'll stop."

She breathed a sigh of relief and nodded.

His head dropped down to her breast and his tongue flicked over the tender bud. A shockwave of pleasure surged through her and she had no choice but to submit to the glorious sensations taking her to the brink of desire.

He slid himself into her. The easy rhythm of the drive took her to new heights of elation. The building friction made her catch fire and flames ignited in her pelvis.

As the frenzy of movement increased, Allison did her best to keep up, not wanting to be left behind. She arched her hips to meet each thrust, causing the springs under the mattress to squeak with each lunge.

His mouth found hers. When she thought she could not stand one more second, her whole world burst into shuddering rapture. Stars exploded behind her closed eyes.

Jayson gave one last plunge before his body tensed and then melted over hers.

Holding his weight above her, he stared at her face and grinned.

She couldn't help but smile back.

In response, he brushed his lips along the top of her nose, each cheek, and then captured her lips in the softest kiss ever. When finished, he lay along her side, enveloping her in his arms, so they were one.

She curled up in his embrace and inhaled his woodsy scent. Her heart drummed in her chest and her breathing shallowed. The intimacy they'd shared overwhelmed her. Nothing at all like she'd expected. Jayson was gentle and caring. There was no pain or selfishness.

A wave of raw emotion surged from inside. Her breath hitched in her throat. Silent tears sprang from the corners of her eyes.

Jayson looked at her with concern. "Did I hurt you?"

"Not at all." She rubbed away the moisture with her free hand. "I don't know what's the matter with me. It was beautiful."

"Aww, come here." He drew her closer and kissed the top of her head.

She sprawled out across his chest and entwined her legs with his. His heartbeat drummed against her ear.

"I've been wanting to touch you for a long time. It was well worth the wait," he whispered hoarsely while stroking her bare skin.

The tears dried as she enjoyed the feel of his large hands roaming over her body, tenderly, adoringly, affectionately.

It was nice to know she was not a cold woman and could enjoy the intimacy of marriage. She no longer feared the act.

A soft contented sigh escaped her. They'd finally consummated their marriage. Annulments were hard to obtain once the deed was done. Jayson would have difficulty casting her aside for another.

Her head rose and fell in perfect rhythm with his breathing. All would be right in the world if not for the nagging vision of Jacquelyn entering the side door of the stable and Jayson following closely behind.

Before she questioned him about the meeting, blackness invaded her disturbed thoughts and sleep carried her away.

~Chapter Twenty-Seven~

The soft mewling cries of her hungry son roused Allison out of a deep slumber. The early morning sun streamed through the partially closed curtains, bathing their hotel room in a warm glow.

With her head on the feather pillow, she peered at Jayson, whose face was inches from her own. Morning stubble broke his skin's surface, although there was no growth jutting from his scar. His even breathing created a soft breeze that stirred loose hair laying upon her collar bone and his hand rested on her bare waist. The sensation of lying beside him without a stitch of clothing on was exhilarating. Nothing like she'd ever experienced before. Never had she enjoyed the feel of her body so much.

It was rare to be awake before her husband, so she perused him as he slept. He lay on his side, the quilt they shared covered only to his hip, leaving his torso fully exposed. Power and strength emanated from every knoll and vale on his brawny form, and she scanned his body appreciatively. She'd seen a good number of bare-chested men while tending the sick and knew her husband was not of an average build. In the past few months when he was shirtless, she'd looked away, too embarrassed to be caught ogling him when she didn't know if he reciprocated the attraction. After last night, she needn't be worried anymore.

The scars on his arm called to her. She longed to reach out and trace the contours of the distorted skin, the ones he was so fond of hiding, in hopes her touch had the power to absorb his anguish over them. But, she held back. There was no need to wake him, not yet. He looked so content.

Father Peter had been right about the angry marks. As time wore on, she noticed the scars less and less. When she looked at Jayson, she only saw the strong jawline, prominent cheekbones, straight nose, and almond-shaped blue eyes. His scars didn't diminish the rugged handsomeness that caused her heart to pitter-patter every time she saw him.

Her eyes traveled over the smooth, well-formed physique of his chest and lower to the trail of hairs disappearing under the blanket toward his manhood. Visions of last night surfaced. She recalled the feel of his muscles under her fingers as she explored his body. How his hands roamed over her curves...

Her insides stirred, and her cheeks flamed as intimate memories flooded her head. Their coming together had been so perfect and felt so right. She never imagined being with Jayson would be so beautiful and chastised herself for the silent tears streaming down her cheeks after the act was done. At that moment, she couldn't hold back her pent-up emotions. He had been so gentle, caring, and kind.

Not like Robert. Never like Robert.

After they consummated their marriage, Jayson didn't dismiss her. Instead, he held her soothingly until she melted in his embrace.

I'm falling in love.

The admission squeezed her chest, and she inhaled deeply.

Jayson was everything Robert was not.

The revelation of her true feelings unsettled her. She wasn't sure Jayson could love her back, not after seeing Jacquelyn. Beautiful, graceful, Jacquelyn, who once held his heart and might still.

A heavy sigh escaped her parted lips. Would her penance for her sins be that she lived out her days with a one-sided love?

Jayson's chest rose and fell in an easy tempo. He looked so relaxed. The tenseness so often tugging on the corners of his mouth was gone.

As she stared at his face, his eyes opened lazily and brightened.

"Good morning." His hand stroked her back, causing a pleasant sensation.

"Good morning. Did you sleep well?"

He grinned slyly. "Like a baby."

"Speaking of babies. Ours is hungry. I'd better feed him before he wakes the entire hotel with his wails." She made a move to leave the bed, but Jayson pulled her back.

"Kiss me first."

Allison's heart beat erratically. She leaned forward to capture his lips. The kiss was soft, sweet and full of unspoken promises.

Jayson brushed a piece of hair off her face and gazed at her deeply. "Come back to bed to feed Brandyn so I can feel you next to me."

Liquid warmth flowed through her as she did his bidding. She covered her nakedness with her thin nightdress, changed her son, gathered him up, and returned to the bed. She sat upright with her back propped on pillows as she fed the baby. Jayson snuggled against her side with a weighted arm resting over her lap in a possessive fashion. He dozed while Brandyn ate his fill.

When the baby burped, Jayson stirred. "Will you put the baby in his cradle… and come lie with me?" His voice sounded apprehensive as if she might not agree to his invitation.

Allison nodded. She knew what she was agreeing to. Her stomach fluttered with excitement. She rose and settled Brandyn in his bed. The baby gurgled and waved his chubby little hands in the air.

At the side of the bed, she dropped the flimsy nightgown from her shoulders and let the silky cloth pool at her feet. Jayson stared at her with a fiery look, his eyes raking her up and down. After their recent intimacy, she welcomed his scrutiny.

He flung the quilt back and offered her a spot alongside him. She gazed longingly at the male body spread out before her, imaging the sensations that were yet to come. Without hesitation, she climbed in and pressed her naked body against his.

He kissed her hungrily and she melted in his arms. They made love with the early morning rays shining upon their bodies. Unlike the urgency of the night before, their coming together was slow and unhurried, giving them time to explore each other's responses.

After one last explosion each, their bodies went limp with exhaustion. Jayson hovered over her as he did the previous night and kissed the tip of her nose.

"That was nice." His voice sounded deep and husky.

Sweat oozed from Allison's pores, causing a sticky film to cover her skin. She placed her hand over the scar on Jayson's cheek and stroked it tenderly with her thumb. "It was."

She hoped he could feel the warmth in her heart.

Jayson rolled onto his side and gathered her close, burrowing his nose in the crook of her neck. He breathed deeply of her scent, making her giggle. "We have to do this more often."

Tranquility came over her and her eyelids grew heavy. She nuzzled closer. "I agree," she whispered before darkness closed in.

***

A few hours later, Jayson escorted Allison to the hotel dining room.

"I'm famished." She rubbed her belly.

"Me too. We'll have to stash food in our bedroom when we get back home." Jayson hooked one arm around her waist and in the other he cradled Brandyn.

She pointed across the room. "There's Daniel and Nathan."

He guided her to the table in front of the window.

"Good morning," Daniel called. An ear-to-ear grin covered his face.

Nathan rose from his seat and pulled a chair out for Allison. "My now, don't the two of you look especially happy this fine morning. Is it safe to say the deed's done?"

Heat rose so fast in Allison's cheeks she thought they might ignite.

Nathan pushed in her seat and chuckled. "I'll take that as a 'yes'"

"You're bad, Nathan McKay." She looked down and straightened her skirts.

"What? What happened?" Daniel asked, and then deftly dodged Nathan's cuff to his head.

"None of your business. Your brother's being a jackass." Jayson took a seat in the high-backed chair and adjusted Brandyn in his arms.

"As usual." Daniel laughed.

Nathan tried to swat Daniel again but missed.

"Did everyone enjoy the ball last night?" Allison poured herself a cup of tea from the teapot.

"Where's Chase and Jasmine?" Jayson asked.

Nathan gave his brother a pointed look. "You're not going to like it."

"I'm not going to like what?"

"After you left, there was a bit of commotion involving Chase."

Jayson leaned forward. Tension returned to his features. "What kind of commotion?"

"Chase got into a big fight," Daniel blurted out.

"He didn't," Jayson said incredulously.

"Seems like an old customer of Jasmine's recognized her. Chase thought it was his duty to protect her honor, and he hauled off and hit the man. The man's friends jumped Chase and we had to pull everyone apart."

Allison's hand covered her mouth. "Oh, no. How's Chase?"

"Chase's face is banged up pretty good, but he'll heal—no broken bones. Jasmine was livid with Chase for causing such a scene. She said she had the situation under control before he stuck his nose in where it didn't belong. She stormed out of the dance. Since then, she's refused to talk to him. Right now, she's holed up in her room." Nathan took a sip of coffee.

Daniel bit off half a muffin and said with his mouth full, "Chase went to get her flowers. She's really mad."

"I should go to her." She pushed her chair back to stand, but Jayson placed a hand over hers, stopping her short.

"Sit. Eat first. Then go." He gave her a look that said he wanted no argument.

She sank back into her chair and glanced longingly at the doorway. Consoling her friend would have to wait.

Nathan reached for Brandyn. "Hand me my nephew so you both can have your meal."

Jayson handed over the baby, and then buttered a muffin and put it on her plate.

Allison took a big bite of the sweet baked good and washed it down with a sip of hot tea. All eyes at the table rose at the same time and stared over her head. She knew without looking who had walked into the room.

"What do you have to say for yourself?" Jayson asked when Chase came up behind her.

Placing her teacup on the saucer, she looked over her shoulder and gasped at the sight of Chase's blue, distorted face.

"I'd do it again," Chase said defiantly.

Jayson huffed. "Of course, you would."

Chase pulled an empty chair up next to Allison. "Jasmine won't talk to me. She locked me out of her room and won't let me have my say. I brought her some flowers and sweet things, but she won't open the door."

Allison felt bad for Chase. "It might take time. Jasmine's a proud woman, and I'm sure she must be mortified that her former profession was disclosed in such a public manner to a roomful of strangers."

He straightened. "You should've seen the way the guy was ogling her."

Nathan glared at his brother. "She was handling things fine. Very discretely, I might add."

Chase dropped his gaze and combed his fingers through his hair. "I didn't like it."

She put her hand on Chase's arm. "I'll go talk with her, but Chase, I'm not sure this is going to resolve itself as quickly as you would like."

"I know. Tell her I'm sorry for embarrassing her." Chase looked away and then said under his breath, "Although, I'm not sorry for hitting that bastard."

Allison pursed her lips. Her brother-in-law was as stubborn as her husband. "I'll tell her."

Jayson wrapped a few muffins in a cloth napkin and handed her the bundle. "We can leave for home any time you ladies want to go. Today, tomorrow, anytime."

"Thank you." Allison smiled appreciatively and left the table.

***

At Jasmine's door, Allison gathered the flowers and brown paper wrapped sweets off the floor and held them in her arms with the bundle of muffins Jayson had given her. She tapped lightly on the wood. "It's me. Let me in."

Soft padded footsteps made their way to the door. The lock clicked, and the door opened a few inches.

"Are you alone?"

"Me and a few peace offerings from Chase," she said.

The door swung wide, and Allison stepped in. Jasmine locked the door behind her, then sprawled out face-first across the bed, making the springs squeak under her weight.

"You heard," her friend mumbled into a fat feather pillow.

"I not only heard, but I also had the displeasure of seeing Chase's damaged face." Allison put her armload down on a small table and sat in the cushioned chair by the window.

Jasmine turned her head to look at her and grimaced. "He deserved it. The whole ordeal was horrible. I've never been so humiliated in all my life."

"I don't think he meant to embarrass you."

"I was taking care of things just fine without his help," Jasmine said angrily.

Allison stayed quiet so Jasmine could vent her frustrations.

"All my life I've known who I was. As a half-breed and a woman, I've always known my place. I've done things I'm not proud of to eat and survive. I had few choices. Until you came along, my life was not pleasant, nor was it happy. Chase let me believe I could let my guard down and be somebody else. The only problem is that I'm not someone else. I've done things that will haunt me forever. He says he's willing to accept me as I am, but he's really not. He's too quick to use his fists. I'm not sure he'll ever be ready."

Allison rose from the chair and sat on the edge of the bed. She rubbed her friends back. "I'm sorry I pulled you into this."

Jasmine rolled over. "Don't be sorry. I'm not sorry I met you. You've changed my life around. I'll always be grateful for your unconditional friendship. I'm just going to have to rethink my relationship with Chase."

"He's trying hard to apologize. Look, he's dropped off all kinds of goodies." She gestured to the table. "What do you say we eat until we feel sick and forget about the McKay men for a few minutes?"

Jasmine sat upright. "Sounds good to me."

"I asked the server downstairs to bring us some tea. Jayson says we can leave for Flat Rock anytime we want. I'm thinking we should leave today. I miss home."

"Me, too." Jasmine walked over to a chair by the table.

Allison followed her and looked in the bag. "Yummy, peppermint sticks...my favorite."

Jasmine scrutinized Allison. "Something has changed about you."

"I don't know what you're talking about."

Her friend stared harder. "There's a warm glow about you. You and Jayson consummated your marriage, didn't you?"

Allison clapped her hands together. "We did. It was perfect."

"I'm so happy for you. It's about time."

"I know. I let it go on too long. Everything is good now." Allison didn't want to share her doubts about her husband's true feelings for her, nor his betrayal of her by going to see his ex-fiancée. Discussing her insecurities and his disloyalty would make her qualms more powerful. Right now, she wanted to focus only on the good moments and let the others fade away.

Some things were better off not said.

~Chapter Twenty-Eight~

"You need to stop meddling."

"Meddling?" Allison sucked in her breath and glared at her husband. "Did you say meddling?"

"Yes, meddling." Jayson rose from the patchwork quilt spread out upon the grass by the stream. The rushing water rippled by over half-submerged rocks, lending to a peaceful sound. He folded his arms across his chest and stood with his legs wide apart.

She lifted her chin and squinted against the bright noontime sun. "It's only meddling if it's none of my business. Discussing Nathan and Daniel *is* my business." Months ago, his hovering over her as she sat at his feet would've intimidated her, but not anymore. Not after the Cattleman's Ball, and the following nights of passion.

"It's no concern of yours." He pressed his lips tight.

"No concern of mine?" She repeated his words deliberately.

Like how it's no concern of mine that you met your old fiancée for a rendezvous? And, after being home a week, you still haven't told me about the meeting?

Her stomach clenched. He didn't trust her with the truth. He continued to keep her at a distance. Rising from the edge of the blanket, she placed her hands on her hips. Her cheeks flamed, and anger oozed from every pore. The man was so infuriating. How dare he put up another wall, just when things were going so well.

"I'm as much a part of this family as you are. You have no right ordering me to keep my opinions to myself. I will not. Nathan and Daniel confided to me, and I'm coming to you with their plans for their futures."

"If they want to talk, they can speak to me themselves."

"So, they can talk to deaf ears? So, you can brush them off, pretend they said nothing?"

Jayson removed his hat and ran his fingers through his thick hair. "That's not true."

"Your brothers discuss things with me because, unlike you, I'm always willing to listen."

"I listen," Jayson said weakly.

"Only to what you want to hear." She gave him a pointed look. "As I said earlier, they are thinking about their futures."

"Their futures are here on the ranch."

"They want something more. Nathan's confidence has returned. He needs to go back East and finish his schooling to become a physician."

"He can practice doctoring without taking the exam. Doc Thatcher is set on retiring soon. Nathan knows what to do. The people around here trust him with or without a certificate to practice."

"He started something, now he has to finish it. Just like you completed your schooling. He needs the same sense of accomplishment."

Jayson clenched his jaw and cocked his head.

Allison knew he didn't like hearing her words and was trying hard to disregard them, but at least she had his full attention. "And, Daniel needs to go off to a university and see some of the world."

"He's too young."

"He's not too young. You've kept him tied to this ranch far too long."

"He's fine right here. I can teach him whatever he needs to know."

"That's the thing. You're not teaching him. You're treating him like one of the hired hands. You bark orders and he does whatever you tell him to do."

He wiped his hands on the sides of his pants. "I'm the head of this family, and I make the decisions around here. They wouldn't be thinking about these things if you weren't meddling."

"I'm a part of this family, Jayson McKay. I'll meddle in whatever I see fit to meddle in."

"Stop trying to change things. They belong here. Leave it be."

She stepped forward and wagged a finger. Her husband stepped back. "Are you thinking about what's best for them or what's best for you? Sometimes, sacrifices need to be made for the greater good of your family."

Jayson rubbed his forehead.

She placed her hands on her hips. "I'm noticing how much you don't like change in your life. I wonder if Brandyn and I are too much of a change for you."

"You know that's not true."

Brandyn fussed. Allison leaned into the big-wheeled, fancy baby carriage to soothe him. Their conversation was going nowhere. Her husband needed time to come around to her way of thinking. He needed to cool off.

She stroked Brandyn's cheek. "All is well, little one. Your father's just being a *jackass*."

Jayson slapped his hat back on his head.

"Oh, Jayson, here's another change you're not going to like." She flipped her hair over her shoulder and looked back at him. "Find somewhere else to sleep tonight."

Without waiting for a reply, she grabbed the stroller handle and walked at a fast clip up the hill, past the sawmill, toward home.

***

Allison and Jasmine each took an end of the baby carriage, carried it up the front steps of the house, and set the buggy in the shade on the porch. She peeked inside. The bumpy journey over the stone path had lulled Brandyn into a peaceful sleep. How she envied her son.

Allison heaved a sigh. "Seriously, Jasmine, that man is so maddening."

"Men often are." Jasmine giggled.

"I really wanted to throttle him, but...because I'm a lady...I instead told him he could find somewhere else to sleep tonight."

"You didn't?"

"I did." Allison chuckled. "Although, I don't imagine it'll come to that. I'm pretty sure he'll come around to my way of thinking before bedtime."

Jasmine nodded. "He will if he knows what's good or him. You're a force to be reckoned with when you're riled up."

Allison smirked. "Especially, when I'm in the right. I also left him to gather up our unfinished picnic. I'm furious his pigheadedness wasted a beautiful afternoon. This morning, I thought it would be fun to surprise him with his mid-day meal down by the stream. I thought a relaxed setting would soften the discussion about Nathan and Daniel moving on. I knew he'd balk at such news. Oh, he's totally clueless when it comes to his brothers. That's why they came to me first."

The two women each sat on a rocking chair under the overhang of the porch. Jasmine poured them a glass of lemonade and set the pitcher on the low table between them.

"Can you believe he accused me of meddling?"

Jasmine touched her fingers to her lips. "He didn't?"

"He did. I never saw anyone dig in their heels so deep. He's got to be the most stubborn man I've ever met." She sipped her tart drink and puckered her lips.

"I think stubbornness runs in this family."

Allison thought of Chase and nodded. "I believe you're right."

Jasmine stared out in the distance and squinted. "We have visitors. Someone's coming down the road."

A buggy and two riders on horseback made their way toward the house. The hired guns at the barn stepped to the corral fence, cradling their rifles in their arms.

"Can you see who they are?" Jasmine asked.

Allison stood at the porch rail and strained to catch a glimpse of their faces. "I think it's Mr. Pearson's carriage. I recognize the canopy. I'm not sure who he has with him, though."

Jasmine joined her as they waited for the four-wheeled carriage to roll into the yard.

Mr. Pearson's face was unsmiling, which was rare. He was usually a jovial man. This was not a friendly visit. The hairs on the back of Allison's neck stood at attention. She couldn't make out the face of the man seated next to him because his fancy hat and the fringed surrey top shielded his features. The armed men on horseback kept pace on either side of the carriage. A woman, who was not Margaret, sat in the back seat.

When the horses reached the white-picket-fence, Mr. Pearson reined in his team. "Whoa!"

Allison glanced at Bob and Ned by the barn, relieved by their presence. Ever since the kidnapping, she was leery of strangers. The men waited for any sign of trouble. They would come to her rescue if need be. Out of the corner of her eye, she also noticed Daniel and Hank walking across the yard from the hay barn.

She left the handrail and made her way to the center of the porch steps to welcome their guests.

The man wearing an expensive hat jumped off the buggy and strode to the gate. "Allison. Sweetheart. It's Robert."

She gasped. Her hands flew to her mouth to quiet the sound.

"I've come to take you and the baby home to Boston. You don't belong way out here." He lifted the latch and stepped into her flower garden. The colors turned gray.

Allison's head reeled.

She shuffled sideways and grabbed the white-washed post.

Oh, my! It can't be.

Jasmine put a hand on her back.

Allison's heart raced to near bursting as she stared at the man she once thought she loved.

How could I have been so wrong?

Months ago, he had dismissed her without a backward glance. Abandoned her to find her way out of a predicament he bore a great deal of responsibility for. She never expected to see him again, at least not in Montana. That he was standing in her yard, saying he wanted her and the baby to return to Boston was so ludicrous, she stifled a hysterical giggle.

This can't be real. Yet here he was.

The shock shook her core. She breathed deep to gather her bearings.

"Wow, you look great. Motherhood agrees with you. I've missed you. We can get this all straightened out. My father talked to the cardinal. He has the power to grant you an annulment. I've been such an idiot. It's time to come home."

"Stop...stop right there," she stammered, putting her hand up to halt his progress.

Jasmine stepped in front of her to block his way. "That's far enough, mister."

Robert paused a few feet from the bottom of the steps. "Honey, what's the matter? I thought you'd be happy to see me."

"What are you doing here?" Allison squeaked. "How did you find me?"

"Like I said, I've come to get you and the baby. I ran into your mother, who told me your whereabouts. She said you got married and had a little boy. Such good news. I have a son."

Her eyes narrowed. Even though she never told her mother who the father of her child was, her mother would guess it was Robert.

Would her mother betray her? It didn't seem possible. More than likely, he paid a maid working for her parents for the information. He'd stoop that low to get what he wanted.

Her chest tightened and her breathing shallowed. She was having a tough time comprehending the situation. Her mind raced with unanswered questions. In her gut, something felt off. He was masking his real intentions with friendliness. Trying to manipulate her, yet again.

She had learned from past mistakes. "Have you forgotten, we are no longer pledged to one another? I'm a married woman. I have a home here, another life."

Robert removed his fancy derby hat and held the rim with both hands. He shook his head. "I was hoping our visit would go smoother. Isn't it enough I want you back? As my wife, you'll be the *Belle of Boston*."

Typical, arrogant Robert. She didn't know how she could've been so blind to his true nature. "Why, Robert? Why do you want me back?"

Robert grimaced. "Because you're the mother of my child. According to the physicians, the only child I'll have, therefore my heir."

"Why can't you have children?"

"Bad bout of the mumps. Nasty business that was. My son is in line for the Winthrop fortune. I want to see that the lad gets what's coming to him."

She sucked in her breath. His presence finally made sense.

He's after Brandyn. Her stomach roiled.

The easiest way to get to Brandyn was to convince her to run away with him. He didn't care about her. She clutched her trembling hands. Her eyes darted to the woman who sat in the carriage behind Mr. Pearson. "Who's the woman?"

"She's a wet nurse. She'll only be needed if you decide not to return with me. The men are here for my protection and to see us safely home."

If she declined to go with him, he had plans to take her son. Without batting an eye, he would tear a mother from her child. *Tear her from her child.* The man was an arrogant bastard. Bile rose in the back of her throat and she swallowed it down.

Think. Think.

"And, if I don't go with you, if I refuse to let you take the baby, what then?"

"I certainly hope it doesn't come to that. As you know, my family is one of the wealthiest in the country. To be married to me would be quite an honor."

When she didn't quickly agree, he continued, "May I remind you, I was sent here by my father to retrieve our family's heir. If, for whatever reason you want to stay, we're willing to pay you for the child. Although, I must warn you that if you instead go against us and try to block the acquisition of my son, we would cause you and this family nothing but pain. I don't advise it."

She reached for Jasmine's arm, afraid she might topple over. A throbbing pain pounded in her temples. "Seeing you is such a shock. I need to think about this."

"I hoped we could settle this now. I'm in a bit of a rush to get home. But, under the circumstances, I'll give you a little time to make the right decision. I'm

242

staying at the hotel in town. I expect an answer by tomorrow, midday. The sooner I get out of this backwoods country, the better."

Robert turned on his heels and headed to the carriage. He sat on the seat next to Mr. Pearson and called out, "Remember, Allison, attempt to thwart me and you'll never see your son again."

A cold chill pierced her innards. Allison held her breath until the carriage headed out. A sob rushed from her chest. She spun around and ran to Brandyn. Tears clouded her eyes. She reached into the baby buggy and pulled out her sleeping son, clutching him against her chest. He squawked in her arms.

Jasmine touched her shoulder.

Allison pulled away. "Not now, Jasmine." She brushed past her friend, ran up the stairs, and slammed her bedroom door. Curling up on the bed, she made a little nest for her fussing son, who was now wide awake.

"What do I do, Brandyn? I can't let him take you away without me. He would, you know. I don't think he has scruples. He brought a wet nurse. *A wet nurse.* As if I would hand you over to him." Her voice came out high-pitched.

"His family has more money than God. If I don't agree to his terms and go back to Boston with him, he might hire people to whisk you away in the middle of the night. Steal you away from me. Or, he might hire people to shoot, maim, or kill, your father and uncles. Hurt the people I love. His father could convince the law to look away." Tears poured from her eyes and she sniffled loudly.

What do I do?

"Robert wants you for his heir, but he didn't have the decency to even look at you. The man is incapable of loving anyone but himself."

Brandyn's little hands waved in the air, and he scrunched up his nose and puckered his lips, getting ready to cry.

"I can't lose you, my little cherub. And, I can't let anyone get hurt because of me." She leaned in, rubbed her cheek to his and inhaled his baby scent. Her hot tears wet his face. She brushed the moisture away with the tips of her fingers, then kissed his button nose.

Her head pounded. She made her decision.

Like she told Jayson earlier. *Sometimes, sacrifices needed to be made for your family.*

~Chapter Twenty-Nine~

*T*his is bad.

Jayson took the stairs two at a time to his second-floor bedroom. Outside the closed door, he removed the kerchief from his neck and wiped the moisture off his brow.

Ten minutes ago, when Jasmine burst through the entrance of the sawmill out of breath, his heart stopped. He hadn't seen her so panicked since the day of the kidnapping. She barely got the words out to tell him about their visitors before he took off toward the house.

Damn. He should never have argued with Allison. Should never have put the notion in her head that she and the baby weren't wanted.

He stuffed the bandana in his back pocket. His hand shook as he reached for the latch. Fear of what he'd find on the other side of the door petrified him. He couldn't lose her.

Not now. Not ever.

He inhaled deeply to control his labored breathing, worked the handle, and stepped into the room. Brandyn smacked his lips innocently while in his cradle, oblivious of the world falling apart around him. Allison stood at the dresser, her back to the door. A drawer was ajar, and she was removing clothing. At the foot of the bed, her traveling trunk was open and half-packed.

His stomach churned. They had lived this scene before. Last time things turned out well. He wasn't sure about this time.

He took off his hat and gun holster and hung them on a wall peg by the door. "Jasmine tells me we had visitors."

Allison stopped folding and stood stone still. "Then you know. Robert came by. Brandyn's real father. He wants to take us back to Boston. Says he can get me an annulment. Wants to marry me. Offered to make me the 'Belle of Boston'." Her voice sounded flat and detached.

Jayson winced. She'd said, *real father.* A rock-hard knot squeezed in the pit of his stomach. His heart raced and pounded in his chest.

"Don't go." His voice had a sharp edge. He shoved his hands in his front pockets as he struggled to tap down the building unease.

She stared at the petticoat in her hand. "You'll be fine. Everything will work out for you. After all, with me out of the way, you can resume your relationship with Jacquelyn."

"What are you talking about?" He lifted a brow. *How did Jacquelyn fit into this?*

"I saw the way she looked at you the night of the Cattlemen's Ball. I know she sent you the note, and you met her in the livery." She glanced over her shoulder and frowned. Her face was red-splotched and teary. "You'll be free to marry. I'm sure the two of you will be incredibly happy together. Just like you always wanted."

She knew. Shit.

Sweat coated his palms. He took his hands out of his pockets and rubbed them on his pants. This wasn't a good time to be talking about another woman. Allison was looking for a reason to leave. "It's not what you think."

"You never told me about your rendezvous." Her voice turned shrill with emotion.

"I didn't want to upset or worry you over nothing."

"You lied when you received the note."

She's pushing me away.

"I didn't lie, just skirted around who sent it. I should've told you. I thought she wanted to apologize for leaving me suffering alone in that dank hospital room, while in horrendous pain, with the smell of burnt flesh stinging my nose. I wanted to hear her say how much she regretted her impulsive decision to cut all ties, and how she should've at least helped me get through the first few days until my family arrived."

Allison turned to face him, her eyes softened. "Did she? Did she say what you wanted to hear?"

"No. She had no intention of asking for forgiveness. Although, she did remark the scar on my face healed better than she thought it would."

"What did she want?"

He shook his head and shifted his weight from one leg to the other. This was the part he wanted to avoid. But, if Allison wanted the truth, he'd give it to her.

"She found out our marriage was one of convenience. That you were pregnant before we married. She assumed we were together for show only. Her new fiancé, a soon-to-be senator, is much older and not all she wished him to be in bed." He brushed his fingers through his hair. *Damn.* This was more awkward than he imagined. "Long story short, she wanted us to resume a part of our relationship where we left off."

A high-pitched hysterical laugh bubbled from her chest. "She wanted to bed you?"

"The woman isn't right in the head. She likes to play games."

"You weren't the least bit tempted?"

"Not at all. I only met with her to give her a chance to apologize for all the hurt she'd caused. I had no intention of getting together with her for anything else. I told her right out I was married, and I take my wedding vows seriously."

He stepped forward and clasped her upper arms. Tears pooled in her eyes and he wanted to take away her sadness. "The second I realized she had no intention of saying she was sorry, I left. All I wanted to do was get back to you, so I could give you the locket, to show you how happy I was being your husband and Brandyn's father."

A soft sob caught in the back of her throat.

He fingered the silver locket hanging from her neck and stared deeply into her moisture-filled eyes. "Allison, you're the only woman I want to be with. The only woman I want to be married to. I'm sorry I hurt you by not telling you about Jacquelyn."

Tears rolled down her cheeks and she brushed them away. Her shoulders sagged. He knew she could no longer use Jacquelyn as an excuse to leave. Her ploy to walk away with a clear conscience vanished.

"I thought you liked living here."

She looked at the floor. "I like it very much."

"Then why are you packing?"

"It's complicated. I have to go." Her legs buckled as she turned toward the dresser.

Jayson grabbed her hips and guided her to the over-sized upholstered chair. He wasn't going to let her get away from him that easily. Sitting on the edge of the opposite chair, he covered her hands with his. "Tell me why you're leaving."

Her body slumped against the chair's cushion in defeat.

"Tell me." He brushed a loose tendril of hair from her face and swept it behind her ear.

She bit at her bottom lip and stared at her lap. "The Winthrop's are a powerful and wealthy family."

Her voice sounded flat and strained, not her usual smooth-flowing pitch. He waited patiently for her explanation.

"They are Boston Brahmins, members of Boston's elite upper class. Their lineage dates back to Boston's founding families. Robert and his family are well-known to other top-ranking socialites all over the country." She locked eyes with him. "They are more powerful than you can imagine."

He stroked the top of her hand with his thumb.

"Robert says he can't have any more children." Allison glanced at the cradle. "He didn't come here for me, he came for Brandyn."

A few tears ran down her cheeks. She freed one of her hands from beneath his and wiped away the wetness.

Jayson knew what it was like to be rejected by someone you once loved. The hurt burrowed deep. "Why do you feel you have to go with him? Do you love him?" The last words stuck in his throat. He wasn't sure he wanted an answer.

"No. I despise him, but he gets what he wants, and he wants Brandyn. He's offering to take me with him. If I go willingly and accept his proposal, I get to remain with my baby. If I resist, he'll find a way to take Brandyn. I might never see my son again if I don't do what he says." Both hands covered her face and a soft sob erupted from her throat.

Jayson leaned forward and pulled her head against his shoulder. He caressed her back. "It makes no sense that you're giving up so easily. It's not like you."

"It is like me. I'm a coward. I've never been so frightened in all my life. Robert has the power and the means to keep me from Brandyn forever."

"You're willing to sacrifice your happiness for your child?"

"As I said earlier, sometimes you have to make sacrifices for family." Her voice muffled against his shoulder.

"True, but you can also lean on family and fight back. Don't forget, you're no longer alone. I'm your husband and Brandyn's father. We said our vows in a church and in the presence of God. We consummated our marriage. Robert might have power and wealth, but I'm not without my own means. I don't want you to go. You've made a life here...with me."

She sat upright. "I'm so confused. I don't know what to do. I can't lose Brandyn."

"Tell me you want to stay. If you do, we'll fight for the right to raise our son together. You don't need to sacrifice yourself to a man who doesn't care for you."

Her chin dropped to her chest, and she covered her face with trembling hands.

"Do you trust me to make things right?" His hands rubbed up and down her upper arms.

She sucked in a deep breath and let it out slowly. "I do. I want to stay here with you."

"Good." His heart filled to near bursting. "We'll get through this. You'll see."

When she gazed at him, her big, brown eyes glistened. "I hope so."

A fierce protectiveness surged within him. He knew her courage was fragile, and it took a lot of resilience for her to be strong. He scooted to the edge of the over-sized chair, pulled her onto his lap, and wrapped his arm around her back. Tilting her jaw, he kissed her lips. He meant the kiss to be gentle and reassuring, to let her know he would lend her his strength.

She surprised him when she delved deep with her tongue. Her warm, tear-streaked skin brushed against his cheek and she pressed him back into the chair. A hint of salt melted in his mouth. She twisted her upper body, pressing a well-formed breast against his chest while squirming on his lap as she settled herself into a more desirable position.

His cock engorged at the onslaught.

He stared at her questioningly. Passion shone in her eyes. The sparkle in their depths dared him to try to deny her what she wanted. He was too far gone to question her need and was more than willing to follow her wherever she took him.

Her fingers unhooked the buttons on his shirt and yanked his shirttails free from his belted pants. She pushed the material from his arms, leaving him bare from the waist up. As she kissed him hungrily, her hands roamed over his chest in an ancient dance of seduction.

His mind drummed. *God, how I love you.*

Jayson's silent heartfelt admission caused her every touch to enflame him like never before. His cock grew uncomfortably stiff and he struggled to keep himself in check, not wanting their coming together to end too soon. The smell of wild roses overpowered him. Her mouth tasted sweet like honey.

Allison took control, leading him to the brink of ecstasy. Her hands were as soft as velvet, rolling over every inch of his naked skin. He came to attention when they traced a path along a cluster of hairs disappearing under his waistband.

Deft fingers undid his belt and unzipped his trousers. She inserted her hand down the front of his pants.

He nearly shot off the seat when she touched his blood-filled shaft. Suddenly, the need to feel her unclothed skin consumed him. She removed her hand as he helped her out of her dress and corset.

Allison sat atop him in her undergarments. The transparent fabric barely concealing her lovely flesh beneath. As he ran his hands up and down her curves and over taut nipples, heat sparked, and the thin cloth moistened against her skin. He pulled off her camisole, baring her breasts which he at once cupped with his hands and gave a gentle teasing nibble to each rosy peak.

A groan resounded in the back of her throat. He glanced up and stared into her passion-filled eyes, framed by long, black eyelashes, begging for more.

He kissed her ripe lips eagerly and his tongue explored her mouth with new fervor. Allison pulled him to stand and loosened his trousers. She worked the waistband over the curve of his buttocks and let them drop in a pool at his feet, atop his boots. His erection emerged from the confines of his pants. Her pelvis ground against his arousal.

A moan croaked in his throat. *Oh, God.*

She pushed him onto the chair with more strength than he thought she possessed. Untying the drawstring of her drawers, the soft material fell to the floor and she stepped out of the pile. Bunching her silk petticoats up her thighs, she straddled his hardness, her knees planted on both sides of his hips. He almost lost all control when she grabbed his manhood, slid her velvety opening over the top, and lowered herself upon him.

An almost animalistic sound rumbled within him.

He buried his face in her chest. Her hips began a slow, rolling rhythmic movement on top of his lap. His buttocks tensed, and his breathing deepened. He circled his tongue over a rounded breast, flicking the tip over first one ripened nipple and then the other. Her back arched as he captured each bud with his lips, sucking gently. A sweet, creamy taste tantalized his mouth.

Allison gazed at him, her wide eyes dark with hunger as she intensified the pace. A panting breath escaped slightly parted, swollen lips as she moved in perfect tempo. His hands rested on her waist and followed her thrusts, each one pulling him deeper and deeper inside her, where her scorching sex encased his stiff cock, squeezing until his head clouded with unbridled desire.

His need grew to near combustion. He cupped her rounded buttocks and stood with her legs wrapped around his waist. She grabbed about his neck, over his shoulders, pressing her breasts into his chest. He finished them there with shuddering explosions coming in consecutive order.

A wave of weakness rushed through him. He sank back into the chair with her on top. Allison laid her cheek against his. Her labored breaths tickled his ear. He wrapped his arms around her body and engulfed her in a deep embrace, waiting for their hearts to slow their drumming beats.

Beautiful wasn't the right word to describe their coming together. *Heavenly*, defined it better.

A few minutes of bliss passed before she repositioned herself and curled up on his lap. He caressed her all over, not able to get enough of her naked flesh. *Mine to touch and enjoy.*

A heady scent of roses mingled with the sweet smell of their sweat teased his nose. Across the room, Brandyn's chubby little hands flapped in the air as he gurgled cheerfully in his cradle.

An overwhelming sense of bliss curled Jayson's mouth in a contented smile. He kissed the top of her head and cherished the sticky feel of their bodies plastered together in one heap.

Allison sealed their deal with unrestrained lovemaking. When the time came to decide her fate, she chose to stay in Montana.

She chose me.

~Chapter Thirty~

Jayson pounded on the closed oak door. The booming sound echoed in the hotel's upstairs hallway. A bed squeaked, and boot heels rapped upon the wood planks on the other side of the door as he waited for a response.

The door opened a crack. A man in a pin-striped suit looked him up and down. Brushing the bottom of his coat aside, the man fingered the gun resting in the leather holster slung across his hips. "Who are you?"

"Jayson McKay." He placed his hand on the door panel to keep it from closing in his face. "I'm here to see your boss."

The man looked over his shoulder, then back. Slowly, the opening grew until Jayson caught sight of an affluently dressed man sitting in a chair by the side of the bed.

Robert.

Brandyn's father was half-shielded by another man, also armed.

Hired guns.

Jayson stepped forward, filling the doorway with his size. A visual trick he learned when studying politics in Washington. Appear as big as possible.

Robert stared at the scar on Jayson's face and winced. "I'm Mr. Winthrop. What do you want, Mr. McKay?"

For the first time ever, Jayson was glad for his disfigurement. Anything making him seem more menacing worked in his favor.

"I've come to inform you that my wife and son will not be joining you." He stared at Robert without blinking and immediately knew what kind of man he was dealing with...arrogant, entitled, self-absorbed.

His desire to protect Allison intensified. There was no way he could hand her over to someone who could never appreciate her finer qualities. Someone who could never love her like she deserved to be loved.

Robert's face dropped. He bolted upright from his chair. The man hadn't expected such an answer. Obviously, he usually got what he wanted. "Is that Allison's decision or yours?"

"I'm speaking for my wife. Allison wants to stay here with me."

Disbelief flashed across the man's face. "How unfortunate. I had hoped to entice her with a better life."

Jayson glared at Robert. "Her life is fine right here."

Robert took a few steps forward and grabbed the iron post of the bed's footboard with one hand. "It's the boy I'm really interested in. A bout of the mumps rendered me unable to have more children. Nasty side-effect. That makes the child my only heir."

"The *boy* stays with his mother, and his mother stays with me."

"If you hand his care over to me, you'll be well rewarded. I'm willing to go so far as to make you a rich man. I'll see that the boy is surrounded by the finest things. He'll lead a life of privilege and want for nothing."

Jayson gritted his teeth. "What makes you think he won't live a privileged life out here?"

Robert retrieved a silk handkerchief from his pocket and placed it under his nose as if the room had suddenly filled with a noxious smell. "Out here? You must be mad. I'm willing to be very generous."

"How kind of you." He couldn't keep the sarcastic tone out of his voice. Every fiber in his body wanted to beat the man senseless. He reminded himself to remain calm. Too much was at risk. "But...my *son* will be staying here."

Robert's face turned ruby red. It finally occurred to the arrogant blackguard that the acquisition of his son wouldn't be an easy one. The man pushed past his hired guns, who kept a constant vigil, and stood before Jayson. "Why do you even care what happens to the boy? The bastard isn't yours."

Jayson's back straightened. "You're wrong. He is mine. He might not be my flesh and blood, but I brought him into this world. Make no mistake, he's mine."

"Then I'm afraid we're at an impasse with few options." Robert blotted his forehead with the embroidered handkerchief he clutched.

"If you're thinking about taking the child by force, I'd advise against it. You'll be dead in an instant."

"Are you threatening me?" Robert's eyes widened.

"Just stating a fact. Be warned, this is my town. Nothing goes on around here without me knowing. I trust you won't attempt anything that might get you killed."

The man cringed. "My father won't allow me to walk away without some kind of fight for my heir."

As expected, Robert wasn't quite as interested in Brandyn as his father was. How far would the scoundrel go to please his father? Did he just need to show some effort?

This was the direction Jayson wanted the conversation to go. "I propose we settle your claim in a court of law and abide by the decision handed down by the judge."

Robert's face brightened. He thought he had a chance at winning. "Good idea. We'll let the courts decide."

"Let's shake on it." Jayson held out his hand.

Robert met him halfway and they shook. "With that settled, we can leave for Boston right away and have our case heard there."

The man's a snake. Sure, Robert wanted the hearing in Boston. He no doubt believed he'd have the upper hand there, where his family had power and influence over those who sat on the bench.

"We won't be traveling to Boston. The child was born here and is a citizen of Flat Rock. The Montana Territory is under the United States jurisdiction and, as such, we follow their laws. A circuit judge will be visiting Flat Rock in three weeks to hear cases and grievances. I suggest you wire your lawyers straight away, so they have time to get here to represent you. I'll do the same. We'll let the law decide the child's fate."

Robert stood with his mouth agape. This was not what he'd wanted. Another three weeks stuck in town.

Jayson suppressed his smile.

***

The hairs on Allison's neck stood at attention as the townsfolk's curious stares followed her into Pearson's Hotel.

This was the day she had both welcomed and dreaded.

Today was court day.

Jayson walked beside her, his arm wrapped around her back, offering support. She cradled Brandyn in the crook of her arm, too worried about the outcome of today's hearing to give him up to Jayson or his brothers to carry. The thought of being parted from her son was terrifying. How could she live without her child?

The palms of her hands moistened, and her heart pounded in her chest. She swallowed hard to stamp down her fear. Walking through the double doors, her footsteps were as heavy as lead.

Brandyn squawked. She glanced down and realized she held him too tight. She loosened her firm grasp and let Jayson guide her into the formal parlor off to the side. He closed the door behind them.

Allison took a seat on the cushioned sofa. He pulled over a chair and sat on the edge, facing her. She unbuttoned her unadorned dress, one she hoped made her look like a well-respected member of the community, and placed the baby to her breast for one last feeding before the hearing started.

Three weeks of self-imposed seclusion had jostled her nerves. Jayson had asked her not to leave the ranch without him, but she dared not venture out at all. The stakes were too high. She couldn't be sure if Robert would wait idly by for the court hearing or take matters into his own hands.

Jayson said he didn't expect trouble but took steps to avert it anyway. He doubled the guards and he barely left her side. Her friends and family took turns visiting the ranch to keep her occupied. Father Peter arrived and spent a few days with her, talking about things going on in Boston. His company was such a comfort. Even Aunt Beatrice came out to the ranch and was surprisingly civilized, gushing over Brandyn as if he was her true-blooded kin.

The passing time still dragged. Sleep was elusive. Her worries were paramount during her confinement. She constantly had to block her negative thoughts, and replace them with more positive ones, but even those were harder and harder to come by.

Now her long wait was finally at an end. A wave of unease flowed through her, and her body trembled uncontrollably. The baby fussed.

Jayson ran his hands along her arms. The heat from his touch quelled her anxiety and she relaxed.

"I'm scared." She stared into his deep-blue eyes.

"This will be over soon enough, and we'll return to our normal life on the ranch."

"I hope so." She wasn't as convinced as he seemed to be. He'd been her rock these past few weeks, always telling her they were going about it the right way. That things would work out.

"I'm sorry you have to go through this. I wish there was some other way, to spare you, but we need the law behind us. I'm not sure Robert and his father will accept anything else."

"I understand." She dropped her head. "All my life I followed every instruction given. I never broke a rule until the night I conceived Brandyn. At the time, I never imagined the consequences that would arise from just one lapse in judgment."

Jayson chuckled and tipped her chin with his finger. "Well, I for one am pleased you're a rule breaker."

His eyes held so much warmth. She smiled.

"We need to talk about the hearing." His facade turned serious. "Judge Wade is presiding over the court. I was in his courtroom when I bore witness against Big Jake, after Jasmine's attack. I've also talked to him a few times when he was in town. He's a fair man. He'll hear both arguments and then decide who gets custody of Brandyn. The only way Robert and his lawyers can win is to convince Judge Wade that Brandyn is better off with him than with us. To do that they will want to paint you as a loose woman who was after Robert's fortune. They'll talk in detail about the night Brandyn was conceived. They want you to squirm, feel guilty, and fall apart. Don't do it. You did nothing wrong. The judge is going to see through their subterfuge and will know the truth."

A heavy sigh escaped her lips. She would have to muster every ounce of strength and courage she had to get through this day.

"Very important. They will make you question your own worth. When you feel yourself faltering, doubting yourself, just look at me and know I'm incredibly happy you conceived little Brandyn and came out West."

She nodded.

"Here, I want you to take this." He untied the black bandana around his neck, exposing his scars.

"What are you doing?"

He stuffed the bunched-up cloth into her palm. "Whenever you feel uncomfortable, roll this around in your hands and know there is nothing you say that will make me change my mind about you. That also goes for all the other people who care about you in Flat Rock. There will be nothing we learn about you today that will make us any less fond of you. Do you understand? *Nothing at all.*"

~Chapter Thirty-One~

Allison sat in a high-backed chair situated at the end of Judge Wade's table and scanned the crowd of onlookers filling the restaurant's small dining room. Moisture dampened the palms of her hands and she wiped them on Jayson's handkerchief. She was slated to be the first questioned in Brandyn's custody case. How she wished it was already over.

The furniture had been rearranged for the court hearing. The judge's table faced two other tables, one on each side of the room. Jayson and Mr. Murdock, their lawyer from Washington D.C., sat at one table. Robert and his attorneys from Boston sat at the other. Mr. Pearson lined the chairs up in rows behind the forward-facing tables. A center aisle separated the two sections. All the chairs behind Robert's table were empty, except for the wet nurse and his two hired guns. Behind Jayson sat his brothers, Jasmine, Father Peter, Melony, Aunt Beatrice, the Thomas's, the Pearson's, the Simpson's, and a man she didn't recognize. Sheriff Hollister stood by the entrance to the dining room.

Earlier, Chase saw to it that the public hearing remained private. He had stationed himself at the entrance of the hotel and scowled ominously at anyone who didn't belong. Word had gone out around Flat Rock, no one outside the family and close friends were welcome, so uninvited townsfolk stayed away.

Robert's team of lawyers had arrived in town earlier in the week. Margaret and Hannah told her the men had taken over most of the rooms at the hotel. Her friends giggled when they shared they were taking advantage of the newcomers by charging them obscene amounts of money for lodging and supplies. Her friends' antics warmed her heart. They were good friends.

Mr. Murdock and Jayson had gone over the proceedings, so she knew what to expect. Even though they kept telling her everything would be fine, she couldn't help but worry that her son might be torn from her arms and given to the wet nurse when the hearing was over. She couldn't fathom life without Brandyn and wasn't exactly sure what she would do if such a horrible thing came to pass. She imagined she'd experience a broken heart and spend every day for the rest of her life curled up in a ball, sobbing.

She glanced at Jayson who held Brandyn lovingly in his arms. He gave her a nod of encouragement and a slight smile. His neck was bare for all to see. Such an unusual sight. She scrunched up his black handkerchief and squeezed it tight. She still couldn't believe he'd offered her such a coveted piece of clothing to soothe her fears.

Robert's head lawyer began his questioning. "Mrs. McKay, did you know Mr. Winthrop was from one of the wealthiest families in Boston?"

Allison took a deep breath and steeled herself to the task ahead. "Yes, I knew he was from a wealthy family."

After the first question her nervousness wore off, and she rattled the rest of her answers off in quick succession, staying calm and concentrating on each query.

"Yes, I knew he hailed from one of the Boston Brahmin families...No, I did not actively pursue him, he was friends with people I was acquainted with. We attended many of the same gatherings and outings ...Yes, my father is a merchant and banker, but he's wealthy in his own right...No, I did not tell Robert to stop, although I'm not sure I fully understood what was happening at the time...Yes, I suppose I would say I consented, I thought we were to marry..."

Her face heated when responding to the last more intimate questions. She tugged at the bandana in her lap and glanced at Jayson. His eyes softened, and the corners of his lips turned up in a smile only she could see. She drew a deep breath before continuing her answers.

"No, I didn't purposely manipulate the next man I met into marrying me. My friend, Father Peter, arranged the marriage. He wanted to help me give my baby a name...No, my parents were not aware of my pregnancy. I was escorted across the country by Father Peter, and Mrs. Elliot, who acted as a chaperone."

The questions kept coming. Her head throbbed. The whole courtroom scene had a dreamlike quality and played out as if it had already happened. She pulled on the corners of the scarf and glanced at Jayson, holding her son. Her husband was right. They were trying to portray her as devious and calculating. A woman who'd seduced Robert with the sole intent of marrying him for his wealth and an elevated position in society.

Then a question Robert's lawyer asked stopped her short.

"Mrs. McKay, is it true you hired the town whore?"

The way he phrased the question made Allison's blood run cold. She glared at Robert who smiled smugly. It was one thing to make Allison defend her actions, opening her up to ridicule, but another to drag poor Jasmine through the mud, a person who had been nothing but good to Allison and her family.

She straightened her back. Anger bubbled within her, causing her chest to tighten. She turned to Judge Wade. "Your Honor, would you be so kind as to let me have my say on the matter?"

"I object. All I need is a yes or no answer," Robert's lawyer squawked.

Judge Wade looked sternly at Robert's lawyer. "I think Mrs. McKay has been more than accommodating today. I see no reason we can't indulge her and let her speak her mind. By all means, Mrs. McKay, go right ahead."

"Thank you, Your Honor." She stared hard at Robert and his table of lawyers. "I take offense to your insinuation that Miss Rose is anything other than a respectable member of the community. I realize most of you don't fully understand what's it's like to be a woman. We live in a man's world. The survival of our gender depends on your charity. Unlike a man, a woman has only a scarce number of work options available to support herself. If she's lucky enough to be white she might have a few choices, but heaven forbid if she's not. Doors are slammed shut. Opportunities dry up, and she may have to choose the only job available. Which happen to be: *servicing men.*"

All eyes were on her and she inhaled deeply. It felt good to have her say. "I see many men sitting in this courtroom today. Imagine what would become of your mother, sister, wife or daughter if no male relatives existed to protect and support them after you die? How would they survive on their own if they had no funds?"

Robert's lawyers looked sheepish, some looked away.

"Miss Rose isn't a saloon girl anymore. A door opened. My husband hired her to help me on the ranch. She does a tremendous job and is a godsend. I will thank you to keep that in mind and address her appropriately."

Allison glanced at Judge Wade who didn't appear ready to halt her tirade so she forged ahead.

"You might wonder how this applies to me. Robert told me he would marry me. When he abruptly cast me aside, pregnant and unable to support myself, I knew I had to do something drastic to survive and not be a burden to my family. I was lucky enough to have been introduced to my husband, who agreed to marry me, sight unseen. Without him, only God knows where I'd be right now and what

I'd be doing to get by. So, take care when you seek to disparage a woman's lot in life."

After her rant, Robert's lawyers had nothing more to say.

Mr. Murdock was next in line to present his questions. Allison took a deep breath in preparation for her lawyer's query's. They had gone over some of the questions earlier in the day, so she knew what to expect.

"Mrs. McKay, were you in love with Mr. Robert Winthrop?"

Allison glanced at Robert and then back at her lawyer. "Yes, I loved Robert, or at least I thought I did." Her breath hitched in her throat. She hadn't counted on the raw emotion Mr. Murdock's first question elicited. There was a time in her life not too long ago when all she could think of was Robert. He consumed her thoughts every waking minute.

She had no time to mourn her lost relationship because Mr. Murdock ramped up the speed of his questions and she had to focus on her answers.

"No, I wasn't after his money...Yes, I had more drinks the night of the ball than normally...Yes, the room had a fire going and brandy set out...Yes, he locked the door...No, I didn't resist, I loved and trusted him...Yes, it was my first experience with a man..."

Allison balled and unballed Jayson's scarf in her hands. The questions caused churning in the pit of her stomach but she vowed to keep pushing through them for Brandyn's sake.

"No, I never had sexual relations with him after that night...No, it wasn't my intention to get pregnant so he'd marry me, he had already said he would...Yes, we talked of a life together and starting a family...No, he never formally proposed but it was implied...Yes, Robert seemed excited when he heard the news I was pregnant...Yes, he said he had to tell his father and get his mother's ring...Yes, that is correct, the next day I received a letter from him. His father didn't think we should marry and threatened to disinherit him if we went through with our plans."

Mr. Murdock held up a crumpled parchment. "Is this the letter you received from Mr. Robert Winthrop before you left Boston?"

"Yes, it is." She wasn't sure why she had kept the letter all these months. More than once she had thought about burning it. The letter was a painful reminder of the end of their relationship. She had forgotten about it altogether until Father Peter asked about it the other day.

Mr. Murdock waved the parchment in the air. "May I have permission to read this letter out loud?"

"You may," Judge Wade said.

Robert squirmed in his seat and whispered a few words to his nearest lawyer. No doubt he remembered how he questioned whether the baby was even his. A ploy to sever his responsibilities.

Allison stared at Jayson as the familiar words poured out over Mr. Murdock's lips. She could recite the letter in her sleep. She'd read the parchment no less than one hundred times during the months following their breakup. Every day, she waited with hope that Robert would change his mind. She prayed he would knock on her door and tell her it was all a mistake. Say that he shouldn't have questioned whether the baby was his, and that he had decided to choose her and their unborn child over his inheritance.

Robert never came.

Instead, he let her simmer in her own insecurities, anguish, and sadness. When she finally realized he wasn't coming for her, she'd gathered her courage and she'd turned to Father Peter for help. Although she didn't know it then, that was the day she began living again.

~Chapter Thirty-Two~

"Mr. McKay, could you please tell the court why you agreed to marry Mrs. McKay, a young pregnant woman from Boston, sight unseen?" Robert's lawyer asked.

Allison's stomach churned. *Oh, how he must hate me right now.*

Jayson sat at the end of Judge Wade's table and was under as much scrutiny as she had been. Usually, he took care to protect his privacy, so it was gut-wrenching to see him sitting in front of so many people, some strangers, while he shared intimate details about his life.

She clutched his handkerchief tighter and bounced her knee to calm her unease. Nathan held Brandyn. She'd taken the baby when she'd finished testifying but her charged nerves made her son fuss, so her brother-in-law offered to calm him down.

As much as she wanted to hear Jayson's reasons for agreeing to marry her, she didn't think it was right for him to have to talk about such matters in public. This was a topic best discussed behind closed doors. She swallowed hard and reminded herself to stay strong.

Jayson kept perfect posture in his seat, shoulders back and chest out. He looked straight ahead at the lawyer questioning him. "There are actually two reasons I agreed."

"Please share your reasons with the court," Robert's lawyer peeked at Jayson over the top of his spectacles.

"My friend, Father Peter Thomas, sent me a wire. He pleaded for my help. He said a friend of his, a young woman from a good home in Boston, found herself with child and he was hoping I could offer for her hand in marriage."

"Didn't the request seem odd to you?" Robert's lawyer asked.

"I thought so. I wired him back to say I wasn't interested."

"And what was his response?"

"He said he was desperate to find this woman a good husband and if I didn't offer marriage to this young lady, he would marry her himself."

"What was your reaction?"

"I was intrigued. I couldn't fathom why my friend would go to such extremes to forsake his vows and marry this girl? I thought he must really think highly of her."

The revelation heated Allison's cheeks. To think Father Peter would've gone to such lengths to spare her the pain of being alone warmed her soul. Such a devoted friend was hard to come by.

"You said there were two reasons, what was the other reason?"

"When I was living in Washington D.C. a few years ago I was caught in a flash fire that ripped through the boarding house where I lived. I sustained burns on my cheek and left arm. After the fire, I returned home and threw myself into my work on the ranch, so I never had time to take a wife. Actually, I didn't try because I felt no woman would have me. Father Peter reminded me it was a perfect chance for me to marry, without having to go through all the normal social venues when finding a wife. He said our marriage would be a mutually beneficial arrangement. He was very convincing. So, I agreed."

As she listened she couldn't help feeling grateful for all that happened before. If any of the pieces, no matter how painful, hadn't come about, she and Jayson would not have come together. Her stomach fluttered at the thought of never having met him.

When asked about his financial stability, he said he shared in his family's fortune along with his brothers. His parents amassed most of their wealth in a gold strike before he was born, and then the assets were built upon through the McKay's cattle and horse business. He also revealed he had inherited a large sum of money from his great-grandfather, a wealthy plantation owner and ex-senator in Virginia, which he reinvested in business deals in the East and reaped repeated benefits from those investments as well.

Allison had no clue he was so well off. They never discussed money matters. If she wanted something in town, the proprietors wrote the amount owed in their ledger and assured her Jayson would take care of it later. She never questioned the way the owners did business with the McKay family.

When Robert's lawyer asked him why he felt he was rightfully the baby's father, her breath caught in the back of her throat. He explained how Allison made him promise the first time they met that he would raise the child as his own. The deal was sealed on the day she went into early labor and he delivered the baby himself. From that moment on, the child was his.

262

Thankfully, Robert's lawyers never questioned Jayson about where the delivery took place or what circumstances were in play, such as her kidnapping. They probably didn't know. In such a small, tight-knit community like Flat Rock, it was one thing for the townsfolk to talk amongst themselves, but quite another to talk to outsiders about one of their own.

When Jayson finished answering questions from both lawyers, he glanced at her and sent her the most alarmingly sweet smile. His eyes lit up and she caught the glimpse of a sparkle. A heartfelt warmth flowed through her along with the reassurance she needed.

He's not mad at me.

When he took the seat beside her, his hand went under the table and rested on her thigh, giving it a gentle squeeze. He leaned in close until their shoulders touched, and she felt strength in his nearness.

While Robert took the seat at Judge Wade's table, Jayson whispered in her ear, "You're doing great. Only a little while longer and this will all be over."

She nodded and caressed the top of his hand.

Robert sat in the front of the room and grinned like a schoolboy. Her stomach roiled. She'd seen his devilish smirk before.

He expects to win.

Allison tensed and held her breath. An all-consuming desire to hold her baby bubbled within her. She needed to feel him against her chest and cradle him in her arms. Needed to protect him and keep him safe. She turned in her seat to retrieve Brandyn from Chase, who was now holding her son. Jayson understood her plight and helped with the exchange. When the baby was safely tucked against her body, she kissed his forehead and inhaled deeply of his baby smell. Her racing heart slowed to a normal beat.

How could she have been so wrong? How could she have loved Robert? Their courtship seemed so long ago. At the time, she thought she knew everything about him, but now she realized it was all a lie.

Allison gave her heart to a man who only existed in her dreams. She had overlooked his glaring faults and put him on a pedestal like the rest of Boston society, making him into something he wasn't.

Were his lawyers, right? Had she hoped to marry a man she barely knew because of his wealth and situation in life? Had she just convinced herself she was experiencing young love because she wanted to be the *Belle of Boston*? How naive she had been not to recognize her fairy-tale world was not based in reality.

Robert's lawyers made their client out to be a saint, a man who could do no wrong. A man who had to cast her aside to protect himself from a woman who had been after his money and the elevated status that came with being his wife. A man who desperately wanted to raise his son, his only heir, in a world of privilege and prestige. They discussed his bout with the mumps and the doctor's prognosis of his infertility. The fact that Brandyn was the only heir to one of the wealthiest families in America was paramount in their case and they made Judge Wade aware of all the ramifications that would arise if there was no one left in the family to take over such a dynasty.

Mr. Murdock, on the other hand, had researched Robert's past and uncovered a few unsavory deals which he shared with the court. Robert's face paled when Mr. Murdock voiced some of his previous indiscretions out loud. He squirmed in his seat and used his handkerchief to swipe away the moisture blotting his forehead as he denied the severity of his actions. Even with all his excuses, he couldn't quite distance himself enough from his past exploits to come out unscathed.

As the questioning of Robert wound down and neared the end, Mr. Murdock glanced over his shoulder at Jayson who silently mouthed a request. Mr. Murdock swiftly turned and faced Robert again. "Mr. Winthrop, one last question. What's your son's name?"

Robert's cheeks turned beet red. He sputtered, "Umm...I didn't name him."

"Just answer the question, sir," Mr. Murdock said.

Robert exhaled a loud huff and shook his head. "I'm not sure. I call him, *The Baby*. I think they call him, Bradly."

"His name is Brandyn, Mr. Winthrop." Mr. Murdock nodded to Judge Wade and turned back to Robert. "Thank you, Mr. Winthrop. You're dismissed."

***

The next people called to the stand were character witnesses for both she and Jayson.

Father Peter testified first. He discussed his relationship with both of them, her volunteer work with him in Boston, the day she told him of her pregnancy, his role in their marriage, his threat to leave the priesthood, and why he thought Jayson would make a good husband and father.

Sheriff Hollister talked about his friendship with Jayson. He explained how her husband helped him keep law and order in the town.

Mr. Simpson spoke about the day she saved his life. He described his injuries and how she closed the wounds and prevented him from bleeding out. He shared how happy he was to be alive and be able to provide for his family, even with his injury, and how he had her to thank for his life.

Hannah shared that years ago, her store was robbed and set on fire. She and her husband lost everything, but Jayson insisted on leading them the money to start over. She said they would always be indebted to him for his act of kindness. Hannah also talked about what kind of woman Allison was, and what kind of mother she was to Brandyn, which made Allison's heart swell with warmth for the older woman.

Melony told everyone about how Jayson hired her a tutor, so she could continue her education to become a schoolteacher without leaving Flat Rock. How he owned the townhouse she and her mother lived in. And, because she didn't make much money as a schoolteacher, Jayson gifted them a generous monthly allowance, so they could live comfortably on their own.

Henry Waite was the surprise character witness for Jayson. Allison had never seen him before and was very curious about what he had to say. He said he first met Jayson when they both lived at Alma's Boarding House, in Washington, D.C., where a lot of young political hopefuls stayed.

One night he returned home drunk after a late-night social event and Jayson helped him unlock the door to his rented room. Once inside, he passed out on the bed. He woke in a fog to banging on his door. By then, smoke filled his room, he could barely breathe, and his throat burned in pain. He had no idea a fire raged around him and that flames had engulfed the building. Jayson broke down his door, pulled him out of bed, and half-dragged, half-carried him down two flights of stairs, through the dense smoke and flames leaping at their bodies. When they reached the foyer, almost out of the house, a burning beam fell from the ceiling and landed on Jayson's shoulder, resting against his cheek.

Jayson used his forearm and the back of his hand to hoist it up and off of his shoulder. While in great pain, Jayson continued to half-carry, half-drag him out the door to fresh air and safety.

Outside, Henry noticed the damage the flaming beam had done to Jayson's cheek, shoulder, arm, and hand. Bystanders helped Jayson into a buggy and they took him to the hospital. The people caring for Henry told him Jayson had made it safely out of the building earlier, but when he realized Henry was still inside he ran back into the inferno to save him at the peril of his own life.

"It takes a special man to rush into a burning building to save another man's life," Henry said decisively. "I wouldn't be here if not for this man. I owe Jayson McKay my life. He's a hero, plain and simple, and would be a good father to any child."

Jayson never talked about the fire, and Allison had never asked about that terrible night. After hearing Henry's testimony, she had never been prouder of anyone. She glanced at Jayson and tilted her head to touch his shoulder. He gazed down at her and gave her a feeble smile.

To relive the horror surrounding the fire must have been hard for him. Now that the events were out in the open for all to hear, she hoped he could come to terms with the decision he made so long ago. The one that changed his life forever. In her mind, the scars were more like badges of courage and honor than blemishes upon his skin. She wasn't surprised they had come about while saving someone's life. She expected no less from Jayson.

There were no character witnesses for Robert. Either his lawyers didn't feel they needed any because his wealth was all that mattered, or his witnesses didn't want to travel so far away from their comforts in the city. None-the-less, no one spoke on his behalf.

Lawyers on both sides made their oral arguments to Judge Wade. He called for a break, so he could review the case and make a decision.

Immediately, after the judge left his seat, Jayson guided her out of the dining room and led her back into the parlor across the hall, closing the door behind them.

~Chapter Thirty-Three~

*T**he court hearing was brutal.*

Allison sat rigidly on the edge of a high-backed wing chair in the hotel's parlor and nursed her hungry son. She stared at Brandyn's chubby cheeks. He appeared so content, unaware of the life-changing events happening around him.

I could lose him. Tears welled in her eyes and she fought to keep the moisture away.

Robert's lawyer's insinuations that she was a bad mother and a woman with loose morals, soured her stomach. The defamatory remarks about her character were a cruel blow to her dignity.

Jayson stood by the window, hands clasped behind his back, looking out over the town. His pensive stance only worried her more. She wished she knew what he was thinking.

Do we have a chance or not?

When he turned and looked at her, his eyes blazed with concern. "Are you okay?"

She gave him a slight smile.

He grabbed a wooden chair, positioned it in front of her, and sat down. Placing his knees on the outside of hers he moved in close, settling his hands on her hips.

Allison felt his energy pass through her, the muscles in his arms and hands encasing her in a bubble of security. His earthy aroma teased her nose, and she breathed deeply of the familiar scent.

"It's going to be fine. You wait and see." He wiped a single tear off her cheek with his thumb.

Her body quaked. "I'm not so sure. Robert's lawyers didn't paint a very pretty picture of me. They've made me out to be a loose woman who chased Robert for his wealth and social status. They suggested that I became pregnant, so he would marry me. They also criticized my friendship with Jasmine."

"All the people that matter know the truth. Robert's lawyer's rantings won't change anyone's opinion of you. I know you to be one of the most courageous women I've ever met. A young mother who was willing to sacrifice everything for the sake of her child. I'm sure the judge will see through their fairy tales and theatrics.

"I feel so dirty and ashamed."

"You have nothing to be ashamed of."

"But, Jayson, I did do what they said. I had relations with a man out of wedlock and we produced a child. The way Robert's lawyers stare at me makes my skin crawl. They have every right to look down on me. I'm a soiled woman."

"I told you earlier, I'm happy he got you with child. When I look at Robert, I'm thrilled he took advantage of you. There are times I want to slap him on the back and buy him a drink to celebrate."

"How can you say that?" His jesting made her feel a little better.

"It's true. If you hadn't found yourself in this predicament, you'd still be in Boston and I'd be alone on the ranch, wallowing in self-pity." He brushed aside a loose tendril of hair from her face and placed it behind her ear.

At his touch, the tension ebbed from her body and Brandyn relaxed in her arms. She looked down at her precious son, suckling at her breast. "I'm afraid we're going to lose him." Her voice croaked with emotion. "If Robert gets custody, I might never see my baby again."

"The court usually sides with the baby's mother in this kind of dispute. I'm glad you kept the letter Robert sent you. The part where he questioned Brandyn's parentage was a big upset to his case. The way he abruptly dismissed his responsibilities to you and his unborn child showed he's not a compassionate or dependable man. His behavior wasn't very fatherly."

"I don't know why I never threw it away." She placed a hand on his shoulder. The well-formed muscles under her fingers reminded her of his strength. "You never told me about Henry."

"I'm sorry. I should've told you about the fire a long time ago. I guess I wasn't ready to talk about it. I asked Henry to testify not only because he's a good character witness but because his father is Morrison Waite."

"I don't understand. Who's Morrison Waite?"

"He happens to be the Chief Justice who presides over the United States Supreme Court and thus the head of the United States federal court system. Robert's lawyers are aware of this fact. Their faces blanched when Henry said his name."

"What does his father have to do with this?"

"His father is incredibly grateful I saved his son from certain death. The Chief Justice's involvement, however once removed, will ensure our interests are paramount. Anyone associated with our custody hearing will tread lightly. If the verdict is in our favor, Robert will have little recourse. The Chief Justice is an immensely powerful man. He will see that Robert's appeals are buried for years. This is how we maintain custody of our son."

A chill made Allison shiver, although the weather was warm. "And what if Robert gets custody?"

"Then we appeal the verdict and our appeal will get pushed through the court system in a speedy manner. I don't foresee that happening though. Judge Wade is a fair man. He'll weigh all the information and come to the right conclusion."

She shuddered. They could still lose.

Jayson stroked the sides of her arms. "I didn't want to say anything earlier because I didn't want you to think I had any doubt about us winning...but it's time to tell you now."

Allison's heart sank.

"You know how I like to prepare in advance. Well, I've been corresponding with your father."

"My father?"

He nodded. "I contacted him right after Robert arrived in town. I explained our situation and told him about the court hearing. I know you didn't want to worry your family, but I thought it was best to keep them abreast of what was happening. Your mother wanted to come to Flat Rock immediately to support you, but she had pneumonia a few weeks ago and your father thought they shouldn't travel at this time. I agreed. In the off-chance Robert wins custody of Brandyn, I've asked your parents if we could move in with them in Boston."

Allison gulped a big breath.

"As a contingency plan, only if things go awry. If they do, I asked Herb at the stage office to book us passage on the same coach as Robert. We'll travel with him to Boston. I'm sure he won't give us any flack for tagging along so long as we take care of Brandyn for him. I doubt he knows what to do with a baby. After all, he didn't even know his son's name," Jayson said with a tinge of contempt. "When we get to the city, we'll stay with your folks. That way you'll be around family while we file our appeal and figure this out. Your father offered me a job to pass the time."

Her jaw slackened, and her eyes grew wide. "You would leave Montana? It's your home?"

Jayson clasped Allison's shoulder and squeezed. "My home is where you and Brandyn are. Before we met, I was miserable and broken. My life had little purpose. Since we married, I feel whole again."

He lifted her hand to his lips and kissed her knuckles. "Wherever you go, I go. Wherever you live, I live. If Brandyn is in Boston, then that's where we should be."

Tears burned Allison's eyes. "Are you sure you could leave everything behind? What about the sawmill and the ranch?"

"Chase can take over. In fact, I've not given him enough credit these past few years. I'm not worried." He placed his palm on her cheek and she automatically leaned into it. "I know I haven't said the words out loud yet, but I want you to know...I love you with all my heart. You and Brandyn are my world."

Allison's pulse quickened. Emotions squeezed in her throat, and she let out a ragged breath. Unchecked tears streamed down her face and dropped on Brandyn's forehead. The baby ignored them and continued to feed. Jayson's words of affection were overwhelming, and she held back a sob.

For a moment, she questioned whether she deserved him. But, as she glanced up, he gazed at her with pure love glimmering in his deep blue eyes, and she knew they deserved each other. She leaned forward, gently crushing the baby between them and captured Jayson's lips in a tender, salty kiss.

Pulling back to look at him, she said in a throaty whisper, "I love you, too. With all my heart."

***

The bang of the anvil on the wooden table echoed in the room.

Allison startled at the sharp sound. The jolt woke her son, who let out an alarmed cry.

Judge Wade sent her an apologetic look.

She gently bounced Brandyn in her arms and watched his eyelids grow heavy as he drifted back to sleep.

Jayson sat beside her, half facing her at an angle. He wrapped his brawny arm around her back and drew her against his chest. She wasn't sure if he was positioned just so to offer his support or if he was preparing to restrain her if the decision was not in their favor.

Judge Wade took off his spectacles and scanned the room. "Today I've been given the task of deciding which parent will maintain sole custody of the infant, Brandyn William McKay. I've reviewed the case very carefully and I feel comfortable my verdict will be in the best interest of the child."

Allison's heart slammed against the inside of her chest. *Just breathe*, she reminded herself when she realized she'd suddenly held her breath.

"Both sides presented sufficient information regarding what took place and why they each believe they should raise this child. It's my job to sift through the information presented and come up with a fair decision. Before I get to that, though, I would like to take a moment and discuss some of my beliefs. First off, I believe at one point in time, both parties had strong feelings for each other. I do not for one minute believe there was any manipulation or subterfuge on the part of Mrs. McKay."

A ripple of joy coursed through her. She couldn't trust what she was hearing. The judge believed her over Robert and his fancy lawyers.

Judge Wade gave her a nod. "I believe your motives were pure, and you honestly thought you and Mr. Winthrop would one day wed. I believe Mr. Winthrop conducted himself in an ungentlemanly fashion the night of conception when he plotted your seduction."

Heat crept up Allison's neck and over her cheeks. Jayson gave her shoulder a little squeeze.

"Mr. Winthrop, I believe you sought to do the right thing and make good on your intention to marry Mrs. McKay but fell short when you chose your inheritance over a life with this young woman. I feel you didn't take your responsibilities seriously when you abruptly cut all ties with the mother of your child and left her to deal with matters on her own."

Judge Wade locked eyes with Allison. "I commend you, Mrs. McKay, for the fortitude and courage it took to uproot yourself from your home and travel across the country to an unfamiliar land to marry a stranger, so your baby could have a name. I hope you realize you're a very lucky woman to have such a good friend in Father Peter. He saw to it you and your unborn child would be well provided for."

Allison looked over her shoulder at Father Peter and gave him a tight-lipped smile. She would always be grateful for what he had done for her.

"Mr. and Mrs. McKay, your character witnesses were quite compelling. I believe you both to be good, decent, and honorable people. Those traits seem to be instilled in your family and friends. I've watched the whole lot of you take turns holding and caring for the baby during this proceeding and from the looks of things, this is a warm and loving community."

Allison snuck a sideways glance at Jayson. He gave her an encouraging smile and she relaxed a little.

"But, I also have a strong belief that a child should be entitled to his inheritance. I don't think it would be fair for him to forsake his birthright, just because his parents are at odds."

Her stomach flipped. She had been so sure but now...maybe not. The back and forth toyed with her emotions. Would the judge rule in their favor, or against them? Jayson's arm tightened, and he pulled her closer.

"Unfortunately, Mr. Winthrop, I doubt you would be a good father to a young child. I have a feeling if I granted you custody, your son would be raised by wet nurses, governesses, and servants. I'm sure he would spend many years in private schools. I doubt the two of you would have much in common until he was a man."

Robert made a sour face as if to deny the allegations.

"So, in light of these observations, I have decided to grant custody of Brandyn William McKay to Mr. and Mrs. Jayson McKay."

A loud whoop went up in the courtroom. Allison's body went limp as the tension drained from her limbs. Judge Wade put up his hand and banged the table with his anvil to regain order.

A quick hush came over the crowd.

"There are stipulations to be agreed upon. Mr. and Mrs. McKay will raise the child until his seventeenth birthday. At that time, he will move to Boston to live with his biological father where he will continue his schooling while acclimating himself to a different way of life. By then, he should have developed a strong moral base and be on his way to becoming a well-rounded man, who will be lucky enough to have an opportunity to experience the best of both worlds."

Jayson gave her a small nod of approval. Brandyn wouldn't inherit a part of the ranch, but he would have his own inheritance, to do with as he saw fit. The benefit being they would have him during the most important years of his life.

I can live with this.

Judge Wade picked up his anvil. "Mr. and Mrs. McKay, do you agree to the conditions I have outlined?"

Together, they said, "We do."

"Mr. Winthrop, do you agree to the conditions?"

Robert glanced at his lawyers.

Judge Wade stared at Robert sternly. "I believe this makes perfect sense for you, Mr. Winthrop. You'll have to wait until your son is almost a man, but you'll still get your heir in plenty of time to teach him all there is to know about being a Winthrop."

Robert's lawyers nodded their approval.

Robert turned back to the judge. "I do."

Judge Wade's anvil hit the wooden table with a bang. "So be it. Courts adjourned."

Excitement filled the dining room, and the noise level grew thunderous. People rose from their chairs and congratulated each other with nervous laughter and cheers. Gentle pats of support and well-wishing landed on Allison's shoulders. Jayson took Brandyn from her arms and helped her stand. When she turned, she faced the bright smiles of her friends and family. They presented Jayson and her with hugs and handshakes, expressing their felicitations and satisfaction with the verdict.

Her whole body shook with relief. The scene seemed surreal, and she couldn't believe the hearing was finally over. She would not be parted from her child.

Margaret ordered the men to start putting the tables and chairs back in their places, so they could celebrate properly with a feast. The women retreated into the kitchen to prepare.

When the crowd thinned, Robert came to stand before her. He appeared to be a different man than the one she knew so many months before, or maybe she just saw him clearer. He no longer had any power over her. There was no fluttering in her chest when she laid eyes on him, only disappointment from crushed dreams.

"Allison, this was not how I had imagined us ending up. You might not believe this, but I'm sorry to have put you through this. The judge is right. I'm afraid I'd make a young child a terrible father. Our son is better off with you and your husband for the time being. I'll have my chance with him later when he can appreciate what he'll inherit. Until then." He tipped his head in her direction and then at Jayson standing at her side.

They watched him walk out the double doors of the hotel with his hired guns following closely behind as they made a beeline to the stagecoach office for the first tickets out of town.

Allison turned to Jayson. "We won. Finally, we can live in peace." Grabbing him around the waist, she leaned in and rested her cheek against his chest, being careful to not squish their son, who remained in the crook of his arm.

Jayson hugged her back. "Now that the court hearing is behind us, the next question is where would you like to live?"

"What do you mean?"

"I was serious when I said I was willing to live anywhere you want. If you want to go back to Boston, I'll be happy to go with you."

Allison glanced up. "Jayson McKay, you are the densest man I've ever come across. I've been telling you for months, but you haven't been listening. The McKay ranch is my home, nowhere else. That's where I want to live with the man I love. That's where I want to raise my family."

Jayson pressed his lips to hers. The heated tenderness conveyed his sentiments without words. When the kiss ended, he said in a husky voice, "Allison, you've captured my heart. To think I almost ruined everything. I can't imagine my world without you."

"I think we were meant to be together."

He stroked her back. "We're going to have a good life ahead of us."

"I'm certain we will. It'll be a new beginning."

~The End~

Many Thanks

Thank you for reading *Fated Beginnings*. I hope you enjoyed my Western adventure as much as I enjoyed writing it.

If you took pleasure in reading this book, help other readers find my story by writing a review on your favorite retailer site, on your Facebook page and/or on other reader platforms you frequent. And, please don't forget to tell your friends!

Visit my website and sign up for news releases at: **www.karen-muir.com**

Friend me on my Facebook page at: **www.facebook.com/karenmuir.writer**

Also, feel free to contact me on either platform to chat about writing or to leave a comment.

Fated Beginnings is part of The McKay Series, a collection of Western Romance stories. Look for Chase and Jasmine's story, coming soon.

If you like Medieval Romances, you may enjoy reading my other Historical Romance, *Dagger's Destiny*, set in England in 1354.

Best Wishes,

Karen Muir

About the Author

I never imagined I would one day be an aspiring Historical Romance writer.

If you asked me years ago what I saw in my future, I would never have said, "I see myself as a writer.".

Writing is hard. It takes a lot of thought. It's time consuming. And, I love it!

My journey began quite differently than most writers. I didn't grow up writing. I didn't spend day after day locked in a room pressing pen to paper or typing.

For as long as I can remember, when my head hit the pillow, I dreamed.

I dreamed about people I didn't know and the lives they might have led. Scenes evolved and aligned themselves in perfect order. Beginnings and endings became clear. Stories emerged. Soon I had a handful of stories taking up space in an already crowded head. There was nothing else to do but write them down, if just to make room for more adventures, pushing their way in, vying for a spot.

I've found that it **was** much easier to dream than to write. In order to share my stories with those who might enjoy them, I studied the craft of writing and joined my words together until I finished my first manuscript. I cannot begin to convey my delight when *Dagger's Destiny* was finally complete.

As I continue on my quest to share my stories with readers who enjoy them, I've embarked on the journey of self-publishing, in the hope that I might touch, in some small way, the lives of those around me.

With Warmest Regards,

Karen Muir